# A BED BY THE WINDOW

ALSO BY M. SCOTT PECK, M.D.

*The Road Less Traveled:*
A New Psychology of Love, Traditional Values
and Spiritual Growth

*People of the Lie:*
The Hope for Healing Human Evil

*What Return Can I Make?:*
Dimensions of the Christian Experience
(with Marilyn von Waldner and Patricia Kay)

*The Different Drum:*
Community-Making and Peace

# M. SCOTT PECK, M.D.

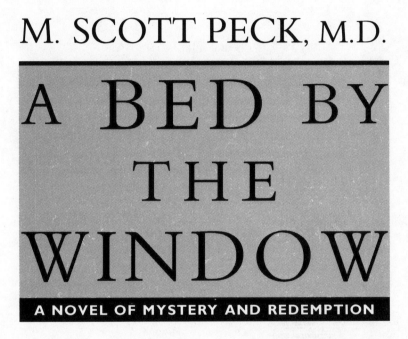

# A BED BY THE WINDOW

## A NOVEL OF MYSTERY AND REDEMPTION

## BANTAM BOOKS
NEW YORK · TORONTO · LONDON · SYDNEY · AUCKLAND

A BED BY THE WINDOW

A BANTAM BOOK / SEPTEMBER 1990

Book design by Jaya Dayal.

LIBRARY OF CONGRESS CATALOGING-IN-PUBLICATION DATA

Peck, M. Scott (Morgan Scott), 1936–
A bed by the window : a novel of mystery and redemption / M. Scott Peck.
p.    cm.
ISBN 0-553-07003-7
I. Title.
PS3566.E2524B44   1990        90-32181
813.'54—dc20    CIP

PUBLISHED SIMULTANEOUSLY IN THE UNITED STATES AND CANADA

Bantam Books are published by Bantam Books, a division of Bantam Doubleday
Dell Publishing Group, Inc. Its trademark, consisting of the words "Bantam
Books" and the portrayal of a rooster, is Registered in U.S. Patent and
Trademark Office and in other countries. Marca Registrada. Bantam Books,
666 Fifth Avenue, New York, New York 10103.

Dedicated to
the Ministry of Nursing Homes
and the people who labor therein.

# ACKNOWLEDGMENTS

My life is hardly my own anymore. Certainly that is true of this work.

Its characters did not arise *de novo*. While a resemblance of any one of them to an actual person is not intended—they are fictional—I am grateful to the lives of all those people who taught me, one way or another, about the richness of nursing home culture.

And to Madeleine L'Engle who, inadvertently, provided part of the inspiration at Christmastime, 1987, when she suggested I might be so frivolous as to read some mystery novels she recommended.

And to Anne Pratt and Susan Poitras, whose diligent hard work and computer friendliness transformed tapes and scribbles into legible literature.

And to Kathleen Fitzpatrick and my agent, Jonathan Dolger, whose enthusiasm for my first draft—a mere germ—led to further drafts.

And, particularly, to my editor, Ann Harris, under whose wise tutelage those drafts were written. If it looks as though I know how to write a novel, it's because she patiently taught me the craft from scratch.

And, finally, of course, Lily.

M. SCOTT PECK, M.D.
Bliss Road
New Preston, CT 06777

# A BED BY THE WINDOW

## *Friday, February 12th*

Mrs. Georgia Bates sat in the back seat of the station wagon, eyeing the dirty ridges of February snow along the edges of Route 83 with distaste. Her son, Kenneth, was driving. Marlene, her daughter-in-law, sat in the front seat next to him. The flat midwestern farmland, still mostly white with the vestiges of the last storm, stretched to the horizon past both sides of the road. Once Georgia had liked to think about the earth lying beneath the snow as pregnant with hidden new life. But it had been decades since she cared to have such thoughts.

When they were halfway there, she broke the silence. "I am being railroaded once again," she announced.

Kenneth exploded. "For Christ's sake, Mother, you know perfectly well you can't live by yourself anymore. Two weeks home and you soaked every piece of clothing you have with urine, and every chair and sofa in the apartment."

"You don't have the right to do this to me," Georgia went on, ignoring him.

Kenneth had heard it before. His voice took on its reasonable accountant's tone. "I have had your power of attorney for the last two years. You are quite free to petition the probate court to change that. Within just a few days the court would appoint a psychiatrist to interview you. Then you and the psychiatrist would appear before the judge, and he would make his determination. It's very simple."

Georgia did not feel the least outwitted. But she had no intention of being interviewed by another psychiatrist. Silence returned to the car and continued until they arrived ten minutes later.

The large single-story building, its three wings extending outward like huge claws, lay sprawled in a shallow hollow next to Willow Creek. Built of cinder block and painted grim brown, it always reminded Kenneth of some anonymous modern factory. A factory for manufacturing what? he wondered. The sign at the side of the short driveway read: WILLOW GLEN EXTENDED CARE FACILITY. Kenneth pulled the car around to the entrance. Marlene leaped out and opened the rear door. "Can I help you, Mother?" she asked.

"I am quite fit, thank you," Georgia replied icily; and, indeed, she climbed out spryly and walked behind Marlene into the foyer while Kenneth parked.

To the left was the Administration Center. Marlene went to the receptionist who guarded its door and announced their presence. Then she crossed to the small reception room on the other side. Georgia had already seated herself and Marlene went to sit beside her, then thought better of it and took the sofa on the opposite side of the room. Kenneth came in and sat beside his wife. The silence was heavy.

As they were waiting, Georgia happened to look down at her lap and noticed a hand resting there. It was a thin hand. The skin was wrinkled, with a collage of overlapping blotches, each with its own history. The veins were like crooked blue threads. "It is an old woman's hand," Georgia thought. There was a brief wave of panic. She jerked the hand away. The wave subsided. "I wonder whose hand that was?" she mused.

The silence was broken when Roberta McAdams strode in. "Good morning, Mr. Bates, Mrs. Bates," she said heartily. "And good morning to you, Georgia! Welcome back to Willow Glen."

Georgia snorted. "Madam Icecube," she said to herself. She did not like Ms. McAdams, the deputy administrator. A slender woman in her early thirties with pulled-back dark hair, everything about her was crisp, efficient, and machinelike.

Ms. McAdams got right down to business. "We can't give you your same room back, Georgia," she said, "but we are going to put you on C-Wing again so you should feel right at home. Shall I call an aide to take you there while I am doing intake with your children?"

"No, thank you," Georgia said firmly, every bit as decisive as Ms. McAdams. "I shall be quite happy to participate in what you call intake. I have no desire for you to be talking about me behind my back, the way you did on my last admission. Besides, I think it is only fair that my children should take me to my room, so that they can see where they are putting me."

Ms. McAdams gave Kenneth and Marlene a look of sympathy. "Come right on in then, all of you," she said, and escorted them across the foyer into the Administration Center. It was a busy place. Three secretaries were typing away, one at a word processor. A computer printer was clacking by itself. They followed Ms. McAdams across to her office. Motioning them to the chairs in front of her desk, she whipped into action, turning on her own computer and punching in the proper code. "Tell me the circumstances behind this readmission," she said briskly, her eyes on the screen.

Georgia sat in silence and Kenneth led off. "The moment Mother was discharged three weeks ago she became incontinent again," he said, his attention carefully directed to Ms. McAdams. "No matter how well Marlene cleans it, that wing of the house is full of the stench. She has to help Mother change her clothes, and she says she's started to develop bedsores from the urine. It's become clear we made a mistake in taking her out. I called Mrs. Simonton, who said you'd take her back. So here we are again after only twenty days."

Ms. McAdams typed away. Marlene shifted, uncomfortable at the awkwardness of her husband's speaking about her mother-in-law as if Georgia wasn't there. She felt many other things as well: guilt at having failed in some nameless way; relief at the clothes and bedding she would no longer have to wash and the house she would no longer have to air daily; and, above all, confusion. Why couldn't Georgia control her bladder? Or could she? Why had she regained control as soon as she'd been admitted to Willow Glen right after Christmas? Yet she had been unhappy there—so unhappy they had felt compelled to take her back home. Why? And why on earth had she immediately lost control again? She glanced at Kenneth, knowing that in his stoic way he was struggling with the same questions.

Barely glancing up from the computer screen, Ms. McAdams explained, "I know this is a readmission, but procedures require that I go through all the data again. Let's see, how old is your mother now?"

"Seventy-six," Kenneth replied.

Until this point, Georgia had been lost in reverie. Now she snapped to attention. "Thirty-seven," she proclaimed.

"What?" Ms. McAdams asked, looking up at her as if she were an unwarranted interruption.

"Thirty-seven," Georgia repeated. "I said I am thirty-seven years old."

Ms. McAdams produced a faint smile of pained understanding. She bent back over the keyboard and punched in "seventy-six." Then she went through the rest of the form: Georgia's date of birth, marriage, number of children, date of widowhood, previous hospitalizations, physical illnesses, medications, financial assets, insurance. Georgia no longer bothered to listen. She was impressed, however, by the precision with which Kenneth answered Ms. McAdams's endless questions. He was not just an accountant, he was a successful CPA, and, while she saw no reason to speak of the matter, she felt quite proud of him. He had done very well for himself. For that matter, so had her two younger children: a son who was a dentist and a daughter who was already an assistant principal. Which meant that she, Georgia, had done well for herself. Success breeds success. She had done her job. And now, thank God, it was over.

And so was the intake. Ms. McAdams ushered them back into the foyer. "Do you need an aide?" she asked.

"I don't think so," Kenneth replied. "We should know the way by now."

Ms. McAdams did a sharp about-face and strode back into the Administration Center.

"I'm going to get the bags," Kenneth announced, leaving his wife and mother alone in the foyer. The two women tried not to look at each other. Then Marlene felt ashamed by the silliness of it. "I'm really sorry, Mother," she said gently. "I know this is upsetting for you."

"If you were really sorry you wouldn't be doing it," Georgia shot back.

"I tried, Mother. I tried," Marlene sighed hopelessly.

Kenneth came back carrying two suitcases, and the three marched silently toward C-Wing. Despite his assurances to the contrary, he was never quite sure he knew the way. The sprawling building reminded him of an airport: one wing looked just like every other wing. Each had its own color code: C-Wing was orange to the best of his recollection, but the fluorescent lighting in the corridors bleached out the tones so it was hard to tell which color was which. Only when one of the bedroom doors was open did daylight get into the hall. The floor was linoleum. It was spotlessly clean. Still, once they passed the foyer, the faint odor of stale urine was unmistakable and pervasive. But he knew that this came with the territory and that Willow Glen met the highest standards for nursing homes.

Halfway down the corridor an elderly woman, imprisoned in a geri-chair, reached out to clutch Kenneth's sleeve. "Have you seen my purse?" she whined. "Do you know what they've done with my purse? Someone's stolen my purse. Where's the doctor? I want to see my doctor. They won't let me see my doctor." Uneasily, he yanked away.

He felt better a second later when they neared the nurses' station and he was able to discern Heather's beaming face like a beacon of light in the gloom he felt. Kenneth was pleased that Heather should be on duty on this otherwise unpleasant morning. Of the licensed practical nurses who staffed C-Wing, he liked her best. Everything about her was soft. Her soft, slightly round young face with its soft skin—she could not have been more than twenty-five—was framed by soft black hair. "Good morning, Heather," he said, smiling cheerfully.

Heather smiled back. "Hi, Mr. Bates. Hi, Mrs. Bates. And hi, Georgia. I'm glad to see you again. I've been expecting you."

Georgia tried to scowl at her, but she couldn't quite do it. Somehow, scowling at Heather took too much energy.

"Peggy," Heather said to the dull-eyed, skinny nurse's aide sitting next to her, "would you take the Bateses down to Georgia's room? It's with Mrs. Carstairs. Georgia, I'll be down to see you later once you're settled in."

Peggy apathetically led them down the hall to Room C–18. The door was open. Through the picture window, the midday February light illuminated a pleasantly furnished two-bedded room. In the bed by the window a pale elderly woman lay snoring softly. Georgia felt a brief flash of envy toward Mrs. Grochowski, the only person on the wing who had a room all to herself. But then, everyone knew why that was. The envy passed quickly, however. Mrs. Grochowski was too gracious to envy for long. Besides, it did not bother Georgia to have a roommate. What she really wanted was the bed by the window. But she remembered Mrs. Carstairs's disease and contented herself with thinking that the ill woman would be moving before long.

"Let me know if there is anything you need," Peggy said, and scuttled out the door too fast for them to answer.

Kenneth hoisted the suitcases onto his mother's bed. Georgia sat in the comfortable rocking chair while he and Marlene unpacked her bags in silence. When everything was hung up and put in the drawers, Kenneth said, "We'll be back to visit you after church on Sunday. Would you like us to bring the children?"

"I don't know why you should bother to visit me," Georgia said, "when the whole point is to put me away."

Kenneth ignored her comment. "Should I arrange for a phone in your room?"

"As I told you the last time, I'm sure you can find better things to spend *my* money on."

"All right, then, you can use the pay phone in the dayroom to call us if there is anything you need." Kenneth bent down and kissed her quickly on the head. Marlene did the same. For both, it was more an act of love than of affection.

They stopped at the nurses' station on the way out. "I want to talk to Heather," Kenneth explained. "I'm so damned confused."

C-Wing, like the others, was Y-shaped, with the circular nurses' station positioned at the junction of the Y. Inside the station were counters and files. Heather was seated at a counter speaking with her other aide. As he waited for her, Kenneth glanced at the wall nearest the station. There was a gurney, a flat, narrow bed on wheels, positioned next to it, and strapped on it he saw an emaciated, dark-haired young man he remembered from Georgia's earlier stay. He had lain in the same place then, also on his side, his hands bent inward like claws, his arms drawn up against his chest like folded wings. Under the sheet that half covered him, Kenneth could see the sticklike shape of his legs, bent to tuously backwards against his buttocks. Catheter tubing led out from under the sheet to a plastic bag half filled with urine.

Instinctively Kenneth averted his eyes. C-Wing was supposed to be for the ambulatory patients who could at least partially care for themselves. Yet this—this *creature*—clearly required total care. What was he doing here? He looked at him again in spite of himself, face to face for the first time.

The young man's eyes met his. There was a moment of shock. The eyes Kenneth looked into were like two boundless black pools. For some reason he thought of lambs' eyes, even though he had never looked at a lamb's eyes. He turned away in confusion, grateful that the aide was leaving.

"I need to talk to you, Heather. Do you have a few minutes?" Kenneth asked across the waist-high wall of the station.

"Sure."

"It's my mother, of course. She baffles me. All last year she became increasingly incontinent. As soon as she was admitted here, she cleaned up her act. She became dry as a bone and she wanted to come home. But the moment she was discharged she became incontinent again. Why? Do you think she was just trying to prove to us that she could make it on her own? Even though she really couldn't? Or do you have some kind of power here that did this? Some kind of magic?"

Heather grinned at him. "Maybe one," she said, "maybe the other. But I would place my bet on a kind of magic."

"Do you know anything about the nature of this magic?" Kenneth inquired.

"I think so. I think maybe it's because we don't expect anything from the patients here."

"I don't understand."

"You see, it really doesn't matter to us whether your mother is continent or incontinent. Because it doesn't matter, your mother is completely free to be whichever she wants."

"I still don't understand. If she wants to be continent, why wouldn't she be continent at home? Why would she behave better here when she says she doesn't want to be here?"

Heather looked at him keenly. "You're feeling guilty, aren't you? Maybe your mother does want to be here."

"I guess I sound stupid, but I don't understand why she would tell us she doesn't want to be here if she does."

"For your mother to say that she wanted to be here would be for her to take responsibility for wanting to be here. Maybe that's something she can't do."

Kenneth began to smile. "You mean to tell me it's possible that my mother became incontinent so that we would have to put her here, because that's what she wanted all along, but wanted us to take the responsibility? You're quite a psychologist."

"Yes, it's possible," said Heather, "but no, I'm no great psychologist. Working here, one simply becomes aware of what makes old people tick. All our lives things are expected of us. It can get pretty tiring, you know. Sometimes it can be a great relief, in the last years of a long life, to come to a place where nothing is expected of you anymore. It can be a kind of sanctuary."

Kenneth had received the information he had asked for, but he was not sure he had digested it. As they walked down the corridor toward the exit from Willow Glen, he said to Marlene, "Well, it's done. I'd been dreading this morning. Maybe Heather's right. Maybe my mother is somehow comfortable here. But if this is what it means to get old, I'd just as soon you put me out of my misery."

"Like shooting a horse with a broken leg?" Marlene asked with mock seriousness.

"You got it." Kenneth smiled at the gallows humor. He put his finger to his head. "Pow. Just do it quickly. But, yes, exactly like a horse."


After Kenneth and Marlene left, Georgia sat in the rocking chair and lapsed deeper into pleasurable reverie. But the reverie was interrupted within ten minutes by a voice from the door: "Georgia, dear, how very, very good to see you again!"

She looked up to see Hank Martin leaning against the door frame, a thin little man with cropped red hair, ruddy face, and bulbous nose. He was already poking the foot of his cane into her room. "I should have known it wouldn't take you long to get here," she said.

"Of course not," Hank said cheerfully. "I came as soon as I heard you were back. Do you mind if I come in?"

"You know perfectly well that I mind," Georgia replied, but there was little snap in her tone, as if she might not be entirely displeased by the predictable attention. "All you want to do is put your dirty paws on me."

"You're wrong there, my love," Hank responded. "I washed my hands thoroughly a mere three minutes ago. But you're right that I would like to get them on you. I've missed you."

"You mean you've missed your fantasies," Georgia said. "I've never let you lay your hands on me yet. What makes you think I'd do so now?"

"I thought perhaps you'd grown up while you were away. Come on, let me in for just a little feel."

Georgia glanced over at her roommate, still sleeping by the window. "Shut up, you old fool," she said, "you'll wake Mrs. Carstairs."

"We could do it in the bathroom," Hank suggested. "Nobody would hear us."

"Do you know what they call you?" Georgia asked.

The question didn't faze Hank a bit. "Sure," he said with a grin, "Hank the Horny."

"Do you think they call you that because you might be just a little bit indiscriminate?"

"That's not true, my love," Hank said mildly. "If you notice, I stay pretty clear of Rachel Stimson. Anyway, it's you I'm after, my love. Come on and let me in."

"You set one foot inside that door and I will immediately scream at the top of my lungs," Georgia retorted. "And with a little bit of luck, they'll move you to A-Wing."

Hank decided to change his tack. "Have I ever told you about the dogfight I was in with the Messerschmitts over the North Atlantic?"

"Yes, indeed you have," Georgia said. "Even if I'd believed you the first time, it was boring the second time, and I told you to shut up the third time you started to tell me."

Hank shifted back again. "It would be fun doing it in the bathroom. We could . . ."

"I do not intend to have sex with you, Hank Martin, in the bathroom or out on the lawn in the snow, today or any day."

Hank wheedled, "Come on, Georgia, you're an old woman and I'm an old man. We don't have much time left. We might as well enjoy what we've got left."

"I am not an old woman," Georgia proclaimed.

"You're about as old as I am, my love," Hank retorted, "and I will be eighty in a few years."

"But I am thirty-seven." Georgia's tone was matter-of-fact and Hank looked at her keenly. "My God," he said. "You talk as if you actually believed it. You don't believe my Messerschmidts, but you believe you're thirty-seven."

"I told you," Georgia said unequivocally, "I am thirty-seven years old."

For the first time Hank was unclear as to how to proceed. But then it was given to him. Both of them jumped at the sound of a raspy voice over the intercom: "Peggy Valeno, would you come to the office, please. Peggy Valeno, to the office."

"Well, I wonder what the commandant wants with Peggy?" Hank said curiously.

Georgia looked blank. "The commandant?"

"Yes, you know, whenever that squawk-box goes, it's the administrator of this concentration camp. I wonder what she wants with Peggy?"

"Well, maybe if you left me alone, you could find out," Georgia said firmly. She wasn't concerned about glum little Peggy, and she had decided that the time had come to be alone again. There was something she wanted to savor by herself.

Her tone gave Hank the message. "All right, my love, I'll try you again later," he said, and limped away from the door whistling.

"Concentration camp," Georgia thought. That was the phrase she relished. "I can use that the next time Kenneth and Marlene come to visit." Contentedly she rocked in her chair, moving from Kenneth and Marlene to the exchange she had just had with Hank. "One of these days I'll have to tell him that I never did like sex," she thought. Then, as she continued to rock, she became aware that her bladder was full. She stood up, and without the slightest hesitation or difficulty, walked into the bathroom.


Mrs. Edith Simonton was not in good humor that morning. But then those few who had known her long would have told you that she had been in an ill humor for at least a decade. Her hawklike sixty-year-old face gave witness to this. It was well lined—almost creviced—but there were no smile lines, no lines of softness. Nor lines of depression. Her eyes were sharp. To some it was a stern face; to others, simply tough.

Mrs. Simonton felt that she had had good reason to be ill-humored. She had been a pioneer. Twenty-five years before, with a modest divorce settlement, she had moved to New Warsaw, the county seat, and purchased a rambling old Victorian house. She fixed it up to turn it into the first private nursing home in the county. The need was desperate. It was filled to capacity within two months. As soon as she had proved she could make a success out of the business, she set about tirelessly obtaining loans, grants, and donations for a much larger, better-equipped facility. Twelve years had passed before her dream finally came true, when the last slap of paint was placed on Willow Glen, the finest nursing home of any kind in the state.

But overnight the dream began to sour. As soon as nursing homes became a major business, the government stepped in. There were tax commissions, Medicare commissions, Medicaid commissions, Social Security commissions, Medical Standards commissions, Certificate of Need commissions. Reports had to be filed for each. Reports. Reports. Reports. And then there were the inspections. Not just the fire department inspections, but the food inspections, the food handler inspections, the Department of Labor inspections, the quality-of-care inspections. It was hard to be polite these days when twice a month she had to answer to some bureaucratic inspection made by a young whippersnapper in his or her first job out of college.

When Peggy Valeno arrived at her office door, Mrs. Simonton was working on yet another report to the state, categorizing the degree of disability of Willow Glen's patients. She was almost relieved, even though this signaled a different kind of unpleasant business.

"You asked for me," Peggy said in her flat voice, standing in the open doorway.

Mrs. Simonton looked at the sullen face, having some acquaintance with the impoverished swamp-hollow family and the relatively uncaring school system from which this nineteen-year-old child had come.

"Close the door and sit down, Peggy." Peggy did so. Mrs. Simonton peered at her. "Do you like working here?" she asked.

"It's a job," Peggy answered.

"Well, at least you're honest," Mrs. Simonton said, pulling out Peggy's folder from under the report she had been preparing. "We need to talk, Peggy. You were hired on a six-month trial basis. You have been here three months now. In this folder I have two sets of ratings on you. One is the patients' ratings, which Ms. McAdams gathers every two weeks or so. Several patients described you as rough. But that doesn't really concern me; they're the type of patients who describe everyone as rough. What does concern me, however, is that *no* patient spoke well of you." She glanced at the sheet of paper before her. "The words they used were: unresponsive, cold, indifferent, careless, untalkative, unpleasant, aloof, distant, and brusque. Not one patient described you as friendly, or warm, or cooperative, or helpful. The other reports I have are from the licensed practical nurses who have been in charge of you on their various shifts.

Every LPN has ranked you as the lowest of any of the aides she has worked with over the past three months."

Mrs. Simonton closed the folder and sat back to watch Peggy's reaction.

"Even Heather rated me down?"

"Heather, in fact, gave you the lowest rating of all."

Peggy gave an audible gasp.

"Do you want to keep working here?" Mrs. Simonton asked.

"I do the best I can."

"That's possible. Perhaps you are indeed doing the best you can. But it is not good enough, Peggy. Given these reports, I could terminate you now. If I let you go on another three months you would have to demonstrate major improvement for me to keep you on. If you did not improve quite dramatically, I would have to let you go then. So if you really don't want to work here, it would be much simpler for you and simpler for me to let you go now."

"I come on time," Peggy said.

Mrs. Simonton sat back and closed her tired eyes. She was quite aware that Peggy had not answered her question. She was also aware that Peggy probably could not answer. The issue of wanting to work was probably irrelevant. It was doubtful that Peggy would want to work anywhere. Peggy was indicating not that she wanted to work, but that she would work, and that she would continue to put in her hours.

Mrs. Simonton opened her eyes again. "Getting here and leaving here on time is not all that is required," she said, looking Peggy square in the eye. "That's just a part of it. An even bigger thing is caring. It is required that you care. If I had to sum up everything that has been said about you in these reports, Peggy, it would be that you don't seem to care. I don't know how to teach you how to care. I wish I did. I don't know how to teach anybody that. But if you do not learn how to care over the next three months, I will have to let you go. God knows how you'll learn to care in three months, but I will give Him and you that time to try."

Peggy had the good sense to know the interview was over. She got up and walked out. Mrs. Simonton shook her head. "It will take a miracle," she thought.

She had seen a few miracles in her time, but she was wise enough to know you shouldn't bank on them. In fact, she didn't even like to think about them. The very notion of supernatural interventions made her uncomfortable. Yet for Peggy such an intervention would be required. Mrs. Simonton sighed and returned to her endless paperwork.

•     •     •

Peggy slammed the waist-high door to the nurses' station behind her when she got back to C-Wing. Heather looked up in surprise.

"Stupid, bossy old bitch," Peggy spat.

"Who?"

"Mrs. Simonton, who else? All she can think about are her papers and reports. Papers and reports. Guidelines. Rules and regulations. I'd like to cram her rules and regulations down her throat."

It was the first time Heather had ever seen her aide's sulkiness erupt into rage. "She can be a tough old bird," she acknowledged, "but she really bends a lot."

Peggy was not to be mollified. "As far as I'm concerned, it's rules and regulations, rules and regulations. I might as well be back in school. She squawks for me over the intercom. It's like being called to the principal's office. Rules and regulations."

"Eheheheh." The bleating sound, halfway between that of a lamb and a goat, interrupted Peggy's tirade. Heather jumped up and went out of the nurses' station to the gurney against the wall.

"Do you want to talk to me, Stephen?" she asked the dark young man lying on it, spastic and helpless.

"Uhuhuhuhuh." The tone was lower. This, she knew, meant "no."

"Do you want to say something?" she asked.

"Ahahahahahah." The higher tone meant "yes."

"Let me get the letter board," she said, and from the head of the gurney she unhooked a thin board eighteen inches square. The board was divided into thirty-six three-inch sections. The first twenty-six were the letters of the alphabet in order; the next was a diagonal slash mark; the remaining sections were nine different punctuation marks. Heather raised the board to Stephen's hands, clutched against his chest.

With the first knuckle of the middle finger of each hand, Stephen tapped in sequence, letter by letter: I/WANT/TO/TALK/TO/PEGGY."

"Peggy," Heather said, "Stephen wants to speak with you."

Peggy came out of the nurses' station. One of the first things she had been required to do when she started to work on C-Wing at Willow Glen was to learn how to talk with Stephen. She held the board for him. He tapped out, "YOU'RE/STUPID."

She gaped at him. "I'm *stupid?*"

Stephen tapped on the board, "YES/YOU/TALK/ABOUT/RULES/BUT/YOU/ DON'T/EVEN/LOOK/AROUND/YOU/TO/SEE/THE/RULES/BEING/BENT.LET/ME/ ASK/YOU/SOME/QUESTIONS.WHY/DO/YOU/THINK/THEY/KEEP/ME/HERE/INSTEAD /OF/IN/A/WING?WHY/DOES/HEATHER/OFTEN/HAVE/ONE/MORE/AIDE/THAN/ THE/OTHER/NURSES?WHY/DO/THEY/ALWAYS/KEEP/THE/OTHER/BED/IN/MRS/ GROCHOWSKI'S/ROOM/EMPTY?THESE/ARE/ALL/BENDINGS.MRS/SIMONTON/

KNOWS/ABOUT/ALL/OF/THEM." Then with a slight thrust of the backs of his hands, Stephen shoved the board away. Peggy hung it back on its little hook at the head of the gurney, and returned to the nurses' station.

Heather looked at her curiously. "What did he want?" she asked.

"He just wanted to ask me a bunch of strange questions," Peggy answered noncommittally.

"Like what?"

"Well, one was he wanted to know why you often have one more aide than the other nurses? Why do you?"

"I guess it's to be sure C-Wing is covered when I have to be away—those times when I get calls from the other wings when patients are dying," Heather answered her. "What else did he ask?"

"Nothing much," Peggy replied. Heather could see that she didn't want to talk about it. She seemed calmer. Yet there still was tension, and a long moment of uneasy silence hung between them. She waited. Peggy looked down at her feet. "You gave me a lousy rating," she finally blurted out.

"Yes."

"But I thought you were so nice."

Heather's eyes suddenly turned metallic. "It's my job to be as nice as I possibly can to the patients," she said, "but it's not necessarily my job to be nice to the aides."

"Then what is your job?"

"It's my job when I'm on duty here to see that this wing is the best-run damn wing in Willow Glen."

"No matter who you step on?" Peggy flashed.

"Have I really stepped on you?" Heather asked.

Peggy wasn't sure. In fact, now she wasn't sure about Heather at all. Her softness no longer seemed predictable. She vaguely recalled a story she had read the year before in high school about Dr. Jekyll and Mr. Hyde. It occurred to her that Heather might be hard under her softness and mean under her sweetness. But there seemed to be nothing further she could do about the lurking distrust she felt.

"What with having to go see Mrs. Simonton and speaking with Stephen," Heather said, changing the subject, her manner rapidly switching back to friendliness, "you're behind on your baths. I'll help you. But since I'm doing the helping, I want to do my favorites: Stephen and Mrs. Grochowski. Okay?"

Peggy nodded.

"Let me know if you need help with Rachel Stimson in case she's in a bad mood." Three times out of four Mrs. Stimson would just lie there in her usual angry silence when she was bathed. But the other times, it would take Heather and at least two aides to hold her down.

When Heather entered Mrs. Grochowski's room, Tim O'Hara, not unexpectedly, was sitting in the chair beside her. Their quiet intimacy seemed to warm the entire room.

"Hi, Tim. Hi, Mrs. G.," Heather announced. "Peggy's behind on her baths, so I asked if I could help her by doing you, Mrs. G."

Tim shifted around in the chair to look at Heather. "Hello, angel," he said. "I'll get out." With great difficulty he lifted himself from the chair. His whole left side was paralyzed, from the lower part of his face down. Still, stroke or not, Heather thought he was the handsomest elderly gentleman she had ever seen. He not only had a pink complexion with beautiful white hair, but a great white walrus mustache. She could never see him without thinking of some full-color advertisement for fine aged whisky, with Tim standing with his glass in front of a roaring fire in the library of an elegant manor house. Heather waited while he picked up his cane and shuffled past her. As he did so, he grinned and said, "The Angel of Willow Glen."

When he was gone, Mrs. Grochowski said, "Tim coined that term, you know. And now everyone knows you as that. Which you are."

"Then you're the Angel's angel," Heather responded without even having to think. It was true. She hadn't been working at Willow Glen for long before she noticed that certain patients somehow uplifted, supported her. Strangely, most often they were among those who were very near to death. The only others who always had this effect on her were Stephen and Mrs. G. Both made her feel lighter—literally lighter—in their presence. It was so striking she occasionally wondered whether the lightness she felt was inside her or inside them. And it wasn't only lightness. There was light itself. Actual light. There were times, looking at them, when she felt she could really see a light coming from them, surrounding them. She went into the bathroom and filled the basin with warm water and brought it back to the windowsill with the soap and washcloth. Gently, she slipped Mrs. Grochowski's left arm out of her nightgown and began washing it.

"I'm sorry I haven't had the time to get in to see you before now, Mrs. G.," Heather said.

Marion Grochowski was the only patient in all of Willow Glen whom Heather did not address by first name. There were other singular things about her. Not only was her room the sole one in which the other bed was never occupied; she and Stephen were the only two totally bedridden patients on C-Wing. She was also the one person Heather had ever met who seemed unfailingly cheerful. In LPN school they suggested that some multiple sclerosis patients might have a kind of brain damage that gave them a peculiar euphoria. But Heather doubted it. Not in Mrs. G.'s case. There was no other sign of brain damage in this fifty-eight-year-old woman whose MS had left her totally paralyzed below the neck. No one could be more alert.

"I've missed seeing you," Mrs. Grochowski said to Heather in a tone which made it feel like affirmation, not accusation.

Heather lowered her nightgown and began to wash her breasts. "And I'm afraid you're going to have to miss me some more, Mrs. G.," she said. "I'm going to be off for the next three days."

"Oh, I realize that; I keep very close track of your schedule. But I'm glad for you. You need all the time off you can get."

It was characteristic of Mrs. G. to know her schedule, Heather realized. It was a strange schedule. While the aides worked ordinary eight-hour days, the licensed practical nurses worked twelve-hour shifts, four days on and three days off. They also rotated between days and nights. One month their shift would be from seven in the morning until seven in the evening, and the next month from seven in the evening until seven in the morning. Mrs. Simonton had established this schedule because of the shortage of nurses—particularly those who were willing to work night shifts regularly.

Heather moved the washcloth to Mrs. Grochowski's right arm. "If the weather's good, I may go skiing," she said. "There's some new place they've built in those little hills northeast of here. I'm a bit scared though. I've never been skiing before."

"Is that new boyfriend of yours, Tony, going to take you?" Mrs. Grochowski asked. She always remembered everything Heather told her.

"That's what he's promised me. I think I'm falling in love with him, Mrs. G."

"Oh, I hope so. It's so wonderful to fall in love, isn't it? Even though it's so painful when it comes to an end."

There was no criticism. Mrs. Grochowski had known Heather to fall in and out of love many times over the three years she had worked at Willow Glen, and while her words held a gentle warning, they also shared with Heather the hope that this would be *the* time.

Heather was finished now. After she turned Mrs. Grochowski on her side, she took the bath equipment back to the bathroom, rinsed the basin, and dropped the washcloth and towels in the laundry bin. "I'll see you in four days, Mrs. G.," she said. "Take care till then."

"How not?" Mrs. Grochowski chuckled. "I haven't got any choice since I can't move out of this bed."

Heather stuck her tongue out at her. "You know perfectly well what I mean."

"Of course I do," Mrs. Grochowski acknowledged. "And you take good care of yourself too."

"I'll try." Heather grinned as she made her exit, leaving the door open for Tim to come back.

Mrs. Grochowski closed her eyes. She both liked and loved Heather. But she had no illusions about her. She realized she got to see Heather at her best, that there were other pieces to the picture, and that the pieces didn't all quite fit together as well as they should. She prayed silently, not only knowing that the young woman's future was unclear, but also sensing that there were storm clouds on the horizon.


Heather walked back around the nurses' station and halfway down the opposite corridor to the short hall that gave way to a small supply room. The medications were here, kept in a locked cupboard, as well as other equipment such as sterile gloves, catheter kits, and surgical sets. From underneath the sink she took out a fresh basin, washcloth, and soap. Stephen had neither room nor bathroom of his own. He lived on the gurney, night and day. It was by choice. He seemed to sleep only in brief snatches, and had he been in a regular room he would have been isolated most of the time. Living on the gurney, he could always be close to the action at the nurses' station and in touch with the life around him.

After filling the basin, Heather reached up to the supply cabinet and got a fresh condom catheter kit. This was a device used for men like Stephen who were able to urinate, so did not need an internal catheter, but who were paralyzed and unable to use a urinal. She took all the equipment out to where Stephen lay, and placed it at the foot of the gurney.

"Peggy's behind on her baths," she said. "So I'm helping by doing you and Mrs. Grochowski. Is that okay?"

"Ahahahahahah." Heather knew this to be an affirmation. Beyond that, she could not tell Stephen's reaction. His spasticity was so great he had no control over his facial muscles.

"I don't know what you did with Peggy," she said, as she sponged him, "but you certainly helped her get out of the snit she was in. You must be a real headshrinker, Stephen. But then I already knew that, didn't

I?'' She did know. She knew that their light was more than just intellectual brightness, but she sometimes also thought that he and Mrs. Grochowski were the two most intelligent people she had ever met.

Stephen lay there quietly—pleasurably, she even imagined—as she bathed him. She left his genitals until last. Looking to see that there were no visitors or other patients about, she removed his diaper. It was clean. She would need to remember to write in the nursing notes that he had not had a bowel movement so far today. She unrolled the condom from his penis, and yanked the tube to which the tip of the condom was attached out from the bag of urine clipped to the side of the gurney. Recovering his loins with the sheet, she unhitched the bag of urine and marched with it and the used condom catheter back to the supply room. She emptied the bag in the sink, rinsed it, and brought it back and reattached it to the side of the gurney. She soaked the washcloth in the basin, rubbed a little soap in it, straightened up, removed the sheet and gently washed Stephen's scrotum and in between his buttocks. When she got to his penis, she was surprised to see what looked like the beginning of an erection. She washed the head of the penis and the shaft. There was no question about it now. It was half erect.

This had never happened when Heather bathed him before and she could have stopped washing him at that point. But there was something in her—urgent, almost violent—that did not want to. Yet she also knew this had to be Stephen's choice. She looked into his face and those unfathomable eyes, asking, "Do you want me to continue?"

Stephen might have answered "ahahahahahah" for yes or "'uhuhuh-uhuhuh" for no. Instead, he made a sound that she had never heard him utter before. It was "mmmmmmmmm," like a purr. She smiled to herself, bent down, soaped the washcloth again, and started massaging his penis. She watched him grow in her hand, delighted by his size, delighted by *her* power to evoke him. When it was fully rigid she finally forced herself from it. She quickly bent back down to the basin, rinsed the washcloth, and then stood up to begin mopping away the soap. "It's beautiful," she said.

"Mmmmmmm."

She picked up the new condom catheter and unrolled it onto his erection. "You've certainly made it easy for me to put it on," she remarked, thinking, I'm jabbering because I don't know what else to say. Then she became all nurse again. She bent down and stuck the tubing into the empty urine container, pulled the sheet back over his loins, picked up the basin, and marched off to the supply room.

"You probably know it," she said when she returned to rediaper him, "but I'm going to be off for the next three days. I just wanted to let you know you can count on me being back in four days." There was, as always, no answering expression on his face, but now she needed a further response. "Does that happen when the other aides wash you?"

"Eheheheheh." The bleat was his signal that he wanted the letter board.

Heather placed it up in front of his hands. With his knuckles, Stephen tapped out, "NO."

"But I've bathed you before, and this is the first time," Heather said. "Why now?"

"I'M/NOT/SURE."

Heather yanked the board away and hooked it back on the gurney. Almost perfunctorily, she turned him on his side and left without even saying good-bye. She was confused. She was quite aware that what she had just done was unprofessional. And above all, she was a professional, wasn't she? There was a sense of embarrassment, of shame. But there was excitement too. Along with the thrill of power. And with that something else—a feeling she couldn't quite identify, a feeling quite new to her, yet one with strange echoes, as if from a primitive past before she had been born.

Kenneth Bates sat in his office at Bates & Brychowski, New Warsaw's largest accounting firm. Established by Polish immigrants at the turn of the century, New Warsaw was a peaceful town of no more than fifteen thousand, but it was also the county seat, serving a much broader area of rich farmland, mostly prosperous farmers, and scattered villages. It was a long way from the excitement of New York City where he had been raised—it was even a long way from Chicago—but it was where Marlene had grown up and where she had wanted to settle after their marriage. It was a good place to raise children. And if there was a certain flat midwestern quality to life in New Warsaw, he was as busy professionally as he would have been in any more urban area.

Particularly now. Fiscal years made every season busy, but the ordinary taxpayers still made the three months before April 15 the most hectic time of year. Since they had admitted his mother to Willow Glen and he had dropped Marlene off at home, Kenneth had not had time to reflect upon the day. His secretary had shoved a sandwich at him between clients and he had run late all afternoon.

It was dark outside his office window. The staff had left. He closed the last file on his desk. But he lingered, feeling a slight sadness. He leaned back in his chair thinking of his mother—once the wife of a successful Wall Street banker—who seemed to have entered widowhood and senility almost simultaneously. After his father's death she had not objected to moving here to live with her oldest child. The house was large enough for her to have a small wing to herself. He did not understand why she had so quickly become irascible and then incontinent. "Senility" was simply the term the internist and psychiatrist had used, but there was no damaged place to point to on the X rays, no physiological malfunction to pinpoint.

And he thought of Willow Glen, lying in the darkness ten miles to the south of town. Here he was well into middle age, the head now of a three-generation family; and he wondered, more clearly than earlier that day, if he would ever end up in such a place. It was not a pleasant thought. He might have shuddered had a word not come back to him from the morning. A "sanctuary," Heather had called it. What did she mean?

Well, it was time he left for the sanctuary of his home, the well-deserved cocktail with Marlene, and the children around them at the dinner table recounting their minor high school crises. He got up and put on his overcoat. Yes, his home was a kind of sanctuary, a safe place. And he was glad his mother was safely ensconced in Willow Glen.

But as he stepped out into the cold night on his way to the car it occurred to him that sanctuary had another meaning. Kenneth was not a religious man. He knew, however, that the term came from the safety a person in flight could find in a church. In fact, he knew that the center of a church was actually called the sanctuary. And even that there was reputedly something holy about such a place. Strange, he wondered as he opened the door to his car, do you suppose there could be something about Willow Glen, that impersonal-looking repository for the decrepit and decaying sprawled out in the night to the south, that might conceivably be holy?

It was an idle thought. As human beings went, Kenneth knew himself to be a rather introspective one. But hardly fanciful. There was certainly nothing to inspire reverence or awe in those cold-looking corridors, in the babbling woman in the geri-chair who had clutched at him, in the eerie, distorted creature strapped on the gurney, in his mother's frosty blame. Unconsciously he straightened his shoulders and turned the key in the ignition, heading very willingly for his real-life home.

## *Tuesday, February 16th*

Heather returned to work with a black eye.

"What happened?" Peggy asked.

"My boyfriend and I got in a fight."

Peggy was still too irritated at her to probe further. "I have to do my baths now," she announced tartly.

Heather sat in the nurses' station knowing it was going to be a bad day. Peggy would not be the only one to notice her eye. And her head throbbed faintly from a hangover. Still, there was some solace in being back at work. She might not be able to handle her love life, but at least she could handle her job; *here* she was competent. She began to review the nursing notes of the preceding three days.

Only two of her patients showed signs of a problem and one of them probably wasn't even a problem. Rachel Stimson had thrown her dinner glass across the day room the evening before. That was not out of character; it was almost routine. Indeed, that kind of behavior was why she wasn't served her meals in the dining hall. Nonetheless, Heather would check on her just to be sure.

The other was significant. The notes from Sunday reported that Betty Carstairs had slept through two of her three meals, while Monday's said that she was too weak even to get out of bed. Like a few other patients, Betty had specifically come to Willow Glen to die. When they had told her six weeks ago that the old cancer of her colon had metastasized to her liver, she had made all the arrangements herself. She'd rejected the oncologist's recommendation of chemotherapy and her children's suggestion of hospice care in their home. She wanted neither a prolonged messy death nor one that would be a burden to her children. Personally, Heather was happy about her choice. She enjoyed working with dying patients. There was something terribly *real* about many people when they got close to death, as if they no longer had the time to waste being inauthentic. She loved that, and besides they were the ones most likely to have that light. In the brief time Betty had been there Heather had been able to establish a good relationship with her. It began to look as though the relationship would not last much longer. Heather got up to speak with her.

She never even got close. Just before the change of shift the night aide would place Carol Kubrick, strapped in her geri-chair—sometimes they called her Crazy Carol—outside the nurses' station against the wall opposite Stephen's gurney. No sooner had Heather walked out of the station than Carol fixed her with her demanding whine. "Have you seen my purse? Do you know what they've done with my purse? Someone's stolen my purse. Where's my doctor? I want to see my doctor. They won't let me see my doctor."

This was Carol's refrain. Heather had never heard her say anything else. She knew what the reaction would be, but she tried as always to give her the benefit of the doubt. Placing her hand on Carol's shoulder, she asked, "Who won't let you see your doctor?"

Carol said nothing. Looking into her empty eyes, Heather asked again, "Why do you want to see your doctor, Carol? Is there anything wrong?"

But, as always, the eyes were blank. Not even confused. That was what was so frustrating. It seemed impossible to connect with Carol. She said the same thing in the same way to everyone. Her words were an incantation. Carol grabbed at everyone, yet it was as if no one existed for her.

Carol was eighty years old. Other than being totally incontinent, she was in very good physical condition. Carol was a wanderer. This was why, except when she was being walked, she had to be strapped into the geri-chair during the day and tied into her bed at night. Unrestrained, she would immediately wander down all the halls of Willow Glen, echoing her refrain. Within the hour, no matter what the weather, she would be out the front door grabbing at passers-by with her litany.

"Is there anything that I can do for you this morning, Carol?" Heather asked.

"Have you seen my purse?" Carol moaned again. "Do you know what they've done with my purse?"

Heather raised her hand in a burst of frustration. For a fraction of a second she was about to slap Carol. Hard. In midair she let her arm drop slowly and ran her fingers through Carol's hair. Then she fled back into the nurses' station to hold her head in her hands.

My God, she'd almost hit a patient! Heather hated it when she couldn't help someone. Hated it. Hated it. And there was no way, in the midst of her emotional turmoil, that she could go visit Betty Carstairs now, no matter how much she wanted to see if Betty had that light.

The thought led her to think of Mrs. Grochowski's light. Instinctively Heather was up and scurrying down the corridor like a lost chick. But she got hold of herself in time to make a joke of her sudden need for mothering as she came through the bedroom doorway. "Hi, Supermom!" she exclaimed.

Mrs. Grochowski's answering smile immediately turned to consternation. "Heather, dear, whatever happened to your eye? Did you hurt it skiing?"

"I wish I could say so, but the truth of the matter is I got in a fight with my boyfriend last night."

"With Tony?"

"Yes, Tony."

"How did it happen?"

"Well, I'm not really sure," Heather began. "You know how fights are? Sometimes they flare up over the stupidest little things, and afterwards you can't even remember how you got into them. We'd both been drinking, so that didn't help."

Mrs. Grochowski looked at her keenly. "Well, I'm sure there must be a little more to it than that, but I don't want to pry. And I don't need to, do I, since I'm not your psychiatrist. I imagine you'll be telling Dr. Kolnietz all about it, won't you?"

Heather grimaced. "I have to," she said. "It's the rules."

"When do you see him again?"

"Next week when I have my break. Six days from now."

"Not until then?" Mrs. Grochowski looked concerned.

"Not when I'm working twelve-hour day shifts. There's no way I can see him any sooner."

"You work so hard taking care of us. I wish people would take better care of you."

"You know you do a great deal for me, Mrs. G.," Heather said. "I came down here out of my need, not yours. I was looking for your sympathy. And I looked in the right place. But we've been spending all this time talking about me, and not a word about you. So you see, I'm not such a caregiver."

"You're a very caring person," Mrs. Grochowski affirmed.

"I almost hit Crazy Carol a little while ago," Heather countered. "That's how caring I am. I was ready to blow my top when she just wouldn't respond to me."

"You almost hit her precisely because you're so caring."

"I don't get it, Mrs. G."

"You're very caring, but you're also very strong willed. That's why you can get so angry, Heather. It's strong-willed people who wrap their golf clubs about trees because that damn little ball won't go where they want it to. You got so angry at Carol because she wouldn't take the care you so much want to give her."

The analogy hit close to home; Heather could feel the rage all over again. She switched the subject. "How do you know so much about golf?"

"I don't, except that my ex-husband used to play. But I do know a lot about strong wills."

"Did he wrap golf clubs around trees?"

"Yes, as a matter of fact. He had a strong will, but I had an even stronger one," Mrs. Grochowski replied, refusing to be diverted.

"You'd have to if you had to live with multiple sclerosis the way you do."

"To the contrary," Mrs. Grochowski replied. "It was my strong will that almost killed me."

"How so?" Heather looked at her in surprise.

"When I was young, my greatest motive in life was to be admired. So I worked hard at being nice so that other people would admire me. It was really totally self-centered, you see, because I was doing it to get their admiration. In order to get it, with my strong will I worked at being just the nicest wife a wife could be and just the nicest mother that a mother could be.

"But while I worked so hard at being nice, things didn't work out so nicely. The first thing that happened was my husband left me with three young children for another woman. I couldn't understand why he left me, since I'd worked so hard at being a nice wife. So I decided that he was a bad man, and then I worked all the harder at being a nice abandoned mother of three children. I did everything for them. But as they got older things continued to not be so nice. They shoplifted. They got involved with drugs. They took up with the wrong crowd. I couldn't understand, again, why I was having such difficulty with them, when I was such a nice mother. So with my strong will I redoubled my efforts at being nice, and I worked myself into a frazzle, rescuing them from this jam and that jam."

Heather was fascinated. In the three years she'd known her, Mrs. G. had never talked about herself so openly. It felt warm, intimate, despite Heather's uneasy sense that there was a message she was supposed to be getting.

"That was when I came down with multiple sclerosis," Mrs. Grochowski continued. "Again, I couldn't understand it. How could God inflict me with this dreadful disease when I had worked so hard at being nice? But I tried not to despair and used my willpower to work even harder so that people would admire me as not only the abandoned but also crippled mother trying to take care of difficult children. Only my multiple sclerosis got rapidly worse. It progressed faster than the doctors had predicted, and I became crippled to the extent that I could no longer take care of my children. They increasingly began having to take care of me.

"And then the strangest thing happened. As soon as they started taking care of me—as soon as I was no longer able to be so nice—my children started pulling their lives together, and things started going better. That was when I became seriously depressed. I began to realize that all of my being nice hadn't worked. Not only were my children doing better now that I was not able to be a noble mother, but I also began to suspect that maybe the reason my marriage had failed was that I had also tried so hard to be nice. You see, I realized that it had been more important for me to look good than it had been for me to make the marriage work. So I realized that in seeking to be admired, I had lived a life totally on a false premise. But I had no other idea how to live it. Here I was, almost totally crippled, and I no longer had a premise on which to live. It was not an easy time. I became seriously depressed. That was when I gave up my will to be admired. I stopped trying to be nice. But you know, it was interesting. That's when my multiple sclerosis stopped progressing so fast. That's why I'm still alive."

Heather was overwhelmed, and full of questions. How could Mrs. G. be so nice when she had stopped trying to be nice? Obviously the story had been pointed at her, but she didn't want to think about that—at least not now. But, as always with Mrs. G., she had gotten what she needed. Although it was confusing, Heather found her story strangely consoling. Her own mother never opened up to her like that, told her stories like this one. No stories at all, in fact. But she didn't want to think about that either. Still, it felt good to know that even Mrs. G. could also experience turmoil, depression. "Thanks, Mrs. G.," she said. "You've helped me, though I don't know exactly why. I expect that you *do* know, but you'll leave me to figure it out for myself. That's the way you usually work."

Mrs. Grochowski grinned at her. "You've figured out my style, at least. Run along now, my dear, I know you've got work to do. But come back whenever you'd like. I'm glad I helped, but you give me a great deal too."

Energized, Heather strode back past the nurses' station and down the opposite arm of the wing to C–18. She was glad to see that Georgia was out—probably still at breakfast. She wanted to talk with Betty alone. Mrs.

Carstairs was lying in her bed by the window, eyes closed, looking even paler than she had four days before. Heather pulled the rocker close to the bed, sat down, and reached over to touch the dozing woman's thin hand. "Good morning, Betty," she announced herself softly.

Mrs. Carstairs's eyes sprung open. The doses of morphine she was receiving did not diminish her alertness. No sooner had she looked at Heather than she exclaimed, "What on earth happened to your poor eye?"

"My boyfriend and I had a fight."

"I'm so sorry."

"Thank you, Betty," Heather replied. "But it will get better very shortly, won't it? Do you think you'll be getting better shortly?"

"Sometimes you get right to the point, don't you, Heather?" Mrs. Carstairs smiled wanly. "That's what I like about you. You don't waste time, and I don't have much time. No, I don't think I will get better."

"Would you like to change your mind and try the chemotherapy?" Heather asked. "It could begin very quickly. We could get you to the hospital today and they could start in the morning." Both knew, however, that at best the chemotherapy might buy her a month or two.

"No," Mrs. Carstairs answered decisively. "You know my husband's dead and my children grown. I've told you how they take good care of my grandchildren. They'll be sad, but they don't really need me anymore. Besides, it might be good for them to learn what it's like to be the oldest generation." For a moment there was almost a twinkle in her eye. Then she continued. "It's been a good life, as lives go; I see no need to painfully prolong it."

"But aren't you afraid?"

Mrs. Carstairs looked at her gratefully. "Yes, I'm afraid," she said. "I don't know what it's like to die. I am a religious person in my own way, but I don't have one of those clear-cut faiths where I know just what heaven is like and am certain that that's where I'm going. I'm going into the unknown. And I guess that's always scary. But it's an adventure too, isn't it?"

"Yes," Heather said. "I think so. I also think you're more right than those people who know all about it. There is mystery to it."

"How do you know all that at your age, Heather?"

"I really don't know," Heather responded. "I don't understand much about who I am." For a full minute of peaceful silence they simply looked at each other. Then Heather reached over to Mrs. Carstairs's wrist and gently felt her pulse. It was regular but the beat had clearly thinned, to a rhythmic whisper now. Heather broke the silence. "I see by the nurses' notes that you were too weak to get up out of bed yesterday. Do you think you might possibly be ready to move to A-Wing?"

Now, for the first time, Mrs. Carstairs actually looked scared.

"They'll be able to keep a much better eye on you," Heather continued, "but I can see it frightens you. What frightens you?"

Mrs. Carstairs lay there for another long moment of thoughtful silence. "It's not the inevitability of A-Wing that scares me," she finally said. "I've come to terms with that. It may seem foolish because they're so small, but two things bother me about it."

"What are they?"

"Well, the biggest thing, actually, Heather, is you. I'd not expected to find you when I came here. You've been a blessing to me this past month. I'd like you to be with me when I die, if that's possible. And it won't be possible on A-Wing."

"Oh, yes it is," Heather assured her. "Every day either the aides or the nurse will be able to tell you whether I'm on duty or when I'm coming on. You can feel free to call for me whenever I'm on duty. Just ask the aide or the nurse and they'll get right in touch with me, and I'll come to you within a few minutes. It happens all the time. It's customary for them to call me from A-Wing."

Mrs. Carstairs looked much relieved.

"You said there were two things that bothered you," Heather prompted.

"Oh, the other's quite small. It's just that I'll miss my bed by the window. I know there's not much to see. Just a little courtyard with a tree, and the snow is usually dirty. But if it snows again, I would love to be able to watch it fall. And occasionally a cardinal or two flies into the tree."

"I tell you what," Heather said, "I'll call over to A-Wing right now. If they have a bed by the window for you, they'll come and take you over this morning. If they don't, I'll come back and tell you, and we'll simply keep you here until they do. Is that all right?"

Mrs. Carstairs looked at her gratefully. "You're wonderful, Heather."

"That I am," Heather said with a grin. She stepped back a couple of steps to look at Mrs. Carstairs in perspective. Yes, there was a faint glow, a light about her. Heather was so glad. "Bye for now," she said. "I'll report back in a little while."

Heather went back to the nurses' station and called A-Wing. They had two open female beds. The woman in one room was comatose, so it didn't matter to her which side of the room she was on. Mrs. Carstairs could have her window bed, and they would be over for her within the hour.

On a roll now, Heather sent word to Mrs. Carstairs and had the energy to check on Rachel Stimson. "From the light to the dark," she thought. Rachel was eighty-two years old and was Crazy Carol's roommate.

Rachel had no feet. Because of diabetes, one leg had been amputated just above the ankle and the other just below the knee. When Heather got to her, Rachel was already in her wheelchair.

Rachel got herself from her bed into her wheelchair by means of a remarkable feat. She insisted upon the wheelchair always being placed next to her bed with the wheels locked. She would swing herself up into a sitting position on the edge of the bed facing it, lean forward, and grab the arms of the wheelchair with her hands. Then she would swing her knees onto the seat, rest for a second, and complete the process with an acrobatic flip, twisting herself around in the chair so that she landed on her buttocks, sitting forward. Although thin, Rachel's arms were as strong as a gymnast's.

"Good morning, Rachel," Heather said, prepared to be undaunted. "How are you today?" Rachel did not answer. Heather sat down in the rocking chair opposite the wheelchair and looked Rachel straight in the eyes. It was a staring match. Rachel's lack of responsiveness was not like Carol's. Her eyes were not vacant or confused. If anything, they glittered, and it was a focused light. Heather thought of lasers.

"Is there anything I can do for you?" she tried again. Again there was no response. Somehow this did not irritate her as much as Crazy Carol had. Carol ignored care; Rachel refused it. She dropped her gaze from Rachel's eyes and quickly checked her out. Her hair needed a little grooming, and she would of course get a bath when Peggy reached her. Her skin color was good. Heather reached forward and lifted the hem of the old woman's nightgown. The stumps looked well. Indeed, after all the years she had been in Willow Glen, Rachel seemed changeless.

"Just let me know if there's anything you want," she said, and got up to leave. As she was going out the door she heard Rachel's voice behind her. It said with measured precision, "He should have blackened the other one."

The parting shot did not faze Heather; its viciousness was customary. As with Crazy Carol, she would inscribe in the nursing notes: "No change." But, of the two roommates, she preferred Rachel. There was life to her—sometimes too much, as when she would hurl dishes, fight against being bathed, or make such hostile remarks. Better a fighting spirit, though, than none at all. Mrs. Grochowski had spoken of strong will. Rachel's will seemed consistently negative, but despite the trouble it caused, there were times when Heather felt a certain admiration for its ferocity.


Clipboard in hand, Roberta McAdams strode through the open door of Mrs. Simonton's office. "Here's the printout of receipts and disbursements, January fifteen through February fifteen," she announced, laying the papers on the desk. "I'll be out of my office for a while. I need to take the bimonthly patient evaluations on C-Wing; it's past the middle of the month."

Mrs. Simonton looked at her deputy with a trace of amusement. There were times she wished she herself could be so well organized. On the other hand, there were times she was very glad she wasn't. "Have you ever in your life been inefficient, Roberta?" She was the only one who ever called her by her first name.

Ms. McAdams looked at her blankly. "Why would anyone want to be inefficient?"

"I don't know. To test the unexpected, maybe. Or to have fun. Like romance. Romance is not very efficient. You're quite attractive, you know, Roberta. Have you any close men friends? Do you date?"

"I have dated," Ms. McAdams answered in a tone that encouraged no further opening.

Mrs. Simonton gave up and switched the subject. "By the way, I have some good news. They called from the State Rehabilitation Office yesterday to tell me they've approved the application for a grant for Stephen's computer. It will be at least six weeks before we get the money, but when you do his evaluation would you let him know? He'll be so happy. Tell him we can't make any promises, but with luck he'll have it by Easter."

"I'll tell him."

"When the grant comes, you're the one who will actually have to buy it. You know how computer unfriendly I am and, as far as I can see, you're the world's number one expert on the things."

Mrs. Simonton had thought Ms. McAdams might look pleased by this tribute to her expertise, but she didn't. She showed no reaction whatsoever. With a faint sigh, Mrs. Simonton waved her away.

Ms. McAdams began with C-18. She found Georgia Bates alone, rocking peacefully. Mrs. Carstairs had already been moved. "How have you settled in?"

Georgia did not particularly want to oblige Madam Icecube, but she couldn't resist trying out the new concept Hank had given her. "As well as one *can* settle into a concentration camp."

"Do you have any complaints about the staff?" asked Ms. McAdams, ignoring the gibe.

Again, Georgia was not eager to respond, but she decided it would be some sort of capitulation not to have a complaint. "That Peggy doesn't seem a very friendly little thing."

Ms. McAdams made a note. "Do you have any questions?" she asked, continuing down her checklist.

Ordinarily Georgia would not have. But the term she had been savoring suddenly sparked a connection and reminded her of a question she'd been meaning to ask during her previous admission. "Speaking of concentration camps, who is that young man who's always lying out in the hall next to the nurses' station? He looks as though he came right out of one."

"That's Stephen Solaris."

"Fine. But why does he look so awful?"

"He was brain-damaged at birth."

"Well, he wasn't born here. How long has he been stuck out there on that table?"

"Over a decade," Ms. McAdams supplied the answer reluctantly. "He was Willow Glen's first patient. And probably its most famous."

"Famous?"

"Yes, there's even been a book written about him."

Ms. McAdams was starting to feel anxious. She never liked to talk about Stephen. Moreover, this conversation was above and beyond the requirements of her checklist. She didn't allot much time for her rounds. But Georgia was persistent. "Why is he the subject of a book?"

"By the time he was two years old they thought he was hopelessly mentally retarded. So he was put in a state school. But when he was five years old an aide at the school suspected he might not be retarded. The book's about how the aide taught him to read and write. It's what they call a human interest story." Ms. McAdams's tone made it clear what she thought of human interest stories.

"Can I read it?"

"It's out of print."

Georgia was not to be put off. "I can't believe this concentration camp doesn't even have a copy of a book about its most famous victim."

Ms. McAdams was growing angry at the garrulous old woman's pertinacity; she had better things to do. She thought of the most time-saving compromise under the circumstances. It was correct that there was a copy of the book in the front office. Obtaining it would be complicated. She was aware, however, that Mrs. Simonton had insisted on keeping a photocopy of the first chapter in Stephen's chart so that the new aides and nurses could read about him. And since it was published material, it was not confidential. "I don't really know whether the book is still around," she responded with forced pleasantness. "But I do know there's a copy of the first chapter in the patient's file."

"Could you get it for me?"

"You can ask the nurse for it," Ms. McAdams cut her off bluntly. "Have a nice day," she added over her shoulder as she turned on her heel,

leaving Georgia marveling. And to think that I called little Peggy unfriendly, she said to herself.

C–17 was next: Stimson/Kubrick. Ms. McAdams glanced down the
corridor at Crazy Carol strapped in her geri-chair. No point in even
talking to her. She neatly inscribed N.R., signifying "no response," in
each of the columns of her checklist after Kubrick. Then she turned into
the room, pleased to see it was occupied so she wouldn't have to go
hunting. "Good morning, Rachel," she exclaimed with her labored hearti-
ness. "Are you feeling well?"

Rachel scrutinized her from her wheelchair, saying nothing. Ms.
McAdams had not expected an answer, marked N.R., and went right on
to the next column. "Do you have any complaints about the staff?"

This time Rachel did respond. "You know perfectly well I can't abide
any of them. Except you, of course. You're the only one I understand."

Ms. McAdams felt no inclination to get her to elaborate. She marked
U.C., for "usual complaints," and moved Rachel right along. "Do you
have any questions?"

Unexpectedly Rachel did. "What is that ugly young man on the gurney
doing here?"

Ms. McAdams allowed herself a moment of surprise. "Rachel, Stephen's been here all the years you have. What's happened that you're
suddenly asking about him now?"

"He's beginning to bother me more and more. He shouldn't be here.
Why isn't he in the state school where he belongs?"

Ms. McAdams felt mixed emotions. On the one hand she was annoyed. Why on earth did everyone decide to be so interested in Stephen all
of a sudden? But she wanted to be particularly careful not to alienate
Rachel. She understood about power and the role that Rachel's husband
played in the community. It was prudent to answer her.

"He *was* in the state school," she said. "But then they discovered he
wasn't retarded. His disabilities are physical—there's nothing wrong with
his mind. He was taught how to read and write and received all the
schooling they could give him. Then regulations required that he had to
leave, since he wasn't retarded any longer. So they moved him to a nursing
home. But he didn't do well. Consequently, when Willow Glen was
opened they transferred him here."

"Well, I wish they'd transfer him out again," Rachel said bluntly,
concluding the interview.

Ms. McAdams gave no thought to why she was the only staff member
Rachel would cooperate with. But she shared Rachel's sense of being
bothered by Stephen. Seriously bothered. He didn't fit anywhere. He
didn't even have a room. It was extra work just to remember to add him

to her checklist. It was all so irregular! And then there were those damn eyes of his and that . . . that sickening *niceness* so incongruent with his condition. But now that he had come to mind, she might as well get him over with. She pushed herself toward the gurney.

As always with him, she phrased her questions so they would not require answers. "I assume you'll let me know if you're not feeling well," she said to Stephen.

He did not respond. Ms. McAdams wrote N.R. "I assume you'll let me know if you have any complaints about the staff." No response. She made the same notation. "And I assume you'll let me know if you have any questions." Again, her third mark.

Eyes still fixed on her checklist, she reported, as instructed: "Mrs. Simonton says that the grant application for your computer has been approved. She said if all goes well you should have it by Easter."

"Ehhhhhh," Stephen bleated.

With distaste, Ms. McAdams unhooked the letter board from the head of the gurney. She did not like to hold it for him because it brought her so close to his grotesque body; moreover, she disliked the inefficiency of such communication. But she did her duty.

"THANK/YOU," Stephen tapped out.

Ms. McAdams hung the letter board back on the gurney without acknowledging him further. She could not stifle—nor did she try—the intense irritation she felt at the thought of Stephen's possessing a computer of his own. He had no right to it. That was her domain. And, if that wasn't enough, she knew Mrs. Simonton intended to waste the time of the Maintenance Department—her own responsibility—in building a stand for his keyboard. Special! Irregularities, exceptions once again for him! But as she returned to her rounds, she glanced at Heather seated in the nurses' station, noted her black eye, and was buoyed by a sense that the rest of the morning would proceed in better order.

When she came back to the wing from her lunch in the dining hall, Georgia spied Heather at the nurses' station. "That unpleasant woman from the front office—Ms. Macadamia Nut or whatever she's called—said you could give me a chapter to read from some book about that young man over there." She motioned toward the gurney.

Aware of how people tended to talk about him as if he wasn't there, Heather announced, "Stephen, Mrs. Bates wants to read about you."

Georgia was chagrined. She realized she'd been tactless. While Heather was opening his chart, she looked at Stephen nervously. Should she apologize to him? But she knew from observing him during her previous stay that he couldn't respond except through his letter board, and she wasn't ready to tackle that yet. She waited helplessly until Heather handed her the clipped-together pages.

She would have fled with it immediately had not Heather said, "You know we moved Mrs. Carstairs out this morning. Probably you'll get a new roommate by tomorrow. If you want to grab the bed by the window, now's your chance."

Georgia was being filled with unaccustomed feelings. First embarrassment, now gratitude. "Thank you. I'd like that," she stuttered, adding, "I'll bring this back as soon as I've finished it." Then she did flee.

Back in the safety of her room, Georgia was elated. She tossed the chapter onto her bed—her *old* bed—and immediately began transferring her belongings from the drawers near the door to the chest on the window side of the room. The picture of the young girl seated in the orchard swing she placed on top of her new bureau. This done, she remembered the chapter. Still excited, she grabbed it and sat down in her new rocking chair, appreciating the better light. The top page, in bold type, read:

# RESURRECTION

## by Stasz Kolnietz

At the bottom of the page was the name of a publisher she'd never heard of.

The print was smaller on the second page and the words fuzzy. Her more familiar mood returned. Why couldn't they make better copies? she wondered as she went to get her reading glasses. She didn't really understand why she should need them yet. But it was just a fact that some people became far-sighted at an early age.

Settling back in her rocker again, she was now able to read the second page. There was the name of the same publisher, the date 1967, and beneath that, written in ink in parentheses—might it have been Heather's script?—(Written while Dr. K. was still in college).

She turned to the next page:

### CHAPTER I

### THE UNSPEAKABLE YES

_____

I CAN'T QUITE remember when I decided to be a lawyer. The New Warsaw Senior High School had a debating team. Perhaps it was making the team in the tenth grade that flamed my ambitions. In any case, it wasn't long before my vision of future fulfillment was the image of myself as a thinner version of Perry Mason, with a competent secretary and private investigator at my beck and call and a commanding presence in the courtroom.

Thus fueled with ambition, I not only became a bookworm but had the hubris to seek a scholarship from colleges of greater prestige than the state university. That hubris was rewarded with the offer of one from Yale. But travel to the East Coast was expensive, the books expensive, and the lifestyle more extravagant. I needed money.

As it was, my parents required my summer labor without pay on the farm. The drought the preceding two years had made the family finances precarious. But my father agreed to let me off by two in the afternoon to find a paying job. The only one available that first summer after my freshman year at Yale, at minimum wage, was working as an aide at the nearby State School for the Retarded.

It was a shock. As an unskilled nineteen-year-old, I was naturally assigned the lowest caste job in one of the male wards for the most severely retarded. It was a plain, large, square room with four rows of five full-sized cribs each. The ages of the bodies in the cribs ranged from two to fifty. It is a dreadful thing to first see an adult man lying in a crib in diapers. Most of the bodies were extremely spastic. The less spastic ones were almost worse. They either lay there in utter limpness, rocked endlessly, or banged their heads against the rails of the crib. Seizures were common.

I was informed that the retarded were divided into three categories: the morons, with an IQ between 50 and 75; the imbeciles, with an IQ between 25 and 50; and the idiots, with an IQ below 25. This was a male idiot ward.

They also informed me that of course they really didn't know the IQs of idiots since, by definition, people so severely retarded cannot communicate sufficiently to be "testable." They lack the capacity for language. Not that they cannot make noise. They scream, yell, babble, and bleat. In fact, the ward was bedlam.

It was also hot. The school could not afford air conditioning. The room stank of feces and urine. But it's amazing how quickly you can get used to even the worst stench.

My job was tediously simple: feeding the inmates and changing diapers. Within two days I had learned the routine and thereafter was in charge of the ward for that shift. I would begin by changing the diapers. Down the rows I would go with a cart containing three buckets and two bins. One bin was for fresh diapers and the other was filled with clean washcloths. One of the buckets was filled with water. The others were for the dirty diapers and washcloths. Crib number one: unpin the dirty diaper, pull it out, dump it in the diaper bucket; take a clean washcloth, soak it in the water, wipe the feces and urine off the buttocks and genitals, and drop the washcloth in the washcloth bucket; take another clean washcloth and use it to scrub the buttocks dry—like scrubbing a wall—and drop it too in the washcloth pail; take a fresh diaper from the bin (they were prefolded) and pin it on; turn the patient if necessary; then move on to crib number two. It took seven minutes a patient. It couldn't be done any faster than that. It couldn't be done any more slowly either. There wasn't the time.

Then I would take the cart down the hall to the kitchen/utility center and park it next to the other used carts. I didn't have to dump or wash the buckets. That was done by the 11 to 7 shift. From there I'd cross the room to get the food cart. The food cart had three bins and three buckets. A small bin held the spoons. The larger ones held bowls and more clean washcloths. One pail was for the dirty washcloths and one for dirty bowls and spoons. The other pail was filled to the brim with baby food. I'd take the food cart back to the ward and begin again down the rows: fill a bowl with baby food, take a spoon, spoon the mush into the patient's mouth; drop the dirty bowl and spoon into the proper bucket; take a clean washcloth, wipe the patient's mouth, dump the washcloth into its bucket, and move on.

This also took seven minutes a patient. I have said that idiots cannot communicate. That's not precisely true. I quickly observed if they did not want to eat or if they had had enough, they would turn their heads away. At such times they would occasionally scream, yell, or bleat. Some ate more slowly than others, and some did not seem to get their fill. But if they hadn't after seven minutes, I had to move on nonetheless. There are not many plump idiots.

At this point Georgia gave up. She simply did not understand why people these days liked to write about such unpleasant things. Certainly, she did not have to read about them. And she wasn't going to.

But then she realized she was in a bind. She had promised Heather she would give back the chapter as soon as she finished it. She checked the last page number. Twenty-one pages, and she'd only finished three of them! Should she keep it and try again? No. She liked Heather, but she was not going to let herself be cowed by a nurse—by anyone—no matter how likable they might be.

She marched decisively back to the nurses' station. "Heather," she asked, "would you be so kind as to come back to my room? I need to talk to you in private."

"Sure. Now's okay."

As soon as the door of C–18 was closed behind them, Georgia explained, "I didn't want to talk with you in front of that young man. You were quite correct in pointing out to me that I'd been rude when I did so before."

"You're sharp, aren't you?" Heather said.

"Thank you. I wanted to give you back the chapter about him."

"You've finished it already?"

"No, and I don't want to. I read several pages and they were most unpleasant."

"The beginning is," Heather acknowledged, "but then it gets quite moving. Besides, it may be unpleasant but it's realistic."

"I don't care," Georgia countered. "I believe people have a right to choose which realities they attend to."

Heather looked at her keenly. "And what realities *do* you choose to attend to, Georgia?"

"I simply wanted to give you the chapter back. I did not intend this to be a philosophical discussion."

With seeming innocence, Heather changed the subject. "How does it feel for you to be back in Willow Glen?"

"It's a nursing home, isn't it? Who wants to be in a nursing home?"

"For many old people, a nursing home like this is just the very best place for them. So it's easier for them to adjust here."

"But I am *not* old."

"How old are you?"

"Thirty-seven," Georgia replied decisively.

Heather sat down in what had been Mrs. Carstairs's chair and closed her eyes. Two minutes of silence went by. It made Georgia profoundly uneasy just standing there. "Aren't you going to say something?" she finally asked.

Heather opened her eyes. "It's hard for me to watch you feeling so guilty when you don't have to be," she said.

Georgia looked at her strangely. "Guilty? Guilty about what?"

"You don't have to feel guilty about being in a nursing home."

"I don't feel guilty about being here. I'm not the guilty one," Georgia exclaimed. "My son and daughter-in-law railroaded me here. They're the ones who are responsible. They're the guilty ones."

"No, they're not. You're just projecting your own guilt onto them."

"Projection, smojection," Georgia snorted. "That's balderdash. I don't know what you're talking about."

"If you could attend to the reality that you're not thirty-seven—that you *are* old," Heather explained, "then you could feel that you have every right to be here. You're entitled to a restful place in your old age. It's all right to give up in certain respects; it may even be good to do so. But you feel guilty about giving up. So, instead of telling your children that you're ready to give up, you blame them for putting you here. You give them the responsibility for being here, when it is really your responsibility. Because you feel too guilty to accept that responsibility."

"I thought this was a nursing home, not a psychiatric hospital," Georgia retorted.

Heather looked her straight in the eyes. "I like you, Georgia. I think you're a good person, and I wish we could be friends. But I only want to be friends with people who are honest with themselves."

"I am perfectly capable of calling a psychiatrist if I wanted to consult with one," Georgia huffed. "Besides, you're too young to be a psychiatrist."

"You're right about that," Heather acknowledged. "But it's not bad to need a psychiatrist, you know. I have one."

"You go to a psychiatrist?" Georgia asked with interest.

"Yes."

Georgia looked at her curiously. "Do you go to a psychiatrist because of your black eye?" she asked.

Heather smiled. "In a way, yes. My boyfriend hit me last night. I don't have a very good love life, you see."

"Have you been going to this psychiatrist for a long time?"

"I've been seeing him for about a year."

"Well, he doesn't seem to be doing you much good then, does he?"

"I'm not sure that's so much his fault as mine." Heather had to chuckle. "It doesn't seem to be very easy for me to change. Sometimes it seems I don't even want to change. So you've got a point. If it's not easy for me to change or even want to change, I certainly can't expect that it would be easy for you to change, can I?"

Georgia did not have to answer. The intercom squawked: "Heather Barsten. Heather Barsten to the office, please."

"Saved by the bell again," Georgia exclaimed.

Heather stood up. "Again?" she asked.

"The other day when that thing went off, it rescued me from Hank Martin's amorousness. And now it's rescuing me from your psychiatric ministrations."

Heather laughed. "I give up." She went to the nurses' station and replaced the manuscript in Stephen's chart. "Now it's my turn to see Mrs. Simonton," she told Peggy. "Would you hold the fort until I get back?"

Heather had long ago come to learn she had nothing to fear from Mrs. Simonton, but a summons always gave her a slightly uneasy feeling in the pit of her stomach. Peggy was right; it was like being called to the principal's office. But the unease faded as she reflected on her conversations with Georgia. She did like the old lady. She could be huffy as all get out and was a bit of a fruitcake, but she pulled it off with a sense of humor. Heather smiled as she thought of McAdams as Ms. Macadamia Nut. She felt calm by the time she knocked on Mrs. Simonton's door.

"Come on in, Heather, and close the door," Mrs. Simonton said.

Heather did so and sat down. "What's up?"

"I wanted to see you because I heard you had gotten a black eye. Almost all rumors in this place are true, but seeing is believing."

"That was fast. How did you hear about it?"

"Spies. I have spies, you know. Ms. McAdams is a very good deputy administrator. Sometimes I am not sure that she has much in the way of a soul, but she gets around, and that's what counts."

"I don't even remember seeing her today," Heather said.

"Well, that's who told me. How she heard about it, I don't have the foggiest idea. But that's not the point, the point is, what happened to you?"

"My boyfriend and I had a fight last night," Heather said for what felt like the hundredth time.

"So when are you going to tell Dr. Kolnietz about it?"

"I suppose when I see him next week."

"You suppose. Would you like to know what I suppose?" Mrs. Simonton asked.

"Sure."

"What I suppose is that by the time you see him next week, you're hoping that most of that shiner will be gone, and what little is left you'll be able to cover with makeup, and that you may just not even remember to mention it to him."

"What goes on between me and Dr. Kolnietz I really think is my business," Heather protested.

Mrs. Simonton grinned at her. "You are quite right, of course. I am being a meddlesome old bitch, as well as a cynical one. I am cynical because I know perfectly well that while there is a part of you that wants to deal with your problems, there is another part that doesn't.

"Your problems are not here at work. So you might think that I have no reason to be concerned about them. But that's just the point. You're the best nurse I have, Heather. There is a vacuum of competence in this world, and when I am able to get some of it in here around me, I value it.

I value you. I worry about you. While I cannot control what happens in your life when you are off duty, I can, to some extent, control what happens when you are on duty. I know that you schedule your appointments with Dr. Kolnietz when you're off duty, and I appreciate that. But that doesn't mean that if there is an emergency, you can't take an hour or two off when you are on duty to go see him."

"But this isn't an emergency," Heather countered.

"It may not be an emergency for you when someone hits you. But if somebody hit me, I would want to talk about it; and because you are a valuable piece of property to me, I myself happen to consider it an emergency. I suggest you get an appointment today or tomorrow. Whatever hours you need to take off are all right with me."

"Thank you," Heather said warily. "I'll think about it."

"You can think about it as long as you want. You can decide not to do it. You can decide never to see Dr. Kolnietz again. But what you cannot do, Heather, is to assume that I am so rigid, and your personal problems so unimportant, that you cannot get a few hours off from work when appropriate. That's all."

When Heather got back to the nurses' station, she sat in front of the phone for two minutes, staring at it. She lifted the receiver an inch, then slammed it down so that the phone gave an involuntary ping in protest.

"Shit," she said, picked it up again, and dialed. To her dismay she reached Dr. Kolnietz without the slightest difficulty. He had an opening, and she made an appointment to see him at noon the next day. When she hung up, she said again, "Shit." She didn't know whether she wanted to kiss Mrs. Simonton or strangle her.


Heather's phone call made Dr. Kolnietz curious. In the year of their sessions together this was the first time she had ever requested an additional appointment. And on one of her workdays to boot. What was up? Well, he'd find out soon enough.

The thought of her at work moved him to think of Willow Glen and, of course, Stephen. His mind jumped back—as it so often did and always would—to that extraordinary night twenty-four years before in the state school.

By the fourth day of his job on the idiot ward he had decided the only way he'd ever survive the summer was by manufacturing an inane kind of unwavering cheerfulness. Going to work each afternoon he'd concoct a stock phrase for the shift such as "I sure hope you've had a nice day" or "The corn's high and it's not even July." Each time he diapered or fed an inmate he'd address him by name—which was easy to do, since each name was printed in bold letters on a card in a slot at the foot of the crib—and repeat his stock phrase. They never responded, of course—they couldn't expect to signal a "no" of protest to unwanted food or a nurse's injection—but it had helped to keep up his morale.

Then the heat wave hit. The second day of it his stock phrase was "It sure is hot, isn't it?" As usual, they didn't respond, at least not until he got to the little five-year-old spastic, Stephen Solaris, in his crib in the middle of the third row. He had said perfunctorily, "It sure is hot, isn't it, Stephen?" and there came back an answering bleat: "Ehhhhhh." At first he had thought nothing of it, but as he was exchanging the diaper cart for the food cart he wondered. Probably it was an accident. Still, it was the only hint of a positive response he'd gotten from any of the twenty patients. Just for his own amusement he'd check it out. When he got to Stephen again—this time with the feeding cart—he'd said, "It sure is cold this evening, isn't it, Stephen?" There was no response.

But he'd continued, "I just lied to you, Stephen. Forgive me, please. It was a kind of test. The truth is it's damn hot. It's even hotter this evening than it was last night, isn't it?"

"Ehhhhhh," Stephen had bleated again.

Kolnietz leaned back in his chair, once again savoring the moment so vividly etched in his memory. He'd rushed through the rest of the inmates with a mounting sense of excitement. At best, all that the others seemed to be able to communicate was a primitive "no" in response to threat. Was it possible that somehow this little boy could respond with a "yes" to an actual question? By the end of the shift Kolnietz had discovered it was. He'd stayed two hours past his shift to work with the child. When they quit at one o'clock in the morning, he had not only taught Stephen how to bleat in different tones to signify "yes" and "no"; the child was able to use the appropriate tone in every single response.

Driving home in the family pickup, his elbow hanging out the window, whipped by the hot dark air, Kolnietz had experienced something akin to exaltation. He did not know anything about neurology then. He did not know whether this child would ever be able to speak intelligibly. He did not know whether he would ever be able to learn how to read or write. He didn't even know the slightest thing about his background. But he did know three things. He knew the boy could not only hear but comprehend human language. He knew the boy could signal to the outside world on the basis of this comprehension. And, above all, he knew that Stephen Solaris was not an idiot.

Kolnietz sat forward and picked the chart off his desk. His next patient was waiting, and he had better things to do than recollect for the ten thousandth time a moment in the distant past. But he did not begrudge himself the recollection. It was only natural he should dwell so often on that moment because it had been, in a very profound sense, not only a new beginning in Stephen's life, but also in his own.

The damn Certificate of Need Commission had requested reports on three of the C-Wing patients to justify their continued stay at Willow Glen. Mrs. Simonton had finished two. The most equivocal remained: Hank Martin's. After a minute's thought, she turned to a fresh page on her yellow legal pad and wrote in longhand:

> Henry Martin is a 78-year-old, chronically unemployed Caucasian male who has been on social security disability since a cerebrovascular accident in 1980 which left his right leg paralyzed. Following this CVA, he maintained himself in a boardinghouse, but represented a problem to the community because of frequent episodes of public drunkenness and inappropriate sexual behavior. For these reasons his admission to Willow Glen was initiated four years ago by the public defender. Since that time he has adjusted well to this facility and been totally sober. His hypersexuality—thought to be the result of cerebral ischemia with consequent cortical disinhibition—has continued but has not posed a serious threat to either staff or patients.

Mrs. Simonton shoved the pad aside for secretarial transcription. She smiled grimly to herself with a certain sense of satisfaction over her phrase, "cerebral ischemia with consequent cortical disinhibition." That would keep them. They always wanted proof that the disability was physical rather than social—as if there really could be proof, the idiots. How on earth could she or anyone know the degree to which Hank's horniness was the result of a stroke or just his chronic emotional immaturity? And what did it matter? The fact was, he was doing perfectly well here, wasn't he? If they dumped him out into a halfway house or something, he'd be a problem once again and cost the stupid state even more. This whole rigmarole was so silly.

Next she reviewed the income/disbursements printout McAdams had handed her that morning. There were no problems, no surprises, although as always she felt irritated when she noted the disbursements for Dr. Ortiz and the RNs. The law required there to be a nurse on duty at all times, but it was the licensed practical nurses—the LPNs like Heather—who really made Willow Glen tick. The registered nurses were an expensive formality. As was Dr. Ortiz. Why did a physician have to sign the death certificates? Any fool could tell when a patient died. Nor was there ever much doubt about the cause—not in a nursing home. And as for the medications he prescribed—usually by phone without even seeing the patient—she could have done better herself. She had learned a lot about medicine over a generation. But the law was the law and Dr. Ortiz had to have his weekly retainer.

Suddenly she noticed the silence. She did not have to look at her watch to know why. The chattering pulse of the typewriters in the Administration Center outside her door had come to a dead halt because it was five P.M.—quitting time. The clerical workers certainly knew how to watch the clock. Wouldn't it be extraordinary if just one of them stayed just five minutes later just once? But then that was the nature of clerks, and how could she expect anything more?

Still, she knew that the morale among the clerical staff was not as high as it might be. Their turnover was far greater than it should have been. She herself supervised the nursing staff, but she had to leave the supervision of the support staff up to McAdams. She couldn't do everything, could she? Nonetheless, she resented her dependence upon McAdams, upon her understanding of computers and record-keeping, and the tight ship she ran. Administratively at least. It was a relief to know she was spared all that, though the turnover was ample evidence McAdams was as ice-cold a supervisor as she was a colleague.

Mrs. Simonton was well aware that her chronic irritation and resentment represented something akin to depression. She had seen too much, experienced too much. It was not easy to keep putting one foot in front of the other when there was nothing new in the world anymore. She thought once again about selling Willow Glen. There would be plenty to retire on. But whom could she sell it to besides one of these new health care conglomerates, who would choose Roberta McAdams—or some other look-alike model of chilly efficiency—to be its director? Anyway, where would she go, what would she do?

She slipped back into a fantasy she'd had of late that someday she'd be able to turn Willow Glen over to Heather. But she knew it was just a fantasy. Thinking of Heather, she wondered whether the girl had made an extra appointment with Dr. Kolnietz. And thinking of that, she wondered if Heather would ever be healed. She hoped so. But the knowledge tugged at her that were she to be healed, Heather would change, and then why would she ever want to keep working at Willow Glen?

Peggy and Laura, her two day-shift aides, had long gone home. Irene, the aide on the three-to-eleven shift, was just starting the evening vital

signs check. Heather savored the moment alone at the nurses' station,
thinking about Stephen. She had deliberately put off going over to him to
the end of the day. She knew it was to be a pivotal moment in their
relationship, and she wanted to put the finishing touches on her plan. The
correct thing to do was unclear, but as she had thought—obsessed, really—
over the past four days about his sexual responsiveness to her, she had
come to know what she *had* to do. He would raise the issue, of course; he
never avoided anything. She had prepared her answer. Now it was only a
matter of execution.

"Hey, baby, you look lonely." The interruption came from Hank
Martin, who had shoved himself up against the outside of the nurses'
station and was leaning half across it with his customary leer.

Heather was glad the barrier of the station was between them. "I'm not
lonely." She eyed him warily. "What do you need, Hank?"

"You know what I need—a good feel."

"Oh, go away."

"You don't even give me the same attention you give the other patients," Hank whined. "Like the way you're always hanging around that
cripple over there."

Heather jumped up. "I'll speak to you in the dayroom," she shouted.
"Now! Get over there!"

Hank limped off quickly, swinging his cane, in obedience to her fury.
She followed after him. "You asshole!" she spat. "Don't you know he
hears and understands everything you say?"

Hank did not look the least perturbed. "You're a nurse," he said.
"You're supposed to take care of me. Yet you won't care for me in the
way I need most."

"You know perfectly well it's not my job to care for patients in that
way."

"Well, I bet you feel *him* up, and I'd think you'd rather spend your time
with a real man."

The insight suddenly came to her. "You're jealous of Stephen, aren't
you, Hank?" Imagine being jealous of someone as hurt, as restricted, as
Stephen! "Well, let me tell you two things," she continued coldly. "One is
that you have every reason to be jealous of him. Stephen is as smart and
caring as you are stupid and thoughtless. The other is that if I ever hear
you talking like that in front of him again, I'll take your cane and
personally wrap it around your neck. Good-bye."

Heather strode out into the corridor. For the second time that day she'd
felt like striking a patient. It was no accident. In his own way, Hank was
just as boring, repetitious, and out of it as Crazy Carol. Only she'd been

guilty about her feelings toward Carol and she wasn't feeling the least guilty now; the little pig deserved it.

Still, he'd been eerily close to the mark, and it called for a slight change in strategy. She'd intended to go straight to Stephen, but it might not look quite right just now. What should she do? She was still angry and needed someone to calm her down. Tim O'Hara, of course. Hank's roommate, as different from him as day from night.

She found him sitting in his rocking chair. His question was inevitable. Before she could even say good afternoon he asked, "Why, angel, whatever happened to your eye?"

"I had a fight with my boyfriend."

"He shouldn't be doing that to you, now."

"Well, it takes two to tango, you know, Tim." Heather smiled wanly. "I expect I'm just as much at fault as he."

"A lot of Irishmen are in the habit of hitting their women," Tim remarked, "but I myself never had the stomach for it. It just doesn't seem very manly to me."

Heather felt defensive. Anyway, Tony wasn't Irish. She switched the subject. "How are you?" she asked.

"Oh, I'm fine, angel," Tim replied. And he did look well, his complexion pink against his beautiful white hair and mustache. But Heather knew otherwise. So did Tim. The angiogram reports demonstrated that his right carotid and vertebral arteries were totally blocked, and only a very small amount of dye was able to get through the arteriosclerosis in his other vertebral and carotid arteries. A surgical attempt to try and open up either of the arteries would far more likely kill him than save him. The question was not whether he would have another stroke; it was when. Tim and Heather had discussed it seriously on a number of occasions. These days, however, they generally joked about it.

"So the arteries are just gurgling away?" Heather said.

"One day at a time, angel; one day at a time," Tim smiled. "I'm a very fortunate man. Whoever would have suspected that God would give Marion to an old man like me? Even if He gave her to me for just one day at a time?"

Heather bent down and kissed him on his pink cheek. "You're a beautiful man, Tim O'Hara," she said.

She had not even straightened up when Tim said matter-of-factly, "Your father's an alcoholic, isn't he?"

Heather straightened up abruptly. *"What?"*

"Your father's an alcoholic," he repeated.

There was a long pause. "It so happens he is," Heather said finally, "but how do you know?"

Tim grinned. "It takes one to know one. I'm an alcoholic myself. Oh, I've been sober now for twenty years through Alcoholics Anonymous, but we're never cured, you know. I'm a recovering alcoholic. That's what we call ourselves in AA."

Heather pulled up a chair beside Tim. She was intensely curious, but she also needed the action to regain her composure. "Whether you're an alcoholic or not, you've never met my father," she said when she was seated. "So what tips you off?"

"All kinds of things."

"Like what, for instance?"

"Like your black eye, for one. I never hit my wife, although I did some things just as bad. But most men who hit their women are alcoholics."

Much as she liked him, Heather became detached—intellectual and sharply skeptical. "Tim, you're full of it," she said. "You've not only never met my father; you've never met Tony. You're jumping to conclusions."

But he seemed to take no notice of her counterattack. "And the women who take up with alcoholics usually have alcoholic fathers," he continued. "It's a pattern. It goes on and on. My wife's father was an alcoholic."

"You're trying to fit me into some kind of formula," Heather protested.

"It's because you fit so well." Tim was unrelenting. "That's why you're such a good nurse."

For the first time since he had come to Willow Glen a year before, Heather felt irritated at Tim. He had no right to be saying these things. And he kept going on and on. "My wife was a nurse," he said, "a real good one, like you. And she took good care of me until she finally became fed up and left me. That's the formula, you see. Her father was an alcoholic. She took care of him. She nursed him. And she liked it in some perverse kind of way. So she became a nurse. But it can become a sort of compulsion, taking care of people. You seek out the kinds of people who have to be taken care of. Like alcoholics and other kinds of cripples or grown-up infants. That's why she sought me out—one more baby to clean up after. I think it gives people like that a sense of power."

Heather thrust back her chair. "You're telling me I'm some kind of power-hungry creep just because I'm a nurse," she said petulantly. "There are lots of reasons people become nurses. All kinds of reasons—good ones. I thought you liked me, Tim O'Hara."

"I do like you, angel. But I just want you to know what you're doing. And I don't want you to get beaten up anymore."

The conversation had not gone as she'd expected. It felt more like a scolding than an uplifting, and a harsh one at that. Yet she couldn't summon up real anger the way she did toward Hank. Even though the things Tim had just said were way off base—they were off base, weren't they?—she felt very differently now. She felt cared for.

"See if I'll come back here to let myself get picked on again," Heather said. They both knew she was joking. "Take care." She was ready now to see Stephen.

He had been waiting for her. Having no alternative, he had grown very good at waiting. Heather, who liked to nurse, had asked him more than once how he stood it, lying on the gurney day after day with so little apparent stimulation. After three years she still tried to ply him with tapes—talking books, lectures, music. Occasionally he accepted, as often as not to please her. The music he sometimes liked, but the books almost always bored him. It sounded so arrogant to tell her that he already knew most of what was in them. "I/HAVE/A/RICH/INTERIOR/LIFE," he tried to explain to her, but how could she understand? How could anyone understand how much there really was to think about unless it was someone equally intelligent and helpless like Mrs. Grochowski?

Particularly the amount there was to contemplate these days! As long as he was parked by the nurses' station there were mountains to digest. Heather's black eye. That was a worry, a deep concern. Georgia Bates's first sign of interest in him. Although Heather had tried to do it quietly, he was aware that the first chapter of Dr. K.'s book had been returned to his chart before Georgia could possibly have had time to read it all. He had surmised the reason, but he did not feel badly; he suspected she would be back. Nor had Hank Martin's obvious jealousy disturbed him, it was so in character. Ordinarily, though, he would have thought more deeply about this had there not been so many other things happening. His computer was coming! Finally, he would be able to write the book he had been drafting in his head for the past two years! Why, however, was Ms. McAdams more unpleasant, more brusque than usual over it? What was that terrible anger she had inside her? But all these thoughts—even his driving preoccupation with his book—were eclipsed by his struggle to solve the mystery of his sexuality, that incredible mystery which had begun a mere four days before.

He had been taught the physiology of sex. As far back as he could remember he would frequently awake from dreams with an erection. Wet dreams had begun when he was twelve. Sometimes the content of his dreams was vaguely sexual—but only vaguely—and would leave him with a faint yearning—but only faint. Often he'd had spontaneous erections while awake, but not because he had conscious sexual thoughts. He never had conscious sexual thoughts. And he'd never had an erection when bathed before. Not until four days ago with Heather, when everything had changed.

Why the change? Why that arousal? And why, at the age of twenty-nine, since that erection, was his mind for the first time running rampant with sexual fantasies, as if a dam had just burst? Fantasies of seeing Heather's breasts, of her putting her nipple in his mouth, of other things she might do to him? And it was not just Heather. Why had he even begun to wonder what young Peggy might look like with her clothes off? It was as if his eyes had suddenly been opened—opened to a whole new dimension.

The first key to unlocking the puzzle had come when he'd realized the question needed to be rephrased. It was not so much why his eyes had suddenly been opened, but why they hadn't been opened earlier. Why had he *kept* them shut? Why hadn't they opened naturally at the age of thirteen or fifteen or seventeen, as he knew happened to normal boys? Why had he unconsciously wanted to avoid—to repress—his sexuality?

Phrased that way, the answer was obvious. The pain. He had wanted to avoid the pain of sexuality. He had had an enormous amount of pain in his life. More than enough. He was not sorry for himself, but it was no wonder that he had wanted to avoid this pain when he remembered his first great pain.

It had come when he was seven. Dr. Kolnietz—he wasn't a doctor then, of course—had taught him to read the summer he was five. By the end of the summer they had moved him to a special bedroom in one of the buildings for the least retarded. In fact, his first truly clear memory was of that move, of being taken from his crib, placed on a gurney, and pushed up the road to the new building; of his first sight of sky and clouds, of buildings from the outside, of automobiles, and of other children walking; of being transferred to a real bed with guardrails in a room of his own. When Dr. K. had left to go back to college, they'd assigned him special aides to continue his teaching. There were so many things to learn. The world became incredibly rich for him. But the richest time was that summer he was seven.

It was geography summer. Unknown to him, throughout the preceding fall, winter, and spring Dr. K. had mobilized the staff of the state school and his classmates at Yale to collect postcards from all across the world—almost four thousand different ones. The two of them began with New Warsaw, with photographs Dr. K. himself had taken of his hometown and the surrounding plains. Then they moved outwards, accompanied by an atlas, with the postcards: cards of Chicago, Minneapolis, St. Louis; of the Appalachians and the steel mills; of Boston, New York City, and the coast of Maine; of colonial New England churches, the Finger Lakes, the Black Hills and the Rocky Mountains, of Mount Rainier and the redwoods; of Seattle, San Francisco, and the California coast; of Death Valley and the Mojave Desert; of the Grand Canyon and Indian cliff dwellings; of giant cactuses and the little arroyos; Phoenix, Santa Fe, Taos, San Antonio and into the South; plantations and Spanish moss; Memphis and the Mississippi; New Orleans and the bayous.

For some reason Dr. K. had saved Florida for last. Stephen didn't know why. Nor did he know—and he still didn't—why it was that when he first saw a picture of a coconut palm he felt shivers down his spine. It was as if he had seen one before; yet he knew he hadn't. He insisted then that they whip around the equator, zigzagging through the tropics and the palm trees of the globe: palm trees in the Bahamas and Caribbean; in Venezuela and Hawaii; Fiji, Bora Bora, Indonesia, Singapore, Malaya, Ceylon.

Then to the date palms on the edge of the Sahara and a tour of the limits of the Moslem world: Tehran, Baghdad, Damascus, Istanbul, Cairo, Fez, Malaga, and Cordoba. That led to ruins: Corinth and Delphi, Delos and the Parthenon, Petra and Angkor Wat, the Forum in Rome, Pompeii, and on to the great Mayan temples of the Yucatan, Chichen Itza, and Uxmal. And palaces: the Alhambra, Versailles, Hampton Court. And cathedrals: St. Peter's, Chartres, Salisbury, Winchester. Then the great cities of Europe: London, Paris, Prague, Leningrad. Together from that little room in the state school, card by card, he and Dr. K. rushed on to explore the Cotswolds and English lake country, the pampas of Argentina, and the rain forests of Brazil, the great animal herds of Kenya and Nairobi, the steppes of Russia, Mongolia, Tibet.

It was late August. Dr. K. had explained there were only two weeks left before he returned to his final year at Yale and had suggested Stephen think of those postcards he most wanted to see again. He'd started to, but then great tears began to roll down his spastic cheeks. It was merely painful to want to smile but not be able to produce a smile with those frozen muscles; it was excruciating to cry without being able to contort his face in grief.

When Dr. K. had returned the next day and asked whether he'd made his selections, he'd signaled "no." The tears started again. Kolnietz saw them. "What's wrong?"

"NOTHING," he tapped angrily.

"Bullshit," Dr. K. had countered. "You have to tell me."

He finally had. "PARIS. NEVER/SEE/PARIS. NEVER. NEVER. NEVER/SEE/A/ PALM/TREE. ONLY/CARDS. NEVER/SEE/ANYTHING/BUT/CARDS."

Dr. K. had suffered the reality with him. Some of the pain was gone by the end of those two weeks, but it was six months more before he could fully accept that his body would forever be confined to a bed or gurney in an institution, and that there was absolutely no hope that he could ever travel anywhere except within his mind's eye.

Since there was no possibility he could ever go there, why yearn to walk the streets of Paris? Why long to actually see and hear the fronds of a coconut palm being brushed by a tropical storm? But that was as far as he had ever consciously allowed his pain to take him. Of course, he had never let himself be sexual. It was more than he could have borne at thirteen, at fifteen, at seventeen, at any age. Since his paralyzed hands could never travel the terrain of a woman's body, why should he have allowed himself such a futile urge? Why become a sexual being when there was no point? Why?

But four days ago—for some reason—that had all changed and he was waiting for Heather. Only the answer to the question—now conscious— was still unclear. One part of him—it seemed to have taken on a life of its own these past four days—was very clear; it was shrieking "YES" to whatever touch, whatever pleasures, might come. The other part was shrinking back from pain to safety, to control, to all that seemed reason and sanity and wisdom. He was both prepared and still very much unprepared when he finally felt Heather's hand on his.

"I'm sorry about the way that scrawny little prick talked about you," she said.

"Ehhhhhh."

Heather unhooked the letter board and held it for him. "NOT/BOTHERED," his knuckles tapped. "BOTHERED/ABOUT/YOU. WHO/HIT/YOU?"

Of course, she thought. He'd been aware of it all day. "My boyfriend."

"BOY? FRIEND???"

"It takes two to tango, you know," Heather said, lamely, repeating what she had just said to Tim.

"YOU/HIT/HIM/TOO?"

Heather shook her head.

"WHY/ARE/YOU/TRYING/TO/DEFEND/HIM?"

Heather was annoyed by the fact that no one—even Stephen—seemed willing to leave the subject of her fight alone. "I may not be as nice as you imagine me to be, Stephen," she said. "If we got closer maybe you'd want to hit me too."

"BUT/I/WOULDN'T/BE/ABLE/TO, WOULD/I?"

She laughed.

Stephen continued tapping. "I/DO/WANT/TO/GET/CLOSER."

"I do too."

"BUT/I'M/SCARED. OF/SEX. ALL/NEW/TO/ME."

"You don't have to be scared," Heather proclaimed with no idea of what was at stake for him. "I've been thinking about it. In fact, I've been having trouble getting it off my mind. It's not something that we can do on days. It's the aide's job to do the bathing, and it wouldn't look right. So it will have to wait until early next month when I'm back on nights. Then I can do something even better than bathing you. I think I have it all figured out."

"DO/YOU?" Stephen tapped, part of him thrilled and part of him astonished at how differently their minds were working. "HOW/DO/YOU/KNOW/IT/WOULD/BE/THE/RIGHT/THING/FOR/YOU?"

"Stephen the Scrupulous," she teased. "Let me worry about me. Don't you want to?"

There was no way with the cumbersome letter board he could explain all that was in his heart. "NOT/SURE," he answered. "MAY/NOT/BE/RIGHT/FOR/ME. YOU/MAY/HAVE/IT/ALL/FIGURED/OUT/BUT/I/DON'T/YET. WILL/THOUGH/WHEN/TIME/COMES — IF/YOU/STILL/WANT/TO."

"You're making me wait," Heather pouted, half seriously, knowing the time had come to change the subject. "Anyway, are you all right? Is everything okay with you?"

"BETTER/THAN/OKAY. I'M/GOING/TO/GET/MY/COMPUTER."

"Oh, Stephen, that's wonderful!" Heather exclaimed. He had been waiting so long for this news, had been, she knew, afraid to let himself believe it would really happen. She shared his joy. "Now you can finally write your book," she said.

"YES," Stephen tapped. "NOW/I/CAN/WRITE/MY/BOOK. IF/IT'S/REALLY/WHAT/I'M/SUPPOSED/TO/DO."

She sensed the doubt behind his words. "Why on earth wouldn't it be?" she asked.

"DR/K/WROTE/A/BOOK. MAYBE/I'M/JUST/TRYING/TO/BEAT/DADDY."

"So what? Why shouldn't you?"

There was silence. His hands lay unmoving on the letter board, as if the words he sought would not come. Finally he tapped: "THERE/MUST/BE/THE/RIGHT/REASONS. I/MUST/NOT/WRITE/FOR/THE/WRONG/REASONS."

"Stephen the Scrupulous again!" she chided, hoping her lightness would ease him. "You write it. You deserve to; you've waited a long time for this."

"DESERVE/IS/NOT/THE/NAME/OF/THE/GAME."

"Now it's Stephen the theologian. But then you're always that, aren't you?"

"HAVE/TO/BE."

"Well, I just hope when I'm back on nights you're not so scrupulous and theological that you won't want to do what I've got in mind for you," Heather said teasingly.

She gave his knee a squeeze and hung up the letter board. She had been so engrossed she had failed to notice Hank Martin propped up against the opposite wall, cane in hand. He slipped away just before she turned back to the nursing station. But he had been there almost the entire time she had been with Stephen, and he had been watching them intently.

# THREE

At forty-three Dr. Stasz Kolnietz was already tired. Specifically, he was tired of fighting. Most of the time the practice of psychotherapy seemed like an uphill struggle. Two years before he had wondered whether he was not already burnt out. He thought it might help to take up a hobby, so he had tried gardening. That too was an uphill struggle: a continual battle against weeds and pests and drought, rabbits and raccoons.

With luck (or was it the grace of God?) the battle of psychotherapy was sometimes won. Only when that happened, it was not long before the patient left, leaving a space to be filled by a new battle to be begun all over again. He sighed, thinking of Heather sitting in the waiting room. This battle still had a long way to go. He stood up behind his desk and went out into the middle of the room. For ten seconds he danced around in the room shadowboxing. He smiled, thinking that if his patients could see him, they would decide he was crazy. His spirits raised, ready to do battle again, he opened the door and said, "Come in, Heather, please."

Heather took her usual chair at one end of the couch, and Dr. Kolnietz the chair at the other. Someday it might be necessary to use the couch with Heather, but not now. She was not ready yet. And with luck, it wouldn't be necessary.

"I didn't really want to come for this appointment," Heather began, "but Mrs. Simonton almost forced me into it yesterday. She thought I ought to talk to you about my black eye. I had a date with Tony the day before yesterday. We drank a good deal and ended up in bed. After we'd made love he wanted to leave. I didn't want him to. I tried to cling to him, so he hit me."

There was a long silence. "That's all?" Kolnietz asked.

"That's all."

He stood up and went over to the window behind Heather's chair. "I am going to give you another lecture," he said. "Actually it's the same lecture I've been giving you before. And I am sure I will have to deliver it again. I have no idea how many more times you will need to hear this lecture before it sinks in."

He stalked to the middle of the room and looked squarely at her. "You are one of the best storytellers I know, Heather," he continued. "You regale me with stories of the patients in the nursing home, about Tim and Mrs. G., about Stephen, about Hank the Horny and Crazy Carol. These stories are filled with detail and pathos. Sometimes they are so funny, I almost split my sides. Sometimes they are so moving, I feel tears come into my eyes. They're filled with richness and detail. They bring the nursing home alive to me. But here you have a story to tell about something most dramatic in your life—about being assaulted—and there are virtually no details, no pathos, no color, no richness, no emotion. It doesn't even begin to come alive. Why?"

Heather was silent.

"You have a neurosis. That term was invented by Freud. In pondering what causes neurosis, he coined another term: 'repetition compulsion.' What that fancy term means is that people with a neurosis have a tendency to do the same stupid thing over and over again. The reason that smart people like you can be so stupid in some area of their lives is that they don't know how to think about that area. They don't know how to think *about* that area because their childhood experience has been such as to teach them not to think *in* that area.

"You came to see me because you have a neurosis, a repetition compulsion. Specifically, you have a neurosis in relationship to men. Although you are bright and beautiful, you take up with one total loser after another. You came to me because you recognized this, recognized that you were spinning your wheels. But we haven't gotten very far yet, have we? You are still relating to men stupidly, over and over again, because you have still not learned how to think in this area. That is why you tell me such a dull, limited story.

"I want you to tell me the story again. Only this time, I want you to think about it. I don't want you to leave out the details. I want you to make it full and rich and come alive for me."

"There really isn't much more to tell," Heather protested. "Tony and I had a date to go skiing. He picked me up at one in the afternoon. We skied from about two-thirty to five. Then we came back to the apartment. I fixed dinner. After dinner, we made love. Then, as I told you, he wanted to leave. I didn't want him to. We fought about it and he hit me and then he left."

Dr. Kolnietz was still standing in the middle of the office, fighting back his exasperation. Finally, he said, "We are going to do something we've not done before. We are going to play a little game. Only it isn't really a game; it's very serious. I call it a game only because I am going to play a role. The role I am going to play is the healthy part of your mind."

He strode across the room and stood behind Heather's chair. "I am going to ask you questions; only you are going to pretend that it is not me that is asking you the questions, but your own mind—the healthy part. You see, part of thinking is asking yourself questions, and when it comes to your relationship with men, you do not ask yourself the questions you ask yourself in the healthier parts of your life. So I am going to bend down just behind your chair and ask the questions as if you yourself were asking them. Do you understand?"

"I think so," Heather replied. She was anxious.

"Good," said Dr. Kolnietz, crouching down so that he could place his lips two inches from the back of Heather's head.

"Tony picked me up to take me skiing at one o'clock," he said. "That is late to go skiing. Why didn't he pick me up earlier?"

"He said he was going to. He said he was going to pick me up by ten. I waited and waited, and he finally arrived at one."

"I wonder why he kept me waiting so very long?" Dr. Kolnietz asked.

"I asked him when he got there, and he said that he had a car to work on—that it was an emergency job."

"Did I really believe him when he told me that?"

"I had my doubts," Heather admitted. "Tony's a mechanic, and I've never heard of mechanics having to work half-days. But I didn't want to question him about it. He would just think that I didn't trust him and would get mad."

"I wonder why he didn't call to tell me that he would be late?" Dr. Kolnietz questioned.

"I didn't ask him. Again, I didn't want to seem to press him."

"Did I have fun with Tony skiing?"

"No. It was all very scary. First we had to rent the equipment. It was strange and new to me. Then he took me out to what he called the 'bunny slope.' I kept falling down. He told me I would have to learn how to turn. I asked him to teach me. He tried for about ten minutes, but we seemed to get nowhere. I'm pretty clumsy, I guess. After that, he said he was fed up and that I would have to learn to turn by myself while he went off on the trails. I kept falling and falling and getting nowhere until some guy came by and taught me a little bit how to snowplow. I fell a little less scared after that. Then Tony came back at five when they shut down the lift, and we went home and fixed dinner."

"Did I feel like fixing dinner?" Dr. Kolnietz asked.

"No. I was tired and didn't want to cook. I hoped that Tony would take me out to dinner. Just a pizza would have done. But he said that he didn't have any money after paying for the skiing. So I bought us two strip steaks and baking potatoes and some ice cream. I had a bottle of cheap gin already in the apartment."

"Did I drink more than I ordinarily would have?"

"Yes."

"I wonder why?"

"I was in a bad mood by that time. I thought it might make me mellow. It did help."

"Did I want to go to bed with Tony?"

"Yes, drinking always makes me horny, and I wanted the evening to end on a decent note."

"Did I enjoy the lovemaking? Did I climax?"

"No. Tony had premature ejaculation. He said it was because of the gin he had drunk."

"Did I believe him?"

"No. I thought if anything, alcohol makes it harder for a man to come. But maybe I'm wrong. It usually makes it easier for me to come. After he had ejaculated, I asked him to help me climax with his hand, but he said he couldn't because he was too tired."

"How did I feel then?"

"I felt abandoned. I just kept hoping something could be made out of the day after all. The thing I most like is to have somebody to sleep with me, to cuddle with, to hold through the night long. If he stayed, that would have made up for it."

"I wonder why I didn't ask him before we went to bed whether he would stay or not?"

"I thought about it, but thought I'd better not. Tony is always telling me that he hates to be pinned down."

Dr. Kolnietz straightened up and stretched. He felt very stiff. He knew that some of the stiffness was because of the awkward position in which he had squatted behind Heather. But it was also the stiffness of someone who had been through a battle. Still, there was more of the battle to come. He went over to his desk and got a tape recorder. Sitting on the edge of his desk, he looked at Heather. "The whole day really was a bust, wasn't it?"

"It sure as hell was," Heather acknowledged.

"I'd like to go back to playing this 'game' we've been playing," Dr. Kolnietz said, "with me asking the questions which you ought to be asking yourself, kneeling behind you, speaking for the healthy part of your mind. Only this time, I'd like to tape our dialogue. Are you willing to have it recorded?"

Heather nodded. Dr. Kolnietz took the recorder and laid it on the couch next to her, turned it on, and crouched back behind her chair.

"Was I angry when Tony kept me waiting all morning?" he asked.

"Yes."

"Did I tell him I was angry about that?"

"No."

"Was I angry that he didn't think to call me that he was going to be late?"

"Yes."

"Did I tell him that I was angry about that?"

"No."

"Was I angry when he finally got there and told me that he had to work on a car, and I didn't believe him?"

"Yes."

"Did I tell him that I was angry about that?"

"No."

"Was I angry at him when he didn't stay with me and teach me how to ski when I needed help?"

"Yes."

"Did I tell him that I was angry?"

"No."

"Was I angry when he wouldn't take me out to dinner?"

"Yes."

"Did I tell him that I felt too tired to cook and that I was angry about that?"

"No."

"Was I angry when he prematurely ejaculated?"

"Yes."

"Did I tell him that I was angry?"

"No."

"Was I angry when he told me he was too tired to help me have my climax?"

"Yes."

"Did I tell him that I was angry at that?"

"No."

"Was I angry when he got up and started to leave?"

"Yes."

"Did I tell him that I was angry that he was leaving?"

"Not in so many words," Heather answered.

"What did I tell him?"

"As he was all dressed and opening the front door to leave and I was standing there in the living room stark naked, I told him that his balls were made out of peanut butter."

Dr. Kolnietz laughed. He couldn't help himself. He got up and walked around in front of her and stretched. "I am sorry if I laughed, Heather," he said, "but that was actually quite funny."

"I'm not really sure what I meant by it. I just said it," Heather responded.

"In eight words you told him that he wasn't a man and that he was like a couple of balls of shit. I suppose that's when he hit you, wasn't it?"

"Yes."

Dr. Kolnietz went back and crouched down behind her. "How did I feel after Tony hit me?" he asked.

"It's as though I didn't feel anything. I really didn't care."

"Frequently when people say they don't care, what they really mean is that they are experiencing many different conflicting powerful emotions all at once. What mixture of emotions was I feeling after Tony hit me?"

"I felt good that I had told him off. I still felt furious at him. I felt glad I'd gotten a reaction out of him. I felt violated by him. I felt I probably deserved it. I felt like a piece of shit, too. I felt he probably treated me like shit because I was."

Now the questions came even faster and harder.

"I wonder how my mother feels when my father hits her?"

"I don't know."

"Wonder, damn it!"

"Maybe the same. Maybe frustration. Maybe hatred. Maybe self-hatred. Maybe just not caring any more."

"I wonder if my mother ever tells my father that his balls are made out of peanut butter?"

"She tells him he's spineless."

"Is that the kind of time when my father hits my mother?"

"Yes."

"I wonder if Tony's like my father?"

"No, my father is an alcoholic."

"I wonder if Tony isn't an alcoholic?"

"He couldn't be."

"Why not?"

"He just doesn't look like an alcoholic."

"I wonder if my father looked like an alcoholic twenty-five years ago?"

"Tony's not passive like my father."

"I wonder if passive men aren't the kind of men who hit women? I wonder if passive men aren't the kind of men who rape? I wonder if passive men don't strike out of weakness rather than strength?"

"Tony's personality's not the same," Heather protested, almost wailing.

"I wonder if my father doesn't keep his promises?" Dr. Kolnietz continued. "I wonder if my father isn't always showing up late? I wonder if he doesn't always seem to have excuses which don't really check out? I wonder if he can be counted on?"

Heather exploded. "I'm not going to do any more of this!" she screamed, at the edge of hysteria. "We've been through all this before. The same old tapes, you're going to tell me. You're going to tell me I'm running according to my parents' tapes. You're going to tell me that I treat men the way my mother does. You're going to tell me that I pick the kinds of men my mother does. You're going to tell me I pick the kind of men who treat me the way my father treats my mother. But it doesn't do any good. I'm sick and tired of hearing all about this damn tape business."

Dr. Kolnietz was standing in front of her now.

"We're both sick and tired of it, Heather," he said, "but we have to keep going at it until you change the tapes. The problem is that you don't know any other tapes yet."

"The problem is that I don't meet any decent men," Heather countered. "There aren't any decent men out there."

Dr. Kolnietz fought back the male psychiatrist's frequent temptation to tell her he could personally show her a decent man. Instead, he said, "There are decent men out there. But you don't notice them when you meet them. You're not attracted to them. They don't compute for you. They don't fit in with the tapes. You wouldn't know what to do with one if he jumped in your lap. You'd run the other way. You wouldn't know how to handle him because you don't have tapes about how to deal with decent men."

She looked exhausted, he thought. Had she observed him, she would have thought the same of him. Quietly now, he instructed her, "A neurosis has a kind of life of its own. It fights back. It tries to preserve itself. That's what we call resistance. We've been fighting against your resistance. It seems so much easier to live with the old tapes, even when they don't work, when you haven't made new ones yet, when the prospect of new ones seems strange and alien. But the more you can become aware of your resistance, the more it will help you. That's why I recorded us. I want you to take this cassette home with you, and I want you to listen to it from beginning to end at least two times before our next session. You're not going to want to replay it. I want you to observe yourself resisting replaying it. I want you to observe how you don't want to hear what's on it.

"It's not just you, Heather. It's anyone with a neurosis. Everyone comes to therapy saying they want to change, and then they start acting as if the last thing in God's earth they wanted to do was change. The neurosis always fights back. I want you to observe how hard you're fighting against changing. I want you to observe how hard you're fighting against me and what I'm trying to do." He went over to the couch, turned off the recorder, ejected the cassette, and handed it to her.

"We already have our next appointment scheduled," he said. "I'll see you then."

Heather stuck the cassette in her purse, but as she left, she thought to herself, "I'm not sure I'll keep our next goddamn appointment."

And after she closed the door, Dr. Kolnietz sat back down behind his desk. He thought about how his training had taught him that psychiatrists are supposed to be aloof, detached, nonverbal, inactive. He wondered if some other sort of therapist wouldn't be better for Heather.


It was luck that Heather had arranged for Georgia to have Mrs. Carstairs's bed by the window because within less than twenty-four hours she had a roommate. Lutzina Stolarz was a tall, thin, seventy-nine-year-old woman whose great dignity could not quite hide her dismay. "Stupid me," she told Georgia, "I never dreamed I'd get myself in such a pickle."

The pickle had been precipitated when, ten days before, she had slipped on the February ice in her driveway as she was returning from the mailbox and fractured her hip. Fortunately, Rob, the tenant farmer, had been driving by in his pickup a mere ten minutes later and happened to notice her lying there. She had not foreseen the fall, but the minute it occurred she knew exactly what was wrong. She instructed Rob to get her several blankets from the house and then call the ambulance. It was routine after that. The ambulance came, took her to New Warsaw General Hospital, and she was operated on the next morning. They put in a pin.

All very simple except for the fact she was a widow who lived alone. Alone, that is, except for Wrinkles, her cocker spaniel. She had gotten him fourteen years before—six months after her husband died—and had named him that because, as a pup, he was all wrinkles. Now, in old age, he was all wrinkles again. His picture, alongside that of her husband, had already been placed upon her bureau. Georgia had pictures of her dead husband and her children and grandchildren, but they were all facedown in her bureau drawer. The only picture on top of her bureau was a card she had received decades before and taken such a liking to she had had it framed—the one she placed there yesterday of that very young woman, no more than sixteen, seated in a swing.

Lutzina—"Call my Lucy; everyone does"—and her husband were both of the Polish immigrant stock that had settled in New Warsaw. They'd not had children, but had worked the largest dairy farm in the county. When her husband died she had sold the cows to a dealer and all but a few of their several hundred acres to one of the burgeoning agribusinesses. She'd remodeled the hay barn into a house—that was where Rob and his wife lived—and had torn down the cow barn and sold the lumber. She had been left quite well-off.

That was the other part of the pickle. She had plenty of money to hire practical nurses around the clock, had they been available. But they weren't. In the hospital they had told her she would need help taking care of herself, as well as physical therapy, for six weeks after discharge. That was when she discovered the region's nursing shortage. And that was when they had suggested a six-week stay in Willow Glen. There was no other choice. "I just never thought I'd end up in a nursing home," she told Georgia. "Not that I've exactly ended up here. I should be going home in six weeks. Still, a nursing home!"

"It is a concentration camp, isn't it?" Georgia commiserated. A loud buzzer sounded. "That's the lunch bell," she explained, "summoning us to the dining room. Do you get to have a tray?"

"No, they want me to use the dining room." Lutzina winced. "They want me to walk as much as I can. It's part of my physical therapy, they tell me. But you go on ahead. I'm awfully slow."

"That's all right," Georgia said. "It's hard to find your way down there at first, and I'm glad to have the company."

Lutzina was not yet able, however, to be of much company while walking. She had to concentrate on every step with her walker. And she was clearly still in pain. "It's the blood in the tissues, they tell me," she explained laboriously. "It's not supposed to hurt much in a couple of weeks more." It was a slow journey, but Georgia didn't mind. She felt like an old hand showing a newcomer the ropes.

Georgia was ambivalent about the dining room. She liked the fact that dessert was already set out—a fruit cup and a piece of cake at each place setting, and a roll on the bread and butter plate. You could sit wherever you wanted, and as soon as you sat down an attendant would bring you your main course, hot from the kitchen. It was nice to be served, no food to be prepared, no dishes to be washed. But it was too brightly lit. The patients' rooms had curtains, polished furniture, and lamps with a warm light to them. But this large room was utterly functional and windowless, all modern and glare. It was institutional. And you never knew who would sit down at your table with you; sometimes she felt trapped.

She didn't feel trapped now. Lutzina was obviously tired after the walk, and they ate together in companionable silence. She had revived by the time they were finished. "How about you?" Lutzina asked. "What are you doing in a nursing home?"

"My children railroaded me here."

"Whatever for? You don't look as if anything's wrong with you."

"There isn't anything wrong with me," Georgia snorted. "I told you I was railroaded."

"But I didn't think they could do that sort of thing any more. Surely there must be some sort of reason."

"I'm feeling rather tired," Georgia announced. "I think I'll go back to the wing now, if you don't mind. Will you be able to find your way back by yourself?"

"Of course."

Georgia had already stood up from the table. She turned on her heel and was gone, leaving Lutzina still sitting at the table with a puzzled expression.


Before she had left for her appointment with Dr. Kolnietz, Heather had wheeled Stephen into the dayroom so he could watch TV until Peggy brought him his lunch tray and fed him. He had not protested. "But, Stephen, you *need* variety," she would have insisted, out of her need to nurse him. But the fact was she had already given him more variety than he could handle. Since learning the evening before that she wanted sex with him—that it was actually on her mind as well as his own—his yearning had become even more urgent. This time his attention had drifted away from the inane TV not in minutes but in seconds. She'd said she'd had something in mind for them, something in store for him. He did not know what it was, but throughout the night and that morning he'd been getting intermittently erect just from his dim imaginings.

Yet, simultaneously, there remained a part of him that was still holding back. Ferociously. It was almost as if there was a voice inside him screaming, "Stop! Don't give in to it! Fight! Beat it down!" Clearly, he had not solved the puzzle. He needed to go deeper. He had not desired sex because he thought he'd never have the opportunity, but now it looked as if he might soon get that opportunity and he was still reluctant, frightened. Why? And then he knew. It was, of course, the Great Pain.

When he had been moved out of the idiot ward, the state school informed his parents that he was not retarded—that, in fact, he seemed to be remarkably intelligent. His parents had refused even to come see him. They had succeeded in putting him out of their lives and were not about to start all over again. But when Dr. Kolnietz had told him about this total rejection in all its stark detail, it hadn't bothered him at all. He couldn't remember his parents. He couldn't remember any home. He couldn't remember being put in the school. He couldn't remember first meeting Dr. K. He could hardly remember the idiot ward; his real memories began the day they had moved him out. As far as he was concerned, Dr. K. was his parents, his mother and father rolled into one, and all the other aides at the school no more than Dr. K.'s helpers. On an intellectual level he knew differently, of course, but the facts were irrelevant.

All that changed, however, when Dr. K.—he was almost a real doctor now—was back on a vacation from medical school in the spring of 1970. "Time is running out," Dr. K. had announced, explaining that the state government was beginning to balk at paying all the extra money for his special education. Being powerless to do anything else, Stephen's appetite for learning had been insatiable and at age eleven he was already handling some college material. "I'll try to hold them off as long as I can," Dr. K. had promised. "We're telling them that the laws guarantee you an education until at least sixteen. But they're balking, and sooner or later they're going to move you to a nursing home, and then it will be almost as bad as if you were back on the idiot ward. They won't be able to do anything more than feed and bathe you. I'm sorry."

"I/CAN/COME/LIVE/WITH/YOU," he had tapped.

Patiently, Dr. K. explained why that was not possible. But it got worse. He had to go on, difficult though it was, to make it clear that he had his own life, and would only rarely be able even to visit Stephen anymore since, as an intern and psychiatry resident far away, he'd have only two weeks of vacation a year. And how eventually there would be marriage and children of his own.

The recriminations began. "YOU/SHOULD/HAVE/LEFT/ME/IN/THE/IDIOT/ WARD. I/WOULD/HAVE/BEEN/BETTER/OFF. I'D/PROBABLY/BE/DEAD/BY/NOW. I/WISH/I/WERE/DEAD."

Psychiatrists called the process "termination," Dr. K. had told him. It was an apt term. He was being terminated. Just like that. Like an abandoned railroad car switched off onto a dead-end track. Abandoned. Forgotten. Terminated.

The process had taken years. Years of agony before he'd had any peace.

It was not only a process of wrestling against giving up Dr. K.; it was also one of wrestling with God. As far back as he remembered, he'd believed in God—a simple child's belief. Now the belief was being tested. Why had God created him? Why was God allowing this to happen? And, toward the end, during one of Dr. K.'s now rare visits: "I'VE/SUBSTITUTED/GOD/FOR/YOU. I/CAN'T/BE/NOBODY'S/CHILD. GOD/IS/MY/PRETEND/PARENTS. FOR/ALL/I/KNOW/I'VE/MADE/HIM/UP. HE'S/NO/MORE/THAN/A/PRETEND/GOD. BUT/I/CAN'T/LIVE/WITHOUT/HIM. THAT'S/NOT/FAITH. BUT/I/HAVE/NO/OTHER/CHOICE. WHAT/KIND/OF/FAITH/IS/IT/WHEN/YOU/DON'T/HAVE/A/CHOICE?  A/FORCED/PRETEND/FAITH?''

The school had somehow managed to keep him there until his sixteenth birthday. By the time they sent him to the first nursing home, he'd accepted his lot. It was not a good place—one of the aides beat him secretly and regularly—and he'd almost died before Dr. K. had engineered his transfer to the brand-new Willow Glen when he was seventeen. By then he'd come to realize that the greatest opportunity for education came not from external teaching, not from postcards, but from contemplation. Helpless to do anything else, he'd become an expert in taking little bits of experience and milking them for all they were worth. His relationship with his "pretend" God deepened almost daily and his growth in understanding became more rapid. He no longer missed Dr. K. He had indeed worked through the termination.

Or had he? Stephen now wondered, lying in the dayroom of Willow Glen with the TV babbling softly in the background. He had succeeded in giving up Dr. K., yes. But apparently he had also succeeded in giving up sexuality. Was it any wonder? The pain of abandonment, coming just at the age when sexuality is normally beginning to blossom, had been almost more than he could bear. It made sense that he should have wanted to protect himself from any recurrence of such pain, that he should have set up barriers against anyone ever becoming that important to him again.

Yes, it made sense. But why should those barriers suddenly begin to break down now, at the age of twenty-nine? He'd once heard a radio preacher say God never gives human beings more pain than they can bear. Like virtually every other absolute statement, he knew it was a half-truth, but certainly he couldn't have borne more at the age of thirteen or fifteen. Could it be that he was able to bear such pain now? The thought that he might have grown strong enough to wrestle with loss once again pleased him, yet still frightened him. If Dr. K. had not been able to stay with him, how would Heather be able to? But, filled with fantasies, he was at this moment confident he could withstand that pain. Somehow it would all work out for the best. They said that love is blind. Well, he was going into this with his eyes open. He could handle it. Or could he really? And was he feeling so confident because he still had two weeks to make up his mind?

Hank Martin had slipped into the dayroom to watch the TV long after Stephen's mind had drifted away from it. At first Hank had been engrossed in the rerun of an old family sitcom. But then there had been a scene where a group of boys had told a younger one to go away because he was too little to play with them. Hank had been small for his age. It was not good to be small in the area of west Cleveland where he'd grown up. He shifted his thoughts to the Messerschmitts.

Were he under oath on a witness stand, Hank would have admitted he'd never seen a Messerschmitt. He was aware of the records to the contrary, records that indicated that when he had tried to enlist in the marines at the age of thirty-two he'd been rejected because of his size and an umbilical hernia. But the army had taken him and, after being recycled once through basic training, he'd actually spent the war years as a quartermaster clerk at Fort Polk in Louisiana. He might have made corporal had he not gotten into a little trouble because of his drinking.

But most of the time he "remembered" it differently. He "remembered" that long before Pearl Harbor he'd recognized the Nazi menace for what it was and enlisted in the Royal Canadian Air Force. His fine instincts and natural abilities as a pilot had been spotted quickly. Promoted to lieutenant, he'd been shipped as a fighter pilot to England to protect its shores against the Jerries. There had been many dogfights with the Messerschmitts. In this particular one he'd managed to bag three of them. As he sat in front of the dayroom TV but not seeing it, he "recalled" how one of his wing struts had been damaged by a Jerry machine gun, and it was a difficult landing. When he entered the mess hall, they'd all stood up and clapped. The wing commander was just about to make a speech before pinning another medal on him when the lunch buzzer sounded.

Hank stood up and observed that Stephen was awake. In fact, the cripple was staring straight at him, although he didn't seem to be particularly aware of him. Well, that could be taken care of. Hank looked around. There was no one else in the dayroom. As he started off toward the dining room, he took his cane, swung it, and gave one of the legs of Stephen's gurney a sharp, hard whack.

At the sound of the lunch buzzer, Peggy went to the dining room to get the tray cart. All but four of the patients on C-Wing ate their meals in the dining room. The first meal Peggy delivered was to Crazy Carol, sitting in her geri-chair in the hallway by the nurses' station. The chair had a straight back with rings attached for the restraining straps, and its own tray in front, which served additionally as a restraint although it had an easily workable latch. As Peggy laid out the dishes for her, Carol recited her usual litany, but when finished she immediately dug into her lunch with gusto.

Peggy took the next tray into the dayroom. Mrs. Stimson had wheeled herself into the room at the sound of the buzzer and was sitting at a table in her wheelchair waiting for it. Good, Peggy thought. Maybe she wouldn't throw any of it today. As expected, Rachel said nothing when the meal was placed before her.

The third tray Peggy took down to Mrs. Grochowski's room. Being totally paralyzed, like Stephen, Mrs. Grochowski had to be fed. Peggy sat down and silently started to do it. It was a time-consuming, wordless process. When it was completed and Peggy had wiped her lips, Mrs. Grochowski commented, "You're a quiet one, Peggy, aren't you?"

True to the observation, Peggy said nothing.

"Well," Mrs. Grochowski continued, "I daresay that's because you don't have anything to say yet. But that doesn't mean you won't. It may not be long before you have a lot to say, and a lot that's worth listening to."

Peggy found that hard to imagine as she carried out the empty tray. Still, she liked what Mrs. Grochowski had said. She didn't mind the possibility that someday she might have something to say that was worth listening to.

The last tray was for Stephen. When she had finished feeding him, he bleated, "Ehhhhhh." She gave him the letter board and he tapped, "GET/ME/OUT/OF/THE/DAYROOM."

Peggy wheeled his gurney back to its place against the corridor wall. He had asked God whether it would be the right thing to complain about Hank Martin. God apparently didn't think the question crucial enough to answer. So, even though he was still frightened, now that he was out of the dayroom Stephen had decided to say nothing else for the moment. But Peggy did want to talk. "When I was bitching about Mrs. Simonton the other day, you asked me some questions," she told him. "One was about why Heather often gets an extra aide. I asked her that and she explained that's because she often gets called away to other wards when they have a death, and I've noticed that. But one of the questions was about you yourself. Why do they keep you on C-Wing when you're bedridden? For that matter, why do they always keep you on a gurney instead of a bed? And why always here next to the nurses' station?"

"I/WAS/IN/A/HOME/FOR/THE/RETARDED. DO/YOU/THINK/I/AM/RETARDED?" he tapped.

"I guess not," Peggy said slowly. Then both her thoughts and words seemed to speed up. "You couldn't be retarded when you know how to write so well. In fact, you write better than I do. In fact, maybe you're very bright."

"I/AM/VERY/BRIGHT," Stephen tapped, "BUT/I/AM/IN/A/RETARD'S/BODY. THINK/WHAT/IT'S/LIKE/TO/BE/VERY/BRIGHT/IN/A/RETARD'S/BODY.  WILL/YOU/ THINK/ABOUT/IT?"

Peggy looked at him, not knowing what to say.

"WILL/YOU?" Stephen tapped again. Insistently.

"Yes, I will think about it. I promise." Already it was dawning on her not only how bright he was but also how fully *human*. Human and humane. And how much healthier he really was than the A- or B-Wing patients who mostly seemed past needing stimulation.

"GOOD."

"There's another question you asked me," Peggy dared to go on. "About Mrs. Grochowski. How come she's bedridden and also on C-Wing?"

"SHE'S/ALSO/VERY/BRIGHT. IT/WOULD/BE/FUN/FOR/ME/AND/HER/IF/I/COULD/ BE/IN/HER/ROOM/IF/SHE/COULD/HOLD/MY/LETTER/BOARD,/BUT/SHE/CAN'T."

"You also asked me to think about why there is always an empty bed in her room," Peggy continued. "Why?"

"BECAUSE/I/AM/ALWAYS/ON/THE/GURNEY/MRS./SIMONTON/CAN/ALWAYS/ HAVE/A/FULL/CENSUS/ON/THIS/WING/AND/STILL/HAVE/AN/EXTRA/BED.  BUT/ THAT'S/NOT/THE/REAL/REASON. THE/REAL/REASON/IS/THAT/MRS./GROCHOWSKI/ HAS/A/LOVER."

"What?" Peggy blurted. "A lover? Who?"

"THAT'S/A/PRIVATE/MATTER," Stephen tapped. "ASK/HER/IF/YOU/WANT/ TO/YOURSELF. ANYWAY/YOU'D/KNOW/IF/YOU/JUST/KEPT/YOUR/EYES/OPEN."

By now Peggy had had all that she could absorb. Besides, it took an enormous amount of energy to follow along with Stephen's laborious writing. Even Heather had her limits. She hung the letter board back on the gurney and went to take care of Carol. She removed the dishes, unstrapped her from the back of her geri-chair, swung its tray out and helped her up. Carol was walked twice a day. Peggy strode with her four times up and down the corridor past the supply room, and then sat her back in her chair. She hooked the tray back in, enclosing her, but she was so preoccupied thinking about what it would be like to be very bright in a retard's body that she forgot to refasten the straps at the back of the chair. Stephen certainly had a way of leading her to think.

She even thought about what it might be like to have no feet when she went into the dayroom to collect Rachel's tray. Rachel was still there, staring into space over the remains of her meal. Emboldened, Peggy asked, "How are you feeling today, Mrs. Stimson?"

Rachel looked at her with a most peculiar expression. "You needn't pretend that you're a nurse with me," she snapped, and backed her wheelchair away from the table, spun it around, and sped straight out the door into the corridor.

Watching her shoot out, Peggy had two thoughts. One was not only how rapidly and effectively Rachel could move—she had observed this before—but also how quiet a wheelchair could be. Rachel had left the dayroom without the slightest sound. The other thought was that it simply didn't pay to try to be nice to people. Listlessly, she returned the tray to the cart and wheeled it back to the dining hall.

As soon as she got back from seeing Dr. Kolnietz, Heather saw Crazy Carol's empty geri-chair in the corridor, its tray swung open, the straps hanging on the floor. Peggy was sitting placidly in the nurses' station. "For Christ's sake," Heather screamed at her, "you didn't tie Carol back properly. Check the corridors of the wing and the rooms. Run! Now!"

Heather sat down in the nurses' station and held her head in her hands. It had been the most godawful forty-eight hours. Tony had beaten up on her. Then in their own way the patients and Mrs. Simonton had beaten up on her too. Dr. Kolnietz had just finished beating up on her. And now this! Couldn't she do anything right? What was wrong with her? Couldn't she even manage a ward decently?

Peggy came running back to announce there were no signs of Carol. Heather called Mrs. Simonton and, barely holding back her tears, told her what had happened.

Mrs. Simonton thought quickly. It was likely that Carol was still in the building. But she couldn't bank on it, and it was well below freezing outside. Every minute might count. She phoned the police to report Carol missing. Then she summoned Ms. McAdams. "Carol's wandered off again. She's not on C-Wing. Notify the nurses on A- and B-Wings to do a search. You search the rest of the place yourself—the dining room, physical therapy, everywhere. Have them call me—you call me—as soon as she's found or not found."

Ms. McAdams exited smartly. If Carol was found in Willow Glen, she could always cancel the police alarm, Mrs. Simonton thought. But the calls came back from the nurses that there was no sign of her. And then, ten minutes later, Ms. McAdams returned to report likewise. Mrs. Simonton telephoned the police again to emphasize the seriousness of the situation. Then, apologetically, she phoned Rebecca Kubrick to tell her that her mother-in-law had wandered off again.

There was nothing else to do now but wait. Mrs. Simonton sat back, anxious and depressed. Why couldn't she take these things in stride? she wondered. It wasn't as if it had never happened before. Why did she care so much? Was it because she was so concerned about Willow Glen's reputation? Certainly that was involved, but it went deeper, she realized. She thought about Carol wandering around in the cold. Carol was probably oblivious to it, but Mrs. Simonton could almost feel the icy wind on her own skin, as if she had somehow exchanged her own body for Carol's.

She wished there were someone she could share her anxiety with. There was of course. Marion Grochowski was always willing to share her burdens. Stephen would have something extraordinarily pithy to say—with his letter board he had developed pithiness into an art—something that would put matters in perspective. It was patients like these who made her life's work worthwhile. And she was not above calling on them—she'd done so before—but not this time. She needed to stay close to the phone. For some reason a fragment of liturgical language returned to her from her distant, vaguely Episcopalian upbringing: "O Lord, make haste to help us; O God, make speed to save us."

Roberta McAdams's thoughts were following a different track. She had been annoyed by all the clamor, as well she should be. Not only was it an interruption; it was unnecessary. Of course there were going to be incidents when you didn't follow regulations. Patients like Carol shouldn't even be on C-Wing. Patients who needed restraint. And patients who were paralyzed like Stephen and Mrs. Grochowski. They ought to be housed on A- or B-Wing.

Were it not for the even greater commotion it would cause, Ms. McAdams would have been hoping Carol could not be found. It would serve Mrs. Simonton right if the old lady froze to death. Then Willow Glen might become a tighter ship.

It would be quite different if she herself was the administrator. There would be much more order. With the demand for beds what it was, she wouldn't even accept those patients who were more trouble than they were worth. And she'd see to it that the nursing staff wouldn't make mistakes such as had just occurred. They needed greater discipline. She'd make sure they received the training they needed.

At the thought of discipline, at the word itself, Roberta McAdams felt the moisture faintly beginning between her trim thighs. She allowed herself to enjoy the sensation for a moment. But only for a moment. This was not the time. There was a proper time and place for everything.

•     •     •

Lieutenant Thomas Petri sat alone behind his desk in his office in the New Warsaw police station, feeling immensely satisfied. He looked again at his name and title embossed on the brass plate at the front of his desk. Damn, that was nice of them, he thought. If he'd stayed in New York or on the East Coast, he'd have had to go buy his own nameplate. But here he'd arrived on his first day of duty to find it sitting all prepared for him. People were still thoughtful—still had a sense of decency—in the Midwest. He was glad he'd come.

Since he was promoted to detective so early in his career, many had wondered why he had taken this small-town assignment when he could easily have obtained more glamorous positions. But he had his reasons, many of them. He had liked the chief when he'd been interviewed, and that first impression had been borne out this morning when the chief had briefed him on procedures. It was a low crime area—prosperous, rural, and stable—and the state police took care of all the routine law enforcement. He liked the fact that it was a small department with him its only lieutenant, only detective. He liked the responsibility of reporting directly only to the chief. But, above all, at the age of twenty-nine, he had spent the entirety of his life in New York City and northern New Jersey, and he was sick to death of disorder and dirt and decay. He had decided to come to New Warsaw precisely because it was quiet and orderly. And, above all, *clean*.

There was a knock at the door. It was Sergeant Bill Mitchell, the top sergeant, the man who would be his primary assistant when he needed one. "Excuse me, sir," he said, "but I wanted to let you know they've found the old woman. Wodjenczi and Roberts spotted her in the doorway of a house about a half a mile down from the home. She seems okay, but they're taking her to the emergency room to have her checked out for exposure just in case. I told them to wait for her there and take her back to the home. But I thought you'd want to know."

It felt a little strange, but not displeasing, to be addressed as "sir" by this veteran twenty years his senior, when he himself had been a sergeant in New York City just a year before. But he respected the tradition that officers should not be addressed by first name except by fellow officers. "Thanks, Bill," he said. "Glad to know she's safe. Tell you what though. If you're not tied down, how about our going to pick her up and take her back to the home? That way I can get acquainted with the hospital and the home and start getting my bearings—particularly with you driving." It seemed to Petri a good opportunity to begin building a relationship with his assistant. "What do you think? Doesn't seem to be much exciting going on."

Sergeant Mitchell assented. They took a squad car. "I guess there aren't many nursing homes that take good care of their patients," Petri remarked with deliberate casualness as they were driving away from the station.

"Oh, Willow Glen's a good nursing home, sir. Best in the state."

"Still seems strange to me that they'd let a patient wander off like that."

"Some of these old people are pretty wily in their own way," Mitchell countered. "It's pretty common for them to wander off."

Lieutenant Petri was quiet, respecting the experience reflected in the older man's voice. Still, as New Warsaw's only detective, he had a major responsibility to assure the order of the community. It was perhaps not criminal, but it seemed somehow outrageous that an old woman should be allowed to wander out into the snow by the very agency entrusted with her care. He didn't voice his thoughts, but it couldn't hurt for him to investigate a little bit, to see this Willow Glen place for himself.

By the time they got to the emergency room, Carol had already been medically cleared. As Mitchell escorted her into the back seat of the squad car, she clutched Petri's sleeve, whining, "Have you seen my purse? Do you know what they've done with my purse? Someone's stolen my purse." Petri would have sprung into action had not Mitchell reassured him. "Don't take her seriously, sir. She's said that same thing every time we've picked her up."

She seemed quiet and peaceful enough when they had locked her from the outside into the back seat. "How many times *have* we picked her up, Bill?" Petri asked.

"Only two or three times the past couple of years." Petri's sense of outrage resurged until Mitchell continued. "But for a while it was once a week, until her family finally put her in Willow Glen."

Ms. McAdams had been on the lookout and met them at the entrance with an aide when they arrived. "Carol, we're so glad you're back safely. I was so worried about you. I've been praying for you," she exclaimed dramatically. "You gave us quite a scare." Carol seemed unaware of the fuss, and trotted back passively toward C-Wing with the aide. "Thank God you found her," Ms. McAdams gushed, addressing the two policemen. "Come on in and see Mrs. Simonton. I know she'll want to thank you personally."

Petri had begun to feel better about Willow Glen. It was modern; the entranceway was clean; the Administration Center seemed busy; and he was favorably struck by the crisp neatness of this young woman who seemed so caring. He was not quite so sure, however, when he met Mrs. Simonton. She was smoking a cigarette, and twin trails of smoke were coming out of her nostrils. An image of an old dragon flashed through his mind. He himself was not one of those who objected to the smell of smoke, but he was always astonished how someone could enjoy such a dirty habit, and eyed the full ashtray on her desk with distaste. She seemed a tough old bird, but she had none of Ms. McAdams's crispness. Indeed, he was struck by the informality with which she greeted them. "Hi, Bill." She turned toward Petri. "Who have we here? I don't know *you*."

But she made him feel welcome after he introduced himself. "Good to have you in town, Lieutenant. Thanks for bringing Carol back and giving me a chance to meet you. I've already notified her children that you've found her and she's all right. They're very grateful to you. Would you like to have a tour of Willow Glen?"

Petri felt a sudden spasm of anxiety. He had never been inside a nursing home before. Unseen, he had had doubts about the quality of care behind these walls, but now he found himself not wanting to see the dying he imagined must be occurring within. Or the aging. Or whether there were more people like Carol to clutch at him. One an afternoon had been enough. "No thanks," he said. "Today's my day for the quick tour of the whole town. I would like to visit Mrs. Kubrick's children, though. It'll give me a chance to see more of the countryside. Would that be possible, Bill?"

Sergeant Mitchell nodded. "I'd be happy to phone them and let them know you're coming," Mrs. Simonton volunteered. Petri thanked her, and shook her hand, thinking how firm her grip was. There might be more to the woman than first met the eye.

From his many trips returning Carol home, Mitchell knew exactly where Rebecca and Henry Kubrick lived. They were a couple of modest means, he explained, solid citizens still trying to work a small farm without selling their homestead to an agribusiness. Petri was pleased by the flat land speeding by, demarcated so precisely by even fences and muddy, narrow, straight access roads. This was the heartland, he thought. The hell with New York and New Jersey.

The Kubricks greeted the two of them, pumped their hands gratefully, and ushered them into the small living room. They sat on overstuffed chairs protected by plastic covers, facing a vase of plastic flowers on the polished coffee table. Rebecca offered them coffee. She and Henry seemed unaccustomed to company but glad for it. "You've been so very kind," Rebecca said. She was a stocky but wholesome woman, and although she was married and at least a decade older than himself, Petri could not help but admire the contour of the firm breasts underneath the bib of her apron.

"Think nothing of it," he said. "Just happy we could be of assistance and your mother's okay. I understand from Sergeant Mitchell this isn't an unusual occurrence."

"That's one of the troubles with Mom, she wanders off," said Henry, a stocky, weather-worn man older than his wife. "It's that darn Alzheimer's disease."

"How long's she had it?"

"Began about seven years ago. It started a bit before Dad died. At first it wasn't bad. She couldn't remember things that happened the day before, but she could remember everything that happened to me as a kid. It was real gradual. But five years ago she started forgetting our names. That was when she began to wander. We took her to the doctors. They couldn't find anything wrong physically, but said she was too young to be that senile."

"Presenile dementia they called it," Rebecca added. "That's when we first heard the term Alzheimer's."

"You must find it a bit annoying that they don't take better care of her at the nursing home," Petri said consolingly.

"Annoying?" Henry snorted. "They take wonderful care of her there. Thank God for Willow Glen!"

"You don't know what it's like, having to tie a person up night and day in their own home," Rebecca added.

"And they do real well down at the Glen," Henry continued. "I'm surprised she doesn't go off more. She's slippery. You'd think being that senile she couldn't untie knots. But she can. She's real slippery. She can get out of anything. She's like a weasel, she is."

"It must have been very difficult for you," Petri commiserated. He liked this plain couple and was beginning to appreciate what they'd been through.

"Keeping her tied up wasn't the worst part," Rebecca responded. "Not even when she lost control of her functions. For me it was before she was tied up all the time. She used to come into the kitchen when I was making dinner. I'd make a nice sauce. Then I'd turn to fix something on the stove, and soon as I'd turn my back again I'd find Mom at the sink, having dumped my sauce down the garbage disposal and washing the bowl, looking all pleased with herself. As Henry said, thank God for Willow Glen." Rebecca began to cry silently.

"And thank God for the state," Henry continued. "We tried not to put her in Willow Glen, but we had no other choice. At least we had no other choice thanks to the state. They pay for it. As soon as Mom's savings were used up, they took over. Before Dad died he knew Mom had started going, so he left the farm to me. If he hadn't done that, the state would have had to take it, even though it's all we have. You know, there are some of these politicians in the capital who are saying people like us ought to pay for it when our parents are in nursing homes. But we couldn't do it. Twenty thousand a year. Why, that's as much as we net. It would take everything. I wish one of those politicians would have to put his mother away. Bet that would change his tune real quick."

"We really did have no other choice," Rebecca said, as if to reassure herself. "No matter how careful we were, she'd slip away every couple of weeks. Sooner or later she would have frozen to death, wouldn't she have, Bill?"

"I believe so, Becky," Mitchell nodded.

"Still, we feel guilty. I guess what we feel guiltiest about is that we don't visit her."

"The worst part for me," said Henry, "happened about a year before we put her away. That was when she began to no longer recognize me anymore." His voice broke, "Me, her own son who's lived with her all her life."

Petri felt an urge to put his arm around Henry's shoulder. He held back, knowing that the familiarity might make him uncomfortable. But God, these people were the salt of the earth.

"Of course, we visit her on Christmas and her birthday," Rebecca clarified. "We feel real bad we don't do it more. But what's the point? When we do, all she says is that thing about someone stealing her purse, and then she looks off into space. She doesn't even know we're there."

"Yes," Henry echoed. "What's the point, Lieutenant? I mean, what's the point?"

Petri had no answer. He stood up. The Kubricks thanked them once more, and as they were going down the walk toward the squad car, Henry Kubrick yelled after them in salute, "Thank God for Willow Glen!"

As Mitchell drove them back into town, Tom Petri was silent. Two things were on his mind. One was the memory of the swell of Rebecca Kubrick's breasts. He was certainly ready to find a congenial young woman of his own. The only thing that had made him uneasy about coming to a small town like New Warsaw was his awareness that it would likely be difficult for him to find eligible women to go out with. Then he recollected Ms. McAdams in her trimly tailored blouse greeting them so warmly at the entrance to Willow Glen. Might she be single? Well, even if she wasn't, someone eligible was bound to cross his path sooner or later and, unlike big cities, that someone was likely to be wholesome.

Even more on his mind, however, was Henry Kubrick. What would it be like "putting away" one's own mother? he wondered. He had not wanted even to set foot in the real inside of Willow Glen. And he thought of his own mother back alone in Newark, New Jersey. Back in the midst of all that urban sprawl and grime and decay. Would the day ever come when he, her only child, might have to take her to a nursing home? It didn't matter, he thought, for the fact of the matter was that, even though she wasn't senile as far as he knew, he already had put her away. And he sure as hell didn't feel guilty about not visiting her. Not on Christmas. Not on her birthday. He didn't write to her. He didn't call. He hadn't seen or talked to her for over four years. And he intended to keep it that way.

"Good evening, Irene," Heather said to the three-to-eleven shift aide when she arrived at the nurses' station at the dot of seven P.M. It was her first time back on nights. Most of the other nurses preferred days, but for Heather both had advantages. Nights could sometimes be boring, but she was often busier than the other nurses because nights were when most of the deaths occurred. It was also when she was freest to talk with Mrs. Grochowski and Stephen. And on this night she had the particular added anticipation about Stephen.

She sat down to read the day-shift notes. She wasn't halfway through when the screaming started. She jumped, then remembered it was Saturday night. "That will be Rachel and her husband," Heather said. "I'll go take care of it, Irene."

It was one of the rituals of Willow Glen, she knew. Every Saturday evening at six-thirty, Mr. Stimson came to visit his wife. Every Saturday evening by seven-thirty, Rachel was screaming at him and they needed to be separated. Then Mr. Stimson would go home until the next Saturday at six-thirty. It had been going on that way for years.

". . . filthy little turd! Subhuman piece of shit!" Heather could hear Rachel's obscenities well before she got to the door. Mr. Stimson sat facing his wife, and Rachel's eyes were bright with fury. "They think you're human. You walk around the town and they all think you are human. But they don't know you. They don't know you the way I know you. They don't know that you are really a lizard. I am a dinosaur compared to you!" Rachel yelled from her wheelchair. "You are just a little slimy lizard, a newt, that just crawled out of the sea, that just crawled out of the sewer all clinging with shit and filth and slime, you asshole!"

"It's time to go," Heather said emphatically. Gently she took Mr. Stimson by the sleeve and led him out to the dayroom without a backward glance at Rachel. They sat down, facing each other across the table.

"Why do you do it?" Heather asked.

"Why do I do what?" Mr. Stimson retorted.

Heather eyed him. Hubert Stimson was still a distinguished-looking man at eighty-two, the same age as his wife. She knew that he was the founder of the largest real estate business in town and a wealthy man. He had been retired for the past five years, but was still regarded as one of New Warsaw's civic leaders. She also knew that week after week, month after month, year after year, without any assistance from the state or welfare or insurance, he paid Rachel's bill. In fact, he was a large donor and a member of Willow Glen's advisory board.

"Why do you keep coming back every Saturday night?" she asked. "I'm not trying to tell you that you shouldn't. I know that for years the staff has suggested you stop coming because your visits always end in a fight. But I'm not concerned about the fighting or the noise, and I'm not trying to stop it. I'm just curious as to why. I would think it would be terribly unpleasant for you. Why do you keep coming back every Saturday simply to go through this torture?"

"Because I love her," Mr. Stimson said stiffly, as if it was obvious.

"But your visits don't seem very pleasing or helpful to her," Heather countered.

"She would die without me," Mr. Stimson said.

Heather did not know quite how to reply to this, but Mr. Stimson continued, "She has nobody else but me. No one else in the world. It is my responsibility."

"She's in Willow Glen so we can relieve you of much of that responsibility," Heather commented.

Mr. Stimson's eyes narrowed. "She needs me," he insisted.

Heather stood up. "Well," she said, "I'll see you again next week." As she watched him walk away down the corridor she wondered vaguely why she didn't feel sorry for him.

At the nurses' station she saw that Irene had gone to do her evening back rubs, and she went to Stephen. His dark eyes were open. She bent over him and whispered, "Now that it's night, we can do what I promised. If you want to. Do you?"

"Ahahahahahah."

"After eleven Bertha will be on, which is good," Heather said. "She keeps her head buried in novels and won't bother us. I'm going to tell her that you want to keep me company while I do my meds at around three o'clock in the morning. Does that sound all right with you?"

"Ahahahahahah."

Heather put her hand on his knee and smiled at him. "I'll see you then."

He had answered in the affirmative. Whatever kind of sexual relationship they were going to have that night, he wanted it. He had decided that a week ago. If Heather still wanted it, he would want it. By way of his erections and fantasies God had told him, Stephen Solaris, that he was ready. Yes, there might be terrible pain again, but to avoid that would not only be to avoid his sexuality but to avoid life. Even to avoid God.

Heather wanted sex with him! The glory of it! His excitement was overborne by something still more powerful: jubilation. Yet, in the midst of it all, he remained uneasy. Heather was so young. How could he be sure it was the right thing for her? If he asked her once more, she'd only reply, "There you go again: Stephen the Scrupulous." Besides, he remembered her black eye. Apparently she could do worse.

Stephen could not imagine being unscrupulous. Once when Heather had asked him why he was so wise, he'd answered, "I/HAVE/A/THIRST/FOR/ MEANING." Searching for the meaning of his seemingly meaningless existence, forced to rely on God, he'd discovered something of the mind of God. Enough to make him even lonelier. But only something. Much of the time he knew he was lost, and he needed his scruples to keep his bearings.

And this was so powerful! His sexuality had come upon him as suddenly as a typhoon, and could easily blow both of them off course. As it was, he was going into uncharted waters. What was she going to do to him? What was better than bathing him? What kind of sex would they have—with him hardly able to move a muscle? Would he like it? Would *she* like it when they were done or would she be disgusted and stop it, leaving him almost as soon as they had started?

But sex and Heather were not the sole cause of his unease. He had been shaken when Hank had struck his gurney with the cane. Nothing like that had happened at Willow Glen before. It had caused him to reflect back on the previous nursing home, and the aide who used to beat him when he was sixteen. It was terrifying to be helpless before violence. He had decided not to tell Heather—or anyone—about the incident. Doing so would likely breed more hatred. If only Hank were willing to use the letter board and talk with him. He thought he understood the way Hank's mind worked, and he didn't think he really had anything to fear from the little man. But he was not sure. Not sure at all.

And he was uneasy about his book. A mere four weeks and he'd actually be able to begin to translate it into reality. But would it be good? Would it be godly? Ambition was dangerous. Inevitably it gave birth to

SATURDAY/SUNDAY, MARCH 5TH-6TH 77

anxiety. Yet some anxiety was necessary and some ambition proper, even required. How he wanted the book to be good, to be the most it could be!

But Stephen sensed his unease went still deeper than these concerns. It had some other root within him. Or was it outside? It was very vague, yet it seemed to be growing. For some reason it felt more as if it was from without, but he couldn't quite pinpoint it.

"Hello. Are you awake?" The voice startled him.

It was Georgia. As long as it could be on her own terms, she was curious. In the two weeks since reading the beginning of the chapter about him, she had been watching more closely how the nurses and aides communicated with Stephen. Could she herself do it? It would obviously have to be on his terms, but the risk did not seem too great and this evening she had decided to take it. "Would you like to show me how to use your letter board?" she asked.

"Ahhhhhhhh," he signaled.

She'd observed enough to know this meant "yes." She unhooked the board and held it for him the way she'd seen Heather and Peggy do it. "HELLO/GEORGIA," he tapped. "IT/MUST/HAVE/TAKEN/COURAGE/TO/TALK/WITH/ME."

Georgia liked him immediately. "Do you get bored?" she asked.

"NOT/MUCH. AND/PARTICULARLY/NOT/LATELY."

"Why not lately?"

"BECAUSE/THEY'RE/GETTING/ME/A/COMPUTER. WITH/IT/I'LL/BE/ABLE/TO/TYPE. I'M/GOING/TO/WRITE/A/BOOK. I/THINK/ABOUT/IT/ALL/THE/TIME."

"What's its title going to be?"

"THE/POWER/OF/HELPLESSNESS."

"What a strange title!" Georgia exclaimed. "What does it mean?"

"BECAUSE/I'M/SO/HELPLESS — BECAUSE/ALL/I/CAN/DO/IS/LIE/HERE/AND/BE/AWARE — I'M/AWARE/OF/A/GREAT DEAL. I/MAY/KNOW/EVEN/MORE/ABOUT/WHAT/GOES/ON/IN/WILLOW/GLEN/THAN/MRS./SIMONTON."

"I'm not sure I understand."

"WHO/BESIDES/ME/DO/YOU/THINK/IS/THE/MOST/POWERFUL/PATIENT/HERE?"

Georgia had never thought about the matter before, but the answer immediately sprang to her lips: "Mrs. Grochowski." Everyone instinctively knew that she was the Dowager Queen of C-Wing.

"OF/COURSE. AND/DO/YOU/THINK/IT'S/AN/ACCIDENT/SHE'S/THE/ONLY/OTHER/PATIENT/ON/THE/WING/WHO'S/COMPLETELY/PARALYZED? SHE/TOO/HAS/LOTS/OF/TIME/TO/THINK/AND/BE/AWARE."

"I still don't understand."

Stephen tried again. "MOST/OLD/PEOPLE/ARE/SORT/OF/PATHETIC. BUT/SOME/OF/THEM/ARE/VERY/VERY/POWERFUL. SPIRITUALLY/POWERFUL. DO/YOU/KNOW/WHAT/I/MEAN?"

"Like Mrs. Grochowski?"

"YES. SOME/OF/THEIR/WISDOM/COMES/FROM/THEIR/YEARS. BUT/MRS./G./ ISN'T/THAT/OLD. THOSE/WHO/ARE/POWERFUL/ARE/ALWAYS/THOSE/WHO/HAVE/ COME/TO/TERMS/WITH/THE/HELPLESSNESS/OF/EITHER/AGING/OR/DISEASE. DON'T/ YOU/FIND/THAT/GETTING/OLD/MAKES/YOU/FEEL/HELPLESS?"

Georgia jerked the letter board away. "I just remembered something I ought to be doing," she blurted. First she'd been afraid of him because he was deformed. Now she really had reason to be afraid.

Georgia would have fled at that point had Stephen not fixed her with an insistent "Ehhhhh." Reluctantly she handed him back the board. "I'M/ SORRY/I/SCARED/YOU," he tapped. "I/GET/TOO/INTENSE. PLEASE/COME/BACK/ AND/TALK/WITH/ME/AGAIN."

Then Georgia did flee, thinking he was a strange young man and unsure whether she would ever come back.

Stephen was furious with himself. He had had a real opportunity and he'd blown it. Sometimes it seemed he had a virtual talent for threatening people. He knew perfectly well that old age was likely to be frightening. Just because he could deal with helplessness didn't mean that everyone was ready to face it. But he'd been so self-absorbed in explaining his message, he'd forgotten and possibly driven the poor woman away for good. Damn. Here he was about to write a book on awareness, and he hadn't even been aware enough of what he was doing to keep from upsetting someone who had actually reached out to him. "Forgive me, Lord," he petitioned wordlessly, "I'm not very grown-up yet."


Because she first had to set up and distribute the evening medications, it was close to ten before Heather could visit with Mrs. Grochowski. She knew she would still be awake. "I'm back on nights," she announced, "and it's time to chat about our love lives. How's yours?"

"You know it's good as long as Tim's alive," Mrs. Grochowski said with a welcoming grin. "I'm glad to see your black eye is all gone. Did you get a chance to talk to Dr. Kolnietz about it?"

"Of course I did. You know I do everything that you want me to do, Mrs. G.," Heather lied cheerfully. "He thinks that I keep taking up with men who are like my father. My father's an alcoholic. He says that men I go out with, even if they're not alcoholics yet, are like alcoholics."

"That is a trap, isn't it?" Mrs. Grochowski commented.

"I guess so. Dr. K. refers to it as a tape or sometimes a broken record. 'Repetition compulsion' he calls it. He says it's a neurosis."

Mrs. Grochowski thought that Heather did not seem as unhappy as she might be under the circumstances. "Have you broken up with Tony?" she asked.

"Well, not exactly," Heather said, "but I've got other irons in the fire." She smiled slightly to herself. People would think Stephen was a very odd iron indeed.

"It's just that I don't like to think of you going out with men who would hit you, Heather. I don't like that kind of repetition compulsion at all."

Heather felt a hint of admonishment. She preferred Mrs. Grochowski's stories. "Let's talk about you for a change. A couple of weeks ago you were telling me how your strong will almost killed you."

"I remember."

"I felt you were trying to tell me something about my own strong will, but I didn't know what. I've never considered myself as having a strong will. I let men walk all over me. Dr. Kolnietz tells me I've got a lot of resistance. I guess you could call that a sort of negative strong will, couldn't you?"

"Quite possibly," Mrs. Grochowski agreed.

"Certainly, Dr. K. makes me feel stubborn sometimes, damn him. Maybe it would help me if you told me some more. You told me how you gave up your will to be admired and that's when your MS stopped progressing. But you also told me you were depressed. You're not depressed now. You're . . . well, you're almost joyful. What happened?"

"Actually, I can pinpoint the change. It's surprising but it's true," Mrs. Grochowski answered. "People are irritable when they're depressed. I'd given up trying to be nice then, but I didn't know how else to be. My oldest daughter was taking care of me as well as her own four-year-old child, Barbara. Barbara came into my room one afternoon and started telling me one of those silly endless stories that children weave. In the middle of it, I told her to shut up and leave me alone. She said, 'You're not interested in me.' I told her to come back and see me the same time the next afternoon.

"At that point, I started doing some really serious thinking. I realized that Barbara was correct, that I wasn't interested in her. In fact, I realized that I had never really been interested in *anybody*. All I had been interested in was being admired for my sake. When I had worked on behalf of others, it was not because I was interested in them, but simply because I wanted to be admired. Indeed, when I got down to that level, the whole idea of being interested in somebody else was a new one.

"So when she came back the next afternoon, I told Barbara that she was correct, that I hadn't been interested in her. But I told her that I would like to experiment with changing. I asked her if she would be willing to give me lessons in being interested in other people. She was, and that's how my education really began. And how I began to cultivate the habit of being interested in other people for the pure sake of being interested. I discovered how hard it is to change. It's still hard. Ever since then, however, I have had a reason—a premise—to live, which has been sufficient to me. But it's a totally selfish reason, still."

"Selfish?" Heather queried. "I don't understand why it's selfish."

"In fact, that's why I came to Willow Glen. My daughter wanted to have her own career, and that would have been impossible with me staying at home with her. She also wanted to continue to take care of me. But you see, it was pretty boring. There are more people to be interested in here than there, just lying in that bedroom. So I decided to come here to be with people like you. Not for my daughter's sake, but mine.

"You've appreciated my being interested in you, Heather. And I'm glad. But that's not necessary. I have not been interested in you in order to earn your appreciation. I really don't care whether you appreciate me or not. I'm interested in you for my own selfish enjoyment—because you're interesting, and your being interesting is what makes me enjoy life."

There was a long pause. "That's neat, Mrs. G.," Heather said. "But why do I still feel you're trying to tell me something about myself? Are you?"

"Well, I suppose you might want to ask yourself what you're doing here, taking care of us old bodies. Is that what really interests you? You're so bright you could go to college. Are you going to spend your life working in a nursing home? You could do so much more."

"I can't go to college. My parents are poor. You know my father drinks everything away."

"There are scholarships, you know," Mrs. Grochowski countered. "You don't have to let anyone walk all over you, including your father. But I don't want to argue with you, Heather. Still, the fact is that you're maybe in a dead-end job here. You might want to ask yourself why. Do you take such good care of us because you really enjoy it—because that's all you want—or are you doing it for some other reason?"

Heather could feel the stubbornness rising up from the bottom of her spine into her chest. "Why are you beating up on me, Mrs. G.?"

"I'm not. But if you really want to see it that way, I feel like answering it the way I did when I was a little girl: you started it. You did ask for it, you know."

To Heather's relief, there was a knock on the open door. It was Irene. "Heather, could I talk with you for a moment?"

Heather went to the doorway.

"Gloria just called from A-Wing," Irene explained in a low voice. "She said Mrs. Carstairs is asking for you."

"I'll go right now," said Heather. "I probably won't be back until your shift is over, so let Bertha know what's up when she comes on at eleven, will you?"

Irene trotted away. Heather turned back toward the room. "I'm sorry, but I've got to leave now, Mrs. G."

"Of course you do," Mrs. Grochowski replied, knowing full well what was happening. "My thoughts will be with you."

When Heather reached A-Wing, Gloria filled her in. "Three days ago she began to spike a fever. The day before yesterday we had Dr. Ortiz see her. He thinks it's pneumonia. He asked her if she wanted antibiotics, and she said that she didn't. She's really been quite peaceful, except for a lot of coughing; but just five minutes ago when I was in she asked for you."

As soon as she entered, Heather pulled the curtain around the comatose patient in the other bed and went to Mrs. Carstairs. She was glad to see that the light still surrounded the frail body, its eyes closed. She heard rapid breathing, occasionally punctuated by a little cough. She sat down at the bedside and reached for Mrs. Carstairs's hand. "I've come, Betty," she said.

Mrs. Carstairs opened her eyes. "I waited," she said. "I knew that you would be coming back this evening. Thank you for coming so quickly."

"Are you scared?" Heather asked.

"No," Mrs. Carstairs replied.

Heather sat quietly, holding her hand and looking intently into her face. A small tear ran from Mrs. Carstairs's right eye. "Are you sad?" Heather asked.

"No, not really."

"Wait just a minute," Heather said. She lowered the bedrails. Then she lifted Mrs. Carstairs into a sitting position, and holding her up, sat herself against the headboard and folded her arms around the frail torso. She began to rock her gently. "You can cry now, Betty," she said.

"I don't want to cry," Mrs. Carstairs protested weakly. But as the rocking continued, one tear, then another flowed down her cheeks; and in less than a minute, interspersed with coughs, she began to sob softly. Rocked in Heather's arms she sobbed what seemed a lifetime's worth of sobs.

Finally, she began to talk between the sobs and faint coughs and gasps for breath. "I don't know why I should be sad. I have no regrets. I told you I have no regrets about my family, and it's true. I guess I'm simply regretting life. It's been a good life. That's why I'm regretting. I want to leave it, but I feel regretful at leaving it. I don't want to lose it. I don't want it anymore. But it's like losing it. I don't want to lose it. But I do. It's so strange. I want to go on, and yet I regret. I'm tired. I'm regretting because I'm tired. I wish that life didn't have to be so tiring. I wish it weren't so tiring for my children and my grandchildren. For all the children. I wish it could be easier. I am glad it's over. But I don't want to give it up. I want to leave. Oh, Heather, it's so silly!"

"No, it's not silly at all," Heather soothed her. "Just be whatever you have to be at this moment, Betty. I'm here and I love you."

"I love you too, Heather."

"And you're so lovely, Betty," Heather whispered. "So lovely. So lovely. So good. So dear."

And as she crooned, Mrs. Carstairs's eyes closed and stayed closed. The little coughs very slowly grew weaker, the breaths more and more shallow. The minutes kept ticking by. "So sweet. So good. So lovely," Heather kept murmuring. And then there came a moment when the light was gone and Heather knew that she was holding only a body in her arms. She sat the body up, eased off the bed, and laid it back down against the sheets. Mrs. Carstairs's eyes were now open, but dead. Heather smoothed her hair and kissed her on the forehead, and left the room. She told Gloria that it was over, and returned to C-Wing.

Bertha was in Irene's place when she got back, very much in place, already ensconced inside the nurses' station with her novel. Heather would have liked to talk to her about Mrs. Carstairs, but it was impossible to hold much of a conversation with this stolid farmer's wife, so settled into late middle age. Given her plans with Stephen later, however, this liability was balanced by the fact that Bertha was not nosy. In fact, she was the least curious person Heather had ever met. Bertha did her work well, with a quiet, uncommitted efficiency. But when there was no work to do she simply sat at the station reading romance novels with astonishing concentration. Nothing disturbed her when she was reading. Bertha's real life lay in between the pages of her novels. The rest of the time probably represented a kind of unwelcome dream for her.

But Mrs. Carstairs's death was reality. It had happened. When she sat back down in the station, idly thumbing through the nurses' notes next to the nonpresent Bertha, without thinking Heather offered Mrs. Carstairs up. "Thank you, God," she said under her breath.

Roberta McAdams did not take ordinary vacations. Instead, without fail, she took off the first Thursday and Friday of each month. She left town early Thursday morning and returned late Saturday night so that she would have Sunday to rest before going back to work. It was well after midnight when she drove her compact Toyota into the parking lot of the apartment complex where she lived. It had been a long drive and she was tired, but she looked as neat and crisp as always.

Despite her fatigue she would ordinarily have had that usual feeling of relaxation that comes with sexual satisfaction. But not on this night. In the midst of her drive she'd turned on the car radio to get some music. Instead, she'd gotten a news report. She was just about to turn to another station when she'd heard the commentator talking about some damn senator or congressman named Stephen Solarz. The name—so similar— was enough for her to switch off the radio in a flash of pure rage.

To Roberta McAdams all the patients and all the staff of Willow Glen fell into a single category: a nuisance of greater or lesser degree. All, that is, except one: Stephen Solaris. He represented far more than a nuisance. She hated him, and she hated his name itself. She had no interest whatso- ever in wondering why his very being was such an insult to her. She was only interested in getting rid of him. Somehow.

Damn him! Why did he have to ruin her afterglow? What could be done about him? She would have to think more about that, she realized, as she carried her valise into her compact apartment and switched on the lights. She went straight to her bedroom and began to unpack. There was only one thing she didn't unpack. She left the medium-sized leather whip curled up in the bottom of the valise as she closed it and put it in her closet. She would be needing it, as always, for her next trip.


Lieutenant Petri had found a modest apartment in an orderly neighbor- hood just four blocks from the police station. It suited him perfectly, except for a few smudges on the living room wall and a small patch of mold on the ceiling. He did not want anything to remind him of the grime of Newark, New Jersey. The landlady had looked at him as if he were mad when he asked her to have the room repainted. But they were reasonable in negotiating the matter, and she agreed to pay for the paint as long as he bought the brushes and did the painting himself.

He had painted all that Saturday, and by evening the job was done. He was immensely pleased with it. The entire space was gleaming white. It had been the kind of day he enjoyed the most: a day where he had made a part of the world cleaner and neater, a day of orderly progression ending with a visible accomplishment. He went to sleep greatly satisfied, well deserving of his rest. Who would have thought that rest would be broken into by the most horrible nightmare of his life? Afterwards, he could only ascribe it to the smell of paint impinging upon his sleeping unconscious. What else could possibly explain it?

The nightmare began reasonably enough. He had finished painting the room and just put the lid back on the paint can. He stood up to take the brushes to the sink for cleaning when his eye was caught by a small dark spot on the wall opposite. He was mildly curious how he could have missed it. He reopened the can, dipped the brush, stepped across the room, and carefully painted over the spot. Returning, he put the lid back on the can. But as he stood up, he saw the spot on the wall once again. He was annoyed. He *knew* he had painted over it. Again, he took the lid off the can, again dipped the brush, again painted over the spot. This time he stepped back a few feet and surveyed the job. There was no doubt about it. The spot was no longer visible in the slightest. It was totally covered over. He returned, covered the can again, and stood up. He glanced at the wall. The same spot was there. Enraged, he leapt across the room. He examined it. It was not quite black. It was a dark, dark green and glistening—like a speck of some sort of slime. As he looked at it the speck began to grow. It became a spot larger than ever. Then it was no longer round. It began to elongate downward, as if the slime were pouring out through a minuscule aperture in the wall. The source of it had to be inside the wall. Frantically, he looked around for something to break through to the source. A curved crowbar appeared in his hand. He began striking at the wall. The crowbar drove through the Sheetrock. The slime kept oozing out. Furiously, he ripped off great slabs of Sheetrock, exposing boards that held back the insulation. The slime was oozing through the insulation. He had to find the source. He wrenched away the boards. He was standing in debris. He tore at the insulation. He couldn't get to the source. He couldn't find it. He couldn't find the source.

He awoke at two A.M. screaming aloud with frustration and rage, and with a pervading sense of both horror and shame as if not only the wall, but he himself and the whole world had become unalterably contaminated.


At three o'clock in the morning Heather announced to Bertha, "I'm going to set up the meds now. Oh, by the way, I'm going to take Stephen with me. You know how much he likes company, and he's asked if he could keep me company when I do the meds."

Bertha did not look up from her novel.

Heather wheeled the gurney down the corridor and turned right toward the supply room. She parked it against the wall, opened the door to the supply room, and turned on the light. Then she came back into the little hall, which was wide enough only for the gurney and herself. She gave him his letter board and held it for him. "How are you feeling tonight?" she asked.

"EXCITED."

"Me, too."

"I'M/ALSO/UNEASY."

"About what?"

"I'M/NOT/SURE," Stephen tapped. "LOTS/OF/LITTLE/STUFF. TOO/MUCH/ HAPPENING. MAYBE/MORE/THAN/I/CAN/DIGEST. IT'S/AS/IF/EVERYTHING/HAS/ STARTED/TO/SPEED/UP."

Heather was uncertain about her response. "Do you need me to back off?"

"GOD/NO. FORGET/IT. HOW/ARE/YOU?"

"I'm fine. Mrs. Carstairs died tonight," she told him. "It was a good death. Easy. And the light was there. Actually, it had been around her for several weeks. They don't all have the light, you know. In fact, most of them don't. Only about one in five do. Boy, what a light Mrs. Grochowski will have when she goes."

"SOMETIMES/I/THINK/YOU'RE/SOME/KIND/OF/DEATH/FREAK."

"Maybe you're right," Heather acknowledged. "I do like the drama of it. There's such reality in dying."

"HOW/COME/YOU'RE/COMFORTABLE/WITH/DEATH/WHEN/EVERYONE/IS/ AFRAID/OF/IT?"

"I *am* afraid of death. My own. When I think of myself dying, I'm terrified. It's just that I'm not afraid of other people's deaths."

"BUT/OTHER/PEOPLE/ARE/AFRAID/NOT/ONLY/OF/THEIR/OWN/DEATH/THEY/ ARE/AFRAID/OF/ANYONE/ELSE'S/DYING. THEY/DON'T/WANT/TO/BE/AROUND/ DEATH/AT/ALL."

"I don't know why that is. I don't understand it."

"BULLSHIT!" Occasionally Stephen was taken aback when Heather acted her age and seemed so dumb. "YOU/KNOW/THAT/PEOPLE/ARE/AFRAID/ OF/OTHERS'/DEATH/BECAUSE/IT/REMINDS/THEM/OF/THEIR/OWN. BUT/IT/SEEMS/ TO/BE/DIFFERENT/FOR/YOU."

"I guess it is," Heather acknowledged. "I've thought about it sometimes. It isn't because I believe in God the way a lot of religious people do. I'm not sure what I believe in. But somehow I don't have the feeling this is our true home, Stephen. And death for me is going home. I think that we're aliens here. Like we've been sent here on a temporary mission to a hostile planet. So I *am* glad when I see other people going home. I know that there are lots of religious people who talk about heaven and whatnot, and also think that this is not our true home. But it seems to me they really don't believe it in their hearts. I do. I don't know why, but I really do believe it. Yet this planet is all that I know, and while I often don't feel at home here, I get frightened when I think about being wrenched away from it. So I'm able to rejoice when others go home, but I'm still scared shitless when it comes to myself."

Stephen was delighted at these moments when they were exactly on the same wavelength. "I'M/SCARED/TOO," he tapped.

"For everyone, or just for yourself?" Heather asked.

"JUST/FOR/MYSELF. I/ALSO/BELIEVE/WE'RE/ALIENS. LOOK/AT/ME. IF/EVER/ THERE/WAS/AN/ALIEN, IT'S/ME. WHEN/I/WAS/SIXTEEN/IN/THE/OLD/NURSING/ HOME/AN/AIDE/ASKED/ME/WHETHER/I/WANTED/A/MERCY/KILLING—EUTHAN- ASIA. THAT'S/HOW/ALIEN/I/AM — THAT/IT/WOULD/BE/A/MERCY/TO/PUT/ME/ TO/SLEEP. I/DON'T/KNOW/WHETHER/SHE/WANTED/TO/DO/IT/HERSELF. I/MIGHT/ HAVE/OBLIGED/HER/IF/I/HADN'T/BEEN/SO/AFRAID."

"Oh, you don't feel like an alien to me," Heather said.

"THAT'S/BECAUSE/YOU'RE/ALSO/STRANGE," Stephen tapped.

"I am strange," Heather said, smiling. "But so are you. You know that light I was talking about that surrounds the ones that are dying? Well, I don't know whether you know it, but the same light is around you. That's not because you're dying. It's been around you all the three years I've known you. In fact, the past month it seems to have grown stronger. I don't know why."

"I/DO."

"Why?"

"LUST."

Heather laughed. "Yours or mine?"

"PROBABLY/BOTH. ANYWAY/IT/MAKES/ME/ALL/THE/MORE/SCARED/OF/ DYING."

"Good. I'm glad that you're scared, Stephen. I'm glad that we're both scared together. Now shut up. You're very talkative tonight. I've got to do my meds. When I'm finished, then I'll have a surprise for you." Heather hung the letter board behind the gurney and went into the supply room to prepare the early morning medications.

It took her twenty minutes to set them up. As she did, she hummed quietly to herself, yet was also aware that she was humming for Stephen's benefit. He lay there on the gurney in the half-light coming from the door of the supply room, listening to Heather humming to him, waiting for what was to come. It was the most magical moment of his life.

When she was finished, Heather reached up into the upper left-hand corner of the cupboard and got out a bottle of baby oil that she placed at the foot of Stephen's gurney. She left the light on in the supply room and the door one-third open. She went into the corridor and looked to see if anyone was there. C-Wing was utterly silent.

"Stephen," she said, "you almost never seem to sleep. I know you do. I know you sleep in snatches. But after what we are going to do, I hope you truly sleep."

Heather pulled the sheet off Stephen's chest and loins. She unraveled the condom catheter and hung it from the corner of the gurney. "I'm not going to bathe you," she said. "That's the surprise. I'm going to use oil instead." She opened the bottle of baby oil and filled her left hand with it. She sloshed the oil onto his penis. What remained on her left hand she rubbed into her right, and with both hands, very slowly, she began to massage his penis. Instantly, she felt it begin to grow in her hand.

They looked at each other. She forced herself to be slow, but in no time he was huge. She took her eyes away from his and looked at it. In the partial light coming from the door, it was the most beautiful thing she had ever seen. Its eye seemed to be looking at her with the same intensity as her own eyes. She bent over him and with a flick of her tongue, licked it. His loins, ordinarily motionless, jerked up ever so slightly to meet her. She straightened up and they gazed at each other for a long moment. Then, no longer able to restrain herself, she bent down and took the whole head into her mouth. Within seconds, everything erupted. Simultaneously his semen burst into her throat and his throat exploded into a roaring noise like nothing she had ever heard. It was a cross between a prolonged death rattle and a wail for all the pain in the world. It seemed to her that it must have echoed throughout every corner of Willow Glen.

Suddenly terrified, she swallowed him and whipped the sheet up over his body. She dashed out into the corridor. No one was there. No steps to be heard. She came back into the little hall and whispered to him, "Darling, you have to be more quiet after this. Promise. I want to do it again, but you've got to be quiet. I'm sorry. I *love* your noise. But we've got to keep it quiet."

Slowly and lovingly she replaced the condom over his softening penis, and put the bottle of baby oil back into the cupboard. She turned the light out in the supply room. Then she wheeled Stephen back out to his place by the wall. In the dim light of the nurses' station, Bertha was still reading, apparently unaware that the world had trembled. Heather herself had not come, but she felt as satisfied as if she had. She bent over Stephen and kissed him lightly on the lips. "Sleep now, my darling," she whispered almost inaudibly. She straightened up and went back into the nurses' station. And Stephen slept.

## FIVE

## Sunday/Monday, March 20th–21st

There were nights at Willow Glen that were simply strange. It did not happen often, but from time to time it was as if some unnameable spirit was stalking the dark corridors. For no reason, the patients would become agitated. But you could feel the ominousness even before they did. Heather and the other nurses and aides would joke among themselves about Halloween or nights of the full moon, but that never seemed to explain it. Those who had worked at other nursing homes said the phenomenon was not unique to Willow Glen. When Heather came on duty, she could feel it immediately: the calm before the storm. "It's going to be one of those nights," she said to Irene.

But it began quietly. Indeed, when she visited Mrs. Grochowski, Heather felt that she had all the time in the world.

"I've been wondering, Mrs. G.," she asked, sitting on the foot of the bed, "have you ever wanted to write a book? Like Stephen?"

"No. Stephen's got something to say. I don't."

"But you could write about your life—all about what you were telling me, about how you stopped wanting to be admired and became interested in people for their own sake."

"Men and women have been writing that story for hundreds of years, and it doesn't seem to have helped too much," Mrs. Grochowski responded. "I'm not saying such stories haven't helped anybody. Yet most readers are unaffected by them. There's more to learning than reading inspirational stories."

"But you really seem to have discovered something special," Heather protested.

"Hardly. There's no point to writing my story precisely because there are too many mysteries, too many secrets I haven't discovered, too many unanswered questions."

"Like what, for instance?"

"There are many, many people who are the way I was, seeking to be admired. Trying to maintain an image. Perhaps most of them stay in that trap for all their lives, until they die or they actually do kill themselves one way or another. Why was I able to get out of that trap? I don't know. Why did I get multiple sclerosis, instead of continuing to work myself to the bone, bitter at my husband for leaving me, bitter at the children for not being the nice children I deserved? Why was I finally able to see the trap I had fallen into? Why was I able to change—what does your Dr. Kolnietz call it—my tapes, and stop trying to be nice?"

Heather was acutely interested. Although, with Dr. K.'s help, she was coming to recognize that there was a part of her that did not want to change, it was all in the service of another part that did. This matter of changing tapes was personal for her. "But you told me you could pinpoint exactly when and how you changed," she reminded the older woman.

"Yes, we can often pinpoint the moments of decision," Mrs. Grochowski agreed, "and it's often clear *how* people change. But we still don't know the *why* of it. Just because people ought to change doesn't mean that they do. I had to have a lot of evidence that my life wasn't working before I began to think about doing it differently. You see Dr. Kolnietz because you've accepted the evidence that there's something wrong with your choice of men. But many would reject such evidence. What's the difference between people like you and me who eventually accept the evidence and those that continue to refuse it? That's a question I cannot answer. I have no idea."

"No idea?" Heather echoed.

"Not really. We Christians think it has to do with something we call grace. Grace is when God somehow intervenes in our lives to soften us up, to help us accept the evidence and grow. I regard it as God's doing, as grace, that I was able to change. But that really doesn't explain anything. Does God intervene in some people's lives and not others? Or if grace is available to everyone, why does it succeed in softening the hearts of some while the hearts of others remain hardened? I don't know."

"But you must know!" Heather protested.

"Oh, sweetheart, you'd like to have an explanation for everything, wouldn't you?" Mrs. Grochowski chided. "But what I'm trying to tell you is that there aren't always explanations. You remembered I told you when I stopped trying to be nice, I became depressed. I mean really depressed. I had lots of medications for my multiple sclerosis. Many times I thought about taking them all and killing myself. I could have done so quite successfully. Why did I never quite take them? And when my granddaughter came around and told me I was not interested in her, since I no longer wanted to be admired or nice, why did I care?"

"What are the answers to those questions?" Heather asked.

"There are no answers to those kinds of questions. At least," Mrs. Grochowski smiled, "not this side of the grave."

Tim O'Hara was equally mysterious when Heather visited him in his room next. She wanted to ask him about something that had been slowly percolating in the back of her mind for the past month. "You told me you stopped drinking when you went to AA twenty years ago," she said.

"That's true, angel."

"And in nursing school they taught us people in AA believe recovering alcoholics should never drink again."

"That's also true."

"Well, Tim O'Hara, you old hypocrite," she chided. "Just what are you doing with a bottle of red wine in your bureau drawer?"

"Ah, I've been discovered, have I now?"

"Not only that; you're the only person in all of Willow Glen who's allowed to have alcohol. It's written in the orders. For some reason Mrs. Simonton has made another of her very particular exceptions to the rule in your case. Why?"

"Ah, she's a nice lady, isn't she? You've never seen me drunk, have you?"

"There you go trying to answer a question with a question. No, I've never seen you drunk. And, as far as we nurses know, Mrs. Simonton gets you a new bottle only about twice a year. But what's going on?"

"Well, I save it for very special occasions, and then all I have is just a little taste. That's all I need anymore."

"What special occasions?"

"Every week or two Marion and I have a special little meal together. Just a sip of the wine and a little piece of bread together. It's a way of celebrating. Eucharist we call it. That's a fancy Greek word for celebration."

Something reverberated in the back of Heather's mind, a resonance of the word she'd heard from other girls when she was a child in school. "That's communion, isn't it?" she blurted out, "like Catholics do at mass?"

"You've got it," Tim replied with a grin.

"Are you a Catholic?"

"Of course. I'm Irish, aren't I? And so's Marion, who's Polish. Most of us Poles and Irish are born Catholic."

"You've always gone to church?"

"Oh, that's another matter. No. By the time I was nineteen, I didn't want anything to do with the Church. I didn't go back until I was sixty, after I'd been in the program for a dozen years or so."

"The program?"

"AA. That's what we call it a lot of the time."

"Why did you go back to church?"

"Oh, a lot of old-timers in AA go back to church after ten or twenty years. Or else start going for the first time. It's a kind of pattern."

"Fine, fine," Heather said with exasperation. "But why?"

"Ah, that's hard to explain, angel. No, I don't think I could explain it to you."

And it was clear he was not even going to try. Heather took another track. "I'm not a Catholic," she said. "I guess I'm not even a Christian. I don't know what I am. But somehow I remember my friends back in school telling me that communion has to be done in church with a priest—that only a priest can celebrate the Eucharist or mass. Or a minister if you're Protestant. How come you and Mrs. G. can do it here by yourselves?"

"Ah, you've got me again, angel. Maybe it's because we're not really very good Catholics. Maybe it's because we've got a dispensation, an authorization."

"An authorization from whom?"

"Well, an authorization from Mrs. Simonton at the very least, don't we?"

Heather still didn't understand. "But you could get a priest to do it," she said. "Father Pulaski comes to Willow Glen at least once a week. I know he gives communion to some of the other patients. He could give it to you and Mrs. G."

"He could," Tim agreed, with a look of mild distaste, "but it still wouldn't be quite the same. I've got nothing against the good father, but he doesn't have much time, and he kind of rushes through it as if he needed to get out of the room. Maybe he's afraid of us in here. So I can't say that I've been able to really get near him. Marian and I, we're very close, you know. And communion has something to do with community, right? It means something extra-special when it's the two of us together in community in Jesus's name."

Confused, Heather continued to prod. "I don't want to challenge your religion, Tim. I'm just curious. Why do you do it? I don't know anything about communion. What does it do for you?"

"Oh, many things, angel, but it's so hard to explain."

"You keep trying to get off the hook, Tim O'Hara," Heather pointed out, enjoying the sparring. "You could at least try."

Tim looked doubtful. "The wine is Jesus' blood. The bread is Jesus' body. When we eat and drink it, it's a kind of cannibalism. The cannibals in the jungle, you know, they don't eat their enemies because of a shortage of meat. Often they eat just the heart. They believe that courage resides in the heart. So when they do it they believe they're taking on the courage of the enemy. Of course we don't think of Jesus as our enemy; we think of him as our friend. But when we eat his body and we drink his blood we take on some of his courage."

"But it isn't actually his body or his blood. You're not actually eating him. You're just eating bread. It's just a symbol."

"No," Tim said with certainty. "We're eating him."

"That's crazy!" Heather exclaimed.

"I thought you said you didn't want to challenge my religion," Tim sparred back with a twinkle. "It's not crazy, but it is mysterious. That's why we call it the 'mystery of transubstantiation.' Now there's a fancy word for you, isn't it?"

"What does it mean?"

"It means the mysterious process by which the bread is actually turned into Jesus' body and the wine actually turned into his blood. And since you've gotten me to ramble on like this, I might as well explain a little more about your earlier question. Good Catholics believe that only a priest can serve communion because only he has the power to cause the process to happen. Perhaps because we're not very good Catholics, Marion and I happen to believe that our own love and faith have the power to transubstantiate. So that's why we don't need a priest."

"I can't believe you're not good Catholics."

Tim smiled. "I hope you're right," he said, "but at the very least you ought to realize that we're renegade ones."

Heather grimaced. "I'm not attacking, but it still all sounds like a bunch of superstition to me. And cannibalism! Ugh!"

"Ah, but it's much more than cannibalism. It's also sexual."

"What? Sexual?"

"Sure. It's a mingling of the juices—of mine and Marion's and Jesus'. It's a sort of way that the two of us couple with Jesus, with God. Yes, it's sexual. And many other things to boot."

"I'm sorry, Tim," Heather said, genuinely apologizing. "I'm just having a lot of trouble understanding it."

"Of course you are, angel. It's like computers. You don't understand computers by listening to a lecture about them, do you now? Or reading a book on them? No, you learn about computers by doing them, using them, experiencing them. You wouldn't be wanting to do that, would you? If you did, if you did want to play around with this communion business, I'm sure I can set you up."

"You do make it sound sexual," Heather giggled. "But, no, I'm not ready to be set up, Tim. It's got to make a little more sense to me first."

"Take your time, angel. Sense, yes, but also remember it's a mystical thing."

"Mystical?"

"Yes, full of mystery. So even when you do play around with it, you won't understand it all. If you have to wait until you understand everything, then you're really not going to be able to understand much at all."

Heather left, if anything more confused than ever. It truly was going to be one of those nights.

Georgia was feeling restless after dinner. So restless she decided to attempt to talk with Stephen again. "I came back," she announced, handing him his letter board. But she gave the responsibility to him for her decision. "You asked me to. Remember?"

"I/DO," Stephen tapped slowly for her benefit. "THANK/YOU. I/KNOW/IT/ MUST/TAKE/A/LOT/OF/CONCENTRATION/TO/TALK /WITH/ME."

"It does," Georgia acknowledged with a sense of pride. "How are you this evening?"

Stephen hesitated. He knew his honesty was one of the reasons he tended to threaten people. But evasiveness had come to be against his very nature. "SAD," he answered.

"Oh. Why?"

Although he was, in fact, very sad, it didn't mean he couldn't gloss over it for her benefit. "BECAUSE/I'M/NOT/NORMAL/I/FEEL/SORRY/FOR/MYSELF/ SOMETIMES."

"Well, I should think you're entitled to."

"PERHAPS. HOW/ARE/YOU/GEORGIA?"

"Restless."

"WHY?"

"I don't know."

"TELL/ME/ABOUT/YOURSELF."

"There's not much to tell. I don't think about myself much."

Stephen surmised this was true. It would not be possible for an old lady to think much about herself if she didn't want to think about aging. But he was not about to point this out to her. He was not going to ruin another opportunity by preaching. "JUST/TELL/ME/ANYTHING — THE/FIRST/ THING/THAT/COMES/TO/YOUR/MIND."

"My parents were good to me," Georgia stammered. "I had a happy childhood."

"THERE! NOW/I/DO/KNOW/SOMETHING/ABOUT/YOU. THANK/YOU."

But even that had been as deep as Georgia wanted to go. "I'll come back again some time," she promised by way of ending the conversation.

"I'M/GLAD. I/LOOK/FORWARD/TO/IT."

Although she felt better about this time with Stephen, it had been disconcerting once again. In spontaneously commenting that she'd had a happy childhood, she knew she'd implied that her adulthood had not been so happy. And that was something she didn't care to dwell upon. Still restless, Georgia prowled along the corridor to the dayroom. Hank Martin latched onto her immediately. "Hello, love. I've just been thinking about us. I've been thinking we ought to leave here for an afternoon sometime."

"What on earth are you talking about?"

"It's not as if we're disabled. If we asked them, I bet they'd let us out for the day."

"And do what?"

"Well, I've got enough saved up for us to go to a motel."

So that was what he'd been leading up to, Georgia thought. Naturally. "Of course it wouldn't occur to you to use your money to take me to a movie instead of a motel room," she countered.

Hank considered the possibility. She probably wouldn't even let him hold her hand. But he was not to be bested. "Well, I might take you to a movie if there was a good World War Two one on—you know, one where I could relive my good old dogfight days."

"The only dogfight you'd ever have had, Hank Martin, is if you worked as a postman."

Hank looked stung. "You don't believe me," he said mournfully, showing her his hands. "I've killed men with these hands," he announced.

"The only thing you'd have the courage to kill," she retorted, "would be a horsefly—if you were quick enough." Georgia turned on him and walked out of the dayroom. She was so accustomed to his being insensitive and taking her snubs for granted that she was unaware how she had succeeded in wounding him.

She went back to her room and found Lutzina reading a circular. She sat down with her. The two roommates had almost become friends.

Lucy had learned to avoid the topic of Georgia's age. Yet she had found there was no problem when she talked about her own. "I've been thinking of moving to California," she said.

"California?" said Georgia in surprise.

"There's a new adult community out there near Santa Barbara. Two of my friends moved there last summer and are urging me to come. They write me that the flowers are beautiful, that it's cool in summer and warm in the winter. No ice to fall on."

"But your roots are in New Warsaw," Georgia protested, "and you're just about to go home." The week before Lucy had graduated from her walker to a cane and was now able to walk to the dining room almost as fast as Georgia herself.

"That's the point," Lucy responded. "I *am* about to go home. When I came here that was all I could think about—getting home. But now it's about to happen and I'm beginning to wonder why. Yes, my roots have been here, but they're rapidly shriveling away. My husband's long dead and the land sold off. Many of my healthier friends have moved, like the two to California, and the sicker ones are dropping off like flies."

"Well, it might make sense," Georgia acknowledged.

"It makes a lot of sense. What happens if I fall again? If Rob hadn't happened to be coming by, I would have frozen to death. It's not good at my age to be living alone. They tell me that in this community out there you can be as independent as you choose, but they also check on you every day. There's a doctor who makes house calls. And if you do have to go to a nursing home," Lucy grimaced, "there's one that's part of the complex and you're guaranteed a bed. Each room has a little kitchenette so you can make your own food, but there's a dining room like here if you don't want to eat alone. They have activities and bus trips. There's much more to do than in New Warsaw. My friends write that they're going to concerts and they just hail a cab when they want to go shopping. It makes a lot of sense."

"When will you go?"

"Oh, I haven't actually decided to go." Lucy's face clouded over. "They won't take pets. I'd have to give up Wrinkles. I don't see how I can do that. I would, maybe, if I could find a good home for him. But nobody wants an old dog. I'd have to put him to sleep. How could I ever do that?"

"Where's Wrinkles now?"

"Rob took him in at first, but then they decided he was too much trouble so they took him to the kennel. You see, no one wants him. I wish there was a good nursing home for old dogs. I can't wait to get him out of that kennel and see him again."

"I can understand how you feel," Georgia commiserated. "But you do need to think about your future."

"What about you, Georgia?" Lucy inquired. "What about your future? Have you ever thought about going to an adult community like the one in California?"

Georgia was startled. "What?"

"Well, there's really no reason for you to be in a nursing home."

"Of course there's no reason for me to be in a nursing home," Georgia snapped. "You know perfectly well my children railroaded me here."

"But if you asked them, maybe they'd be willing to send you to California."

"One doesn't ask my children anything," Georgia pronounced. "They're not about to give up control of me. I'm stuck here."

It was clear to Lucy she had gone too far. "Well, I think I'll go for a walk and exercise my leg some more," she said with delicacy.

Georgia was left sitting in her rocker with an unpleasant mixture of annoyance and confusion. Why couldn't people understand the reality of her situation? she wondered. But she began to feel better when she looked at the picture on her bureau of the girl swinging in the orchard. It was so much like the orchard her parents had when she was a child. And then she was back there in reverie—back before she'd had children, back before she'd been married, back when she'd still been free.

Edith Simonton licked the envelope flap of the last of a small pile of letters she had written. She was sitting in the easy chair in the living room of her two-bedroom house. Few visitors came to the house, but those who did immediately felt comfortable in it. A Victorian clock she'd inherited from her parents ticked noisily away on the mantel over the fireplace.

The letters on the coffee table in front of her were not letters to relatives. She had two sisters, seven nieces and nephews, and a dozen cousins, but she found them insufferably dull. She was quite content with their Christmas card relationship.

Nor were they letters to friends. She had more than enough friends through her work. Not many, but enough. True peers like Stephen Solaris, Marion Grochowski, and Stasz Kolnietz. She was not, in the ordinary sense, lonely. As a contemplative person, in fact, she often needed to be alone.

They were letters to prisoners. She had been writing to men in prison for the past dozen years. Her motives were compassionate. And platonic. Indeed, after two of them visited her when they were paroled, she had learned to discourage their sexual fantasies as well as her own. She made a point of quickly writing the others that she was ugly—something she believed true—and that she was happily married—which was a lie.

There was, however, an indirect sexuality to this letter writing. She wrote them out of a particular empathy, she realized, because she too was a prisoner—a prisoner of her body. She hated her body. Ever since her divorce almost three decades before, she had felt herself to be unattractive. She'd made no attempt to date again. She'd tried to not even think of herself as feminine. Yet she could not deny the reality that she was a sexual person. She especially hated her body because of the power it had over her, the extraordinary power of those urges to be taken, to be filled and saturated.

She knew that as the world looked at these things, her attitude would not be considered "healthy." She'd even gone to see Dr. Kolnietz for a while when he'd first opened his practice in town. They'd talked about her childhood and parents, exploring the usual Freudian psychodynamics. But it went deeper. It wasn't long before they both realized these dynamics were irrelevant. "Of course I want to be fucked," she'd said. "You know that. But I don't want to be married again. I don't want one-night stands either. And I don't want my close relationships to be complicated by sex. I don't like to sit in front of my mirror and put on makeup. I never did. I don't like to go shopping and I don't care what I wear. I used to think I wanted romance, but now romance just seems silly. I don't like games. I don't want sexual power. So what are you going to do with me, Doctor? I want to be fucked, but I don't want anything that goes along with it."

"Maybe you're just not called to sexual love," Stasz said mildly.

"Then why in God's name am I so horny?"

"Maybe it is in God's name."

She stared at him, aware of stirrings of fear—no, something more intense than fear. Terror. "What are you talking about?" she protested.

"Most monks and nuns and priests feel called to celibacy," Stasz had continued, "yet many of them struggle for years with strong sexual desires."

"You keep using this word 'called.' What do you mean?"

"Maybe God is calling you through sex. Maybe God wants you for Himself."

"Would you care to be just a little bit more edifying, Doctor?" she had retorted sarcastically.

"We psychiatrists are trained to be skeptical of religion," said Kolnietz, "so I don't want you to go around telling people what I'm about to say to you. But I haven't totally rejected my good Catholic upbringing and I remember that Saint Augustine once said, 'You made us for yourself, dear Lord, and we cannot find true rest except in You.' Maybe you're like Saint Augustine, looking for true rest."

"Oh, so I'm a saint now, am I?"

"Possibly." Dr. Kolnietz blandly ignored the attempt at provocation. "Most people—even most who believe in God—seem to have relatively secular souls. But there are a few who have a particularly burning desire for closeness with God. Or maybe it's because God has a particularly burning desire for them. And there does seem to be something sexual about it. Go back and read the Song of Solomon, Edie. This business about God being the 'Bridegroom' didn't come out of thin air, you know. When I talk about calling, I mean that your sexuality may possibly be what it is because you are one of those few whom God made very specially for Himself."

Yes, it had been terror. In some way she knew that they had hit pay dirt. But she was not in the least bit willing or ready to deal with it. Nor had Stasz been particularly anxious to push her on it—"I suspect these things require gradual evolution," he'd said—and shortly afterwards she had ceased her visits to his office.

That had been fifteen years ago, and she still wasn't ready to deal with it. But closer. Maybe much closer. Lately, in particular, almost in spite of herself, she had been discovering herself nibbling at the edges of this terrifying core of truth more and more often. But that had no effect upon the urges of her body, and she still hated them. She remembered how, as a child, she had learned to refer to her periods as "the curse." Well, her periods had tapered off eight years before, but her sexual need had not stopped in the least. Sex was the curse of her body. Sex was God's curse.

Agitated, she got up and went into the kitchen. The bottle of whisky was there. She checked the level before pouring the first drink. Daily she wondered if she was an alcoholic. She knew that her friends in AA would tell her that if she had to wonder about it that much, then she was. But she didn't care. Alcohol was God's blessing to balance the curse. It never hurt her. Maybe she couldn't give it up, but she could control it very exactly. She never got drunk. She titrated herself only in the evening and precisely to that sweet level of anesthesia where the body was calm, where she no longer needed that *thing*—the vibrator—that sat at the bottom of her top bureau drawer.

She poured herself the second drink. It usually took two and a half, three at the most. She accepted now that her yearning was ultimately not for another human being; it was for the very One who had placed it in her. Yet He, She, or It who had cursed her with this yearning refused, except for the very rarest of moments, to ever be palpably present to her. It was so damn *unfair*. And while she occasionally resorted to it, masturbation seemed to her the loneliest thing on earth.

At two A.M. it started. The wail echoed down the corridors of Willow Glen like a siren, rising and falling in waves.

"I knew it," Heather said. "I knew it—or something—would happen tonight. It's probably Carol Kubrick. Would you go and check, Bertha?"

Bertha put down her romance novel and lumbered down the corridor. Within a minute she was back. "You're right. It's Crazy Carol, as usual."

Heather unlocked the medication cabinet in the supply room to prepare a syringe. Mrs. Kubrick had a sedative prescribed for nights like this. They didn't happen very often—only once every couple of months—but the wailing would continue indefinitely until the sedative put her back to sleep. Carrying the syringe on a little tray, Heather went down to the room Mrs. Kubrick shared with Mrs. Stimson. She flipped on the light. Carol was lying on her back wailing. Rachel, in the bed by the window, was lying on her side simply staring. "What's wrong?" Heather asked Carol, not expecting any reply. The wailing went on as if Heather had not even entered the room. Heather rolled up Carol's nightgown, rubbed her thigh with an alcohol sponge, and slipped the needle in.

Heather turned to Mrs. Stimson. "I am sorry Carol woke you, Rachel," she said. "She should be asleep within ten minutes. Is there anything that I can do for you?"

Rachel continued to look at her silently. There was no acknowledgment. There was nothing for Heather to do except turn out the lights and leave. But as she was doing so she thought she heard a faint whisper behind her. It sounded like "Don't go." She looked back into the room. "Is that you, Rachel?" she asked. "Do you need me?"

There was no answer from the darkness. Heather waited another minute, then decided she had only imagined it.


Tim O'Hara woke up when Crazy Carol began wailing. He lay in bed in the darkness until it ceased. Hank Martin's breathing sounded as if he were asleep. Tim slid out of bed and, laboriously dragging his paralyzed leg behind him, shuffled in the darkness past Hank's bed and out into the hall. He went down to Mrs. Grochowski's room. Able only to use his right side, he hoisted himself with difficulty up onto the bed and lay down beside her. "It's me, Marion, darling," he whispered to her.

But Hank was not asleep. He, too, had been awakened, and he knew where Tim had gone. Everybody's getting theirs except me, he thought. Wasn't he manly enough? And then he remembered Georgia's gibe that he didn't have the courage to kill anything larger than a horsefly. But what did she know? Yes, what did she know? She *would* know if he took his cane to her and slammed her down. Maybe he hadn't really shot down the Jerries, but that didn't mean he couldn't kill *someone*. His shame having turned to rage, Hank continued to brood alone in the darkness.

•    •    •

At three A.M., Heather wheeled Stephen on his gurney into the narrow hallway outside the supply room. "It's one of those weird nights again," she said to him. "Did you hear Crazy Carol wailing?" She unhooked the letter board from the gurney and gave it to him without his asking. Over the past two weeks she had come to treasure the intimacy of these times tucked away in the narrow little hall in the half-light. "How are you feeling this evening, dear Stephen?" she asked.

Stephen tapped out, "HOPELESS."

Heather was startled. This was the first time she had ever known Stephen to be depressed. "My God," she exclaimed. "What's wrong?"

"YOU'LL/SOON/BE/BACK/ON/DAYS."

"I've been sorry about that too. I'll miss being together at night. But in another month, I'll be back on nights again. And while it won't be the same, at least I'll be able to talk with you when I'm on days."

"NOT/THE/PROBLEM," Stephen tapped. "I/CAN/DO/WITHOUT/SEX/FOR/A/ MONTH. I/KNOW/YOU'LL/COME/BACK. THEN/YOU'LL/GO/AGAIN. AND/YOU'LL/ COME/BACK/AGAIN. BUT/SOMEDAY/YOU/WON'T/COME/BACK/AT/ALL."

"Oh, Stephen," she said. "I'm sorry. I haven't been thinking about the long-term future."

"BUT/I/HAVE. AND/FOR/ME/IT/SUCKS. SOMEDAY/YOU'LL/LEAVE/HERE/FOR/ A/BETTER/JOB. OR/YOU'LL/WANT/TO/LEAVE/FOR/A/REAL/MAN."

"You are a real man, Stephen. You're more of a real man than I have ever known."

"THEN/THAT'S/YOUR/PROBLEM. I/AM/A/GOOD/PERSON/BUT/I'M/ALSO/A/ HOPELESS/CRIPPLE. SOONER/OR/LATER/YOU'RE/GOING/TO/PUT/ME/AWAY."

"Put you away?" Heather repeated dumbly, but with the dawning knowledge that there had to be possible truth in what he was saying.

"YES/PUT/ME/AWAY. I'M/A/HOPELESS/CRIPPLE/WITH/A/HOPELESS/FUTURE. IT'S/ MY/OWN/STUPID/FAULT. I/THOUGHT/I/COULD/HANDLE/MY/FEELINGS/FOR/YOU. I/EVEN/KNEW/THE/LOSS/WOULD/COME. I/THOUGHT/I/COULD/HANDLE/THE/ LOVE/IS/BLIND/BIT/BUT/I'VE/BEEN/THE/BLINDEST/FOOL/THAT/EVER/CAME/ ALONG. I/REALLY/DID/BELONG/IN/THE/IDIOT/WARD."

"Oh, Stephen, I hate to hear you talk like this. You know that isn't true," Heather protested.

"MOST/IS/TRUE. LOVE/IS/BLIND/AND/I/DO/LOVE/YOU. BUT/I/KNOW/NOW/ THERE/IS/NO/FUTURE. THERE/IS/FOR/YOU. BUT/NOT/FOR/ME."

"There's always a future."

"WHAT/DO/YOU/MEAN?"

"I don't know. It's hard to talk about." Heather stumbled, searching for words. "Remember when I was talking about Mrs. Carstairs's dying and the light she had surrounding her? The kind of light that you have all the time? That's growing? I remember learning in nursing school that there is no single moment of death. Even with a heart attack. Even if there is a single moment when the heart stops beating, it takes thirty seconds or so before the person becomes unconscious, and it takes several minutes before there is brain death. So when people die who have that light, you would think that it would just gradually fade away over those several minutes. But that's not the way it happens. When I hold people with the light who are dying, that light is just there, and then it's gone. It doesn't fade away. It's gone in a second. Rather than fading away, it leaps away. I think it leaps free. I think it leaps somewhere. I know it leaps somewhere."

"SHUT/UP! I'M/NOT/INTERESTED/IN/METAPHYSICS," Stephen tapped with urgent speed. "I'M/NOT/TALKING/ABOUT/DEATH. ABOUT/AFTERLIFE. I'M/TALKING/ABOUT/US. AND/THERE'S/NO/FUTURE. THERE'S/NO/FUTURE/FOR/US. IT'S/HOPELESS."

"Oh, my dear, I'm so sorry. Would it make it easier for you if we stopped having sex?"

"NO. IT/HELPS/ME/TO/SLEEP, REMEMBER?"

"You're bitter."

"DAMN/RIGHT. BUT/THAT'S/NOT/BECAUSE/I/TAKE/OUR/SEX/SO/LIGHTLY. IT'S/BECAUSE/IT'S/SO/PRECIOUS/TO/ME. I/LOVE/IT. I/LIVE/FOR/IT. I/WOULD/DIE/FOR/IT." There was a pause. Then he continued tapping. "MAYBE/YOU'RE/RIGHT/ABOUT/THERE/BEING/A/FUTURE. GEORGIA/HAS/STARTED/TO/TALK/TO/ME. MAYBE/I/HAVE/AN/OLD/LADY/IN/MY/FUTURE. BIG/DEAL. I/DO/HAVE/MY/BOOK. AND/AT/LEAST/THERE'S/ALWAYS/TIME. AS/THEY/SAY, TIME/HEALS/ALL/WOUNDS. MAYBE/TIME/WILL/HEAL/THIS/ONE/SOMEHOW. I/DON'T/KNOW/HOW. BUT/MAYBE."

"Does that mean you still want to have sex tonight, even though you are feeling so sad and angry and bitter?"

"OH/HEATHER/I/NEED/YOU/MORE/THAN/EVER."

Heather took the letter board and hung it back on the head of the gurney. "I've got to get to work and do my meds now," she said. "And when I'm done, I'll put you to sleep, my darling."

Among those awakened by Crazy Carol's wailing was Georgia Bates. She got up to go to the bathroom and returned to bed. When the wailing stopped, she thought she would go back to sleep. And she did, in a fashion. But it was not like real sleep; sleep and dreaming and wakefulness all blurred into one. As soon as she thought she was awake, she drifted off. As soon as she thought she was about to enjoy a good dream, it would slip away. Elusive images of numbers, of vague shapes, of words without meaning circled around in her mind. She had a sense of struggle, but it seemed to go nowhere, to have no purpose, to be endlessly repetitive. Finally, after—was it minutes or hours? she did not know—her frustration turned to anger. This is ridiculous, she thought. I'd rather be up and about.

She put on her soft slippers in the darkness, but did not bother with her robe. She made for the door in her nightgown, passing by Lucy, and went out into the dimly lit corridor. They turned off the fluorescents at night. There was only a dim light coming from the nurses' station. She moved toward it, thinking she might have some conversation. When she got there, however, Bertha was buried in a book. Bertha, she remembered, was hardly a conversationalist, and besides it would be rude to interrupt her for no reason. Maybe she would go into the dayroom. Then she noticed a ray of light emanating from the opposite corridor. Curious, she circled around the station, passed the engrossed Bertha, and realized the light was coming from the supply room off the little hall. She walked into the light and saw Heather in her white uniform bent over the form of Stephen on the gurney. Heather's head was at Stephen's groin. Some things are better not watched, Georgia thought, and she turned back.

This time she did go to the dayroom, again going around the nurses' station without Bertha's looking up. She turned on a floor lamp and sat down to read a magazine. Nothing in it could catch her attention. What a dreadful night, she thought, switching off the light and going out into the corridor. I might as well go back to bed. Then something in the opposite direction impinged on her awareness. She peered down the hall into the darkness. Was that a shape moving across the hall? Was it something slightly lighter than the darkness or something slightly darker than the darkness? She couldn't tell; it was as vague as everything else had been in her dreams. She was conscious of it only because it moved. Or was she just imagining it? If it moved, it moved in total silence. By the time she peered more closely, it was gone. That is, if it ever existed.

This night gets stranger and stranger, Georgia said to herself, as she circled past Bertha and returned to her room and her bed. She wondered whether it would be like before. But this time, blessedly, she fell into a deep sleep.

## Monday, March 21st

Peggy Valeno was late for work that morning. Her brother had used the car the night before and left the lights on, so the battery had run down. She had to awaken her father to help her jump-start it from the tractor. He was slow and grouchy. It's not my fault, she kept thinking. It wasn't her fault that her brother had left the lights on. It wasn't her fault that she had to wake up her father. And it wasn't her fault that she was going to be late. She remembered telling Mrs. Simonton that she got to work on time. Now she couldn't do that. And the other week she hadn't tied Carol up. Probably Mrs. Simonton would fire her. But it wasn't her fault. By the time she reached Willow Glen, the refrain had been transformed in her mind into "I don't care."

When she got to the C-Wing nurses' station it was seven-thirty, and Heather was already gone. "I'm sorry I'm late. My car wouldn't start," she said to Susan, the day-shift nurse. "Where would you like me to begin?"

Susan looked at her coldly. "Just get going on your baths," she answered. Peggy thought she would start with Stephen. She always began with the pleasantest or easiest patient. Today she really didn't care. Probably she wouldn't even talk to him. But if he did want to talk, at least he was more interesting than the others.

She went to the supply room and filled up the basin with warm water. She carried it and the soap and washcloth to the gurney and set it down on the floor. The sheet was half covering Stephen's face; he must still be asleep. But even as she began to lift up the sheet, she had the sense that something was awry. The color of his forehead was wrong. She pulled the sheet down to his waist and screamed. Protruding from his chest was a pair of scissors. One blade had been driven up to the hilt into his chest. The other blade lay horizontally over his breastbone.

She screamed and screamed. Susan shot out of the nurses' station and saw the scissors. "Laura!" she yelled. The other aide came running. "Hold Peggy. Don't touch anything. I'm going to call Mrs. Simonton or Ms. McAdams."

And Peggy continued to scream. Georgia padded out of her room. Hank Martin, still in his bathrobe, came from the dayroom. As they began to crowd around, Laura held Peggy with one arm and motioned them to keep their distance.

Tied into her geri-chair on the opposite side of the corridor, Crazy Carol demanded, "What's happening? What's happening? Is someone having a baby?" But no one heard her or noticed that at last she had said something different. And Peggy went on screaming.

Thomas Petri felt excited as he drove with Sergeant Mitchell toward Willow Glen. He had worked on several murders as a sergeant, but this was the very first time he would be in charge. This would be his case. Still, his excitement was mixed with a certain sense of chagrin and irony. Who would have thought that his first case would be a murder in a nursing home? A murder of the already near-dead?

Ms. McAdams met them at the door and ushered them straight into Mrs. Simonton's office. "Well, Lieutenant," Mrs. Simonton said, "I'm afraid you will get to have a tour of Willow Glen after all." She looked tense and grim.

"What have you done so far?" Petri asked.

"Not much other than calling you. I didn't think anything should be disturbed, and there wasn't anything we could do for Stephen. An aide is guarding the body. The patients on the wing have all been restricted to their rooms."

"Bill," Petri said to the older man, "would you take the aide's place and see to it that nobody, but nobody, goes near the body? I'll be down just as soon as I've talked with Mrs. Simonton."

Sergeant Mitchell picked up the large case that held the investigation kit. Ms. McAdams volunteered to lead him.

"Would you fill me in, please?" Petri said when the door closed behind them. He opened his notebook. "Tell me anything you know about this."

"Not much, Lieutenant. The body was discovered an hour ago—just about seven-forty-five, shortly after the day shift came on duty—by one of the aides when she went to bathe him."

"What about the victim?"

"Stephen Solaris. He was twenty-nine. He was Willow Glen's first patient and has been here longer than any soul other than myself. He's had severe cerebral palsy since birth. They also thought he was severely retarded and he was placed in the state school when he was two. When he was five an aide there discovered he wasn't retarded and began to teach him. In fact, the aide discovered he was remarkably intelligent and he wrote a whole book about him. I dug it out for you. I thought you might want to look at it. It will give you some flavor of his past." She pointed to the worn volume on her desk. It had no jacket.

"Thanks," Petri said. "I'll take a look at it later. How'd he come to be in Willow Glen? I thought this was a place for elderly patients only."

"Most are, of course, but there are no limitations put on us about the age of our patients. And I had a special request to take him in. By the time he was sixteen the state, in its great wisdom, decided that since he wasn't retarded he didn't belong in the school anymore. So they shipped him to a nursing home. Not one as good as this, however. The man who wrote the book found out he wasn't doing well there, so he asked if I would take him when Willow Glen was opened. Stephen was seventeen then. He's been here ever since."

Petri looked at her. Was it an accident, he wondered, that he'd come here twice in a month's time? That one patient should wander out into the snow and now another patient be murdered? Was Willow Glen really as well run as this woman and Sergeant Mitchell and the Kubricks thought? "Do you know of any reason why the victim might have been murdered?" he asked.

Mrs. Simonton looked back at him with equal concentration. She noted his All-American-Boy face. Was he mature enough to handle this ghastly event? She observed his neat manner. Almost prissy. At least, he's likely to be thorough, she thought. "No," she said. "I don't know of anyone who would want to kill him. Many people didn't take the trouble to know him, but I don't know of anyone who doesn't like him."

She was switching back and forth between the past and present tenses. Petri was glad to note this sign of dismay. It was common when death was a shock, when the fact of death was still being absorbed. He would be needing her fullest cooperation. He stood up. "Thanks for filling me in. We might as well go down and see the body now."

As she led him past Physical Therapy and the dining room and turned into C-Wing, Tom Petri realized his excitement was now colored by a sense of dread. It was not because he was about to inspect a corpse; he had viewed many of them in his young life as a policeman. It was the sense that he was walking into so strange a world. What kinds of weird people were hidden for the moment behind all those closed doors? To distract himself from his own anxiety, he resumed his questions. "You said the murder was discovered about seven-forty-five?"

"Yes."

"I don't want anyone who was in the building at the time to leave until I give my okay. What time was the change of shifts?"

"Seven."

"Has the night-shift staff all gone home?" Mrs. Simonton told him they had. "Who was on the night-shift staff on the victim's wing?"

"Heather Barsten was the nurse. Bertha Grimes was the aide."

"I'll need them back for questioning. Could you arrange that?"

Sergeant Mitchell had already set up the portable light. The corpse lay under the glare. Petri deliberately looked away from it and at the nurses' station. Peggy was sitting there, still pale with shock. Susan and Laura had gone to reassure the patients and keep them to their rooms. "Could I go in and get one of those chairs?" he asked.

"I'll get it for you," Mrs. Simonton said.

He peered over the counter of the station as she did so, noting its architecture: the placement of the gate that latched from the inside, the counters, and the file rack. He took the chair from her and wheeled it over to a position five feet from the gurney and just outside the circle of light.

"I want to be left alone here for about fifteen minutes with Sergeant Mitchell," he said to Mrs. Simonton. "Maybe you might use that time to call the night-shift staff. Then I'll be wanting to talk with you and other people on the staff."

He sat down on the chair. "Bill," he said to Mitchell when they were alone, "you have three jobs. One is to keep everyone away from him except us. The second is to take notes. The third is to make sure that I do not leave here for at least fifteen minutes."

Mitchell looked puzzled at this final instruction.

"I had a mentor," Petri explained, "an old detective I used to work with when I was a sergeant. He was the reason I volunteered to take all those special courses on evidence and interrogation and whatnot. I thought he was a genius. I still think so. Just before I was promoted, he took me aside. There's only one real difference between a good detective and a poor detective, he told me. A good detective thinks good, he said, and a poor detective thinks poor. But he made it clear that it isn't a matter of brain power. A poor detective thinks poor because he doesn't take the time to think. A good detective thinks good because he does. Good thinking takes time. Always take the time, he told me."

Sitting there, Lieutenant Petri was at eye level with Stephen's body on the gurney. The sheet covered only the loins. The body lay half on its side and he could look directly at both the face and the scissors. Neither, however, commanded his first attention. What assaulted him above all was the horror of how crippled the body was. The limbs were mere skin taut on bones. Everything was drawn up as in spasm, even the fingers. He remembered a mummy he had once seen in a museum as a child. Except that it wasn't dark and leathery, this body looked as though it had been dead for three thousand years.

It took him a full minute before the horror began to pass. He found himself wondering whether whoever had killed Stephen Solaris had seen it as a mercy killing. Then he told himself to set that thought aside. "Keep your mind as free as possible from assumptions," his mentor had told him. The issue of motives could wait. They had emphasized in school that it is not motives, but the small details, the little facts, that are likely to crack a case.

So Petri cleaned the slate and looked at Stephen's face. It revealed absolutely nothing of the mind that once had inhabited the crippled body. That itself was remarkable, he thought. The faces of the dead usually reveal something of who they had been. He tucked the thought into the corner of his memory.

Next he scrutinized the scissors. The blade lying across the breastbone was the blunt-ended one. The sharp blade had been inserted into the chest about an inch and a half to the left of the lower end of the breastbone. There was merely a trace of blood around the wound. He could see no sign of other wounds. Whoever did it seemed to know exactly what he or she was doing, he thought. The attacker had gone straight for and into the heart. No fuss. No muss. Again the thought of mercy killing entered his mind, and again he pushed it aside.

He asked Mitchell to hold up the sheet. There were no stains on it. The loins were diapered. He observed the tubing extending from the diaper down to the bag of urine hooked on the bottom of the gurney. "Lay the sheet at his feet. Do you think you can unfasten the diaper without disturbing anything else?" Mitchell assented. The genitals seemed to be the only part of the body that were not deformed, but they revealed nothing except the condom catheter. "Put the sheet back where it was for now," he said. "Later we'll need to send it to the lab to be checked."

As he sat looking at the body, Petri realized that it lay half propped up on its side facing him. "Something must be supporting him," he said to Mitchell. "Could you bend down on the floor, Bill, and grab the gurney by its feet? Now pull it out a couple of feet from the wall." Mitchell obliged. "Now, without touching the gurney anymore and trying not to touch the wall, would you go back behind him and tell me what you see?"

Sergeant Mitchell went on the other side of the gurney. "He's propped up by a pillow, braced against his lower back," he reported.

"Lift the sheet again. Check his buttocks. Then his back, the back of his neck and his scalp. Any sign of wounds?"

"No, I can't see anything abnormal at all. But, my God, he's thin."

"Come on back then."

Petri sat in silence for another two minutes. Then he said, "Okay. It's time to call the medical examiner. We need him down here pronto. The sooner he gets here, the more accurately we'll be able to determine the time of death. After you've called, dust for fingerprints. Dust the sides of the gurney. Dust the wall behind him. And dust the scissors. Remind the examiner to be real careful removing the scissors. It ought to be done with a clamp. I don't want anything to screw up the fingerprints on those scissors."

Mitchell scribbled furiously. When he was finished, Petri asked, "Are my fifteen minutes up yet?"

Mitchell looked at his watch. "It's been twenty."

"Okay. I'll stay and watch the body until you get back from calling the M.E. When you do, remember I don't want anybody but you to touch *anything* until he gets here."

While waiting, it occurred to him that the victim's age was the same as his own. It was not a pleasant thought. It made him uneasy to have any identity with someone so deformed. It was hard to think of living in that spasmed body. "Poor bastard," he muttered under his breath.

When Mitchell came back, Petri decided to set up his interviews in the dayroom. He began with Mrs. Simonton. She still had vestiges of shock on her face and she sat down on the couch with a heavy sigh. He took the easy chair facing her. "He was terribly crippled, wasn't he?" he began.

"Yes."

"Could he do anything for himself?"

"No. He had to be bathed, turned, fed."

"He could speak though."

"No, he couldn't even do that."

A vegetable, Petri thought. But then how could a vegetable be liked by those who knew him? And what about that intelligence she had mentioned? "I thought you said he was very bright. And likable, that people liked him."

"They did. He couldn't speak, but he could communicate. It's all described in that book I mentioned. There's a board of letters hanging from the head of the gurney. When you held it for him in just the right way, he could tap out messages with his knuckles."

Petri kicked himself for missing this. "I should have noticed that," he said. "Excuse me for a moment." He left the dayroom to look at the board and add it to Sergeant Mitchell's fingerprint list. Mrs. Simonton was relieved that the young man didn't try to pretend he was perfect.

"We were just about to get him a computer," she told him sadly when he returned. "It was supposed to be here by Easter. He wouldn't have been able to write any faster than on the letter board, but it would have been visible on the screen and would have been easier for others to understand and communicate with him. Not only that, but he would have been able to write by himself. In fact, he was going to write a book."

"A *book*? About what?"

"Its title was going to be *The Power of Helplessness.*"

Suddenly Petri's head began to spin. For the second time he had a feeling—only now much more intense—that he had entered into a very strange and unsettling culture. Two minutes ago they'd been talking about a vegetable. Now they were speaking of a man who was planning to write a book about power. It made no sense. "Writing a book is an ambitious project," he commented warily.

"Not for Stephen. I think you may be confusing his physical crippling with his mind. *That* wasn't crippled. It's hard for you to imagine how bright he was, Lieutenant. That's why I think you ought to read that book about him. Before he left the state school, they tested him as having an IQ of one thirty-five. That puts him in the very superior range. But the psychologists added that the test results were adversely affected by his physical limitations and clearly stated their belief that his true IQ was much higher. In some ways he was, without question, a genius. I suspect, Lieutenant, that he was considerably brighter than either of us."

It still did not add up. Here was a person who wanted to write a book about power, yet who could not even speak or move, who had been stabbed to death as easily as if he had been a bag stuffed with straw. What kind of power was that? Petri felt an urgent need for routine, for the daily and mundane. "Could you get me his chart?" he asked.

He went with Mrs. Simonton to the nurses' station; he didn't want to give anyone the chance to alter it in any way. He would have to take into account that it might already have been altered. The nurse handed it to her, and she gave it to him. It was thick. He opened the cover and skimmed the top page. The most recent notation on the form read: "4:00 A.M. No change" and was signed H. Barsten.

"I'm going to have to impound this," Petri said as they returned to the dayroom. "And I'll also need to impound any other records you have of the decedent. Will you be able to produce them for me before I leave?"

"Of course," Mrs. Simonton replied. The *decedent*! she repeated to herself. The jargon grated, even though she recognized the youthfulness behind it.

"Did he have any visitors?" Petri asked.

"Only one; the man who discovered he wasn't retarded, the man who wrote the book about him. He's stayed very much interested in him, and he comes four or five times a year."

"No relatives, no family?"

"His parents placed him in the state school when he was two. I think it must have been very painful for them. Having a child so hopelessly deformed is a terrible tragedy. In any case, three or four years later, when they discovered he wasn't intellectually retarded, the school got back in touch with his parents. They said they'd given him up, and they couldn't turn back the clock on their lives."

"That seems harsh."

"Harsh, but understandable. Having once gone through the pain of deciding to give him up, I can see why they didn't want to stir up more pain—and probably guilt as well. The message we have is that they're to be contacted only in the event of his death. Which is one of the things I shall have to do today. Anyway, to the best of my knowledge, they've not seen him for twenty-seven years."

"No one else?"

"No one."

"Who pays for his care here?"

"The state. Maybe that's another reason his parents decided to sever the relationship with him. The state might have wanted them to pay."

Petri wrote in his notebook for several minutes. Mrs. Simonton watched him, wondering. He was obviously not an incompetent young man, as young men in the world went. But would he be able to *understand*? That was very much open to question.

Petri finished his notes. "I'll certainly see you before I leave, and I may want to see you sooner," he said. "Now, though, I'll need to question the staff. Would you bring me in the aide who discovered the body?"

Peggy Valeno was ashen-faced and still shaking. "I can see this has been very upsetting to you," Petri said reassuringly. "I understand you were the one who discovered the body." Peggy nodded. "Could you tell me about it?"

"I just went to bathe him, the way I do every morning." Her voice trembled. "The sheet was pulled half over his face. I felt something was wrong—his color—as soon as I lifted it. Then I saw the scissors. Then I started screaming."

Petri felt sympathetic. She was just a little slip of a girl, probably just out of high school, and hardly prepared for something like this. No one could be prepared. "Did you touch the body in any other way?" he asked.

"I'm not sure. I don't remember."

"Did you touch the scissors at all?"

"Maybe with the sheet. I don't know. I can't remember. I don't think so."

"Is there anything else you can tell me?"

Peggy shook her head.

"Do you know of any reason why anyone, including yourself, might have wanted to murder him?"

Peggy shook her head again.

"Is there nothing you can tell me about him?"

"I liked him," Peggy said, her voice quavering. "He was real smart. I don't know why, but I felt he understood me."

Petri thought she was about to cry. He wasn't sure how bright she was, but something about her struck him as being genuine. He thanked her and told her he would be in touch with her if he had any further questions.

The other C-Wing day staff had nothing to offer beyond what Peggy Valeno and Mrs. Simonton had already told him. Then Bertha Grimes arrived. "It's terrible, isn't it?" She introduced herself, but Petri noted that beyond her words this heavyset woman, almost elderly, seemed unperturbed. It was so different from Peggy, from the feeling she'd clearly had for Stephen.

"You were on duty last night?" Petri asked.

"Yes."

"Who was on duty with you?"

"Heather."

"That's Ms. Barsten?"

"Yes."

"When did you last see the deceased alive?"

"About midnight," Bertha said laconically. "That's when I turned him. He needed to be turned every four hours. Prevents bedsores, you know. We didn't talk, but he was like he always was. He wasn't dead. I would have noticed it if he was dead."

Clearly, her lack of emotion was her characteristic style. "So, as far as you know, he might have been killed anytime after midnight?" Petri asked.

"Well, I wouldn't say that," Bertha answered. "About three in the morning, Heather always takes him into the hall outside the supply room when she sets up the medications. So I don't need to turn him again. They talk then. They're real close. She took him as usual last night. So he must have been alive then."

"What time did she bring him back?"

"I don't know. I don't keep that close track of time. It was probably about four."

"So you think he must have been killed after four?"

"I don't know. I suppose so."

"What did you do after four?"

"Nothing until about six A.M. That's when I go take vitals."

"Vitals?"

"Yes, vital signs. You know, temperature, pulse, and sometimes blood pressure."

"Well, was the victim alive then?"

"I don't know. I don't do vitals on everyone. Only the ones the doctor orders. Stephen was stable. There was no reason to do vitals on him. They're not ordered."

"What did you do between four and six?"

"Nothing."

"Nothing?"

"Well, not nothing. I read. That's why I like this job. It's real slow at nights. I get to read a lot."

"What was Ms. Barsten doing at this time?"

"I don't know. At six when I go off to do vitals, she goes off to do meds."

"Meds?"

"Yes, you know, distribute the medications. Before that she was probably just sitting there doing her nurses' notes. No, that's not true. I remember now, she told me that she was going for a walk."

"A walk?" This sounded strange for a nurse on duty in the middle of a cold night.

"Yes."

"What time was that?"

"I dunno. Maybe about four-thirty."

"What time did she return?"

"I dunno. Maybe about five."

"Does she usually go out for a walk?"

"No. Can't ever remember her doing it before."

"Do you know why she took a walk last night?"

"Nope."

Petri was struck by Bertha's extreme taciturnity. And she was so passive. She seemed totally unmoved by what had happened. She gave him the facts, but only the facts. Beyond that she hardly seemed alert.

"So as far as you know, Ms. Barsten brought the deceased back on the gurney and left him by the wall next to the nurses' station at around four o'clock. At around four-thirty, she went out for a walk and returned around five. At around six, you both left the nurses' station, you to do vital signs and she to distribute medications. When Ms. Barsten was on her walk, or at any other time between four and six, did you leave the nurses' station?"

"Not so as I can remember."

"Are you sure?"

"I said not so as I can remember."

Petri gave up. "Do you know any reason why the deceased might have been killed?" he asked.

"No, he seemed like a nice enough young man to me. I can't tell you more than I already have."

Petri was afraid this was true, and dismissed her. He was still writing up his notes when he heard cries out in the hall.

"I want to see him. Oh my God, you've got to let me see him. Get out of my way! Stephen, Stephen!"

Petri shot out to the nursing station and saw Mitchell struggling with a dark-haired young woman in a white uniform. Petri grabbed her arms from behind. She wrestled against him. "You've got to let me see him," she wailed. "Oh, Stephen, what have they done to you?"

Petri held her in a viselike grip. "Stop it!" he shouted. Then in a normal voice he identified himself. "I am Lieutenant Petri of the police department. I am in charge here. Neither you nor anyone else will do anything without my permission. Now just calm down."

Heather stopped struggling when she heard the authority in his voice. Still, she seemed oblivious to anything but her plea. "I've got to see him," she moaned.

"You are seeing him," Petri pointed out. "You're looking right at him. He is in full view."

And so he was. Behind Sergeant Mitchell, Stephen's body lay on the gurney as it had been left, the scissors still imbedded in his chest, the sheet still pulled down to his loins. Fingerprint powder covered the sides of the gurney and the letter board. Mitchell's camera was on the floor surrounded by a pile of exploded flashbulbs. The medical examiner had not yet arrived.

"I want to touch him. I want to hold him," Heather wailed.

"You cannot touch him," Petri said forcefully. "No one will touch him until the medical examiner gets here. If you have to touch him, you can do so when he's in the funeral home." He forced her around and looked her in the face. "Who are you?" he demanded.

"Heather Barsten."

"You're the nurse who was on duty last night?"

She nodded.

"Come into the dayroom with me then, Ms. Barsten," Petri said, now holding on to her right arm, tugging her along. For the first time she seemed to be aware of him, and she allowed herself to be led.

"This has obviously been very distressing for you," he said when she was seated, conscious what an understatement it was. Indeed, he thought she was hysterical. He also thought she would have been pretty had she not been so distraught. "Is there anything you can tell me about this?" he asked.

Heather sat in the chair looking at him blankly. "What can you tell me about this?" he repeated.

She burst into sobs. Petri felt torn. One part of him wanted to console her, responding to what felt like genuine grief as well as shock. The other part of him couldn't understand why a nurse in a nursing home should be so grief-stricken over the death—even the death by murder—of an obvious basket case. He waited as she sobbed.

After several minutes her sobbing was clearly abating. He thought it might help to be purely factual.

"You are Ms. Barsten, the nurse who was on duty last night in this wing?"

Heather nodded.

"What time did your shift begin and what time did you leave here?"

"Seven P.M. last night. I left at seven A.M.—no, it was a little after seven, maybe seven-fifteen. I stayed to brief the day nurse." She seemed numb, but at least she was responsive and otherwise composed.

"What time did you last observe the deceased alive?"

"I think it must have been about four o'clock in the morning."

"How do you know the time?"

"Because that's when I finished my meds. I take Stephen with me when I set up the medications. We talk while I do it. When I'm finished, I take him back."

"Back where?"

"Back to the wall next to the nurses' station." Heather's voice caught. "Where he is now."

"So he was perfectly well when you left him there at four A.M.?"

There was a strange pause before she answered, "Yes."

"You seem uncertain," Petri commented.

"Well, he was perfectly well physically. I mean, well for Stephen. Emotionally, he was upset."

"What was he upset about?"

Again, there was that odd hesitation. "About being crippled," Heather finally said. "He felt he had no future. It's hard to be in a cripple's body."

Petri could understand that. "What did you do after you left him?" he asked.

"I sat down and started to write my nurses' notes. But then I went out for a walk. When I came back I finished them. Then I just daydreamed for a while until six o'clock, when it was time to pass out the medications."

"What time were you out walking?"

"From about four-thirty to five, I imagine."

"So you don't know what might have happened during that half an hour when you were gone?"

"No. But Bertha was here."

"Here?"

"In the nurses' station."

"You assume she was there." Petri pointed out the flaw in her logic before going on to ask, "Do you usually take a walk at that hour, Ms. Barsten?"

"No."

"Why did you go out for a walk last night?"

"Because I was upset."

"What were you upset about?"

"I was upset about Stephen being upset. And I was upset about my love life. My love life's all screwed up."

The answer was frank enough. He was curious. There was something of the voyeur in most detectives, he supposed, something that gave them a certain delight in probing the personal, the hidden. But he also knew the urge needed to be balanced with tact, and right now he was more interested in what was going on inside Willow Glen than outside of it. "You seem to have been quite attached to the victim," he commented.

"Of course, I'm attached. I love him."

As with Mrs. Simonton, Petri automatically noted the present tense, the sign of genuine shock. But he was stunned by the simple intensity of her statement. "You *love* him? Why do you love him?"

"He's beautiful."

For the third time that morning he had that disconcerting sense of being in a new world so crazy that, among other things, he didn't even understand the language. The body lying out there in the hall was the most hideously crippled human being he had ever seen, and this passionate young woman was calling him "beautiful." He did not know how to proceed. He felt confused. When confused, take notes, his training courses had taught him. So he did. While this strange young woman sat across from him in silence, he wrote for five minutes. Her story and Bertha Grimes's checked out to a T.

But he was still concerned. Even allowing for the shock of a brutal murder, her reaction seemed extreme. After all, death came with the territory if you were a nurse, and in a nursing home with its large population of aged and infirm, it had to occur even more often than in a hospital. And she was taking it so *personally*.

He looked at her. Her face had gone slack, empty of expression, like an automaton. It wiped out all possibility of further responsiveness. He'd need to talk with her more, but he decided this was not the time. "That's all I have to ask you now," he said. "I may have more questions in the future, but you can leave now. This has obviously been a great shock to you. I don't want you trying to touch the body. Can I help you to your car?"

Heather stood up. "No, I'm all right now," she said.

"Oh, Ms. Barsten, one other thing. Do you have any idea who might have done this? Or why?"

Heather shook her head. "No." She started to turn, then stopped and looked at him with suddenly blazing eyes. "But if I do, you can be damn sure I'll tell you." Then her eyes dulled again and she left.

When he went back to the nurses' station, the medical examiner had arrived. Petri introduced himself and they spoke briefly about the details. Mitchell had completed his tasks and was waiting. There was nothing left to be done on C-Wing for the time being. "Let's go, Bill," Petri said. "We'll be needing to report to the chief."

They stopped at Mrs. Simonton's office, and Petri was surprised to see that she had been crying. The reddened eyes seemed incongruous in her sharp, formidable face.

"I'm sorry this has happened," he said. "We're done for the moment. The medical examiner is here now, and he'll take care of the body. As far as I'm concerned, you can let the patients out of their rooms as soon as the body's gone. I'll be back tomorrow morning for more questioning."

"I'm glad we'll be able to let the patients out," Mrs. Simonton said, "but they're likely to be frightened. Is there anything you can suggest I say to reassure them?"

"Reassure them about what?"

Mrs. Simonton glanced at the lieutenant sharply. Was he being obtuse? "Reassure them that there's not going to be another murder, that they're not in danger."

"Sure," Petri replied. "You can tell them that serial murders are really quite rare."

It was Mrs. Simonton's turn to be obtuse. "Cereal murder?"

"Yeah, repetitive murder. Most killers kill only once, maybe twice in their lifetime. The public always gets upset about some homicidal maniac on the loose—like the 'Son of Sam'—who stalks victim after victim, but what they don't realize is how uncommon that is. It's statistically unlikely."

Mrs. Simonton did not find the statistic particularly comforting. She changed the subject. "I've notified his parents. They already have a family funeral home and are making arrangements. I'll let the medical examiner's office know."

Except for the evidence of her eyes, Petri would have never known she'd been anything but composed. "Yes, that would be helpful. By the way, I do have one question that you might be able to answer. Usually you can see a lot in a dead person's face, no matter what caused his death. But the victim had a strange face. I couldn't tell anything from it."

"Stephen's facial muscles were spastic like the rest of him. He had no control over them. They couldn't express emotions."

"I've gathered from you and others that he was a remarkable young man. Certainly Ms. Barsten seemed particularly attached to him."

Mrs. Simonton looked at him. "If you get to know Willow Glen well enough, Lieutenant, you will find that there are many remarkable people in here. The public tends to think of nursing homes as simply dumping grounds. They are a great deal more. But, yes, Stephen was a particularly remarkable person."

Petri stood up. "I have to go now and fill in the chief. He'll be needing to talk to the media as quickly as possible."

"The media?"

"Sure; the newspapers, TV, the radio stations in the county. In fact, all across the state. This'll be big news for them. It's not like New York City. They'll be hounding him for the rest of the day. In fact, they'll be hounding him until the whole thing is over. You call me if something else happens or you have any questions. Otherwise, I'll be back around eight-thirty in the morning. I'll probably want to start by interviewing the patients on the wing."

"As you wish, Lieutenant." To him it was a matter of course, but she had been subdued by the reality of publicity. "Here are Stephen's past records you wanted to impound. And also the book I told you about."

Petri had all he could carry. He and Mitchell went out to the squad car. As they drove off, Petri mused about the enormous difference between the night nurse and the aide. Grimes acted as if nothing of consequence had occurred and Barsten as if the whole world had caved in. Then he looked at the spine of the book lying on top of the pile of records in his lap. The title was *Resurrection*, he noted, and the author's name was Stasz Kolnietz.


Peggy Valeno had been busy feeding patients since she had spoken to the lieutenant; because they were still confined to their rooms they all needed to be brought their lunch. She returned the huge pile of trays to the kitchen. When she came back to C-Wing, she saw that the medical examiner was wheeling Stephen's body away. She went to the nurse and asked if she could leave two hours early.

Susan eyed her coldly, knowing not only that Peggy was on probation as an aide, but also remembering that she'd arrived late to begin with. "That's not a matter I can decide," she said. "You'll have to ask the front office."

Ms. McAdams listened to Peggy and was in the process of refusing her when Mrs. Simonton came out of her office. "I'll take care of it," she said. "Come in, Peggy."

Mrs. Simonton closed the door behind her and sat down at her desk. She saw the tears in Peggy's eyes. "You'd like to leave early?" she asked. "Why?"

"I'm upset," Peggy answered.

"It is upsetting to discover a killing," Mrs. Simonton said matter-of-factly.

"I don't understand it."

"It seems to affect you," Mrs. Simonton commented.

"I don't understand it."

"That's good," Mrs. Simonton said. "You shouldn't be able to understand it. Yes, you can have the rest of the day off, Peggy. But be sure to come back tomorrow. Go home now and feel what you have to feel, think what you have to think."

Peggy left. Mrs. Simonton stared after her. Already she had sensed the staff, including herself, slipping back into routine, doing what needed to be done. Life must go on, of course. But it was proper, even healthy, that someone, thank God, couldn't go on, couldn't cope so smoothly. She crossed the fingers of her right hand.

Then she sat back in thought. All morning she'd been worrying about the patients and how they would need reassurance. But until the lieutenant had mentioned it she had not even considered the media. It would not be long before they would be calling her too. How could she handle them? She knew the chief of police. Obviously he was expert in such matters. More to the point, she knew him to be a sensitive man. The best thing she could do was to be closed-mouthed with the press and simply refer all the inquiries to the police. Still, with the media attention, in short order there would be the relatives, also wanting reassurance, criticizing, maybe even wanting to withdraw the patients. Should she try to beat them to the punch, to phone them all and tell them that everything was in hand? Over a hundred families? No, it was more than she could manage. Besides, did she really know that everything was in hand with a murderer on the loose in Willow Glen? Hardly. She had better have McAdams hire round-the-clock security guards. Beyond that there was really nothing she could do. Strangely, the title of Stephen's never-to-be-written book came to mind: *The Power of Helplessness.* She could only sit back and watch the drama play itself out.

Her mind was flooded with thoughts, feelings. Guilt: had she left something undone? Could she have done something to protect Stephen better? Simultaneously she was aware that these self-recriminations were irrational, that they were an instinctive part of the early grieving process. Everyone went through them. What could she have possibly done to prevent a totally unexpected murder committed against a helpless victim by a murderer whose identity—and motive—she couldn't even begin to guess?

Side by side with these questions was her awareness that she just didn't know a damn thing about *anything*. How did she know that there wasn't some kind of rightness in Stephen's dying? Had he not already suffered enough for a lifetime? Blessings in disguise were as much the rule as the exception. For all she knew, life itself was some big blessing in disguise.

But she didn't feel that way. Because, above all—above and beyond these speculations—was her overwhelming sense of personal loss. Loss of her first patient in Willow Glen. Much more, loss of a friend, a peer, a person of astonishing insight. Never again would she benefit from one of his one-sentence sermons. "WHY/DO/YOU/NEED/TO/BE/SO/ATTACHED, EDIE?" he'd tap out in response to some tale of woe she regaled him with. Why, indeed? But she was attached. To him. Not his sermons, not his friendship, but him. There was a loss of *him*. Something indefinable and unique in the universe was gone. She choked back a sob.

Mrs. Simonton glanced at the office door through her tears to make sure it was shut. Not caring otherwise, knowing the staff might hear something strange, she looked over at the couch as if God Himself were sitting there smirking, and she hit her fist on the desk. "I don't trust You," she half screamed. "I've never trusted You. You've never deserved it, and I don't intend to begin trusting You now!"

The moment passed. Tiredly she heaved herself up from the desk. After talking with McAdams about the security guards, she would go down to C-Wing to speak to Susan about reassuring the patients and see what she herself might do to fill in during Peggy's absence.

## Tuesday, March 22nd

Georgia had slept well after the full day before. There had been so much going on. Among the other patients, she herself had been a center of attention. She was not only one of the few who had actually *seen* the scissors protruding from Stephen's chest; she was one of the few who had ever communicated with him at all. This had caused her some discomfort. It seemed unfair. Why couldn't they have murdered someone who was just a body? Or someone who was mean? Slight though it was, however, her knowledge of him had been in demand among those patients who wanted to talk about the murder. They were agitated, fearful, and curious as they crowded around her at the dinner table. Lucy, unfortunately, had not been one of them. The bad part of the day had been when they'd been shut in their room all morning without being able to see what was going on and Lucy unwilling to speak about any of it.

But the body had been removed and they'd been let out of their room shortly after lunch. And this morning, as they sat together in the dining hall for breakfast, Lucy, if not more cheerful, was at least communicative.

"I knew I shouldn't have come here," Lucy said. "I have to get out. At physical therapy yesterday afternoon they told me I need about another ten days, but when I go there today, I'm going to see if I can't get out now. I don't see why one of those therapists can't come to my home. I want to get out today."

"Why are you in such a terrible hurry?" Georgia asked.

"Why? Because I'm afraid, of course."

"Afraid of what?"

"Afraid of what?" Lucy repeated with surprise. "Why, I'm afraid of being killed, that's what. I'm terrified. Aren't you scared with a murderer running around on the loose?"

"Well, I haven't really thought about it that way," Georgia replied. "Actually, I find it rather exciting."

Lucy looked at her in amazement. And then she had an insight. She suddenly realized not only that Georgia was strangely childlike, but that in some way she lacked a normal adult's desire to live—or, perhaps so often obviously lost in fantasy, a normal adult's fear. At the same time she realized that she herself, Lutzina Stolarz, was not the least bit ready to die.

As he had promised, Lieutenant Petri was back in Mrs. Simonton's office by eight-thirty. She fixed them both a pot of coffee. He was feeling challenged by what the day would reveal, but he kept his voice deliberately calm when he asked her if she had anything new to report.

"I've hired three security guards, one for each shift," she told him. "Sometimes I'm selfish enough to wish there weren't a labor shortage in the state. Ms. McAdams had to go over a hundred miles to find one of them. They're instructed to spend half of their shift on C-Wing and the other half patrolling the rest of Willow Glen. Each wing has a fire door. They're locked from the outside so no one can get in through them, and an alarm goes off when anyone goes out one of them. I thought about locking them on the inside too, but I called the stupid fire department and they refused to give me a dispensation to do so. Not even under the circumstances. Would you believe it? One of the secretaries is watching the front door during the day, and I've got an aide coming in to do it from five to eleven. Then that will also be locked until seven in the morning. We're keeping a log of everyone entering and leaving. Does that meet with your approval?"

"Sounds very thorough. What else?"

"Well, the whole staff is agog of course. Edgy, too. And most of the more alert patients are frightened. The nurses are telling them about the security guards to try to reassure them. But some of them aren't so easily calmed, and I can't say that I blame them."

"Anything else?"

"The reporters started calling me as soon as I got home last night. Fortunately, they stopped by midnight. I simply bucked them back to you. I told them I knew nothing beyond what the police already knew. I haven't seen the papers yet, but I suspect the relatives will start hounding me shortly. A few even called last night."

"Anything more?"

"No. I didn't get quite as much sleep as I would have liked, but under the circumstances I did all right."

Petri examined her closely. She did look reasonably rested. He'd talked to the chief about her. The chief had echoed Sergeant Mitchell's and the Kubricks' assessment of Willow Glen, adding his opinion that Mrs. Simonton was a woman to be trusted. Well, he was still not about to trust her totally yet, nor was he about to tell her everything. But he could foresee no risk in telling her the major facts.

He took a long slow sip of his coffee, watching her take deep inhalations of her cigarette. "I am afraid at this point," he said, "that your staff—either Ms. Barsten or Mrs. Grimes or both—must be under serious suspicion, given the circumstances of the murder. What do you think?"

"I think, Lieutenant, you must be barking up the wrong tree. If you are asking me about the kinds of persons they are—with which I am very familiar—I would have no choice but to give you my opinion that neither has the type of personality which is capable of murder. But then, undoubtedly, you are in possession of facts of which I am not aware."

Petri looked at her appreciatively, thinking that if they were ever to play chess together he might well come out the loser. "The medical examiner went through the usual ifs, ands, and buts about the degree of lividity and the unreliability of rectal temperatures, and how this was a particularly difficult case due to the victim's spasticity interfering with the estimation of rigor," he announced, imagining how experienced he sounded. "But when I finally pinned him down, he guessed the time of death to be five A.M., give or take thirty minutes. That would indicate that the victim was killed between four-thirty and five-thirty. According to Ms. Barsten and Mrs. Grimes, the victim was situated adjacent to their nursing station throughout that period, and one or the other of them was in the nursing station when he was stabbed to death. Since it is hard to imagine someone being stabbed to death in plain view of a nurse on duty ten feet away, that would suggest that either one of them is lying or that one of them is the murderer, or both."

"That does sound logical, Lieutenant. But in my experience, this strange world is not always logical."

"Another remarkable fact," Petri continued, "is that there were absolutely no fingerprints on the handle of the scissors. Do you know what that means? It is impossible for anyone to hold a pair of scissors in their bare hands and not leave some kind of fingerprints. It means that whoever stabbed the victim used gloves. It was a most professional job. The blade went directly into the heart. There was no poking around. Whoever killed Mr. Solaris used gloves and knew exactly how to do it."

"Like a nurse, you would suggest?"

"*Possibly* like a nurse," Petri said, and grinned at her. "Believe it or not, we are trained not to jump to conclusions, logic or no." He pulled a clear plastic bag containing a pair of scissors out of his coat pocket and laid it on Mrs. Simonton's desk. "This was the murder weapon. Is there anything you can tell me about this pair of scissors?"

Mrs. Simonton inspected them through the plastic. "They're the kind of scissors we sometimes use. They look like the same make as our surgical scissors. That doesn't mean you couldn't find them elsewhere. You could certainly find them in other hospitals and nursing homes. For all I know, they may even be sold in hardware stores."

"You're suggesting that anyone might be in possession of such scissors? The patients, for instance?"

"I have no idea. There are some patients we would not allow to keep a pair of scissors, since they might hurt themselves. But other patients have scissors they use for needlework or sewing."

"But where in Willow Glen would I be most likely to lay my hands on a pair of scissors like these?" Petri asked.

"In the supply rooms on each wing."

"Would we be likely to find a pair in the supply room on C-Wing?"

"Probably."

"Let's go look, then," Petri suggested.

Mrs. Simonton led him down the corridors to C-Wing. She felt a clutch of pain at the absence of Stephen's gurney as they went past the nurses' station on to the supply room. She opened the left lower cabinet and pulled out a package wrapped in brown linen, handing it to him. "There are two more pairs here," she said.

Petri opened the package, which was fastened by a piece of tape. He matched the scissors from his pocket against the pair he had just unwrapped. They were identical. "Why are they wrapped?" he asked.

"To keep them sterile. They're sterilized that way."

"If a nurse came in here to get a pair of these scissors and unwrapped them, what would she do with the wrapping?" Petri asked.

"She would throw it in the linen hamper."

"If somebody threw the wrapping into the linen hamper on the night of the murder, would it still be there?"

"No. The linen hampers are collected every day and then sent out to a commercial laundry. It would be gone by now."

"Damn," Petri said. "I should have thought to check the linen hamper when I was here yesterday morning."

Mrs. Simonton again noted how he blamed himself. He was conscientious. "You can't think of everything," she said consolingly. "You couldn't have known about the way our scissors are wrapped."

"You mean to tell me that there is no way I could trace the wrapping of a pair of these scissors if it was discarded the night of the murder?"

"I don't think so."

"Do you keep an inventory of these scissors, so that whenever a nurse opens a new pair she makes a notation?"

"No. We already have more than enough paperwork to do here at Willow Glen, Lieutenant."

"Do they keep the gloves here also?"

"Yes, I'll show you. We have two kinds." Mrs. Simonton drew another brown linen package from the left lower cabinet. "These are sterile rubber gloves," she said. Then she reached for a box on the counter, opened it and showed him that it was filled with white powdered plastic gloves. "These are the unsterile gloves. They're used for rectal examinations and the like."

"And I suppose you are going to tell me that there's no inventory kept on these either, and that if a pair of either of these gloves was discarded on the night of the murder, there would be no way for me to find that particular pair?"

"That's the case."

"Damn and double damn," Petri kicked himself once more. "I really should have searched. Only the nurses can come into this room?"

"Generally only nurses and aides come in here. Our staff doctor or one of the visiting doctors might. But, in fact, anyone *could*."

"You don't keep it locked?"

"Not the supply room. The medicine cabinet is kept locked. But the rest is unlocked."

"So what you are telling me is that theoretically anyone could have walked in here at any time, night or day, and picked up a pair of your surgical scissors and some gloves?"

"Theoretically, yes."

"Let's go back to your office," Petri said. "I have to think."

Mrs. Simonton freshened his coffee for him and sat with him in silence for several minutes. "Where to now, Lieutenant?" she asked, thinking that she had her own work to do.

"What I'd like to do now is to interview all the patients on C-Wing and ask them if they have any information to contribute. I'd also like to look at each patient's record. Is that all right with you?"

Mrs. Simonton thought quickly. Technically, the patients' charts were confidential medical records. She realized, however, that this was a murder case; if she refused, he would simply subpoena them. "Yes," she said, "I'll tell the nurses that you can look at the patients' charts, but I would appreciate it if you would do so only inside the nurses' station. Even then, as you may realize, I am bending the rules. I can't allow you to go carting them off. Also, at this point, I can't allow you to make any copies of them. As far as talking with the patients, I realize it's necessary to do this, but I hope you will talk to them in such a way as to not get them unduly upset. Most of them are frail, and they're very shaken by the murder."

"Yes, of course," Petri said. "I'll be as sensitive as I can."

He left her and ambled back toward C-Wing, thinking that there was one little piece of information he had not given her. Probably it meant nothing. But the medical examiner reported that he had found fresh semen at the tip of the victim's penis. Apparently Stephen Solaris had ejaculated sometime shortly before his death. The examiner had told him that it was routine for men to ejaculate at the time of certain kinds of deaths, like hanging, but as far as he knew, it would not happen in the case of a stab wound to the heart. Certainly, Solaris would not have been able to masturbate. Probably the young man just had a wet dream.

He also thought about the fingerprints on the gurney. They had been a waste of time and good film to boot. He could get prints from Barsten and Grimes, the most natural suspects, but what would be the point? Since they both handled the gurney in the course of their duties, you'd expect to find their prints on it. And if someone else was the murderer, seeing as how he or she had used gloves, it was improbable—to say the least—that that person would have left prints on the gurney. No, forget that blind alley; the right thing at this point was to turn his attention to interviewing the patients on the wing.

It was a thoroughly unproductive morning. Some of them, like Mrs. Kubrick and Mrs. Stimson, seemed unable to answer his questions at all; they simply sat there in silence. A few, like Hank Martin, appeared unconcerned. Most, like Mrs. Stolarz and Mrs. Grochowski, were clearly fearful. But none had any information to offer. The process had also been deeply disconcerting, since he never knew despite his cursory review of the charts in what shape he would find his next subject—terribly ill and crippled or surprisingly healthy. He was hungry and agitated and beginning to feel disheartened. It was well after lunchtime when he finally came to Georgia Bates, the last of his list of patients on the wing. Lucy was at physical therapy and Georgia was alone in the room when he knocked on their door. "I'm Lieutenant Petri," he introduced himself. "I'm a detective with the police department, and I'm investigating what happened to Mr. Solaris. Do you mind if I sit down and ask you a few questions?"

Georgia scrutinized him. He looked a bit young to be a detective, she thought, but he was quite handsome, and it should be interesting. She had never talked to a detective before. "Not at all," she said.

"You're aware of what happened here the night before last?"

"The murder? Yes, of course; I could hardly not be aware. It was a dreadful thing, wasn't it? Some of us patients are even afraid for our own safety."

"So you can see what a terribly important matter this is. You may possibly be able to play an important role in helping to solve the case."

Georgia liked the idea that she might play an important role. And this young man seemed most pleasant. She wanted to be obliging. "I'll do whatever I can," she said.

"Do you have any ideas as to how or why this might have happened?"

Georgia racked her brains. "No," she finally said. "I'm afraid I don't."

"Do you know anyone who might have had a motive for killing him?"

"No, I'm afraid I don't," Georgia said. She wished she could be more helpful.

"Do you know anyone who had a special relationship with the deceased in any way?"

Ah, there was a way she could be helpful after all. "Yes," she said, "Heather did."

"Heather? Ms. Barsten, the nurse?"

"Yes, they were very close."

"I have become aware," Petri said, "that Ms. Barsten felt a good deal of affection for the victim."

"That, and more," Georgia commented.

"More?"

"Oh, yes," Georgia said. "They also had a sexual relationship."

Suddenly every nerve in Petri's body came alive. "How do you know that?" he asked, keeping his voice matter-of-fact.

"I saw them."

"You *saw* them?"

"Oh, these kinds of things are difficult for a person like me to talk about," Georgia said primly. "But, yes, I saw them having sex."

"When did you see them having sex?"

"Actually, it was the night of the murder."

"What time was that?"

"Oh, I am afraid I can't tell you," Georgia said. "One of the patients was screaming," she explained, "and it woke me up. I tried to get back to sleep. I have no idea how long it was I lay there, but I couldn't fall asleep again. Finally, I got up and went for a walk. I saw them having sex in the little hallway by the supply room."

"The victim was terribly crippled," Petri said. "I am not sure I understand how he could have had sexual relations."

"Oh, Lieutenant, you do make me talk about the most embarrassing things, don't you? They weren't having intercourse. They were having—well, she was doing—what do you call it?—oral sex with him."

Petri made a deliberate effort to hide any sign of emotion. "What happened then?"

"Well, I certainly didn't want to disturb them or watch them. That wouldn't be nice. So I just turned around and walked into the dayroom. I tried to read for a while, but I soon got bored, so I came back to bed and was able to get to sleep."

Petri had first felt shock, now revulsion. What kind of woman—what kind of *animal*—would perform oral sex upon someone so hideously crippled? But a piece seemed to have fallen into place. This would explain the fresh semen that the medical examiner had found. "Is there anything else that you can tell me about the victim or Ms. Barsten or their relationship?"

Georgia was thoughtful. "No, I don't think so. I didn't know the young man well, although I'm one of the few who took the trouble to talk with him. He was quite intelligent. He was going to write a book, he told me. As for Heather, she is *very* nice. She's the nicest nurse they have."

"Yes, I've gathered that she is popular," Petri said, barely able to hide his disgust. "There's nothing more you can tell me about her?"

"Oh, yes," Georgia remembered. "She goes to see a psychiatrist."

"How do you know that?"

"She told me. It was some time ago. We were having a conversation, but I can't remember what it was about."

It was certainly appropriate that Ms. Barsten should be seeing a psychiatrist, Petri thought. "Anything else?" he asked.

"No, I'm afraid that's all, Lieutenant."

"Well, that's a great deal. I'd like to thank you. You have been extremely helpful, Mrs. Bates."

Georgia was very pleased.

Leaving her room, Petri went to the nurses' station and asked to see Mrs. Bates's chart. He was beginning to feel the excitement of the chase until he read her diagnosis: "Senility." Damn, he had jumped to conclusions. Mrs. Bates had seemed perfectly rational. Physically, she looked well. But then what was she doing in a nursing home? He had bought her story hook, line, and sinker; but for all he knew, she had made it up. For all he knew, she was totally demented.

He went back into her room. "Would you mind if I asked you just a few more questions, Mrs. Bates?" he asked.

"No, of course not, Lieutenant."

"What day is it today?"

"Oh, good heavens, I don't keep track of that," Georgia said. "They're always trying to tell it to us, but it really doesn't seem very important, does it, when you're stuck here in a concentration camp?"

Petri hid a wince. "What month is it, then?" he asked.

"Oh, good gracious, I couldn't hazard a guess."

"Try."

"July?"

Ah well, he thought. "Go to the window, Mrs. Bates," he commanded, "and see if you can tell me."

Georgia got out of her chair nimbly and looked out the window. "Oh, you are clever, Lieutenant," she exclaimed. "The tree is bare and there's some snow on the ground. I guess it couldn't be July, could it?"

"When were you born?" Petri asked.

"Nineteen-twelve."

"And how old are you now?"

"Thirty-seven."

"Thirty-seven?"

"Yes, Lieutenant, I am thirty-seven years old."

Petri excused himself. He felt as though he'd been Alice in Wonderland talking to the Cheshire cat. Maybe he should have stopped for lunch. He was both starved and frazzled by the time he got back to Mrs. Simonton's office. But there was still work to do. "How's it going?" he asked her. She no longer looked rested.

"The newspapers are out and so are the relatives—in droves, just as I feared."

"That must be a strain," he said, "but it was inevitable. Can you tell me anything about one of the patients on C-Wing, Mrs. Georgia Bates?"

"Not much," Mrs. Simonton answered. "She hasn't been here all that long. She was here for a short stay back in early January, then went home. She's a widow in her mid-seventies with a diagnosis of senility. We readmitted her because she was incontinent at home, but she isn't when she's in Willow Glen."

"At times, I thought she seemed to be quite normal," Petri commented, "and at other times she seemed totally out of it."

"That's rather typical of mild senility, Lieutenant. Patients can be perfectly lucid one minute and totally foggy the next. It's amazing sometimes how well they pull themselves together when they want to."

"Want to? What do you mean? You make it sound as if senility's something voluntary."

"Yes, sometimes it can be."

"Then how do you know when someone's senile or not?"

"Sometimes we don't."

Petri felt frustrated by the ambiguity. "How can I learn more about Mrs. Bates?" he asked her. "The chart isn't enough."

"I suppose you could talk to her son, Kenneth. He has her power of attorney," she answered, restraining her curiosity. Obviously something about Georgia—she couldn't imagine what—had caught the lieutenant's particular interest. But if it was important, she would learn soon enough. She waited.

"What can you tell me about Ms. Barsten?" Petri asked next.

"Heather's the best nurse I have," Mrs. Simonton replied. "The patients love her. Some of them even refer to her as the Angel of Willow Glen. If I had a whole staff of Heathers, I wouldn't be sitting here talking to you. I'd be in the Bahamas."

Angel, indeed, Petri reacted to himself. What would Mrs. Simonton think of her paragon if she'd heard Georgia Bates as he had. Maybe Bates was senile, but there could well be a kernel of truth to it. Angels in nursing homes? Angel of life? Or angel of death? Hadn't there been an "angel" in some hospital or another, he recollected, who had turned out to be a mass murderer of her patients? Was it that pediatric nurse in Texas? He couldn't quite remember, but his brain sprang into action. "Are you pretty well computerized here?" he asked.

"Yes, but you'll have to ask Ms. McAdams about that. She understands all about those things. I'm too old to be a computer person. Do you want me to get her?"

"Would you, please?"

Mrs. Simonton pressed the buzzer on her desk. She could almost hear the wheels working in the lieutenant's mind. Well, let them, she thought. Only let them work in the right direction, she added to herself in an approximation of prayer.

Ms. McAdams appeared within seconds. Petri was struck again by the crisp efficiency of her manner. "I understand you handle the data processing," he said. "Do you happen to punch in the times of the patients' deaths?"

"Of course."

"Does the computer also store shift records—like which aide or nurse is on which shift on any particular day or night?"

"It does."

Petri looked at her appreciatively. He could not help but compare these two women in the same room with him. Mrs. Simonton seemed, if anything, older than she was; Ms. McAdams looked to be no more than thirty. Mrs. Simonton's face was lined, practically fierce; Ms. McAdams's, framed by a high-collared blouse and neatly bunned auburn hair, was definitely attractive. Mrs. Simonton often had a disconcerting quality; Ms.

McAdams radiated organization and focus. It was no accident she was the computer person. "Is there any way you can match up both these data for the past year on the computer?" he asked.

"Yes," Ms. McAdams replied without hesitation.

"You mean you could actually get me a printout that would have the times of death of every patient in Willow Glen over the past year on one side and the nurses and aides who were on duty at that time on the other?"

"No problem. How soon do you want it?"

"Could you have it for me by the morning?"

"No problem."

Petri realized he was reluctant to signal that he had no further requests; he hoped he would be seeing McAdams again. When she left, Mrs. Simonton said, "I have the feeling there are some things you're not telling me, Lieutenant."

"You're right," Petri acknowledged. "There are a number of things. I'm not really trying so much to keep anything from you as I just don't know what to make of them. There's a lot of confusion. This is a strange place, you know."

"Strange? In what way?"

"It's as if it's a different world in some ways, and I haven't learned the rules yet. Things are not what they seem."

"Such as?"

"Such as someone who looks sane is crazy; or someone who looks crazy is sane. Or maybe even both angelic and demonic."

Mrs. Simonton was pleased to see that he had at least some dawning appreciation of paradox. "Is that so strange, Lieutenant? Isn't that the way it is with most people?"

"Now you're talking like one of them," Petri said with a grin, enjoying, almost despite himself, this momentary foray into philosophy. "I'm not sure you're always what you seem, either. I know you're the director of a nursing home, but somehow I get the feeling you're something more."

"Well, I should hope so. But I am glad you're getting to know a bit about this strange world. You'll need to know it to ferret out the truth, won't you? Actually, once you come to know it, I don't think you'll find it so strange. I think you'll just find that it is a bit more focused than the so-called ordinary world."

"More focused? I don't understand."

"Lieutenant, all the people in Willow Glen, one way or another, are closer to death than people in the ordinary world. Or at least they are more aware of how close to death they are. Things tend to become a bit more focused when you're close to death."

Petri had had enough of death, disease, and aging for one day. He felt the anxiety rise in him. "I'd better get out of here while I still can," he responded, trying to make a joke of it. He had come to sense this woman knew her business, but it was not a business he was eager to get too close to. "I expect to be back at eight-thirty again in the morning. Okay?"

"See you around the campus, Lieutenant," Mrs. Simonton assented.

As soon as he got back to the station house, Petri phoned Kenneth Bates to make an appointment for the end of the afternoon. Then he stopped by Mitchell's desk. "Bill," he announced, "that young nurse who was on duty at the time of the murder—Heather Barsten—looks like she's got some pretty weird stuff going on. Would you check her for priors before you go home?"

Mitchell had a fair idea of what the check would reveal. "Sure, sir. But wouldn't you like to sit down and talk a bit about it?"

"I can't now," Petri answered him. "I'm famished. It's three o'clock and I haven't even had lunch yet. And I've got an appointment in a little over an hour."

"Sure, sir."

"Take it easy, Bill," Petri flung over his shoulder. "I'll see you in the morning."

Mitchell watched him go, feeling glad to be a sergeant, glad to be just who he was and not a detective. Petri was the fourth detective he had worked under in his twenty years in New Warsaw. In a way, they were all the same, always in a hurry, always trying to get somewhere. One had burned out quickly and had some kind of breakdown. The other two had gone on to become chiefs. What would happen to this new one? he wondered.

It was a funny thing about ambition—why some people had it and others not. Mitchell suspected it was a question to which no psychologist had the answer. You had to have some kind of ambition to go on to being a detective in the first place. He, himself, had never even thought about wanting it. He doubted he would ever be able to understand what made someone like Petri tick, and he imagined that Petri probably couldn't fathom why someone would be content to stay on being an ordinary sergeant.

But content he was. Ambition could make you, but it was more likely to break you. It could be almost ludicrous. Hell, just over twenty-four hours ago Petri had been giving him a spiel about how important it was for a good detective to take time, and today the kid was running around like a chicken with its head cut off. It must be a kind of curse to think you're so important that the world's going to collapse if you take time off for an ordinary lunch. Or sit down and learn some of the information right at hand. Yes, ambition could make you or break you, and he didn't know which it was going to do to Petri. But he did know—it was as clear as the nose on your face—that his new lieutenant was already pushing himself close to the point of being off balance.

Sergeant Mitchell, in no hurry, rose from his desk to go make the check on priors.

When his secretary signaled him that Lieutenant Petri had arrived, Kenneth Bates told her to say that he was tied up and would see him in ten minutes. It was not quite true that he was tied up. The truth was that he wanted some time to think.

He had no sooner gotten to the office that morning than Marlene had called to say she'd just read in the paper about the murder at Willow Glen. She had wondered whether they shouldn't take his mother out of there. He'd reassured her and told her to keep cool; they could talk about it that evening. He did take the time to get the newspaper from his secretary and read the story himself. It sounded as though the victim was that terribly crippled young man into whose uncanny eyes he had looked the day they'd readmitted his mother. Then, the season being so busy, he'd immediately become caught up in work and had not had the opportunity to give the matter further thought.

His partner, Gus Brychowski, and their two junior CPA associates conformed to the stereotype of accountants as people without much insight, types interested only in numbers. But Kenneth had never fitted the mold. As long as he could remember, he had been of a thoughtful bent, and the six months of psychotherapy he had received a dozen years before to help him deal with his anger at his father had served to reinforce his contemplative nature. He was a person who needed time to sort things out.

Now this police lieutenant—Detective Petri—wanted to talk with him. Kenneth assumed it had something to do with the murder and his mother, but had no idea what. Before he talked to the lieutenant, he needed to think. He'd been quick to reassure Marlene because he had absolutely no desire to go through the whole process of taking his mother out of Willow Glen once again. But might she be in danger? And—an uncomfortable thought—to what extent did he care? These days his predominant feeling about her was one of being fed up. They had tried to do the very best they could for her, and she'd virtually spat upon them for their efforts. His resentment, he realized, was the reason he'd so easily put the matter out of his mind, but now he had to face it. He was responsible for her if she was in jeopardy, whether he liked it or not. He buzzed his secretary and asked her to bring the detective in.

He was surprised by Petri's youth. "Good afternoon, Lieutenant," he said. "I'm sorry I kept you waiting."

Petri was struck in turn by this large office, quiet and uncluttered, so different from the smaller offices and cubicles buzzing with activity that he'd just passed. Kenneth Bates was clearly a successful partner in a successful firm. "You've heard about the murder at Willow Glen?" Petri asked.

"Yes. My wife read it in the papers this morning and phoned me about it. I think I even noticed the victim when we visited my mother. It sounds rather bizarre."

"It is," Petri acknowledged. "The reason I asked to see you is that your mother may be a peripheral witness, not to the murder, but possibly to a couple of related incidents. But I have some questions as to her reliability as a witness. Could you tell me something of her history?"

Kenneth obliged, recounting the story of his mother's gradually increasing incontinence that compelled her admission and readmission to Willow Glen.

"But what about her thinking? Does she think clearly?" Petri asked.

"Well, it all depends upon what you mean by thinking clearly. She doesn't seem to have a very clear grasp of her situation or the consequences of some of her behavior. She genuinely feels that my wife and I railroaded her into Willow Glen for no reason, and in that respect she's not thinking clearly. She's become antagonistic toward both of us. I'm not saying we're saints, but I really don't think we've done anything to merit her hostility."

"How about her memory?"

"It seems to be good enough when she wants it to be. There are a number of things she forgets that ordinary people would remember, but generally they're inconsequential, not very important. It's more as if she just can't be bothered. But when she's interested in something, her memory seems to function better than my own."

"She told me that she was born in 1912," Petri said, "and then quite emphatically proclaimed that she is only thirty-seven."

"Yes, that's another area where she's obviously not thinking quite clearly. She's been on that thirty-seven kick for several years now. It started right after my father died."

"It's always thirty-seven?"

"Yes, she's quite consistent about it."

"I wonder why specifically thirty-seven?"

"Well, that's a very interesting question," Kenneth mused. "I hadn't asked myself that before. Why thirty-seven? I really have no idea."

"Tell me, does your mother make up things?" Petri asked. "Other than her age and being railroaded into the nursing home?"

"Not that I can think of."

"Has she ever made up any sexual things? You know, the way some senile people can, like people trying to rape them or falsely accusing people of adultery, or having fantasy lovers?"

"Lord, no. Mom has never been into that sort of thing. In fact, it would surprise me if she ever was. She's never seemed to be interested in sexual matters. It's not that she's prudish so much as she's not really a sexual person. No, that doesn't seem likely."

"In general then, other than this age business and her feelings about you, would you say that your mother would likely be a reliable witness?"

"Yes, I would say so."

"Thank you, Mr. Bates, you've been helpful," Petri said. "I appreciate your time."

"Would you mind spending an extra minute, Lieutenant?" Kenneth asked. "I have a question for you."

"Of course."

"Is my mother in danger? Do you think that we should take her out of Willow Glen?"

"I can't answer that," Petri replied. "I can tell you that Mrs. Simonton has hired around-the-clock security guards. To my knowledge, there has never been a previous murder at Willow Glen. We have no evidence at this point to suggest that it is likely to be a repetitive phenomenon."

"Thank you, Lieutenant. That's all the information I could expect."

As Petri left he was quite aware that, while he refrained from telling Mr. Bates, it was just that kind of evidence he thought Ms. McAdams might have for him the very next morning.

Kenneth lit a pipe and sat back reflectively. He felt reasonably reassured about his mother's safety. But Petri's questions haunted him. "Why thirty-seven?" indeed. He himself was now forty-nine. How old would he have been when his mother was thirty-seven? He calculated swiftly: ten years old. What was it like when he was ten years old?

And then he remembered. He remembered lying fearfully in his bed, listening to the arguments. His parents would scream at each other. He could even remember his mother yelling one night that she wanted a divorce.

But then the arguments had stopped. Just about the time he was ten. Why had they stopped? He thought about what it must have been like for a woman back in 1949 who wanted a divorce. A woman with three children, himself the eldest. A woman married to a prosperous and authoritarian man who was never prone to give in or change his ways. A man who was so domineering that it had caused him and his brother and sister great difficulty growing up.

It was as though she had just caved in at about that time, he realized. Capitulated. She had allowed herself to be bossed around by his father for the rest of his days. He remembered how the life had seemed to go out of her around then. She had cared for them very well, but he'd always had a dim sense that she was going through the motions—fulfilling her duty, doing what she had to do—without her heart being in it. It was as though something had died in her. Maybe that was why she now thought of herself as thirty-seven. Maybe that was when she had stopped living.

He wondered how she had survived the next thirty-six years under his father's thumb. What was the price she had had to pay? It was as if she had given up thinking for herself anymore. Perhaps that was why she had become senile at a relatively early age. Perhaps she had gotten out of the habit of thinking.

For the first time in a long while, Kenneth felt genuinely sorry for his mother. Maybe they should bring her back home once again. But his surge of empathy did not make his resentment disappear; it just made him feel more torn. He would talk about it with Marlene. But there was no point in overreacting. The murder would probably be solved in a few days. They certainly had no real reason to think she was in jeopardy. The lieutenant had not seemed alarmed. Probably the best course was to wait a little while at least. And there was a security guard now. Still, he wasn't quite sure what the right way to proceed was.


Before dinner, Mrs. Simonton visited Crazy Carol in the corridor and Rachel Stimson in their room to offer them words of reassurance. The words might have fallen on deaf ears. There had been no response, no dialogue.

It was, of course, very different when she entered Mrs. Grochowski's room. "Edie, you look tired," the voice immediately came from the bed, alert and concerned. "You must be exhausted, poor dear. What a terrible thing it is! And how terrible it must be for you!"

Mrs. Simonton gave her friend a penetrating look. "I came to comfort *you*, Marion."

Marion Grochowski ignored the gibe. "You may not realize how important Stephen was to me, Edie. Every six months or so, at his request or mine, one of the aides would wheel him in here on his gurney. We'd just lie and look at each other. That was really all that we did. Then, after twenty minutes, they'd take him out again. But, it was enough. We didn't need words to connect. He and I had a kind of attachment that would be difficult for someone who's not paralyzed to understand. But our attachment was nothing compared to yours. What a loss it must be!"

"Yes, it's a loss for me. A great loss. But, as I said, I came to comfort *you*. And to reassure you—aren't you afraid?"

"A little bit. But of course it's mostly imaginary. Just because there's been one murder hardly means there's going to be another, does it now? No, I think we probably have much less to worry about than we might think, Edie."

Edith Simonton's explosion was a minor one. "Damn it, Marion, you're a bedridden woman, you've got deep feelings, and you're always trying to act so goddamn strong."

Mrs. Grochowski chuckled. "You've got me there. That's my neurosis, isn't it? Yes, I always have to be the strong one, don't I?"

"Well, if that's your neurosis, it doesn't seem to bother you very much. Yet it bothers me." Perhaps it was her own tension, but Mrs. Simonton refused to let her friend off the hook. "What might help me more than anything else you could say would be for me to be able to help you. Only you never need help, do you?"

Mrs. Grochowski's face clouded over. She remembered thinking the same thing about Heather's neurosis, how the girl could acknowledge her problem, yet remain appallingly committed to it. How easy it was for a supposedly smart pot to call the kettle black! "I'm sorry, Edie," she answered, crestfallen. "You're dead on target. The only thing I can say in my defense is that a neurosis isn't like a pebble you can just kick out of your way; it's more like a huge boulder you have to keep chiseling away at year after year—maybe for a lifetime. And that's the kind of task I do need help with. Yes, I am scared there will be another murder and scared that I might be its next victim. But you wouldn't even be here to see me if you weren't doing every other possible thing you can do. I know you. So there really isn't any way for you to reassure me, is there? But you did help me. You prodded me just where I needed prodding, and I'm sure I'll need it again, and I hope you'll be here to help me when I do. I do need you, Edie."

The buzzer for dinner sounded.

"And I need you, Marion," Mrs. Simonton rejoined. "The timing isn't accidental. I've already talked to many of the C-Wing patients individually, but I thought maybe I ought to talk to them as a group in the dining hall this evening. They're not like you. They don't have everything figured out. Maybe they do need what little reassurance I can give them.

But I don't know. I'm worried. I'm worried that in attempting to calm them I'll just agitate them instead. What do you think?"

"I think that's one of those imponderables. I also don't think it's the real point. I think they need to know that you care, Edie. And knowing *that* may be more reassuring than any words you have to offer—just your presence; you being present for them, as you've been for me."

Mrs. Simonton had gotten what she needed. She did not like to talk to groups. She hated that awful moment of anxiety—of panic—when she still had the option of turning heel and walking from the room with dignity preserved—that moment of clearing the throat when there was nothing left except to begin. But the anxiety was not the point. The point was simply to do what needed to be done. Commissioned to act, she left Marion Grochowski and strode down the corridor toward the dining room.

She wasted no time when she arrived. She walked to the front of the room, the side with the entrance to the kitchen, and straight to Hank Martin's place. The patients had not yet had dessert. "Excuse me, Hank," she said, picking up his spoon and tapping it loudly against his half-filled water glass. Then the clearing of the throat. She watched as forty pairs of eyes turned toward her.

"As you know," she began, "there was a murder on C-Wing early yesterday morning. We do not yet know who did it or why. There was no motive for it. The victim—Stephen Solaris—was a good man. A very good man."

Here Edith Simonton's voice caught. Damn, why was grief so . . . so unexpectedly *physical*? She forced herself to continue.

"Certain measures have been taken for your protection. I have hired security guards around the clock. One of them is on duty at all times. You can get out through the fire doors, but as always, they are kept locked from the outside in such a way that no one can get in. The front door is being locked at night and watched during the day. The detective in charge of the investigation—Lieutenant Petri—I think many of you have already met him—may look a bit young to you, but I've spent a good deal of time with him, and I can assure you that he is very bright and that he is most thorough and conscientious."

Mrs. Simonton paused, looking out at the small sea of faces. Some appeared alert, others not. They were all worn and old. Many were frail. They were so vulnerable. "Feed my lambs." The words came into her mind, unbidden. She brushed them immediately aside.

"I'm sure you have some feelings of anxiety," she continued, "but we have no reason to believe you are in danger. Nonetheless, such feelings are quite normal. Accept them. And feel free to talk about them. I encourage you to do so. With the aides. With the nurses. With me, if you so desire."

Mrs. Simonton stopped here. Had her little speech been any reassurance whatsoever? "Are there any questions?" she asked after a pause.

Lutzina Stolarz spoke up. "How can you possibly say that we're not in any danger?"

Of course it would be Lucy, Mrs. Simonton thought. Someone who would be leaving, someone who had a life ahead of her on the outside, someone not the least resigned. "What I said is that we have no reason to believe you're in danger," she explained. "The fact that there has been a murder does not imply that there will be another."

"A murderer is on the loose somewhere, isn't he?" Lucy demanded.

"Yes," Mrs. Simonton acknowledged, "and what you're afraid of is that that person may murder again. As I said, your apprehensiveness is perfectly normal. But it is also true that a second murder is very unlikely. Repetitive murder—what the police refer to as serial murder—is, they tell me, statistically rare." She was unexpectedly glad to have had the benefit of Lieutenant Petri's professional categorization.

Lucy was persistent, however. "Just because it's rare doesn't mean that it's out of the question, does it?"

"No. You're correct. I cannot tell you that it is completely out of the question," Mrs. Simonton replied. For better or worse, the issue was out on the table. "Thank you, Lucy. Are there any other questions?"

There was an entire minute of silence. Were they apathetic or was it because *the* question had already been asked? Suddenly Mrs. Simonton realized she had no idea how to end the meeting. What she wanted to say was "I love you." But that would be too emotional, wouldn't it? A strange instinct arose inside of her to leave them with a blessing: "May the Lord bless and keep you. May He lift up His countenance upon you. May . . ." She silenced it. How ridiculous! "Thank you for your time," she said instead. "We'll keep you informed. And, as I indicated, please be sure to come to any of us if you need us." She left the dining hall shaken by a sense of ineptness. Oh, hell, she thought to herself. Marion said all they needed to know is that I care. Well, if I was sitting in their place, I sure as hell wouldn't have felt reassured. She walked into her office, slammed the door behind her, and lit a cigarette with trembling hands.


Every few minutes, Tom Petri stood up and paced around his apartment. The chief had gone home by the time he returned to the station. He considered calling him at home to tell him he had a possible suspect, but he discarded the thought quickly. He'd seem to be jumping the gun.

Still, even after his dinner, Petri continued to feel pressured. And outraged. All afternoon he'd been sitting on his feelings, hiding them, acting unperturbed. But the truth was, he was appalled. Working with the lowest of the low in the bowels of New York City he thought he'd heard everything. Yet now, in this clean little midwestern town, he'd encountered the ultimate in degradation. There was Heather Barsten looking all soft and feminine in her white uniform and an image of a black widow spider came to his mind. Or was it a scorpion or a praying mantis? Some female insect that murdered its mate after copulation.

He was quite aware that at this point he had nothing to go on other than Georgia Bates's account. But his talk with her son had confirmed his gut impression that this account was probably correct. He didn't underestimate the problems ahead. It would be difficult indeed to convince a judge that an old lady who was clearly senile was also clearly an accurate witness. But there had to be a way, for as far as he was concerned, he did have a possible suspect. A real one. A woman who would perform oral sex on a hideously deformed patient was obviously someone who was capable of anything.

Lieutenant Petri's day began well. He met Mitchell at eight in the station house, and the sergeant reported that Heather Barsten did not herself have an arrest record. But—very intriguing—she had been involved in two arrests, both violence cases. Four years previously the police had been summoned to a barroom brawl. Ms. Barsten had been beaten and was a material witness. Two years ago the police had been called to her apartment by neighbors. Again she had been beaten. She had agreed only reluctantly to press charges against the man. He'd been given a suspended sentence and six months later had committed murder in another state.

Angel indeed, Petri thought to himself. Mrs. Simonton might be smart in a lot of ways, but she'd sure allowed herself to be sucked in by her sweet little nurse. People didn't attract violent behavior without cause. And anyone with even a little knowledge of psychology knew the roles of victim and victimizer were closely linked—close enough for these roles to reverse under the right circumstances. "Thanks, Bill. Good work," Petri said. "Something's certainly odd here. She apparently sees a psychiatrist. Do you know anything about the shrinks in this area?"

"There are four of them in the county. Three do mostly hospital work. Only one does outpatient work primarily and has a private practice: Dr. Kolnietz. There's also a bunch of social workers who do psychotherapy at the mental health clinic, but if it's a psychiatrist she's seeing, it's probably Kolnietz."

Petri remembered the book he'd been reading about the victim. "Does this Dr. Kolnietz happen to have a first name spelled S–T–A–S–Z?"

"Yes."

"How do you pronounce that anyway?"

"Stash," Mitchell answered with a chuckle. "After you've been here a year you'll be able to say these Polish names like a native."

It computed quite nicely, Petri thought as he drove by himself to Willow Glen. This Dr. Kolnietz was apparently the person who'd written the book. Mrs. Simonton had told him the author was the victim's only visitor. It would be natural for Ms. Barsten to seek help from this man connected with both Willow Glen and with the victim with whom she'd been having a sexual relationship. He grimaced involuntarily at the thought of that relationship.

As she had promised, Ms. McAdams was ready for him with the computer printout. She provided him with a table and chair in a corner of the Administration Center together with several pencils and sheets of paper. Petri had two thoughts as he sat down to work. One concerned the difference between this space and the wings. Except for the intermittent wails or moans on A- and B-Wings, the corridors where the patients had their rooms were strangely hushed, muted. Here the word processors tapped and the printers clacked away and the clerical staff bustled about in bright light. This was clearly the nerve center of Willow Glen. The other thought concerned Ms. McAdams. Was she married? he wondered. Engaged? He wanted to find out; he liked what he was seeing.

The printout was voluminous, but the task was easier than he had anticipated. Within an hour he had the figures: the average daily patient census was 120; in the twelve months immediately preceding Stephen's murder there had been sixty-two deaths at Willow Glen, almost all on A- and B-Wings; Heather Barsten had been on duty at the time of thirty-four of them.

This means that 54.8 percent of the deaths had occurred when she was at the nursing home. The figure would be closer to sixty percent were the victim's death included. Yet working twelve-hour shifts, four days on and three days off, with at least two weeks a year thrown in for vacation and a week or two for sick time, she would have been on duty no more than one quarter of the total period, he estimated. Petri was both slightly horrified and quite pleased. She had been on duty no more than twenty-five percent of the time, yet more than fifty percent of the deaths had occurred on her shift. The pieces were continuing to fall into place.

What next? If he went straight back to the chief with these statistics, would he be impressed? Maybe not. He and Simonton were apparently buddies. Likely he'd ask, "What does Simonton think of all this?" And the same thing with wholesome little Nurse Barsten's bizarre sexual appetites. After all, when it came to death statistics and the behavior of nurses

Simonton was the natural expert. Petri wanted to impress the chief and the chief would naturally want her reactions. Willow Glen was her bailiwick.

But that was the very problem. Maybe the chief trusted Simonton, but could he? He remembered her red eyes from two days before, her muted but obviously genuine grief and shock, so different from Barsten's histrionics. And if anyone had anything to lose from the victim's murder, it was she. Her first patient in Willow Glen. Her reputation. The standing of her nursing home. Yes, he could probably trust her. Certainly she was the most appropriate person to test his findings on, knowing all she did about Willow Glen. On the other hand, he sensed that this testing might be something of a battle. She had already stated her belief that Barsten did not have the personality of a murderer and was her best nurse to boot. No, it was not likely to go smoothly, but just as his findings needed to be tested, so did Simonton's faith in a demented nurse.

"It's time I brought you up-to-date," Petri began, seemingly calm, after she ushered him into her office. "I need your help with some matters. However, I also need you to assure me that our discussion will be absolutely confidential."

"You have my assurance," Mrs. Simonton promised.

"Well, to begin with, I'm afraid I have some bad news about your 'Angel of Willow Glen,' " he announced.

"Then tell it to me."

"We have already established that the victim was murdered at a time when either Ms. Barsten or Mrs. Grimes was in the immediate vicinity. We have also established it is probable the murderer had the knowledge that only a health professional would ordinarily possess; and, moreover, had access to a murder weapon that a health professional in Willow Glen would most likely have access to."

"Go on."

"We now have a considerable amount of additional information. One piece of that information is that it is highly likely that Ms. Barsten was having a sexual relationship with the victim." He looked closely at Mrs. Simonton to see how she would respond. But he was not prepared.

"Was it masturbation or fellatio?"

Petri almost jumped out of his chair. "You're not surprised?"

"Those are the only two alternatives, given Stephen's physical condition," Mrs. Simonton replied. "Now, let me tell you three things. One is that you should not interpret my lack of surprise as condoning Heather's behavior. The issue of a nurse having sexual relations with a patient has profound implications. Second, however, is that you can interpret my lack of surprise as representing a respect for your own abilities. I do not know you very well, but I do know you well enough to know that you would hardly state that something was highly likely unless it was. If you tell me it is highly likely that Heather was having sexual relations with Stephen, then I agree with you: it is highly likely. Finally, you may attribute my lack of surprise to my age and career. I am in the human being business, and I have been at it for a long time. There is not much that surprises me anymore."

The battle was going to be worse than he had expected. Petri was indeed glad he did not play chess with Mrs. Simonton. "We have another piece of information," he continued. "Over the twelve months preceding the victim's death, sixty-two other deaths occurred at Willow Glen. Ms. Barsten was on duty during thirty-four of those deaths, or fifty-five percent of the time. Yet my estimation is that nurses are on duty only around twenty-five percent of the time. In other words, the rate of death in Willow Glen when Ms. Barsten is here is more than twice that of what would be expected statistically." For the first time Petri was grateful for the almost unbelievably dull course in statistics that he had had to undergo in night college.

"So?"

The feeling that he had wandered onto a different planet returned. Petri looked at this obviously intelligent woman with astonishment. "*So?* So it looks as though you have a mass murderer on your hands. I gather Ms. Barsten has been working here for three years. I certainly intend to get Ms. McAdams to gather data for me from the two previous years. But even as it is, do you know what the statistical improbability is of these figures? And I suspect with additional data, the statistical improbability will become even higher. There would seem to be a unique connection between Ms. Barsten and the occurrence of death in this nursing home."

"Yes, and I suspect that if you gathered the additional data the statistical connection would be even more compelling," Mrs. Simonton said.

"My God, aren't you the least bit upset?" Although he was not aware of it, Petri had lost his cool.

"We talked yesterday about logic," Mrs. Simonton continued, unperturbed, "and we each acknowledged, Lieutenant, that it has its limitations. Logic makes connections on the basis of certain data. You have certain data in your possession that I don't have. But I have certain data in my possession that you don't have. Consequently, you hypothesize that these data signify Heather to be a mass murderer. Having a different knowledge base, I simply interpret the data to indicate that she is an unusually good nurse."

Petri gaped at her. "And just how might you interpret the data differently?" he asked caustically.

"It's quite simple, Lieutenant. Many patients at Willow Glen wait to die until Heather's shift so that she can be with them when they do."

"Run that by me again."

"Most of the patients at Willow Glen not only like Heather; they love her. They also know that she understands dying the way very few people do."

"Understands dying?" Petri broke in. "What's to understand?"

"She's not frightened the way most people are by the dying," Mrs. Simonton explained patiently. "Because she's comfortable about it, and because she loves them, when many of them are about to die, they want Heather to be with them. So they wait until her shift and then they call for her, and she helps them die."

"It's obvious she helps them die, all right. And it's pretty obvious she's comfortable about it."

"I'm not sure you heard me, Lieutenant."

"I heard you. What you're saying is that these patients schedule their deaths. You're as wacky as everyone else in this place. People don't schedule their deaths."

"That's where you're wrong, Lieutenant. Certainly, you would be correct that not all people schedule their deaths. Stephen certainly didn't, and that's one of the reasons we call it murder. Some people who die of natural causes don't either. But many do."

Petri looked at Mrs. Simonton with a mixture of skepticism, resentment, confusion, and profound discomfort. "Prove it to me," he said.

"I'm afraid that I can't, at least not very quickly. All that I can do immediately is to question your own concept of proof. You assume that the statistics you have gathered are proof that Heather is a mass murderer. I have pointed out to you that they don't prove that at all, because there is an alternative, quite reasonable hypothesis. Only it doesn't seem very reasonable to you. That's because we are in possession of different facts, different sets of experiences.

"Yesterday I told you that this is a place where people are closer to death than they are in other places. I have worked in this kind of environment for twenty-five years. It is only natural that I should know some things about dying that you do not. But if you hang around long enough in this strange world, as you call it, you will have the same kind of experience. You will come to learn that yes, many people do schedule their deaths. You will have your proof. But not until you get to know this strange world better.

"And one other thing, Lieutenant, since we're into statistics. You're correct that, whatever the cause, the incidence of death on Heather's shift is a statistical aberration. But it might be of relevance in your calculations to know that the death rate at Willow Glen as a whole is probably normal. It's hard to tell what's normal, given the fact that virtually every nursing home has a different flavor. Some serve more as rehabilitation centers than others. Some take only ambulatory patients like those we generally have just on C-Wing. Some don't take ambulatory patients at all. Some serve as hospices. But as far as I can ascertain, Willow Glen's death rate is no greater than would be expected."

Petri was annoyed at the way this woman had taken the wind out of his sails. But there were other breezes, other tacks. "There is some additional information in my possession," he said, realizing he sounded pompous. "I had Ms. Barsten checked for priors. She herself has never actually been arrested, but she's been involved with two men who were, who'd beaten her up. One of those men later committed murder. Your Ms. Barsten certainly seems to have a certain predilection for violence as well as for natural death."

"On that score, Lieutenant, our databases are similar. Unfortunately, you are quite correct. Heather does have a very clear tendency to take up with the wrong kind of men."

"To your knowledge, does Ms. Barsten see a psychiatrist?"

Mrs. Simonton hesitated. There was no good way out of the trap. If she said no, she would be lying. If she said yes, she would be divulging a confidence. And if she refused to answer, Petri would know that the answer was yes, anyway. "I am afraid I cannot answer that question, Lieutenant, since that kind of information is customarily held confidential."

"Is it Dr. Kolnietz?"

"I cannot answer that question either, on the same grounds."

Petri leaned back in his chair. "I am afraid I must ask you, temporarily, at least, to relieve Ms. Barsten of her duties here," he said.

"Is that a formal order, Lieutenant?"

Petri realized he had slightly overstepped his bounds—he would probably need the chief's permission to make an actual directive. "No, just a reasonable request," he snapped back.

"Then I am afraid I must decline," Mrs. Simonton responded.

"My God, why? You've got a potential mass murderer at large here!"

"For two reasons, Lieutenant. One is that I need her services. The other, as we have discussed, is that I have no reason to suspect Heather of being a mass murderer."

"Aren't you concerned about the danger to your patients? I know for a fact that some of *them* are."

"Yes, Lieutenant, that concerns me very deeply, more deeply than you might suspect. Only not in relation to Heather."

"Well, could you at least put her on the day shift where she's more likely to be observed?"

Mrs. Simonton thought for a moment. "Yes, that's something I think I can do," she responded. "She's due to go on days in a week anyway. I'll move it up."

Petri stood up. Yesterday he had rather liked this old dragon lady. Today he found her enormously frustrating. He wanted to return to the station. He wanted to get out of this crazy world and back to where he could think. She might not be concerned about Ms. Barsten being a homicidal lunatic on the loose, but he was. It was his responsibility to see that this thing got wrapped up just as quickly as possible. "I'll call when I need to see you again," he said coldly.

"One more thing, Lieutenant, please," Mrs. Simonton stopped him. "I'm sure you don't ordinarily make serious mistakes. You're a bright man. And conscientious. So I'm puzzled. I can understand perfectly well that you must feel in a hurry. But it seems like more than that. It's as though Heather's become some kind of cause for you to fight against. What's eating you?"

With an about-face, Petri was gone. He didn't even bother to try to answer her.

As soon as he returned to the station, he telephoned Dr. Kolnietz. It was another frustration. When he explained how and why he wanted to talk to Kolnietz about one of his patients, Heather Barsten, the psychiatrist had replied, "I understand that your concerns are legitimate, Lieutenant. But please realize that my inability to respond to them is also legitimate. Legitimate means according to law. According to the law of this state, I cannot divulge any information to you about any patient of mine without his or her written permission. I cannot even tell you whether the person you mention is or is not a patient of mine. Should the person in question happen to be a patient of mine, and should that person give me written permission to talk to you about his or her case, then and only then would I be happy to facilitate your investigation. I hope you have a nice day."

When he was a sergeant, Petri had watched detectives have this sort of experience with shrinks. Every damn one of them had an obsession with confidentiality. Part of him had anticipated this, but another part was furious. He had forgotten that less than two hours before he himself had pledged Mrs. Simonton to confidentiality. At this moment all he could feel was that these two health professionals—Kolnietz and Simonton—simply seemed bent on obstructing the process of justice. The time had come for him to speak with his superior.

The chief had gone out to lunch. Petri strode out of the station and one block down to West Main and the Warsaw Tea Shoppe. He ordered an egg salad sandwich on white—he was too agitated to be hungry for more—and while he ate, he prepared himself by pulling out his notebook and compiling a list of the seven factors that pointed suspicion at Heather Barsten:

1.  No alibi—timing and access to victim.
2.  Access to weapon and accessories.
3.  Knowledge of anatomy—expertise.
4.  Bizarre relationship with victim.
5.  Statistical tie-in with other deaths.
6.  Violence in personal life.
7.  Under psychiatric care.

He went back to the first item on the list: no alibi. If Barsten's story was correct—if she had, in truth, taken a walk at four-thirty in the morning—then it would be Bertha Grimes who would have been alone with the victim for the next half hour, who would have the least alibi of all. But the matter had been nagging him in the back of his mind for the past two days. Did Barsten really go for a walk? What a strange time to leave her post! Why would she go out in the predawn winter cold on that particular night of all nights? Yes, the time had certainly come to focus more deeply on this additional peculiar behavior of hers.

The chief had returned when he got back from lunch. Petri sat in the chief's cluttered old office and went over every item on his list. He kept his voice impassive, hiding his revulsion over the suspect's sexual behavior and his amazement at Mrs. Simonton's calmness in response to it. The chief could draw his own conclusions. But he was careful to present Simonton's counterexplanation of the death statistics.

"So I think I need to interrogate Barsten again, sir," he finished. "I still don't actually know she had sex with the victim. All I've got is the old lady's word for it, and I need to be sure. I also need her permission to talk to her psychiatrist. And I want to be able to see her reactions when I confront her with all this. But I can't do it unless it's a formal interrogation, and that means I have to read her her rights."

The chief leaned back in his swivel chair and closed his eyes. He liked his new detective and wanted to support him in every way he could. Someone as bright and energetic as Petri didn't wander into New Warsaw every day. But you didn't stay chief of police in the same town for fifteen years if you made many mistakes, particularly political ones. He knew almost everyone. He knew this Barsten girl's parents. They'd be no problem. He reviewed everyone else he could think of who might have a concern. He could see no reason not to proceed. An arrest, however, might be quite a different matter.

The chief sat forward and opened his eyes. "Yes, I think you do have enough to go ahead with a formal interrogation, Tom," he finally said. "But I want to make it clear that it's not near enough to detain her. Some of the things that point to Barsten could equally well point to the Grimes woman. And the other stuff, while it's interesting, is all just circumstantial. Added together it looks like a lot here, but that's not worth a damn in a courtroom. You know that. If an attorney makes one or two pieces look dubious, then the whole sum becomes dubious. The last thing we need is a false arrest—or even one that doesn't lead to a conviction. Yeah, go ahead and do your interrogation. And if you come up with something big, for God's sake let me know. Any time, any place, day or night. I want to be kept closely informed. It's a small town and the murder's drawing a lot of attention."

Petri knew that what the chief had said was only reasonable, but he still felt as if he had somehow been chastised, like a little boy. Well, he'd earn the man's respect one way or another, sooner or later. Maybe sooner. Maybe this very afternoon. He went straight to Sergeant Mitchell. "Bill," he said, "everything points to that nurse, Ms. Barsten. It's time for a formal interrogation. It ought to be done here. I'd like you to call her and ask her to come down here to the station as soon as possible. If you can't get her, let me know. I'll want you here with me as a witness. I also want the recorder going from the moment she enters the door."

"Sir?" The tone in Mitchell's voice was tentative.

"Yes, Bill?"

"Don't you think you might be moving just a little bit too fast?"

"What do you mean? Say what's on your mind, Bill."

"Well, it's hard to put into words." This was clearly difficult for Mitchell. "I'm not saying there shouldn't be an interrogation. That's not my place. I don't mean to be critical, but it's just that . . . well, you seem a little bit pressured."

"I checked it all out with the chief, Bill," Petri responded impatiently. "He was quite thoughtful before giving me the go-ahead."

Mitchell gave up. He'd done all that he could, he figured. But he knew in his bones that something about this seemed wrong.

Petri was not upset by his sergeant's attempt at intervention; merely oblivious to it. As far as he was concerned, it only remained for him to think about the style of the interrogation. Should he be soft or tough? Or a mixture of both? He wasn't sure yet. But he did know he was going to get some answers. She wasn't going to get out of the door unless she delivered on those.

•    •    •

After Tim O'Hara shuffled back to his room from lunch, he went to visit Marion. The afternoon sun, beginning to grow a little stronger now, was bathing the motionless woman on the bed next to the window. "How are you doing, my darling?" he asked.

Mrs. Grochowski looked at him gratefully. "Physically okay," she said. "But I'm feeling scared, Tim."

"About the murder?"

"Yes. It's the first time I wished I had a roommate. I feel so defenseless. I keep remembering that Stephen was the only other patient on C-Wing who was totally paralyzed. Is that an accident? I wonder. I keep thinking maybe I'll be next."

"Oh, my dear, how horrible. Even I've been frightened, and at least I could hit someone off with my cane. For you it must be awful!"

"Who did it, Tim? Why would anyone want to murder a helpless man like Stephen? Who could have done such a thing?"

"I don't know, my darling. I wish I did."

"All I can do is lie here and wonder, Is it this one, is it that one? Then I get suspicious, but my suspicions only make it worse, waiting for him to come. Or her."

"Who do you suspect?"

Mrs. Grochowski gave a hollow laugh. "Suspicions are only that. Several people keep running through my mind, but I wouldn't want to label them at this point—not even to you. But I'm so damn helpless."

"And I'm helpless to help. If only there was something. Let me talk to Mrs. Simonton and see if she can't have me moved in here with you."

"You'll do no such thing, Tim O'Hara. She has more than enough to worry about at a time like this without you bothering her over such a little thing. Besides, she already stretches things to the limit. What kind of fix do you think she'd be in if it got out that there's not only been a murder at Willow Glen, but she also has men and women sleeping in the same room?"

"I guess you're right. But I wish there was something I could do to make it less scary for you."

"There is, my love," Mrs. Grochowski responded. "We can have a Eucharist."

"Ah," Tim said. "That's not something I can do, it's something He can do. But isn't it a coincidence? It just so happens that I brought a piece of toast back with me from lunch."

"Oh, Tim, that's wonderful," Mrs. Grochowski exclaimed.

Because his left arm was paralyzed and he needed the other to hold on to his cane, it took Tim two trips to bring the half piece of toast and the bottle of wine back from his room. He laid the toast on top of the bedclothes. The bottle of wine he placed on her nightstand. He went into her bathroom and returned with a glass. Picking up the bottle, he sat down on the chair and set it between his thighs so that he could unscrew the top with his one good hand. This done, he got up and poured an inch of wine into the bottom of the glass. He reseated himself. These simple preparations took him ten minutes. Mrs. Grochowski had gazed at them in anticipation.

She was the first to break the long silence that followed. "We always say the mass to honor Jesus. Could we also say this one to honor Stephen?"

"Of course," Tim agreed. "Jesus," he continued, as if addressing another man in the room, "you sacrificed yourself for us, and now Marion and I offer ourselves back to you as living sacrifices. We do so this afternoon in honor not only of you, but also of Stephen. We ask that you number him among your most beloved martyrs."

"Amen," Mrs. Grochowski said. Another minute of silence passed before she added, "And, Jesus, please watch over me. And Tim. And all who are being threatened and are in danger." For a reason she could not explain, the image of Heather briefly flashed through her mind—so briefly she gave it no thought.

"Amen. And be with the souls of murderers, for their own sakes and that they may not murder again," Tim prayed.

"Amen." An even longer silence followed.

Then they were ready. Tim stood up and over the bed. "On the night before He was handed over to suffering and death, our Lord took bread," he intoned. Had someone been listening outside the closed door, they would only have heard murmuring within, but inside the room Tim's voice resonated as if in a cathedral.

He picked up the piece of toast in his right fingers and held it high above Mrs. Grochowski's chest. "And after He had given thanks to You, He broke it." At this point there was a slight flick of Tim's fingers. The piece of dry toast split in half with a crack that was audible throughout the room.

"And then He turned to His disciples," Tim continued, "saying, 'Take. Eat. This is my body which is broken for you. Do this in remembrance of me.' "

Tim put one piece of toast in his mouth, munching on it slowly. After a minute he swallowed. Then he held the other piece to Mrs. Grochowski's lips. "Marion," he said, "this is the Body of Christ, broken for you." She opened her lips and eagerly took it in.

Tim limped down to the foot of her hospital bed and cranked the head up so she was in more of a sitting position. In wonder, Mrs. Grochowski watched him hobble back to the nightstand, pick up the glass, and say, "After supper He took the cup of wine . . ." Here again he raised it high above her chest. ". . . and after He had given thanks to You, He gave it to his disciples saying 'Drink this, all of you. This is my blood of the New Covenant shed for you and for many for the forgiveness of sins. Whenever you drink it do so in the remembrance of me.' "

Tim lowered the glass and took a small sip. Then he held the glass to her mouth. "Marion," he said, "the Blood of Christ, the Cup of Salvation." He tipped the glass and she took two good swallows. He placed the glass with a small amount of wine left in it back on the bedside table. One by one he carefully picked up each crumb of toast that had fallen on her bedclothes and dropped it in the glass. He swirled the mixture of crumbs and wine around and with a quick gulp emptied the glass. He replaced it on the table.

Then he sat down and took her hand. "I love you, Marion," he said softly.

"I love you, too, Tim," she replied. They sat together in silence for a long time, and peace was between them and in them and with them.


Sergeant Mitchell ushered Heather into Petri's office slightly before four that afternoon. She was wearing jeans and a tunic. Petri had two impressions. One was that she looked exhausted. That may be helpful, he thought, in breaking her down. The other was that, despite her fatigue, she was beautiful. He noticed this much more powerfully than the first time. He was startled. Was it a shame or was it only natural, he wondered, that the angel of death should be beautiful?

"Thank you for coming down here so promptly, Ms. Barsten," Petri said formally. "I wish it could be under more favorable circumstances, but the fact of the matter is that the situation is very serious. Indeed, before you say anything, I must warn you that our entire conversation is being tape-recorded. Furthermore, I must warn you that anything you say might be used against you. You therefore have the right to remain silent at any and all times, because you have the right not to say anything which might incriminate you. You also have the right to contact a lawyer and not proceed any further without the help of counsel."

Heather looked at him dully. "It sounds like you're accusing me of murdering Stephen."

"I'm not accusing you at the moment, Ms. Barsten," Petri said, "but, yes, you are under suspicion. That is why I wanted to be sure you understood your rights. Do you want a lawyer?"

"No, I don't need one, thank you," Heather replied.

"Why are you so sure you don't need one?"

"Because I'm not guilty."

"I am not certain you realize how serious this is, Ms. Barsten."

"Look, Lieutenant," Heather said irritably, "I told you I am not guilty. But even if you make some mistake and conclude that I am, I couldn't care less at this point. I'm so tired and so sick at heart over Stephen, as far as I'm concerned you're quite welcome to lock me up and throw the key away. But why am I under suspicion?"

Petri was surprised. He had expected her to be fearful at having been summoned to a police station and read her rights. Instead, she seemed oblivious to her surroundings and to what he had told her. Was it because she was so depressed? She couldn't actually have been in love with him, could she? No, he had seen the body. Pity, perhaps, but not love. Maybe she was hiding how afraid she was. Well, she had asked why she was under suspicion, and he would tell her. He would begin to tighten the screws and see if she showed a little fear.

"Mr. Solaris was apparently murdered," Petri recounted, "ten feet away from the nurses' station at a time when either you or Mrs. Grimes or both were present. The murderer used surgical scissors and gloves such as you would have access to. The murderer seemed to have the kind of medical knowledge such as a nurse or physician would possess. You had access to the victim, to the weapon, and to the skill."

"But all that's also true for Bertha," Heather protested.

Ah, she'd come alive, Petri noted with satisfaction. Yes, there was some fear there. He would let it build a bit. He said nothing.

Heather broke the silence. "I wish I hadn't said that. I have no reason to point the finger at Bertha. Please disregard it. I only said it because you must have some other reason for suspecting me."

"Yes, indeed, Ms. Barsten, I have some other reason for suspecting you. In fact, *reasons.*" He looked at her coldly. "One way in which your and Mrs. Grimes's situations differ is that on the night in question she stayed at her post while you reported that you went for a walk. Where did you walk to, Ms. Barsten?"

"No place really. I just went out the front door and walked five or six times around the parking lot and then came back in."

"Around the parking lot?" Petri's voice reverberated disbelief. "Do you like to walk around parking lots, Ms. Barsten? Is it your custom?"

"No, I told you it wasn't."

"How often *do* you take walks when you're on duty?"

There was a slight pause while Heather recollected, "I don't think I've ever taken one before."

"Oh, why not?"

"Well, I wouldn't ordinarily want to leave the wing when I'm on duty, and I never had reason to before except when I've been called to another wing."

"It must have been cold out there in the parking lot, wasn't it?"

"I don't know. I took my coat with me. Otherwise I don't remember."

Petri's tone was icy. "I understand that you've worked at Willow Glen for three years, Ms. Barsten. Isn't it a bit strange that there should just happen to be a murder at the very first time in years you've left your post supposedly to walk around a parking lot at four-thirty on a cold winter night for no discernible reason?"

"I told you, I was upset."

Petri idly shuffled a few papers on his desk to give her a little more time to sweat. Then, with deliberate suddenness, he looked up at her piercingly. "Ms. Barsten, did you have a sexual relationship with the victim?"

"Yes."

Petri was put slightly off balance. There had been definite fear in her eyes after he shot the question at her. But he had not expected the rapidity with which she had responded. She was either strangely honest or without conscience. It would be interesting to see how she handled the details. He would hit her with them fast and hard. He struck. "For how long had you been having sex with the victim?"

"For about three weeks before his death."

"What was the nature of your sexual relationship?"

"We had oral sex. Or, at least, I performed oral sex on him."

"Did you perform oral sex on him the night of the murder?"

"Yes."

"Where and when was that?"

"It was in the hallway outside the supply room, just after I prepared the meds. It would have been about four o'clock in the morning."

Petri was annoyed. He could detect no defensiveness in her tone. In truth, her matter-of-factness was shameless. "Is there a connection between your sexual relationship with the victim and his murder?" he asked.

"Not that I know of."

"What do you mean, not that you know of?"

"Just what I said. Not that I know of. But I gather that somebody must have known about our sexual relationship and reported it to you. For all I know there might be a connection to that person. Or people. I didn't think anybody knew about it. Who did?"

Petri was focused on firing questions at her. "Mrs. Bates," he snapped, plunging ahead, not noticing Mitchell's wince. "Isn't it true, Ms. Barsten, that your sexual relationship with the victim gave you motive to kill him?"

"No, it's not true."

"You have already told me that the victim was distressed at being locked up in a cripple's body. Isn't it true, Ms. Barsten, that you killed him in order to put him out of his misery?"

"No, it's not true."

"Isn't it true, Ms. Barsten, that you have assisted many patients at Willow Glen in dying?"

"Yes."

"How do you do that? What do you give them?"

"My time."

"No, I mean what medication do you give them to help them die?"

"I don't give them any medication to help them die."

"You're a very popular nurse, Ms. Barsten. You seem to be a very humane person. Working with so many terribly ill and old people, people crippled, people in pain—people whose lives are no longer useful—it must be a great temptation to help them out of their misery."

"No, it isn't."

"Why not?"

"Because it's not my job. It's not my job to play God."

"Is it your job to have sex with patients, Ms. Barsten?" Petri was jabbing at her, first with a left, then with a right.

"No."

"Then why do you do it?"

"I . . . I don't have sex with patients. Only with Stephen. He was the only one."

She had begun to stammer. Good. He was starting to get to her. "Was that because he was helpless to fight you off?" Petri bored in.

"No. He wanted it," Heather answered, but it was clear she was uncomfortable.

"And how do you know that?"

"He told me."

"Told you?"

"With his letter board."

"Do some of the other patients want to have sex with you too, Ms. Barsten?"

Heather thought of Hank. "Yes."

"And you oblige them?"

"No."

"Oh?" Petri raised his eyebrows quizzically. "And why not?"

"Because I'm not attracted to them."

"But you were attracted to the victim?"

"Yes."

It was obvious to Petri that she had to be lying. "Come on now, Ms. Barsten. Mr. Solaris may have been closer to your age than the other patients, but he was hardly someone who was sexually attractive."

"But he . . . he was good," Heather stuttered. "He had a kind of light."

"A light?"

Heather knew there was no way she could make this man understand. How on earth should she respond? The reality would sound so lame. It even seemed awkward in her own mind. But she said it. "I loved him."

Petri looked at her in total disbelief. Yet he realized that he could take it no further, that a shift was required. "Do you love other patients too, Ms. Barsten?"

"Yes."

"And is that why you kill them also? Out of love?"

Heather stood her ground. "I don't kill anybody, Lieutenant."

"Are you aware, Ms. Barsten, that the death rate in Willow Glen doubles when you come on duty?"

"Not in those terms. I know that more patients die on my shift than on others."

"And how do you explain that?"

"Some of the patients want me to be with them when they die."

"So?"

"So they wait for my shift."

Petri wanted to explode, but there was no place to explode to. She was going to give him the same crazy argument that that damn Simonton woman had made. "You know, Ms. Barsten, you're a pretty odd young woman. You have sex with one of your patients. At least one. Your patients somehow *want* to die when you're around. Yes, pretty odd. Some might even say weird. This is not the first time you've had to come to this station, is it, Ms. Barsten?"

"No."

"In fact, you've been here twice. In fact, those two times you've been here were also associated with violence, weren't they?"

Heather did not answer. She knew the question was purely rhetorical.

"I'd like to return to the subject of your supposed walk on the night of the murder," Petri continued. "You told me you took this walk because you were upset. What you were upset about was your relationship with the victim, wasn't it, Ms. Barsten?"

"Yes."

Finally, maybe he was getting somewhere. "You had a fight?"

"No. Not really. He was bitter and angry because he couldn't see any future for our relationship. He thought that I was going to leave him."

"And were you?"

"No. At least I had no intention to. But he was so filled with despair he made me think about our long-term relationship. I hadn't thought about it in the long term before. I was feeling guilty. That's why I was so upset."

Petri had something to chew on. "So, Mr. Solaris was bitter and angry. Did he threaten to expose you?"

Heather's reaction was swift. "Of course not. He wouldn't have thought of such a thing. Stephen wasn't anything like that. Anyway, I told you it wasn't a fight. He wanted our relationship to continue."

Petri was not to be put off. "But you said he was angry and bitter."

"Yes."

"And filled with despair."

"Yes."

"You told Mrs. Grimes that you were going on a walk. But that doesn't mean you actually did go for a walk, does it?" Petri could see the picture quite clearly now. "There was, in fact, nothing to prevent you from wheeling Mr. Solaris back down the hall—maybe back down to the supply room—to where you couldn't be seen. It was a simple solution, wasn't it? There could be no danger of anyone finding out about your sexual relationship. You wouldn't have to worry anymore about leaving him. And you could put an end to his despair. Quickly. He wouldn't have to feel despair anymore, would he? And then you could just wheel him back to his usual place and announce to Mrs. Grimes you were back from your walk."

"I didn't kill Stephen," Heather said simply. "I loved him."

Petri grimaced. Love did not fit into the picture. "Did anyone actually see you walking in the parking lot that night, Ms. Barsten?"

"Not that I know of."

"So it's not an alibi, is it? At best, from where I sit, it's a conjecture, and a poor one at that."

Until now Heather had felt herself in a weak position, trying only to be honest and compliant. Suddenly—only for a moment—for no known reason, her need to comply was replaced by clarity, by a vision of Petri and Mitchell and herself sitting together in that office at a minute in time that was utterly peaceful and piercingly clear. "*You* have nothing but conjecture, Lieutenant," she said.

Her response had multiple effects on Petri. One was the recognition of its truth. His vision was, in fact, still conjecture. Another was an increase in the certainty of his vision. The details were conjecture, yes, but he *knew* she was guilty. Her brazenness confirmed it. Yet he also realized that the interview was essentially at an end. There was nothing left for him to do—now—except to restrain his fury and play his only remaining card for the day. There would be new cards in the days ahead. "Do you see a psychiatrist, Ms. Barsten?"

"Yes. Did Mrs. Simonton tell you?"

"No. It's my job to ask questions here," Petri scolded, pushing forward. "Who do you see?"

"Dr. Kolnietz."

"How long have you been seeing him?"

"For about a year."

"Why do you see him?"

"Because I seem to pick the wrong kind of men."

"Would you have any objection if I talked with Dr. Kolnietz about you?"

"No."

"Would you give me written permission to that effect?"

"Yes."

Petri was discomfited. The interview had not gone at all as he had hoped. Ms. Barsten had been entirely cooperative. She merely acknowledged what he already knew. He had succeeded in making her uncomfortable, but she'd given him absolutely nothing to sink his teeth in. "Bill," he said to Sergeant Mitchell, "would you write up a piece of paper for Ms. Barsten's signature to the effect that she gives me full permission to talk to Dr. Kolnietz about her? Then get her to sign it and you witness it."

While he was doing this and she was sitting there—quite placidly, damn her—Petri went over the interrogation in his mind. He'd so much wanted to get something to impress the chief. But there was nothing. He'd review the tape that evening, but there wasn't even any point in playing it for his boss. At that moment, thinking of how the tape would sound to him, Petri froze. He'd made a serious mistake, he realized. He had let Barsten know it was Georgia Bates who'd revealed her sexual relationship with the victim.

Damn, how could he have been so stupid? His first formal interrogation and he'd blown it. Even that idiot who'd been trying to make detective at the same time he had was aware you didn't let your suspect know the identity of your informant. How could he have made such an appalling blunder? He'd moved too fast. Mitchell had been right. He should have taken more time, been cooler, more dispassionate. But he wasn't dispassionate. How could you be dispassionate when you were dealing with a monster? He didn't want to be a kind of person who felt neutral in the presence of a woman who molested and murdered cripples. No, damn it, he did not feel neutral about Ms. Barsten, and he never would. Yet he couldn't deny that he'd broken a cardinal rule of police practice. And that he'd possibly placed old Mrs. Bates in jeopardy. For all he knew, Barsten would go after her next. He had to make sure that didn't happen.

"Ms. Barsten, you have been cooperative," Petri said. "But I want to warn you. You are currently the prime suspect in this case. You are free to leave but you had better not feel complacent. I have a responsibility to the public. I do not want to see anyone else killed at Willow Glen. So I want to let you know that you are being watched. I am watching you very carefully, Ms. Barsten, and I will continue to watch you. You may go now, for the moment."

The day that began so well had not ended well. Petri not only felt frustrated; he felt stupid. She had gotten as much out of him as he had out of her. Still, he'd gotten permission to talk to this Dr. Kolnietz. Maybe he'd get something there. Surely the psychiatrist of so bizarre a woman would have interesting information to offer. He was not discouraged. But, while he was not ready to confront his blunder more deeply, Petri was left with a sense of shame over the fact that his conduct of the interrogation—for some reason he didn't fully understand—had been peculiarly clumsy, even immature.

# NINE

Stasz Kolnietz opened his desk drawer, took out the brown paper bag, and dumped its contents on top of his desk: an apple and, in a plastic bag, a tuna fish sandwich on whole wheat. Prepared with loving hands; his own. It had been a year since Marcia, his wife, had fixed him lunch. She was divorcing him. They were staying, for the moment, in the same house only for her convenience. He was paid to assist people develop better relationships, and he couldn't even make his own marriage work. He was paid to help them to feel better about themselves—usually—and he himself felt a failure.

Surprisingly, however, he was not depressed. Tired, yes, but not depressed. He was tired of fighting with Marcia, tired of trying fruitlessly to push her into marriage counseling, tired of the frustration, tired of his own guilt, tired of trying to make it work anymore. He was ready for it to be over. He was uncertain about his capacity to be a single parent for two adolescent boys, but he would try. He would try his damnedest. But, as for his marriage, he was finished trying.

He wasn't even depressed about Stephen. As soon as he'd heard about the murder, he'd gone through all the usual self-recriminations that accompany grief. How clearly he could remember the boy tapping, "I/CAN/COME/LIVE/WITH/YOU!" That termination had been excruciating—for both of them. In sixteen years of professional psychotherapy practice he'd never experienced anything to match that pain. He had seriously considered the possibility of taking Stephen home with him, of sacrificing a medical practice, marriage, and an ordinary family just to take care of him. Very seriously. Perhaps that was why, after Edie Simonton had called him

Monday afternoon, the breast beating—"I should have taken him home. He'd still be alive if I had"—didn't last for long.

And there was something else. He'd been shocked when Edie phoned. Yet a part of him had not really been surprised. Why not? As a physician Kolnietz had always known Stephen's life expectancy would be less than normal. People so spastic, so crippled and immobile, were more prone to infection. But not murder, of course. So why his lack of surprise? It was not the body; it was the mind. Kolnietz remembered how it had first dawned on him when he was twenty-two that the eight-year-old Stephen knew many things that he didn't, was in some ways wiser, more mature, than he himself. And, as the years passed, the strange discrepancy had only increased. It was never mentioned in medical school, never in psychiatric training, never in the journals, but Kolnietz knew there was a word for it. Stephen himself had used that word in referring to it almost a decade ago. During one of his visits to see him at Willow Glen the young man had responded to some question by tapping out, "I/HAVE/AN/OLD/ SOUL." Kolnietz didn't understand it, but for a long time he'd had a sense that Stephen was close to being ready to go home.

And he knew this same sense was at the root of his comparative lack of grief. Was it T. S. Eliot who had said, "Middle-age is when they keep asking you to do more and more, and you're not yet decrepit enough to turn them down"? What with the boys—God, how he loved them, but God, what a responsibility—the shopping, the house, the taxes, the lawyers, his busy practice, Kolnietz was feeling profoundly middle-aged these days. He loathed the notion of the murder—though the death must have been very quick, Edie had told him—but he could not grieve deeply for one he envied, and because he loved Stephen that envy was almost akin to rejoicing. For there were moments of increasing frequency when he wished he himself was close to being ready to go home.

But he wasn't ready. "Get on with it," he said to himself, aware of the lieutenant sitting in the waiting room. He assumed the detective's visit to have something to do with Stephen's murder, but he'd said he wanted to talk about Heather. What was the connection? Well, it would become clear quickly enough.

Although Petri was not yet aware of it, psychiatrists are even better trained in observation than detectives. He would have been astonished at the rapidity with which Kolnietz sized him up: young, likely new at his job; dark hair, slightly aquiline nose, probably northern Italian as his name suggested; coat and tie, very neat, hair cut short, obviously conservative unless it was a self-disguise; sexuality unclear, of course, but intuitively he suspected a heterosexual orientation, although there was some question, something not quite right there; direct eyes, firm chin, suggesting intelligence and strong-willed determination; supple, athletic body, moves quickly, maybe too quickly for his own good. "I hope you don't mind if I eat my sandwich while we talk," Kolnietz said. "You said you wanted to see me as quickly as possible, and my lunch hour was the first time I had."

Despite himself, Petri felt a twinge of anxiety, although this middle-aged man looked unthreatening and appeared mild-mannered. When he was a sergeant it had always been the detectives who talked to the shrinks—alone. It was the first time he had ever been in a psychiatrist's office. The office, like the man, seemed comfortable. But Petri, still berating himself for divulging the information about Mrs. Bates the preceding afternoon, was on this day unsure of his professionalism. More than that, he had the uneasy sense he was about to be found out for something, although he had no idea what that something might be. "I'm grateful for the time," he said, feeling like a boy taking his first dive into deep water. "It's about the murder at Willow Glen. I've read much of your book and know how close you were to the victim. It must be a great grief to you."

"My greatest grief," Kolnietz said, "is that I didn't thank him enough."

Petri was taken aback. Why would this man be grateful to someone so impotent, someone for whom he had been caretaker, the rescuer? "*Thank* him enough?" he repeated blankly.

Kolnietz gave him a slight smile. "If you finish reading the book, Lieutenant, you'll realize its title, *Resurrection,* refers not so much to Stephen's resurrection from the grave of the back ward of a state school for the retarded as to my own. It was through working with him I first became interested in the mind—not just his, but my own. I became more interested in helping people rather than making money from them or prosecuting them. It changed the direction of my life. Without Stephen, I would have become a lawyer. I don't know how good a psychiatrist I am, but I would have made a lousy lawyer."

The title of the victim's intended book, *The Power of Helplessness,* returned to Petri's mind. The paralyzed young man had clearly mattered—had meant something oddly profound in the lives of more and more people, he was coming to realize. He wondered for the first time whether Stephen had not been so impotent, whether he did have some strange kind of power? But the notion was uncomfortable. It still didn't fit with the hideously crippled corpse he had seen. "The victim must have also been extremely grateful to you," Petri said.

"Yes, Stephen was grateful. But I'm not sure you came to see me to talk about Stephen's and my relationship. You said it was about Ms. Barsten, and you have her written permission to speak with me."

Petri handed him a photocopy of Heather's authorization. Kolnietz glanced at it and slipped it into his desk. "How can I possibly be of help?"

"Your patient, Ms. Barsten, is the prime suspect."

Kolnietz's first reaction was to laugh, but he suppressed it. "That's surprising," he said mildly.

"Why are you surprised?"

"After you've been in this business of psychiatry for a while, nothing surprises you very much. So surprise has become an unusual emotion for me. But Heather simply isn't the kind of person who would kill."

Petri sprung it on him. "Were you aware that Ms. Barsten had a sexual relationship with the victim?"

"No."

"Why weren't you aware of it?"

"Because she didn't tell me."

"Why didn't she tell you?"

"I don't know," Kolnietz replied placidly. "I presume because she was embarrassed by it. Technically, patients in psychotherapy are supposed to tell their therapists everything. But they virtually never do. It's routine for them to withhold significant pieces of information, at least until the very end of therapy. And Heather is not near the end."

"So you're not surprised by this information?"

"No."

"Don't you think it is rather bizarre for a beautiful young nurse to routinely perform oral sex on a hideously crippled patient?"

"Yes."

"But you're not surprised?"

"No."

"I am somewhat puzzled, Doctor," Petri pushed on. "I tell you something very bizarre that your patient has done, and you tell me you are not surprised; but then you tell me you are surprised that she should kill."

"Many people are not terribly well integrated," Kolnietz explained. "It is common for the right hand not to know what the left is doing. Consequently, it is not surprising when I learn that someone who generally looks normal has done something quite bizarre. But the lack of integration I am talking about is relatively superficial. At the deepest level of the personality—I guess you might call it the soul—there is usually integrity and congruence."

Here Kolnietz paused reflectively. "Please realize that most psychiatrists don't talk much about the soul, and I'm on shaky scientific ground here. Even shaky theological ground. Most people seem to me to have good souls. But a few seem to be sick even at that deep level. It's as if they're integrated in the wrong way. But Heather has a good soul. Good souls don't murder. That's why it's not surprising to me that she should do something bizarre, but it would be most surprising to me if she had done something evil."

Petri shifted in his chair. The psychiatrist had acknowledged that this was shaky ground, but as far as he was concerned it was more than shaky—it was off the wall. Maybe this shrink was even weirder than most. "So you believe it is highly improbable that Ms. Barsten should murder a man with whom she was having a bizarre sexual relationship, and that improbability is the basis of your surprise?" he paraphrased.

"Yes."

Petri plunged ahead. "Ms. Barsten is on duty roughly one quarter of the time at Willow Glen. Over the past year there have been sixty-two deaths at Willow Glen. Thirty-four of them have occurred when she was on duty. That is an extraordinary statistical correlation. The laws of statistics clearly point to a connection. It is extremely improbable that by chance alone over the course of a year the death rate at Willow Glen during Ms. Barsten's shifts should be more than twice what is expected. As a physician and a scientist, does that improbability surprise you?"

"No."

"Why not?"

"Because the statistics you describe are not the result of chance alone. There is, as you say, an obvious connection. It is indeed statistically highly improbable that the sun should rise each morning for the next year or millennium by chance alone, but the sun's rising is not a matter of chance. Similarly, death is usually not a matter of chance."

"And why isn't it?"

"Stephen's death was not a matter of chance. Someone murdered him. That's why you're here. Similarly, if you were investigating an automobile accident, and you learned that the driver was extremely drunk, you would not determine that the fatal accident was the result of pure chance. You would more likely determine that it was the result of the driver's being drunk. When an alcoholic dies of cirrhosis of the liver, we generally do not feel that his cirrhosis occurred by chance; it was the result of his alcoholism. People who are fatally ill will frequently hang on until a certain family member can visit them. Dying patients at Willow Glen routinely hang on until Heather can be with them."

Christ almighty, Petri thought to himself, these health professionals sure were birds of a feather. Probably they were even in cahoots. "Have you ever talked to Mrs. Simonton?" he asked with annoyance.

"Yes, many times."

"When was the last time?"

"Oh, about two months ago, other than when she called me Monday to tell me about the murder."

"Have you ever talked to Mrs. Simonton about Ms. Barsten?"

"No, never. Why do you ask?"

"Because the two of you sound just alike."

Kolnietz grinned. "That also might seem statistically highly improbable on the basis of chance alone," he said, "were it not for the fact that once again there is a connection. You see, even though the two of us have never talked about Heather, we both know her quite well, and we know the kind of nurse that she is."

"And what kind of nurse is she?"

"Extraordinarily competent."

"Why does Ms. Barsten see you for psychotherapy?" Petri asked.

"Because her relationships with men are so poor."

"Would you say that Ms. Barsten is extremely incompetent when it comes to relating with men?"

"Yes."

"I must say, I am somewhat puzzled, Doctor, why you can tell me that Ms. Barsten is extremely incompetent when it comes to relating with men, and yet assure me that she is an extremely competent nurse."

Kolnietz became aware that Petri had an instinct for logic, but also realized that he had not yet begun to learn its limitations. "Remember I told you, Lieutenant, that it is common for there to be a lack of integration of different parts of the personality, except at the very deepest level. It is not only common, it is the norm for people to be competent in some areas of their lives and incompetent in others."

Sometimes logicians are particularly responsive to scholarly authority, Kolnietz thought, trying to adjust himself as best he could to Petri's personality. "But you don't have to take my word for it," he continued. "I could refer you to some articles in the professional literature on the subject, and if you wanted to do the research, you could probably find several dozen more. Indeed, the phenomenon is so frequent that there is a standard term for it in psychiatry: 'conflict-free areas of ego.' "

"And what does that mean in plain English?" Petri was unable to prevent a touch of sarcasm in his tone.

"I'm sorry it's hard for me to talk about this without using jargon," Kolnietz replied mildly. "The ego we think of as the governing part of the personality. It is routine for this governor to be in conflict over certain matters. In such matters, the governor behaves very stupidly and inefficiently. But there are other areas where it is routine for the governor not to be in conflict, and therefore capable of behaving with great wisdom and efficiency and power."

Petri was impatient, almost bored. Talk, talk, talk. Theory, theory, theory. There's a real corpse, a real murderer, a real body of evidence pointing to Barsten, and all he was getting was denial that she could have done it on the basis of a bunch of theories and words. "Integration."

"Conflict-free areas of the ego." And then there was the word power again. "So you believe Ms. Barsten operated powerfully as a nurse?"

"Yes. Heather is a very powerful nurse."

It occurred to Petri that powers often clash. If Stephen Solaris was so strangely powerful, perhaps Ms. Barsten resented that power. Perhaps it threatened her control, her own power. It was an interesting thought. "But she's not powerful in relation to men?" Petri asked. "There, somehow, she's incompetent or conflicted, as you call it. Why?"

"Heather's mother is an angry, depressed woman. Heather's father is an alcoholic who batters her mother—not without provocation—quite frequently. Heather received little, if any, love from her mother. Indeed, her mother frequently told her that she was worthless. Still tells her. What little love Heather received was from her father. Consequently, she is attracted to men like her father who are passive and potentially violent."

"But what has this to do with the stuff about conflict?"

"Heather knows that there is a pattern in her making poor choices of men, and she wishes she could have a better love life. So she is in conflict. That's why she sees me. Eventually, we hope, she will be able to resolve the conflict. But for the moment she is not able to, if for no other reason than because her mother's kept telling her that she is worthless. There is a part of her which, in imitation of her mother, does not feel she is worth better men."

"Go on."

"But none of these factors affects her professional life. Surely, Lieutenant, you must know of similar cases: extremely competent business executives who are terrible fathers; powerful politicians who are impotent lovers; loving mothers who are frigid wives. It's all very common."

Unfortunately, Petri did know of such cases. It generally made sense. But there was still something missing from the psychiatrist's picture. Petri pounced on it. "You have described Ms. Barsten as an unusually competent nurse. In your opinion, would a competent nurse have sex in a hospital with one of her patients who is quite helpless?"

"Willow Glen is not exactly a hospital, although that's not the point, of course." Kolnietz sat back thinking of his own frequent—sometimes intense—sexual attractions to a number of his patients, including Heather, particularly the past few years as his marriage had gone sour. "It's quite normal for a nurse to sexually desire a patient now and then," he answered, "but no, it is probably not a good thing for her to act on that desire. I would say in this instance that Heather compromised her competence. However, in my opinion that compromise was less the result of any deficiency in her nursing abilities than the deficiency in her romantic competence."

Petri had had it. He stood up. It was clear that the psychiatrist had given him all he was going to get, which wasn't much.

Kolnietz looked at him. "Just one thing more before you leave, Lieutenant. I told you that Heather had not informed me of her sexual relationship with Stephen. But that doesn't mean that she never talked to me about him. In fact, she talked a great deal about her patients, and him in particular. This is not meant to condone her sexual behavior, but I thought you might want to know. It has been clear to me for some time that she cared for him deeply."

"You've been most kind," Petri said. But that was not what he felt. What he felt, as he was leaving, was overwhelming frustration. Conflict-free areas of the ego! he thought derisively. He was not one iota ahead of where he'd been twenty-four hours before.

But he was hardly stymied. There were other avenues, other stones to be turned. He remembered his mentor's favorite word: thoroughness. Thoroughness took time. Thoroughness took patience. It's the little details. What he would do was to thoroughly go over the death reports of those thirty-four patients. And there were other people he could talk with. The Grimes woman, for instance. The chief would insist upon that, but it could wait until he got more on Barsten.

Then there was Ms. McAdams. After all Kolnietz's and Simonton's gobbledygook, *that* ought to be more productive. It would be a relief to get some common sense at last. She really seemed competent and level-headed, as well as good-looking. She might have some very useful things to tell him about Willow Glen. In fact, he could go right over there after his own lunch and talk with her. Petri got into his car eagerly, looking forward to the remainder of the day after all. He might even get a chance to know her better so that after the case was closed he could ask her out. Not before, of course. He was not one to mix his personal with his professional life.

Heather thought she might be going insane. The snatches of sleep she'd gotten the night before were even sparser than on the previous ones. She had barely been able to get through her morning work. It seemed like eons since she had truly slept. She wished she *could* go insane. It would be a relief.

She knew she needed to talk to someone, but need and desire were quite different. Her scheduled appointment with Dr. Kolnietz was tomorrow, and she wasn't even sure she would keep it. How could she possibly face him? She couldn't hide it from him. He'd probably heard about it already. For all she knew, the lieutenant was talking with him that very moment. And what would Dr. K. be telling him? That she was resistant, certainly. That she was sex-crazed, probably. That she was evil? That maybe she was crazy after all?

She had no place to turn. No mother, no father worth turning to. Mrs. Simonton? Who must also know? Why else would she have suddenly switched her to the day shift a week early without giving her any reason? But she couldn't know yet about her sex with Stephen. Otherwise she would have been fired. No, she couldn't face Mrs. Simonton either.

She heard a rattle and looked up from the nurses' station to see Peggy starting to wheel the lunch trays back to the dining hall. That meant Mrs. Grochowski had been fed. Heather raced down the corridor. Somehow it was better not to stop and think about it.

"I've got to talk to you, Mrs. G.," she exclaimed breathlessly when she reached the older woman's door. "I know you like to nap after lunch sometimes, but I've got to. Please?"

"Of course you can talk to me. This would be a fine time." Mrs. Grochowski eyed her in alarm. She had never seen Heather look so haggard. "Are you sick? What's wrong, darling?"

"I'm in deep trouble, Mrs. G."

"Is it your boyfriend again?"

"No, I mean *deep* trouble. The police think I'm the one who murdered Stephen."

"*What?* You a murderer? How ridiculous! What police?" Always attentive, Mrs. Grochowski's mind now switched into the very highest gear. "You don't mean that young lieutenant?"

"Yes."

"That's absurd! He seemed like such a nice young man. I wouldn't have thought he could possibly be so silly."

The loving disbelief was not what Heather wanted to hear. She needed to be taken seriously. "That's the problem, Mrs. G. He's not silly. He's got a lot of reasons to think that I did it. He even had me down to the station yesterday afternoon and read me my rights. I'm as good as arrested."

"Oh, you poor dear, how frightening. You must be so worried. But I don't understand how he could possibly suspect you."

"He thinks that the murder was committed by somebody with medical knowledge who had access to the supply room. That's me. He knows that Stephen was murdered lying right next to the nurses' station when I was on duty, so that's me again. Then he's found that an unusual number of patients die on my shift, so that's me again."

"But isn't all that what they call circumstantial?" Mrs. Grochowski protested. "And any fool would know why the patients tend to die on your shift."

"Maybe anybody who really knew about Willow Glen. But it must look strange to an outsider. And I'm afraid that's not all, Mrs. G."

"Oh?"

Heather was silent. Mrs. Grochowski watched her face. It was flushed and almost contorted with tension. "You've got to get it out, Heather," she commanded.

"I feel horrible talking to you about this. I haven't even told Dr. Kolnietz. I know I shouldn't have done it. I feel terribly guilty."

Heather was silent again. Mrs. Grochowski could feel her shame although she had no idea of its cause. Again her instinct was to assert her authority. It would lessen Heather's feeling of responsibility for telling her what obviously needed to be told. "Go on, Heather," she ordered. "I won't let you stop now."

"For several weeks before his murder, I had a sexual relationship with Stephen." Heather rushed through the words. "Not intercourse. He couldn't, of course. But, you know, oral sex. I feel so horrible. You're the only one I could talk to, Mrs. G. I hate myself, but somehow I thought you wouldn't hate me."

Mrs. Grochowski now understood the occasion for the shame. There was, indeed, reason. But Heather was being quite hard enough on herself. This was not a time for admonition; it was a time for consolation. "Why do you hate yourself?"

"Because it wasn't good for him. I did it for my own selfish reasons. I didn't think about it. He wanted it. I wanted it. He liked it. I liked it. It gave him hope and joy, he said. But then the very night he was killed, he was telling me that he was feeling terrible because he couldn't see any future for us. I made him feel terrible on the very night he was murdered." Heather broke into exhausted sobs.

For the first time in a month, Mrs. Grochowski wished—and wished harder than she ever had before—that she was not paralyzed. Her whole mind shrieked to reach out and touch the child, to hold her. But she could not move. "One part of me is sorry with you that Stephen felt badly the night he was murdered" was all she could say. "But the larger part of me rejoices."

"Rejoices?" Heather peered at her through tears.

"Because he was able to die fully human. We do not have to have sex to be human. But sex has a way of making us even more human."

Mrs. Grochowski reflected on her agony that she could not feel Tim inside her when they made love, and his agony that her senseless paralyzed body could not respond to him. She thought of her continuous dread about those damned clogged arteries in his neck. "*You* did not make him feel terrible, Heather," she went on. "The pains of love made him feel terrible. If it hadn't been for you, Stephen would have died without ever knowing the joys and the pains of love."

Heather continued to weep, now feeling understood. In between her sobs she spluttered, "I never looked at it that way. You don't hate me?"

"I could never hate you, Heather. You know that." Mrs. Grochowski thought of Stephen. Between his paralysis and hers they never had been able to talk together. Yet, through talking with others like Heather and Edith Simonton and the mutual sensitivity of their shared afflictions and spirits, they had known so much about each other it was as if their very minds had intertwined. "Stephen was much, much more than your other young men," she added. "I know how lovely he was. But I don't understand what all this has to do with the lieutenant thinking that you have murdered him."

"Because he learned that we were having sex, and he thinks it gave me some kind of motive."

"How on earth did he learn about it?"

"Apparently Georgia Bates was up and around walking one night and saw us. Somehow or the other she told the lieutenant about it."

"That's terrible!"

"There's still more. He also knows I'm seeing a psychiatrist."

"And how did he learn that?"

"I don't know. Maybe Georgia again. I'd mentioned it to her a few weeks ago."

"Georgia certainly has trouble keeping her mouth shut," Mrs. Grochowski said furiously.

Strangely, Heather felt like protecting Georgia. "He probably would have found out sooner or later. I'm in the police files. They were called a couple of times when I've had fights with men. It really looks bad for me, Mrs. G."

"Well, perhaps there is something I can do."

"I didn't expect you to do anything, Mrs. G. I only needed to talk to you. It's been wonderful just to talk. How can you do anything?" Heather asked. She'd stopped crying now.

"I can't do much, can I? I can't even reach up and hug you. But there's always a little something I can do. I can pray."

As soon as she left Mrs. Grochowski's room, Heather began to yawn. Over the past four days she had no more than a total of five hours of sleep, but this was the first time she had yawned. She remembered an old nurse in school telling the class that yawning was a sign of health, that often it occurred when patients were released from great burdens.

Certainly she did feel remarkably relieved. It was relieving to have told Mrs. Grochowski about sex with Stephen and not be hated. And though she didn't understand it, she also found it oddly relieving to know that Mrs. G. was praying for her.

Roberta McAdams did not seem surprised when Petri asked if he could talk with her. "Of course, Lieutenant. Come right in."

"Has Mrs. Simonton filled you in on any of the details of the investigation so far?" he asked as he seated himself in her small office.

"No."

"So you don't know anything about it?"

"Nothing except that you asked me for that computer printout."

Well, at least the dragon woman had kept her pledge of confidentiality, he thought. "What do you think of Mrs. Simonton?"

Did he detect a very slight pause before her answer? "Mrs. Simonton's a wonderful director, a very dedicated person."

"What is your opinion of the aide, Mrs. Grimes?"

"Oh, Bertha's very competent. She's worked here for many years. There's no nonsense about Bertha."

"What about Ms. Barsten?"

Here there was most definitely a pause. "The patients generally like Heather a great deal," Ms. McAdams answered.

"Yes, but what do *you* think about her?"

There was another distinct hesitation. "Well, and of course this is just my own opinion, I feel Heather's a bit too friendly with the patients for my taste—you know, a slight bit too personal."

If only she knew how well she had hit the mark, Petri thought. She was not merely an attractive woman but a most perceptive one. "I hope you don't mind if I ask you a few questions about yourself," he said. "No specific reason. I'm just interested in getting to know Willow Glen better and the people who run it. And the citizens of New Warsaw, for that matter, since I'm new in town." Here he smiled. "And I gather you fall into both categories."

Ms. McAdams did not smile in return. "If you mean do I live in New Warsaw, yes." She was on guard. She was always on guard. Indeed, it never ceased to amaze her when some fools seemed quite willing to let their guard drop. Didn't they realize how dangerous the world was, that it was always a matter of survival of the fittest? And of power? And this man, of course, represented a particular threat to her.

"Married? Family?" Petri was continuing.

"No, I'm single."

"So am I," Petri said. "Are there any singles clubs in the area?"

"I've heard that several of the churches have them."

He clearly was not going to get to know her better through a singles club, but at least she wasn't married, Petri thought. "Have you always lived in New Warsaw?"

"No. Just the past four years."

"Is that how long you've worked for Willow Glen?"

"Yes."

Petri was feeling slightly discomfited by the brevity of her answers. It was not yet turning into the easy conversation he had hoped for. "Where did you live before you came here?" he persisted.

"Oklahoma City."

"Was that your home?"

"Yes."

"Born there? Family there?"

"Both."

"You don't sound like an Oklahoman."

"How do Oklahomans sound?"

She was doing absolutely nothing to help the conversation along. "I really don't know how they sound. It wasn't meant as a criticism," Petri said. "Relax. This isn't an investigation. You can ask me about myself, if you want. I'm from New Jersey and I guess I can't tell you how someone from New Jersey sounds either."

Ms. McAdams suddenly realized there was a possibility that this asshole detective was not suspecting her, that he was actually trying to flirt with her. She stifled the impulse to laugh and said nothing.

"You went to college in Oklahoma?" Petri asked to break the uneasy silence.

"Yes. Oklahoma State."

"What did you major in?"

"Business administration with a minor in computer science."

"Then what did you do?"

"I worked as the comptroller for a small hospital in Oklahoma City."

"How come you moved here?"

"I wanted to live in a smaller town."

"That's why I moved here, too," Petri said. "All my life I've lived in New York or northern New Jersey, and northern New Jersey's nothing but urban sprawl. I'm really glad to be out of it."

For the past few moments Roberta McAdams had actually been considering the possibility of a sexual relationship with Petri. In one sense it could be possible. He might identify someone else as the killer so that she herself would never be a suspect. Or the murder might go unsolved and the whole thing eventually blow over. Yes, in that sense, it was a theoretical possibility. But she had already discarded it. There was nothing about him to suggest he would enjoy true discipline and humiliation. The asshole had a kind of integrity. It was amazing how quickly you could spot the types who needed real submission and degradation. Petri was not one of them. She said nothing in response to him.

"How about you? Do you like it here in New Warsaw?"

"Yes."

The uneasy silence returned. Petri thought he would give it a final try. "Do you have any hobbies?"

"Computers."

"Do you have one at home?"

"Yes."

"What kind?"

"A Macintosh." She wouldn't even volunteer the type.

"Any other hobbies?"

"Reading."

"What kind of things do you like to read?"

"History."

"That's a broad subject. Any particular kind of history?"

"Early Scottish history."

"Well, that's the reverse, super-specialized. Why Scottish history?"

"I'm of Scots descent."

Petri gave up. Ms. McAdams was one of the most difficult people to talk with he had ever encountered. Perhaps it was because she was frightened of him because of the investigation; the police made a lot of people uneasy. But it felt like something more than that. She seemed to freeze up whenever he tried to be personal. Maybe she just didn't like men, he thought. Maybe she was lesbian for that matter. He didn't know. What he did know was it was clear she was not welcoming any relationship with him. He might as well go back to the business at hand. "Is there anything you can tell me about why the victim was murdered?" he asked.

"No."

"What was the nature of your relationship with the victim?"

"Well, it wasn't a personal one, of course, since he was a patient and I an administrator." Here Ms. McAdams became more voluble. "But I liked him. He was extremely bright, you know. It was a shame that he died just before we were able to get a computer for him. I'd been looking forward so much to picking out just the right system to suit his needs and to teaching him how to use it."

Petri stood up. "Thank you for taking the time to talk with me," he said. "There is one more thing you can do for me. The printout you gave me related to the deaths which have occurred in Willow Glen over the past year. There were sixty-two of them. Would it be possible for you to dig up the charts on all those sixty-two patients for me? If they were long-term patients, I'm not interested in their back records—just the ones that would describe their last days and their deaths. Could you do that?"

"Of course. I'll have them for you by the time the office opens in the morning."

"Oh, and could you also do the same kind of printout you did for me to cover the two previous years as well?"

"Of course," she answered.

Driving back to the station, Petri thought he could cross Ms. McAdams off his list of potential women to date. She hadn't shown a smidgen of interest. It was too bad, but there'd been no chemistry between them despite his initial attraction. It had not been a totally wasted interview, however. He had learned something. He had learned that not everyone liked the "Angel of Willow Glen."

## Friday, March 25th

After breakfast Lucy headed for the dayroom to watch TV, but Georgia went straight to their bedroom to settle into her usual beloved, aimless reverie. Shortly, however, that reverie was interrupted. "There's a call for you on the pay phone." It was Lucy at the doorway. "You can ask them to call back on my phone if you want some privacy."

"Thanks, Lucy, but I don't think I'll need it. And thanks for coming to get me." Georgia hid her annoyance from her friend. The call could only be from Kenneth or Marlene. When she took it and heard Kenneth's voice asking after her, she was blunt. "Why are you calling?"

"Because of the murder. You must be worried, and we've been concerned about you."

"Your concern for me is touching." Georgia's sarcasm was unmistakable.

"Under the circumstances we thought you might want us to visit you this weekend rather than wait till next."

"The circumstances are not such as to compel you to extend yourselves beyond your perfunctory obligation."

Georgia enjoyed the irritation her stiff response provoked in Kenneth's voice as he replied, "All right, we'll see you a week from Sunday as usual."

Georgia was hardly back in her room before she was interrupted again. This time it was Peggy. "Mrs. Grochowski asked me to see if you would come down for a talk with her as soon as possible."

This time Georgia felt both pleased and surprised. She was pleased because she liked Mrs. Grochowski; everyone liked her. Several times she had gone into her room to chat and she had always felt good afterwards.

Mrs. Grochowski held the status of queen of Willow Glen, so that it was almost an honor to be in her presence. But this was the first time she had ever been summoned to see her. She had not heard of anyone else being so summoned. There seemed to be something momentous about it.

When Georgia arrived for the audience, Mrs. Grochowski wasted no time with amenities. "Are you aware that Heather is suspected of murdering that young man?"

"Heather? Oh my, no. Why would anyone suspect Heather?"

"Because of you."

"Because of *me*?"

"Yes, because you told the lieutenant that she was having a sexual relationship with Stephen. You also told him that she was seeing a psychiatrist, didn't you? And now she's in serious trouble. They might put her in jail."

"But I didn't think that I would get her into any trouble," Georgia protested.

"That's the problem with you, Georgia," Mrs. Grochowski said sternly, "you didn't think about it. You don't think much, do you? In fact, it is a pattern for you not to think. It is, I suspect, a very prolonged pattern. I suspect you stopped thinking a long time ago, Georgia."

It clearly was not going to be a pleasant audience. Georgia felt uncomfortable and had not the slightest idea how to behave.

"The facts are these," Mrs. Grochowski continued. "The young man was murdered at a time when either Heather or Bertha, or both, were at the nurses' station only a few feet away from him. He was stabbed with scissors that probably came from the supply room and by someone who probably had medical knowledge, like a doctor, nurse, or aide. For these reasons, both Heather and Bertha are natural suspects."

"I can't help any of that," Georgia protested.

"What you could have helped is that the lieutenant thinks because Heather was having a sexual relationship with Stephen, this somehow gave her a motive. Because of you, he also learned that she was seeing a psychiatrist and that makes him believe she is mentally unbalanced. He knows that she takes up with the wrong kind of men. Furthermore, he knows that the patients in Willow Glen tend to die on Heather's shift. What he doesn't understand is that this is because she is a good person rather than a bad person. He has a slanted view of things which is going to have to be corrected. You have helped give him this slanted view, and I think you, therefore, have a responsibility to help him correct it."

"But what can we do about it?"

"You mean what can *you* do about it? I have done my part. It is up to you to figure out what to do about it."

Georgia began to get huffy. "I am an old woman. I don't see how you can expect . . ."

"It would not be difficult for me to be angry at you right now, Georgia," Mrs. Grochowski snapped. "You go around trying to pretend that you're a young woman, and then as soon as any responsibility is given to you, you protest that you're a senile old lady. Well, you certainly aren't young but you're certainly not that old and, above all, you're certainly not senile. Other people may think so, but you and I know better. You're quite capable of figuring out what to do, and you have the responsibility to do it."

Georgia felt as if she had been the target of a whole barrage of arrows, and had been stung by their accuracy. She looked frantically for a way out. It was clear Mrs. Grochowski would not accept a pretense of confusion. All right, she would use her wits. She became crafty. "I'm not sure why I have a responsibility in this matter. I did not create the information that I gave the lieutenant, and the simple fact that I gave it to him doesn't make me responsible."

"You have the responsibility of giving people the whole picture."

"But I'm not sure what else there is in the picture."

"How can you be until you think about it?"

"I am still not sure that this is my responsibility. Why can't *you* think about it, and give him the whole picture?"

"You are correct, Georgia, that simply making amends to Heather is not the only reason this is your responsibility. There is a deeper reason. Do you believe in God?"

Georgia was taken aback. "I don't know. I guess I've never thought about it much."

"There you go again, not thinking about anything very much. Especially God. Well, I do believe in God."

"So?"

"So I talk to God, and He talks to me. I talked to Him a great deal last night. I asked Him what could be done to help Heather. His answer to me was very clear. He told me that I was to give the task to you. God told me that He has specifically chosen you to be the one to straighten out the lieutenant's mind. He was quite clear about it. He told me He did not want me to do it. He didn't tell me that anybody else should do it except you. He very specifically told me that He was appointing you to be the one."

"But . . ."

"I'm tired now," Mrs. Grochowski said. "Please go. You already have your orders."

When Georgia got back to her room, her mind was in turmoil. There was guilt, a profound unease that somehow she had indeed done something very wrong. There was anger at Mrs. Grochowski. How could anyone possibly be so haughty? There was enormous resentment at even the possibility she might be required to think. There was helplessness. There was fear. There was confusion. But as the hours passed, all of these filtered—at least partially—away, while one thing increasingly rose to the top. It was this odd idea that God had appointed her to do something.

In some ways it was a deeply uncomfortable idea. People didn't talk much about God back in New York and Westchester. It was not in good taste. And they certainly didn't talk about actually having conversations with Him as if He was some kind of real person. No, she wasn't senile, but maybe Mrs. Grochowski was. Georgia could not entertain that escape route for long, however; the woman was just too sharp.

She'd been accurate when she'd said she had never thought much about God. Georgia wasn't even sure He existed. But, if He did, she vaguely knew He must be terribly important. And were that the case, she had received an important appointment. Throughout her married life, Georgia had served on occasional women's committees—garden clubs and auxiliaries. She looked back on them with distaste. They'd been perfunctory, inconsequential, and, above all, boring. The thought of the girl being put in jail was unconscionable. She really didn't know about this God business, but the notion that she might, for once, have received a truly important appointment was exciting. Maybe she would put on her thinking cap after all. On the other hand—damn that Mrs. Grochowski—maybe she wouldn't.

After she had finished doing her morning baths, Peggy wanted a break. It wasn't so much that she was tired as that she was feeling thoughtful. No, that wasn't quite it either. She didn't know what she was feeling these past few days. But she did know she wanted to be alone. She went into the dayroom and was glad to see no one there except for Hank Martin watching television in one corner and Lucy who had fallen asleep in her chair. She sat down in the opposite corner and stared out the window.

She was so lost in thought she did not hear Hank come up behind her.

He placed both his hands on her shoulders and she leapt up in terror. She backed herself against the window, her eyes wide with fright. "Don't touch me!" she snapped.

Hank was accustomed to being told that. He was not accustomed to what happened next. Peggy started to cry. Huge tears rolled down her face without stopping. They went on and on. He did not know what to do. "What's wrong?" he finally asked.

"I thought you were trying to kill me," Peggy sputtered. "I thought you were the murderer."

"Oh, no," he protested. "I was just trying to touch you," he said.

"Coming up behind me like that, you could be anybody." To his consternation her tears turned into sobs.

He had no idea how to deal with them, so he stood there in mute confusion. Gradually, Peggy's sobs eased.

"I've been so upset since the murder," she told him.

"What's so upsetting?"

"What's so upsetting?" Peggy looked at him in amazement. "Somebody's been murdered, and you ask what's so upsetting? You don't care?"

"Why should I?"

"You're cold as ice, Hank Martin."

Hank had always thought of himself as passionate. She was right about him sometimes, however. He could be cold as ice when his finger was on the trigger and there was a Messerschmitt in his sights. And at other times, too—times more real and recent. "But I didn't even know him," he said.

"Well, I did. I touched him. I bathed him. He was a real human being. No, he was more than that. He was good."

"Good? What was so good about him?"

"He cared about how I felt. He asked to talk to me one day. He didn't ask for his sake. He asked for mine. I never reached out to him. He was so crippled, yet he was the one who reached out to me."

"I'll reach out to you any time," Hank said with a leer.

"You reach out purely for your own sake. He reached out purely for mine. That's why no one likes your pawing. His reaching out was good."

"So he was good. So what? He was just a cripple. Why are you so upset?"

Peggy looked at him with horror. Without a word she turned and ran out of the dayroom. The nurses' station was empty. But it was not a private place. She had to find a private place. She ran past it and into the hall to the supply closet. She switched on the light and closed the door behind her. She turned the spigot on the sink, cupped her hands, and splashed handful after handful of cold water on her face.

Finally she calmed down. Why was she so upset? It was not just that cold, stupid, oversexed man. It was his stupid question: "So he was good. So what?" How could anybody be so indifferent? Stephen hadn't even mattered to him. Of course, no one mattered to him. But Stephen mattered to her. Why? To be honest, she didn't really miss him. Just because he'd been nice to her one day didn't make an attachment. It didn't even mean that on one level she wasn't glad that there was one less body for her to bathe. So why did he matter? Why did anything matter?

Peggy would never be able to answer that question in the language of words. But a wave of rage suddenly foamed through her blood into her heart. Stephen had been human. And alive. He was human no longer. He was dead. The human being she had discovered was dead. Murdered. It was evil. Whoever murdered him was evil. The killing was evil.

The wave of rage was followed by another one of boiling confusion. Stephen had been good, and she'd simply accepted it. But now, because of his murder, she was left facing the reality of his goodness. She was left facing goodness and, also for the first time in her life, evil. And she had no idea how she would deal with these realities.

Mrs. Simonton was sitting in her office worrying about Heather. She would be off duty until Sunday. Where was she? Sitting in her apartment alone? By this time she would surely know that the lieutenant was on her case. Hard on it. She must be wondering why she'd suddenly been shifted back to days. What must she be feeling? Would she be able to talk to Stasz about it?

Then there was Heather's sexual relationship with Stephen. As administrator, sooner or later she would have to counsel her about it. Damn, how could the girl be so impulsive? But, try as she might, she could not summon up any real anger. What bothered her most about Heather's behavior was the simple fact that it had gotten her into trouble, put her in jeopardy. The truth was, she could imagine perfectly well why the girl had done it. Had she herself been down on the wing, in daily contact with him, required to bathe him, able to give that extraordinary man any pleasure whatsoever, able to take him into her mouth. . . . Mrs. Simonton brought the fantasy to a halt. The reality was, she was not down on the wing, that it wasn't her job to bathe the patients, that she was called to be up here, loveless, sexless, and in charge. "I've become an old nun," she sighed to herself.

And not even a mother superior with any real power. Throughout the morning she'd been aware of Lieutenant Petri sitting out there in the Administration Center as if he'd taken it over, as if he were in charge of Willow Glen. He hadn't asked her permission, hadn't even acknowledged her presence for the past two days. He was obviously angry with her for having challenged him. But what else could she have done? She would have challenged him if he'd been God almighty. He needed it. For that matter, he still needed it. She got up and went out to the center, where he was working at the desk McAdams had allotted him. "Would you mind coming into my office, Lieutenant?" she asked. "I'd like to talk to you for a couple of minutes."

"Well?" Petri asked curtly when they were seated.

"I have a feeling you've been avoiding me, Lieutenant."

Petri looked at her without interest. "I've not had any need to talk to you."

"But I need to talk with you," Mrs. Simonton said. "I gave you a pledge of confidentiality the other day, and I need to be released from it. At your request, I shifted Heather to days, but I wasn't even able to tell her why."

"So?"

"So I'm sure she's wondering."

"Let her," Petri said, thinking it might make her sweat even more.

"Have you talked to her?"

"I'm not sure you have any need to know," Petri answered. He had learned his lesson; he was not going to release any unnecessary information.

"I do have a need. She's my nurse. She's probably in a good deal of distress at the moment. I'd like to be able to speak with her."

"You do not need my permission to speak with her about anything you want, as long as you don't tell her any of our conversation of Wednesday morning. And you have failed to convince me you have any need to know about any interactions I may have had with her."

"Aren't you being a little bit inhumane?"

"Murder is not a humane business, Mrs. Simonton."

She would never have believed he could turn into such an officious little bastard. Well, she could fight fire with fire. "You seem to be very busy out there, Lieutenant."

"Yes."

"What are you doing?"

"I'm not sure you have any need to know that either."

"I'm sorry, very sorry, that we seem to have fallen into an adversarial relationship, Lieutenant. Isn't there any way we can get out of it?"

"I'm doing my job," he said coldly.

"Then I have to do mine, Lieutenant. You seem to be reading charts. The charts in Willow Glen are legally my property, and I'm entitled to know what you're doing with them."

"They're not the charts of current patients. I promised you I'd read those at the nurses' station, and I keep my promises," Petri responded testily.

"You've told me what charts they aren't. You haven't told me what ones they are."

Petri realized that in this instance she'd gotten the upper hand and would persist until he was specific. "They're the charts of other patients who have died on Ms. Barsten's shift," he acknowledged reluctantly.

"You're still after her, aren't you?" Mrs. Simonton said. "Heather's not the only person in the world. Why do you keep harping on her? Isn't there anyone else for you to suspect? Aren't there any other avenues to explore?"

Petri stood up. "Mrs. Simonton, with the exception of advising you to take Ms. Barsten off duty, I've not made any attempt to tell you how to do your job, and I'll thank you not to tell me how to do mine."

With a sinking heart, she watched him go out the door and back to his pursuit. All she'd achieved was to make matters worse. She felt utterly helpless. There was nothing she could do other than pray. Well, what else were old nuns for? Do we invent God because we're helpless, she wondered, or does God render us helpless in order that we might pray? She didn't know. She never expected to know. It didn't even matter anymore. "Dear Lord," she began, "I don't know how I'm supposed to talk to you, but . . ."

Heather had been tempted to break her appointment with Dr. Kolnietz. But she assumed Lieutenant Petri had already seen him, and she knew if she didn't keep it Kolnietz would be calling her within fifteen minutes after her scheduled time. Indeed, she was no sooner seated in his office than he asked, "Why haven't you come to see me sooner?"

"Because I didn't have an appointment until now."

"This must have been a terribly tough week for you."

There was a part of her that wanted to cry in response to the sympathy in his voice. But the larger part of her was not going to give an inch. She said nothing.

"It grieves me, Heather," Kolnietz continued, "that your resistance to therapy is so great that you can't even call me when you need me. It grieves me not to be able to be of help to you in a time of need."

"I kept my appointment, didn't I?"

Kolnietz ignored this. "A man you deeply loved is murdered, and you don't feel you can call me. Then you are accused of being a murderer, and still you don't feel you can call me. I'm really sad that I can't be there for you."

"Do you think I murdered Stephen?" Heather blurted.

"Of course not."

"Did the lieutenant tell you that I had had a sexual relationship with Stephen?"

"Yes."

"I feel so ashamed. There have been moments I've wanted to call you," Heather acknowledged, "but I felt too ashamed."

"What are you ashamed about?"

"Because I hurt him."

"Because you *hurt* him?"

"The night he was killed, he was miserable. He told me he felt hopeless. Because he was crippled, he could see no future for our relationship. I hadn't thought about how it would affect him. I hadn't thought about how it might hurt him. I should have thought about it first."

"Yes, I think you do have some reason for guilt. But it's hardly a terrible thing, is it? I agree, ideally you should have thought. But how many twenty-five-year-olds think that much about what they are doing in romantic relationships? And sooner or later love always brings some kind of pain with it."

"So you understand why I'm so ashamed?"

"No. I understand why you have a little guilt." Kolnietz wished he did not have to be tough with her at a time when she was under such pressure. Had he seen her the day before he would have held back. But after her talk with Mrs. Grochowski she had been able to sleep. She no longer looked haggard and he decided she could handle it. "And I think you would have wanted to talk to me about your guilt," he continued. "It's usually a relief to confess guilt. Over the past year you've had no trouble doing so on a number of occasions. I don't think it was your guilt that has held you back from seeing me. I think you used the proper word when you said that you were ashamed. Shame is different from guilt. I think you do feel guilty about hurting Stephen. But I also think on another level you feel ashamed about your relationship with Stephen. It's that shame that has kept you away. Why are you ashamed of your relationship with Stephen?"

"Because it was sexual."

"So? You've not been ashamed of your sexual relationships before."

"Because he was crippled."

"I think we're getting closer. What's so shameful about having a sexual relationship with a cripple?"

"I don't know. I loved him."

"You're right, you did love him. And there is nothing shameful per se about having a sexual relationship with a crippled person, particularly someone whom you love. I think your shame goes beyond that."

"I guess I am ashamed because he was my patient. You shouldn't have sex with a patient."

"I think you're getting still closer, Heather. But you're not quite there." Kolnietz continued to press her. "Certainly a psychotherapist should not have sex with a patient. But you weren't Stephen's psychotherapist. And, as you say, you loved him and he loved you. So why should you be ashamed of having sex with a patient?"

Heather began to blush. "It's like . . . it's like patients are in trust to you," she stammered. "It's like a nurse should be sort of trustee."

"Why?"

"Because they're helpless."

"Yes, he was weak and helpless. And it has been your pattern to have sexual relationships with weak men, hasn't it?"

"But Stephen wasn't weak. Where it counts, he was more of a man than I've ever known."

"But he was still so helpless in many ways."

Heather's mind flashed back to the night of the murder. She had told Stephen, "You're more of a man than I have ever known." And she remembered with excruciating clarity how bitingly he had replied, "That's your problem." Maybe she did have a problem. But damn it, it wasn't her fault he was helpless. "I know you're going to say it's my tapes," she said angrily, "that I have this genius for picking weak men. You talk as if I didn't want to have a good love relationship. But maybe it's weak men who are attracted to me. If there are any strong men, they haven't come around. Maybe there aren't any strong men." But even as she said it, Heather was aware that she had repeated this lament before.

As was Kolnietz. He was also aware the time had not yet come for her to give it up. Soon, he hoped. Oh, how he hoped she would give up the struggle. But not today. Today was more a time for mothering than confrontation. "Stephen really was beautiful, wasn't he?" Kolnietz said.

Heather began to weep.

He sat with her silently, absorbing her grief yet sensing there was

more than that behind her tears. "You don't hate me?" she finally
asked.

"No. Why should I?"

"Because I had sex with Stephen."

"I can't tell you I wholeheartedly approve of it, but I can certainly
understand it."

"I also told Mrs. Grochowski about it yesterday," Heather said. "She
didn't hate me either."

Kolnietz saw the opportunity. "You expected us both to hate you?"

"Yes."

"Twice in a row your expectations were unrealistic. I wonder why?"

Heather looked confused. "I'm not your mother, you know," Kolnietz
said softly.

"Tapes again?"

"Yup. You expected the same kind of vicious disapproval from us that
you get from your mother, even though you should know very well by
now that neither of us is at all like your mother. Transference, we call it.
Remember?"

"I remember," Heather wryly acknowledged.

Kolnietz thought of pressing home the advantage, but instinct told him
this too was not the right time. He waited. "Stephen's death must have
been hard for you too," she said after a lengthy period of silence.

"In some ways." He was deliberately noncommittal.

"You never tell me anything about yourself," Heather protested.

The Chinese word for "crisis" flashed across his mind, with its two
characters, the one signifying danger and the other hidden opportunity.
"You've never really asked me," he replied.

"I don't even know whether you're married. Well, that's not true. I've
heard from some of the nurses you are. But I don't know if you have
children."

"So?"

"So I want to know. I want you to tell me about yourself for a
change."

There were a half-dozen different moves Kolnietz could have taken at
this point. Whole chapters in textbooks had been written about the moment when a patient first asks about the personal life of his or her
therapist. The standard gambits were ones of deflection. Even "Why do
you ask?" would have bought time. But her expressed curiosity about him
for the first time in over a year struck him as inherently healthy. Despite
all the rules to the contrary, despite all the potential traps he could foresee,
it was not in him to respond to a sign of possible new health with
evasiveness. In most other cases, yes, he would have responded more

warily, but something in Heather led him now to take the riskiest—and honest—path.

Still, it was with trepidation that he told her. "Your information is correct: I am married. But not for much longer. My wife is in the process of divorcing me. I have two children, both boys. Well, adolescents really. Mark is thirteen and David's fifteen."

There was a long pause as she digested this. "Do you like your sons?" she finally asked.

It was a discerning question, he thought. "Yes, I love them. And I also like them both very much—at least most of the time," he added with a smile.

"So you'll miss them after the divorce," Heather commented.

"No. They'll be staying with me."

"She's giving them up?" There was incredulity in her tone.

Pitfall number one, Kolnietz thought. "It will be a temptation for you to think of me as the good guy and she the bad one," he replied, "but I suggest you try to avoid it. Yes, Marcia—that's my wife—is something of a free spirit, and she's chosen not to be encumbered by their care. But you should also remember that I married her precisely because she was a free spirit in the first place. Often—not that it's necessarily healthy—we marry people who complement us, who have what we lack. The good old Puritan work ethic is in my bones. I don't know how to play very well. So it's no accident I was attracted to a particularly playful woman."

"So you're trying to tell me that it's a no-fault divorce."

Kolnietz admired her succinctness. That was precisely the conclusion he himself had reached, although it had taken him four years to get to it. "Yes. Better stated, however, you might say it's a both-fault divorce."

The pause this time was brief. "If Mrs. Simonton agreed to let me take the time off work, could I see you more regularly and a little more often?" Heather asked.

Pitfall number two. "That's an interesting question. And not unwelcome," Kolnietz responded, "but to even begin to address it, I need to know why you're asking it, particularly at this time."

Heather blushed. "I'm not sure. I hadn't planned to ask it. It just sort of popped out."

"Go on."

"It does have something to do with your telling me about yourself."

"Go on."

"Well, somehow . . ." she stammered, "somehow it just makes you seem more real, more vulnerable."

"More vulnerable or more eligible?"

"What do you mean?"

"I've just told you I'm getting divorced," Kolnietz explained. "That suddenly makes me a man eligible for romance. Do you have romantic feelings toward me?"

Heather blushed again. "I don't think so."

"I'm not trying to tell you that you should," Kolnietz went on, "but the fact of the matter is it's extremely common for patients to harbor romantic feelings for their therapists, and all the more so when they know he or she is even conceivably available."

"I know that," Heather blurted, as if she had been a child who had been talked down to. Then she became more thoughtful. "I can't be certain, but I really don't think that's it. Somehow knowing you've got marriage problems makes you seem less perfect. Less remote."

"It's proper you should realize that I'm not perfect," Kolnietz commented. "That's the reality. More often than not, the process of psychotherapy is one of the blind leading the blind."

"I'd rather be led by a humble blind man than some cold-fish psychiatrist who thinks he's got it all together."

Kolnietz was aware that the hour was almost up. He was also aware of all the further pitfalls ahead. "It may be just the right thing for us to see each other more regularly and frequently," he said, "but it's not the kind of decision that you should make on the spur of the moment. For one thing, you do have to ask Mrs. Simonton first whether she's willing to let you off regularly on your workdays. And even more important, it means we will have to wrestle with the question of romantic feelings on an ongoing basis.

"As you wrestle with this question," he continued, "you need to realize two things. One is that I am not eligible to you for romance. That's not because I don't find you attractive, because I do. In fact, there's a part of me that wishes I could be eligible. But I can't be. For better or for worse, I'm your therapist, and that means we're sexually off limits to each other. Period. No ifs, ands, or buts. Yet just because I say that doesn't mean you're going to believe it in your heart. It's not only likely that you're going to have sexual and romantic fantasies about me; it's going to be incumbent upon you to tell me about such fantasies, no matter how uncomfortable the telling might make you. Do you understand?"

Heather nodded.

When she was gone, before he prepared himself for his next patient, Kolnietz smiled painfully to himself, knowing just how difficult it might be for him to keep her off limits, but also thinking that maybe Heather's willingness to see him more frequently represented the beginning of a breakthrough, and that maybe, just maybe, he had made the right move.

•    •    •

It was only very occasionally that Georgia missed the cocktails she and her husband used regularly to have before dinner back east. Her life usually was no longer stressful, thank God. But as she and Lutzina sat in their room this evening waiting for the dinner buzzer, her body was churning for something that would take the edge off. It was hard for her to concentrate. It had been a most upsetting day.

". . . so I've decided to put him to sleep, if necessary," Lucy said.

Georgia sat upright. *"What?"*

"So I've decided to take Wrinkles to the vet and have him put to sleep, if that's what I have to do," Lucy repeated.

"But that's murder!"

"You certainly have a way of being blunt, Georgia."

"I'm sorry," Georgia apologized. "I just wasn't thinking. But why would you put him to sleep when you love him so much?"

"Haven't you heard a word that I've been saying? I was explaining it to you. You're right, it would be murder. But the murder of that poor young man made me realize how much I value my own life. Even more than that of Wrinkles. And it's either him or me. It would be no life for me just sitting around New Warsaw waiting for poor Wrinkles to die."

"But it's a terribly difficult decision for you, isn't it?" Georgia sympathized.

Lucy's eyes brimmed with tears. "I still hope I won't have to do it. There'll be a four-month wait at least for a room in Santa Barbara, and maybe Wrinkles might die naturally before I go. And I will try to find a home for him. But you know, something's been consoling me. The past couple of days I keep hearing the words in my mind. Something Jesus said. 'I am come that they might have life, and have it more abundantly.' We're supposed to live abundantly, and I can't do that in New Warsaw."

Georgia became very alert now. "I didn't know you were religious, Lucy."

"I'm not. It's just something I remember from church when I was a child. Funny how these things can come back to you. Actually, I'm a very secular person. I want to be in this world. I want parties and concerts and shopping trips. And somehow those words tell me that's what I ought to have. But what about you, Georgia? Are you religious? Do you believe in God?"

"I don't know, but I've been wondering a bit about that very subject ever since this morning." Georgia smiled reflectively. "And I guess I've also been thinking about living life a little more abundantly."

Lucy beamed with excitement. "Oh, Georgia, that's wonderful! Does that mean maybe you'll ask your children about coming into the adult community with me?"

"No, it doesn't mean that. I don't want parties or concerts or shopping trips. I had all of those I wanted when I was married and back in New York City and Westchester."

"Then what does a more abundant life mean to you?"

"I'm not sure, Lucy."

"Does it mean you're going to do something different?"

"I'm not sure, Lucy. Maybe. Maybe not. All it means is that I'm thinking about it a little."

The dinner buzzer sounded, cutting off Lucy's questioning. Georgia was grateful. One could do just so much thinking and that was enough.

## ELEVEN

## Sunday, March 27th

Petri had worked by himself not only Friday, but all day Saturday in the Administration Center of Willow Glen. He'd reviewed the charts of all thirty-four patients who had died there the past year while on Heather Barsten's shift. The final nursing notes were discouragingly similar: "Patient failing rapidly, asked for Ms. Barsten. Ms. Barsten called." and "Patient expired with Ms. Barsten in attendance. Death peaceful. Dr. Ortiz notified." There was nothing else revealing.

Then he had gone over the computer printouts Ms. McAdams had prepared of the deaths of two and three years before. The results were no different than he had expected. For the first six months Barsten was at Willow Glen, the death rate on her shift was average. Then over the course of several months it jumped to double the average. Obviously, she was not going to start killing right away; she'd want to gain people's trust first. But he knew Simonton would use that very same fact to make the opposite case: that it was because they came to trust Heather that the patients started to *decide* to die when she was on duty.

He'd had a solitary dinner at the Tea Shoppe Saturday night. When he got back to his apartment he turned on his new TV, but his mind was too preoccupied to concentrate on it. Something had to break. The first murder in the county in four years, and no arrest. Oh, he knew that these investigations usually took time—lots of time—but a murder in a nursing home surely ought to be more simple, not less. He'd made good progress the first two and a half days, but the last three he'd gotten nowhere.

After switching off the light, he'd tossed and turned for over an hour

before he finally got to sleep. He knew he felt the need to prove himself as
the officer in charge of this investigation. He was also aware of how much
he wanted to please the chief. But it was more than these things. The chief
had not been putting any pressure on him, but Petri knew how much
pressure was being put on the chief: the persistent phone calls from the
reporters; the dismally similar daily communiqués in the newspaper and
on the radio—"An arrest has yet to be made in the case of the brutal
murder at the Willow Glen nursing home. The police report that they are
continuing to follow leads." The evasions couldn't work much longer,
and then what?

It seemed he'd hardly gotten to sleep when he had the nightmare again.
It was exactly the same as the one three weeks before: the spreading stain
on the wall of his freshly painted living room; the same filthy, dark-green
slime that kept recurring; the crowbar in his hand, and his hacking away at
the Sheetrock; the stain spreading through the insulation; his inability to
locate its source; the same sudden awakening; the sweat and the overwhelming feelings of frustration, rage, shame, and terror.

After the intense emotion subsided, he was puzzled by the dream. The
first time he could ascribe it to the fact that he'd actually been painting the
day before and the apartment was filled with the smell. But what could
account for it this time? When he thought about it, however, it actually
made more sense on this occasion. Did it not reflect the intense frustration
he'd been feeling over Willow Glen? And did not the inability to pin down
the source of the stain represent his failure so far to obtain enough hard
evidence to pin the murder on Heather Barsten?

But these realizations did not put his mind at ease. The feeling associated with the slime, the disgust and the shame—why shame? he wondered—
continued to linger, and it was two hours before he was able to get back to
sleep.

No wonder that when his phone rang a few minutes before nine
Sunday morning, it thrust itself on his sleep as an outrageous insult. It was
Mrs. Simonton. She was calling from home to inform him that Georgia
Bates had asked to talk with him. "I have no idea what it's about. It's not
the sort of thing I would expect from her. But she said it was urgent."

Simonton offered to come in too, but he told her it would not be
necessary. He would call her if she was needed.

Driving to Willow Glen, Petri felt a twinge of excitement. Georgia
Bates was a strange old woman, but the information she had given him
was accurate. Indeed, it had all but made his case. Maybe now she would
give him the one piece that still seemed to be lacking.

"Have you seen my purse? What have they done with my purse?"

Crazy Carol attempted to grasp him as he moved into the wing, but he was accustomed to her now, and merely brushed her away and proceeded eagerly to Mrs. Bates's room.

Georgia was dressed for the occasion. She had even dispatched Lucy to the dayroom. She welcomed him with the manner of someone pouring tea. "Thank you for taking the time to come, Lieutenant," she said.

"You're quite welcome." Petri sat down. "To what do I owe the pleasure of this invitation?"

"I wanted to tell you that I am guilty."

Petri's mind went blank with astonishment. After a long pause he asked, "Guilty? Guilty of what?"

Georgia did not answer him. In the silence that followed, Petri's head swirled. He had been so fixed on Heather Barsten and now . . . could she mean . . . ? Unaware of how he was being maneuvered, he finally broke the silence. "Do you mean that you are guilty of the murder?"

"No, but I could have been," Georgia replied placidly.

Damn it, Petri thought, why was this abominable place so confusing? "What do you mean, you could have murdered him?"

"Just that. I could have murdered him if I wanted to."

"Mrs. Bates," he said patiently, "the young man was murdered between four-thirty and five-thirty in the morning. As far as we know, he was murdered while lying on the gurney only ten feet away from the nurses' station. During that time either Ms. Barsten or Mrs. Grimes, or both, were sitting in the nurses' station. How could you possibly have murdered him ten feet away from them?"

"I certainly could have murdered him when Mrs. Grimes was in the nurses' station."

"Why Mrs. Grimes?"

"Mrs. Grimes likes to read novels," she told him. "She reads them with great concentration. She buries herself in them, you might say. When she is reading, a bomb could go off next to the nurses' station and she wouldn't know it."

"Why are you telling me this?"

"I told you that on the night of the murder I had woken up and gone walking and had seen Heather and the young man having sex. What I neglected to tell you was that during that same time, Mrs. Grimes was sitting in the nurses' station reading. In fact, I passed by the nurses' station three times during that walk. On none of them did Mrs. Grimes even look up. I doubt very much that she was aware of me. I think it is quite possible that I could have stabbed that young man and she wouldn't have been aware of it at all."

Petri sat back in his chair. This was a new piece of information. It was not the one he had wanted, but maybe it was significant. He remembered that when he had interviewed Mrs. Grimes, she had not seemed terribly alert. But again, could he trust this apparently senile woman? Because she'd been accurate before didn't mean that she was now. And she was one of those people who liked Barsten; maybe she was trying to cover up for her.

And it was hard to believe that the Grimes woman, no matter how immersed she might be in a book, wouldn't even notice a murder occurring ten feet away from her on a quiet night. Still, if it was true, it didn't mean that Barsten wasn't the murderer. In fact, it simply confirmed the possibility that she could have stabbed the victim, while he was lying there on the gurney, without Mrs. Grimes knowing it. But it also raised another more disconcerting possibility: maybe *anyone* could have stabbed the victim without Mrs. Grimes knowing it. Maybe someone who did it when Heather Barsten had gone for her walk. But who? He recollected, with a start, that Mrs. Bates had said she was guilty.

"You said that you did not murder the victim, but you could have. You also said that you were guilty. If you didn't murder the victim, what are you guilty of?"

"I am guilty of withholding information. Mind you, I did not withhold it consciously. But as I have thought about things, I have become aware that when we last talked I failed to give you the whole picture."

"How?"

"Well, I've already given you one example. I told you that I was wandering about the night of the murder, but I failed to tell you that Mrs. Grimes was unaware that I was doing this. That's one part of the whole picture I left out. There are others."

"Go on."

"I told you that Heather and the young man were having a sexual relationship. But I am not sure that you have been able to put that fact in perspective. I had not realized you might think it to be something quite unique. Had I given you the complete picture, I would have had to tell you that lots of people have sexual relationships in here."

He gaped at her. "Lots of people? Like who?"

"Like us patients. That young man was hardly the only patient who had a sexual relationship. There's a man here who paws at everyone. There's another couple who sleep together with some regularity. You had not thought of there being sex at Willow Glen, had you, Lieutenant?"

Petri acknowledged he hadn't.

"That's one of the troubles with people," Georgia continued. "They don't think about these sorts of things. They think of us patients in a nursing home as people who are already dead. They don't think of us as having real lives. They don't even think of us being capable of committing murder."

"Are you suggesting that one of the patients is the murderer?"

"I don't know, but it's certainly a possibility. I've already explained to you that I, myself, could have been the murderer. It's certainly something you should consider."

Lieutenant Petri again sat back thoughtfully. He had gotten used to the fact that when he had come into Willow Glen he had wandered into a territory quite foreign to him. Now it was also beginning to dawn on him that he had wandered into it with a lot of preconceptions. Perhaps he had not given the patients sufficient consideration. He leaned forward. "Do you know, Mrs. Bates, who the murderer is?"

"No."

"Do you have any particular suspicion?"

"No. But there is still another piece of information I unwittingly withheld from you."

"Yes?"

"I told you that Heather was seeing a psychiatrist, as if that was also something unique. I should have added that it's possible there are lots of people here who are seeing psychiatrists. Or at least have seen one. I, myself, had to see one a year ago. He thought I was senile. I, myself, thought he was rather dense for being a doctor."

"Was that a Dr. Kolnietz by any chance?"

"No. It was a Dr. Hassle down at the hospital. Good name for him. He was a hassle."

"Do you know of anyone here—patients or anyone else—who is seeing a psychiatrist?"

"No, but that doesn't mean that they aren't. I thought you might want to look into it. And there's something else you might want to look into as well."

"What is that?"

"I understand that you have been considering Heather as a suspect partly because the murderer seemed to have medical knowledge. There might be other people here besides the staff who have medical knowledge."

"You mean, like the patients again?"

"Yes. We do have pasts, you know."

Petri looked at Georgia with a mixture of admiration tinged with resentment. She had certainly succeeded in opening his eyes. But he was also annoyed that this old woman could be so far ahead of him. And there was still his doubt as to how reliable a witness she might make. Perhaps he could take her down a little peg. "When were you born?" he asked.

"You inquired about that before. 1912."

"And how old are you?"

Until now Georgia had felt most pleasantly in control of the situation. She had not fully thought, however, about the price she would have to pay. It was a terrible price. But it had to do with Heather and Mrs. Grochowski and with God. Spasms of pain crossed her face as she began to calculate. They kept posting the date all over the place. She couldn't ignore it. It was 1988. How many years were there between 1912 and 1988? She looked down at her hands sitting in her lap. They were an old woman's hands. Finally, she looked up. "I am seventy-six years old, Lieutenant."

Just before lunchtime, as she was walking along the corridor exercising her hip, Lucy Stolarz heard a faint call for help coming from behind the door of Mrs. Grochowski's room. She opened it to find Tim O'Hara, who had been sitting on the chair next to the bed, slumped to the floor. "Get Heather," Mrs. Grochowski commanded.

Swinging her cane, Lucy practically ran to the nurses' station. "It's Tim O'Hara," she said excitedly. "He's on the floor in Mrs. Grochowski's room."

Heather shot down the hall and into the room. She bent over Tim. His eyes were open, but he was not responding. She listened to his breathing. It was regular, but slow and noisy. She straightened up. "I'm sorry, Mrs. G., but I think he's had another stroke. I'll call for the doctor."

"No. Please don't," Mrs. Grochowski said.

"No?"

"No. We have always known if he had another stroke it would be his last. He's dying, Heather; there's no point in getting the doctor. I want you to get some help and lift him up onto the bed. I want to be close to him when he dies."

Mrs. Grochowski's voice was calm, but Heather knew it was that strange kind of calm that could come at times of devastating crisis. Devoted to Tim, yet so differently from Mrs. G., Heather was in agony. She forced herself to look at his face again. Spittle began to dribble out of the corner of his mouth and down his chin. Would she never again be able to see him standing? Standing erect, with that beautiful ruddy complexion and mane of white hair, so peaceful yet so manly?

Well, it would be as his lover wanted, as he himself would have wanted. Heather rushed out. She was back with three aides, one from each wing, five minutes later, and they moved Mrs. Grochowski farther to the window side of her bed. Then they gently lifted Tim's great body, and laid him on the bed next to her. "I'm afraid that I do have to call the doctor, Mrs. G.," Heather said. "Maybe I could get by without it some other time, but the police are watching me. I also need to call Mrs. Simonton."

"I understand. Don't worry about it. The doctor will probably take hours. And I suspect Tim will be gone by then. Please just leave us alone now."

Heather understood. She wished she could kiss Tim good-bye, but instinctively she realized that this hour belonged solely to the older woman. "I love you, Mrs. G.," she said. "I'll check back every twenty minutes." Then she quietly closed the door.

After speaking with Georgia Bates—it had been more like being spoken to, he realized—Petri drove to the police station. He found the number in the phone book and called Bertha Grimes at her home. She did not seem surprised that he wanted to see her and asked for directions to their farm. But then he had not expected her to be surprised, not the phlegmatic woman he'd met six days before.

Petri had made the appointment for late in the day because he needed time to think. He had been so certain! Now the Bates woman was forcing him to consider the other possibilities. But it still didn't mean that Barsten wasn't the one; just that he had to be more open, and he was finding that difficult. He realized he was having some trouble operating without a focus. Barsten had been his focus; now he had to direct his attention elsewhere. Yet at the same time she remained his most likely suspect. Damn her, why couldn't he get her out of his mind?

Elsewhere? Where? He had no other focus. Mrs. Bates raised the possibility of the patients. He had simply glanced at their charts when he had interviewed them. Tomorrow he would go over them more thoroughly. But her suggestion was merely that. It could be anybody. Mrs. Grimes came first because she was the next most obvious suspect. She could have done it when Heather was out on her walk, but she had hardly seemed the type. Still, he would put the pressure on her that very afternoon. Suppose the visit revealed nothing? It could be one of the other nurses or aides. It could be anyone on the staff. It could be one of the doctors. It could be a relative or visitor. Hell, it could be anyone. Who? Why? He felt as if he were in a vacuum—lost in space, in darkness.

The Grimeses' farm reminded him of the Kubricks', except that it was more run-down. The sitting room furniture was threadbare in places and lacked the plastic covers. There was dust on the coffee table. Bertha Grimes was not the world's best housekeeper, Petri thought. "I'm sorry to bother you on a Sunday afternoon," he said, "but a murder investigation doesn't wait. We don't want to have another killing, do we, while we doodle around?"

Bertha said nothing. Petri examined her impassive face, guessing her to be around sixty, but sensing nothing other than her chronic absence of animation. "Tell me about yourself," he asked.

"Nothing much to tell."

"Married?"

"Sure. Couldn't work this farm by myself."

"So it's a working farm?"

"Sam's out milking right now."

Petri smiled, trying to warm her up. "Dairy farmers have to work on Sundays, just like detectives, don't they? It must be a hard life."

"And no money in it anymore. We're thinking about retiring."

"Do you have children?"

"Sam and I, we got three, but they're grown now and moved away."

"Do you have any hobbies?"

"Nope. Just reading."

"Oh, what do you like to read?"

"Love stories pretty much. You know, romance novels."

"How many of them do you read?"

"I dunno. Maybe five, ten a week."

"Wow, that's quite a bit. How do you get time to do all that reading?"

"No problem since the kids are grown and I got the job at Willow Glen. It's pretty quiet on nights."

"So you get to read a lot when you're on duty there?"

"Yup. Read at home too. But it's real good there."

It checked out.

Petri changed the subject, knowing he would come back to it. "What kind of person was Mr. Solaris?"

"He wasn't a problem."

"Not a problem?"

"I mean he was easy to take care of."

"Did you like him, Mrs. Grimes?"

"Sure. Everybody did."

"Did you find him intelligent?"

Mrs. Grimes possibly was slightly flustered. "Well, I really can't say. I never talked to him much. Using that letter board was real hard on me. But the others said he was real bright."

Petri could believe that Mrs. Grimes had never talked to him much. "Do you have the slightest idea who might have murdered him?" he asked.

"Nope."

"Ms. Barsten had access to him. She could have done it in the little hallway outside the supply room."

"Heather's too nice to do anything like that."

"How about one of the patients? Do you know any of them who might do such a thing?"

"Nope."

Petri switched directions again. "Was it pretty quiet the night of the murder?"

"Well, Crazy Carol—that's Rachel's roommate—got to wailing around two. She does that now and then. But Heather gave her a shot and that got her back to sleep. After that it was real quiet."

"None of the patients up and walking about?"

"Not so I remember."

"How about around four A.M., when Ms. Barsten was doing her meds with the victim by the supply room? Anyone up around then?"

"Nope."

"You didn't see Mrs. Bates wandering around?"

"Nope."

"You told me that about four-thirty, Ms. Barsten went out for a walk and came back about five."

"That's right."

"So you were alone in the nurses' station during that period?"

"Yup."

"During that period, did you see any of the patients up and around?"

"Nope."

"Did you see anyone at all?"

"Nope."

"Really, no one?"

"Don't expect so."

"Why not?"

"I would have seen them."

"But you told me you read a lot at night. Isn't it possible you might have been reading when Ms. Barsten was out for her walk? And that you might have been so absorbed in your book, you didn't notice someone go by?"

"I suppose it's possible," Bertha acknowledged reluctantly, "but it's not likely."

The time had come to get tough. "I disagree," Petri said. "I think it *is* likely. Isn't it a fact, Mrs. Grimes, that the other aides and nurses tease you about your reading, about your concentration on your novels and how a bomb could go off and you wouldn't even notice when you're reading?"

For the first time Petri saw real emotion in her. Bertha blushed, then looked afraid. "Yes, they do tease me," she said.

It had been a slight guess, but only slight. Georgia Bates had, indeed, turned out to be a most reliable witness. And now that Grimes's composure was shaken, it was time to keep the pressure on. "I also disagree, Mrs. Grimes, that you have no idea who the murderer is. I think you do know who it is. It was Ms. Barsten, wasn't it?"

But she stuck to her guns. "I told you. She's not that kind of person. I don't think so."

"Then who did do it?"

"I told you, I don't know."

"You don't know any of the patients who might have done it?"

"Nope."

"You like all the patients?"

"Sure."

Bertha's laconic composure had returned. It needed to be really broken this time, Petri thought. "I'm not sure you realize the seriousness of the situation, Mrs. Grimes. Of *your* situation. You're one of the prime suspects in this case. You had access to the victim. You had access to the murder weapon. You were alone with the victim during the time period when he was killed."

"I didn't do it!" Bertha almost jumped out of her chair in her own defense.

Petri suspected this to be true, but by now he had learned the right strategy with this woman was to keep the pressure on. "It is likely he was killed when Ms. Barsten was out for a walk," he continued. "You have no alibi. I think you'd better cooperate, Mrs. Grimes."

Bertha looked terrified. "I'll do whatever I can."

Petri went on pushing her. "You said you like all the patients. I don't believe that, Mrs. Grimes. I don't believe that all the patients are equally likable."

"Well, some aren't as likable as others. I can't say that I like Crazy

Carol with that whine of hers over and over about how someone's stolen her purse. And, of course, I don't like Rachel."

"Rachel?"

"Rachel Stimson. She's Carol's roommate."

"You said 'of course.' "

"Sure, no one likes her."

"Oh, why not?"

"Well, she hardly ever talks except to say something mean. And then she bites."

"She bites?"

"Sure. There's not a nurse or aide in Willow Glen who doesn't have Rachel's teeth marks in her arms."

"How does she bite them?"

"Sometimes when they bathe her and she's in a bad mood. Then it takes three or four aides or nurses to hold her down. That's when she bites. It hasn't been much of a problem for me because I'm on nights, and we don't do baths on nights. But once or twice a year, like when there's a big storm, they call me in to help out on days. So even I've been bitten once. I've seen her. She's vicious."

"So, do you think it's possible she killed the victim?"

"Oh no, I don't think so."

"Why not?"

"Because she's a double amputee. She's got no legs."

Petri had begun to be excited, but now his spirits sank. "She's bedridden then?"

"No, she can use a wheelchair. She can even get from her bed into it by herself. She's real strong."

Thinking back, Petri now thought he remembered her when he'd been interviewing the patients five days before. Then she was just another old lady who was clearly of no help to him. But she was probably the one sitting in a wheelchair in front of her bed. She'd seemed completely mute, responding to none of his questions. He had a thought. "You wheel her around then?"

"No. She wheels herself. She can whip around in that chair like a real pro."

"Are there some other patients you don't like?"

"Well, one other. No one likes him either."

"And who's that?"

"Hank Martin. He tries to paw all the women."

"Paw?"

"Yup. For sex. Hank the Horny we call him. He steers clear of me, though," she added with a pleased smile.

Damn, Petri thought, already the woman was starting to relax again. "Remember you're under investigation, Mrs. Grimes," he reminded her. "Do you think this Hank the Horny could have been the murderer?"

"Doubt it."

"Why not?"

"Well, no one likes him, but everyone thinks he's kind of harmless."

"What makes him harmless?"

"I dunno."

"Is he weak or bedridden?"

"No, he's ambulatory. Good health. I don't even know why he's in Willow Glen. Has a little limp, that's all."

"So he would be physically capable of killing someone?"

"Sure."

"More so than the rest of the patients?"

"Come to think of it, probably yes."

Petri paused to reflect. There had not yet been any discussion of motive. "What was the relationship like between the victim and this Hank the Horny?"

"Dunno."

"Cooperate, Mrs. Grimes," he reminded her.

"You couldn't talk with him except through his letter board. Most of the patients didn't try."

"And did Hank Martin?"

"Not that I know of."

"Is there any reason you know that might have caused Mr. Martin to dislike the victim?"

"Not that I know of."

"How about that other patient—what's her name?"

"Rachel Stimson."

"Yes, did she communicate with the victim?"

"Doubt it. Rachel doesn't usually even talk with the people it's easy to talk to."

"And is there any reason she might have had to dislike the victim?"

"Not that I know of."

Petri sensed he had probably exhausted both Bertha's knowledge and her imagination, but he persevered methodically. "Are there any other patients you don't like?"

"Nope."

"Are you sure?"

"Yes. Of course there are some I like better than others. Mrs. Grochowski, for instance. Everyone likes her. But there are no others on C-Wing I dislike."

Petri took notes. It would be impossible to keep this woman on the alert for long, but it was still best to not let her off the hook. "Thank you for your time, Mrs. Grimes," he said, "but I want to remind you that you are still one of the major suspects in this case, and I am going to require your cooperation. I do not want you to talk to anyone, not anyone, about this interview or its substance. Is that clear?"

It was.

Driving back into New Warsaw, Petri reflected on how little he still had to go on. Mrs. Grimes continued to be a suspect, although he had exaggerated this with her; she just didn't feel like a murderer. Clearly he needed to have a talk with this Hank the Horny as soon as possible. The Stimson woman might also be a lead, at least worth checking into. But Ms. Barsten remained the most likely candidate. Still, he could not help but be struck by the irony of a person who might be so buried in the fiction of a romance novel that she was unaware of a real-life murder occurring ten feet away.

## TWELVE

## *Monday, March 28th*

Peggy Valeno was in the nurses' station when Petri got to C-Wing at eight A.M. He explained that he needed to sit there to review all the patients' charts. His inclination was to go straight for the charts of Hank Martin and Rachel Stimson, but having decided the day before that there could be danger in excessive concentration on one suspect, he was determined to go through them in the order in which they were arranged. That was by room number. Only when he had scrutinized them all would he begin to draw conclusions—if any.

He had just seated himself when Heather came back from her rounds, crisp in her starched white uniform. It was an awkward moment for them both. He elected to ignore her presence. She was tempted to do likewise. But then she realized it was an opportunity to make a dig at him, to make him uncomfortable, to give him back some of what he'd dished out. "Good morning, Lieutenant," she said. "You told me you were going to keep a close watch on me, but I didn't know it would be *this* close."

Petri continued to ignore her. Her remark made him all the more embarrassed. Damn her, he thought, and reminded himself she was still his prime suspect. Was not a stance of aloof detachment only appropriate under the circumstances? He looked down at the first chart and his empty notepad, and settled down silently for a long morning's work.

What would ordinarily have been a dull weekend for Peggy had passed with astonishing rapidity. In between the dishes and other chores required of her at home with her swamp-hollow family, she had been lost in thought. She had never known that thinking could be so sustained.

What was she to do with the facts of Stephen's goodness and the evil of his murder? She either had to run away from them or go deeper. She would never know exactly why she chose the latter course.

By Saturday night Peggy didn't know whether she wanted to laugh or cry. She wanted to laugh because the confusion was over. She wanted to cry because of the clarity of the burden. The clarity was her acknowledgment that good and evil were *real*. The burden was that this acknowledgment gave her a choice. She had a choice of which kind of person—what kind of Peggy—she was going to be.

She had sat with that choice all day Sunday. Now, having learned of Tim's death as soon as she was back at work this Monday morning, she realized that she had her first opportunity to act on her acknowledgment. Mrs. Grochowski would, of course, need to be bathed. That was her job, but there was no law to say that she couldn't choose to do a little bit more than her job.

She was surprised by the effort it took as she walked into Mrs. Grochowski's room. Partly it was shyness. But partly it was an effort totally new to her: the effort of deliberate action. "I just wanted to tell you," she said, "how sorry I am for you that Tim died yesterday."

"Why, thank you, Peggy," Mrs. Grochowski smiled wanly.

"How are you holding up?"

"Well, I knew all along—we knew all along—that Tim would go soon. It's not as if it was a surprise. I'll be all right."

There didn't seem to be anything more for Peggy to say. Feeling somewhat deflated, she turned to the bathroom to get the washbasin.

"Peggy," the voice came from behind her, "come back."

Peggy turned back.

"I want you to know I really do thank you," Mrs. Grochowski said. "I'm grateful. I'm glad that you care. I'm very good at caring, but I'm just learning how to be cared about. Thank you."

Peggy beamed. Then she awkwardly shuffled her feet before saying, "It was nice of you to pick up that I was trying."

Mrs. Grochowski smiled at her. "It's more blessed to give than to receive, they say. And perhaps they're correct when you're young. But when we get older we need to learn how to receive again. I really don't know much about how to receive caring, Peggy. It's a big problem for me. For me, I think it is really more blessed to receive than to give."

"Well, I'm still young," Peggy replied, "and for me I'm just beginning to learn how to give care. In fact, you're a kind of experiment. I decided to learn how to care. But I don't know how."

"Maybe wanting to is just about all that's necessary," Mrs. Grochowski suggested. "Maybe you really don't have to do anything except care. You came to tell me you were sad about Tim. That's enough. That's all I need. I think one of the problems people have when they want to care is to feel that they have to do something to prove it. I don't need you to *do* anything, Peggy."

"But what do I do now then?"

"Maybe you would just sit here with me and hold my hand."

Peggy sat down next to Mrs. Grochowski's bed and took her hand. "But what should I say?"

"I don't want you to say anything. Just hold my hand," Mrs. Grochowski said. And then she added, "please."

Peggy held her hand. The silence seemed interminable. But finally Mrs. Grochowski began to talk. "I gave you only a part of myself, Peggy," she said. "I told you it was no surprise. And for part of me, it wasn't. The thinking part. But the heart is another matter. I don't know why it should be a surprise to the heart, but it is. I had even rehearsed it, you know. I had thought that if it took him a while to die, I would ask them to lay him next to me. And so it was. I had the last hour with him. It was just the way I wanted it, and I'm very glad for it. In one way it was very beautiful. But I didn't know it would be such a shock."

Peggy looked up and saw that Mrs. Grochowski had begun to cry quietly. "I believe in heaven, you know," Mrs. Grochowski continued. "I believe that Tim is better off now than when he was here with me in Willow Glen. But I wish I had died first. It's selfish, but that's the way it is. I'm not sad for him. I'm sad for myself. I wish he hadn't died."

Now the tears were coming faster. Peggy began to cry with her. But while Mrs. Grochowski's tears were ones of grief, hers peculiarly were ones of gratitude—almost joy. She didn't fully understand it yet, but she felt strangely privileged.


If anyone with a cane and slight limp could bounce into a room, Lucy did. "They just told me at physical therapy that I can go home tomorrow," she announced with a broad grin. "I've already called Rob and he's coming to pick me up in the morning. And on our way back we'll stop at the kennel for Wrinkles. I'm going home, Georgia. I'm going home!"

Georgia responded with delight tinged with sadness. "That's wonderful, Lucy. I'm so glad for you. But I'm going to miss you. It's been very good having you as a roommate, and I can't imagine I'll do so well with the next body."

Lucy decided to give it one last try. "But you don't have to have another roommate, Georgia. I can't believe your children can keep you here against your will. You can come home with me and then you can go to Santa Barbara with me."

"No, Lucy, I need to stay here."

"But why? You're in good health. You're not senile."

Georgia took her time to answer this woman whom she liked, yet who was so different from her. Lucy did not know all that had been going on in her mind these past three days; she had hardly begun to understand it herself. But she understood enough to reply firmly, "I need to stay here to learn."

"To learn? To learn what?"

Georgia sought for the right word. She was a little surprised at what came forth. "Power, I guess."

"Power? What do you mean?"

"Well, *you've* learned something about power here, Lucy. You've made several very powerful decisions. You've decided your life is even more important than Wrinkles's, and you've decided to totally uproot yourself and move across the country. You've taken charge of your life, power over it."

Lucy thought for a moment. "I suppose that's a good way of putting it. But I don't think it's happened because of Willow Glen, and I still don't understand about you, Georgia. What can you learn about power in this dreadful place?"

It was a good question and Georgia took her time in answering it. More had happened to her—or, rather, inside of her—over the past few days than had happened to or within her for many years. And while it was very new, it felt *right*. She felt alive. It might seem strange to Lucy and even stranger to those on the outside, but Willow Glen was a place where things happened. There was still more to sort out, but she no longer even attempted to hold on to the illusion that it was a "dreadful place" or she had been involuntarily consigned there. She thought of Heather and, above all, of Mrs. Grochowski. "There are teachers here for me, Lucy," she finally replied. "I guess people have different paths they need to travel. You have a lot to learn from concerts and Santa Barbara. The things I need to learn, for the moment at least, are in here."

"Well, I can't say that I understand it, Georgia. But it's true, you do seem more powerful than when we first met."

"Thank you. I hope you'll write to me when you get out to Santa Barbara and let me know how it is. And, Lucy, I know you don't want to—but I've thought, maybe even prayed about it—and if you do have to put Wrinkles to sleep, it's the right thing. I know it."

The tears of being understood flooded Lucy's eyes. "Georgia, you
know it's still hard for me to bend down. Would you get out of that chair
and give me a hug?"

Georgia did. It was the first embrace either of them had received in
many years.


Petri had gone back to the station for lunch and returned to finish the
charts. Now that he had reviewed them all, there was indeed some reason
to focus on the two patients Mrs. Grimes didn't like: Rachel Stimson and
Hank Martin.

Eight of the C-Wing patients had records of psychiatric consultations in
their charts. Mrs. Bates, who was one of them, damn her or bless her, had
certainly hit the nail on the head. But unlike Heather Barsten, none of the
patients was receiving any kind of ongoing psychiatric treatment. With a
single exception, the reports on them, like those of Mrs. Bates and Mr.
Martin, all centered around the issue of senility or brain damage. The
exception was Mrs. Stimson, whose report differed in other respects as
well: it was the only one that had been written by Dr. Kolnietz; it was the
only one that had been requested by Willow Glen itself to assist in patient
management; and it was the only one that made no diagnosis and suggested no concrete treatment plan. Written three years previously, it was
extremely brief: "This chronically hate-filled woman, who probably would
not be judged truly psychotic (although the issue is equivocal) demon-
strates destructive behavior that, in my opinion, is unlikely to respond to
therapeutic doses of psychoactive drugs. I therefore have nothing to rec-
ommend other than what you have already been doing: occasional brief
use of restraints, when appropriate."

The term "destructive behavior" had caught Petri's attention. It applied
only to Mrs. Stimson and Mr. Martin. The problems of the others, such
as Mrs. Bates's incontinence or Mrs. Kubrick's wandering and repetitive
refrains, could certainly be considered a nuisance—and perhaps self-
destructive—but were hardly assaultive. The theme of violence, however—
even viciousness—ran throughout Mrs. Stimson's records: incident reports
of aides and nurses who had been bitten; the vituperative weekly quarrels
between her and her husband; sudden silence alternating with unpredictable verbal assaults; and frequent mention of extraordinary strength for
someone so thin and elderly. In a different way Mr. Martin's records also
revealed a clear assaultive pattern: frequent episodes of public intoxication
and belligerence before his placement in Willow Glen and repeated

instances of unsolicited sexual advances—more than advances, actual grabbings almost bordering on attempted rape.

There was nothing in his chart to suggest that Hank Martin had had any medical training. That didn't mean he hadn't, of course. Surprisingly, however, Mrs. Bates had scored again. Even the charts alone gave witness to the fact that at least three of the C-Wing patients had in their past at some time been directly involved in health care. One was Mrs. Stimson, whose very admission note, eight years previously, began: "This seventy-four-year-old retired nurse. . . ."

But what particularly intrigued Petri was the issue of Hank Martin's residence at Willow Glen in the first place. Yes, he had had a small stroke, but hardly a disabling one. He used a cane, but a number of notes in the chart suggested he really didn't need it. Yes, he apparently had delusions of grandeur about being a flying ace in World War II, but so what? Even the state had repeatedly questioned his need for medical care. Of course, his sexual assaultiveness might possibly stem from some kind of brain damage, as Mrs. Simonton's recent report suggested, yet, as Mrs. Grimes had noted, he was physically C-Wing's most hardy patient—certainly hardy enough to commit murder. And the whole tone of his chart made him seem more like a candidate for jail than a nursing home.

Petri decided he would begin with Hank Martin. He found him sitting in the dayroom, a short and slender little man with a cane by his side. Petri noted that he looked considerably younger than the age on his chart, his short cropped hair still thick and red. "Good afternoon, Mr. Martin," he announced himself. "You may remember I spoke with you briefly early last week. Now I'm talking with some of the more alert patients at greater length to see if they can help me solve the vicious murder of the poor, helpless young man."

It pleased Hank to be recognized for his alertness. "Sure, I'll do whatever I can to be of help."

"Do you have any idea who might have done this dreadful thing?"

"I wish I did. If I had I would have grabbed him by now and brought him down to the police station."

The word "pip-squeak" came to Petri's mind. "It sounds as though you had a close relationship with the victim."

"Nope."

"Well, what kind of relationship did you have?"

There was sufficient pause for Petri to look closely at his eyes as Hank said, "We didn't really have any relationship. He wasn't easy to talk to, you know. The letter board and all."

There was fear in the eyes already, Petri thought. "You had no relationship at all?"

"No, I never spoke with him."

"What feelings did you have for him?"

"Oh, I liked him."

Petri pounced. "How could you like him when you never spoke with him, when you had no relationship at all with him?"

"Well, everyone seemed to like him," Hank said lamely. "That's what I meant." His hands started to shake.

"What are you trying to cover up, Mr. Martin?"

"Nothing."

"I don't think you're telling me the truth, Mr. Martin."

"I'm not a liar," Hank blustered, trying to sound tough, despite his trembling hands.

Petri knew exactly how to proceed. "Did you ever serve in the armed forces, Mr. Martin?"

"Yes, I was a fighter pilot during World War Two."

"Oh, when did you join up?"

"It was before Pearl Harbor," Hank said with pride. "Early 1941. I could see it coming, so I was one of those who enlisted in the Royal Canadian Air Force. Fought the Jerries over the North Atlantic."

"What were you doing before that?"

"Odd jobs. Construction mostly."

"What was the longest you'd worked at one of those jobs?"

It was a question for which Hank was not prepared. "A couple of months," he blurted out.

"When were you born, Mr. Martin?"

"Nineteen-ten."

As expected, it didn't hang together. Whether or not this pip-squeak was the killer he didn't know, but Petri did know that he was dealing with a liar, and not a likable one at that. He had no hesitation in breaking him down. "If you're telling me the truth, which I don't believe, that means you were thirty-one when you joined the service. It also sounds like you were pretty much of a deadbeat, doing odd jobs. They didn't train thirty-one-year-old deadbeats to be fighter pilots, Mr. Martin."

Hank's right hand was spasmodically scratching his left forearm. "I served my country," he said.

"Of course you would have a discharge certificate," Petri continued. "But even if you were to tell me you'd lost it, it wouldn't matter. There are records of these things. It would be simple for me to check them, although I certainly hope you wouldn't want to put me to any unnecessary trouble."

Hank looked miserable. "I was an auto mechanic in the army during the war," he confessed. "I've never been overseas."

"Thank you, Mr. Martin; that sounds more realistic. But I'm still not pleased with you. Five minutes ago you emphatically told me you weren't a liar and then you immediately lied to me. What are you trying to cover up, Mr. Martin? That you're a coward and a weakling?"

"I'm not," Hank protested.

"Let's arm-wrestle then." Petri got up and moved a small magazine table between their two chairs. He could tell that Hank, trying to prove himself, was not holding back. They did both arms. Petri, young and vigorous, could have beaten him with either, but made no attempt to bring the match to a conclusion. He had learned what he wanted: that Hank Martin was quite strong indeed for a slender man of seventy-eight—if that was, in fact, his age—and certainly strong enough to drive a scissors blade into another man's heart.

"Have you ever had any medical training, Mr. Martin?"

"Yes." Here Hank could honestly say that there had been some glamor in his life. "I've worked for several fire departments and as an ambulance technician."

"Point to your heart."

With instant accuracy Hank touched his index finger to his chest two inches to the left of his lower breastbone.

"Mr. Martin, it's quite possible you murdered Mr. Solaris," Petri said matter-of-factly.

"I didn't," Hank said emphatically.

"But how can I believe you when I already know you've lied to me at least once this afternoon?"

Hank looked terrified. "I told you I didn't."

"What were you doing between four and six A.M. on the night of the murder?"

"Sleeping in my room."

"Is there anyone who can witness to the fact that you were asleep in your room during that period?"

Hank thought of Tim O'Hara, who had left the room that night and, in any case, was now dead. "I don't know," he said, "I was asleep."

"I wish I could believe you, Mr. Martin, but the fact is you have no alibi."

Hank looked even more terrified. Petri had sensed him to be a cowardly man, but the depth of his fear—so much greater than Barsten's had been—seemed inordinate, even under these circumstances. That is, unless he was guilty. Petri thought he had been covering up something from the very beginning, something to do with a relationship with the victim. He sustained the silence, both to plot his next strategy and to let Hank squirm. "You told me you had no relationship to the victim," he said at last.

"That's right."

"I don't believe you, Mr. Martin. I believe you're covering something up."

"I'm not. I'm not covering anything up."

"I'll tell you what, Mr. Martin. I was thinking back there a minute ago how I ought to take you down to the station, book you on suspicion of murder, and put you in a cell. You've been in a cell before, haven't you? But I've decided to be kind to you. I've decided to give you a night to think about it. What I'm going to do is come back in the morning—oh, about eight-thirty probably—and I'm going to have another little chat with you again, and that's when you're going to tell me what you're covering up. In the meantime, I don't want you to do anything rash. I'm going to ask the security guards to keep a close check on you. You can go now, Mr. Martin. See you in the morning."

Petri watched him scurry out of the dayroom. His chart was correct. He had a slight limp, but he truly didn't seem to need his cane and he could move speedily. Yes, Hank Martin was very much a suspect. Petri wrote up his notes.

Then he turned his attention to Mrs. Stimson, obviously a less likely suspect being a wheelchair-bound double amputee. Still, there was this theme of viciousness running through her records, and he was beginning to resist his tendency to concentrate on a single suspect. His interview with Stimson deserved its own strategy.

He found her alone in her room, sitting in her wheelchair, not reading, doing nothing, as if waiting. Waiting for what? He pulled up the rocking chair and sat down. "I'm Lieutenant Petri," he announced. "I don't know if you remember it, but I spoke to you briefly last week when I was just beginning to look into the murder of Stephen Solaris. Now I'm talking to each of the patients in a bit more detail. I need your cooperation. Would you help me?"

Rachel stared at him, but said nothing. Petri found the stare intriguing. It gave nothing away. The face was old—very old—although the tight, thin skin was oddly smooth and said nothing of the person behind it. Slightly reminiscent of the victim's face, he thought idly, except that the eyes were dulled neither by death or age. They were bright, piercing, and utterly unrevealing.

"Is there anything you can tell me that might help me to solve this terrible affair?"

Silence.

"Well, I didn't really expect you to be able to. Mainly at this point I'm just interested in getting to know the people in Willow Glen better—particularly those on this wing and particularly the old-timers. I understand you've been here about eight years?"

Silence.

"How did you happen to come to Willow Glen?"

Silence.

Petri looked at the uneven stumps of legs visible against the fabric of her lap robe. "I imagine it must have something to do with your diabetes and your amputations. It must be difficult for you to be bound to a wheelchair." His tone was sympathetic.

Silence.

"I gather you used to be a nurse. I suppose it must be doubly difficult for you to have to be taken care of when you used to do the caring."

Silence.

Petri had been expecting it. He had also prepared a possible provocation. "Well, I guess it's not possible for you to carry on a reasonable conversation," he said. "There was no reason for me to count on help from someone who's over the hill, who's senile."

There was no rise to the bait. Was it because the fish was too sluggish or too smart? The eyes did not look sluggish.

Well, he had lined up another provocation, this one more legitimate. "I'm sorry about that last remark. It wasn't very kind, was it?" he said. "But detective work often isn't kind. It's more about justice than kindness. And that gives me a problem with you, Mrs. Stimson. Your records suggest that you are not senile; that you can speak quite lucidly and to the point when you want to. So apparently you do not want to answer my questions. But do you know what we call it when someone refuses to answer a police detective's questions? We call it obstruction of justice. You don't want to be guilty of obstructing justice, do you?"

Petri waited for two minutes and there was still no answer. "Well, you are old and ill," he continued. "I suppose you've done the best you could. It's your roommate's turn next: Mrs. Kubrick. I like to interview privately. You wouldn't mind if I wheeled you into the dayroom, would you? So I can bring Mrs. Kubrick back here?"

Although it was the very thing he was watching for, Petri was startled when Rachel Stimson, with a series of amazingly coordinated flicks of the wrist, whipped her wheelchair around his right side, then past him. He turned around just in time to see her reach far forward, turn the knob, pull the door open into the room and hold it wide open while she sped out into the corridor.

He ambled into the corridor himself. She was already out of sight. He walked to the nurses' station and turned left to where he knew he would find Mrs. Kubrick in her geri-chair. She clutched at him immediately, whining her predictable refrain. Petri was not disconcerted. Maybe he was getting used to this crazy place, he thought. He wheeled her back to the room she shared with Rachel and placed her chair in the center of the floor. Then he closed the door, pulled the rocking chair around to face her, and sat down. "Well, Mrs. Kubrick, we meet again," he said.

There was no response.

"How do you like your roommate, Mrs. Stimson?"

There was no response.

"Who do you think might have stolen your purse?"

No response.

"Why won't they let you see your doctor?"

No response.

"Mrs. Kubrick, is there anything you can tell me which might help me solve this murder? I really need your help."

Carol's eyes were utterly vacant. Petri was not surprised. In fact, the little interview had been a ruse. Its real purpose had been to make Rachel Stimson believe the statement that he was routinely interviewing all the patients and to give him the opportunity to see how she worked her wheelchair. Bertha Grimes had been right; Mrs. Stimson was indeed a pro on wheels. He had also not failed to notice how quietly the chair moved. He had noted some other things as well. The door was quite heavy, not that easy to pull open, and its knob was at approximately the same level as a gurney. "Thank you, Mrs. Kubrick," he said. "You've been of more help than you know." And he wheeled her back to her accustomed spot outside the nurses' station.

But what was he to do now? Petri drove back to the police station with mixed emotions. It felt like a successful day. He was pleased with the way he had conducted the interviews with Mrs. Stimson and Mr. Martin. He had definitely succeeded in uncovering two new suspects. But the success was chiefly productive of confusion. Over the past thirty-six hours his focus had moved from a single suspect to four—which was no focus at all. And how many more suspects might there be? If this was progress, it was progress only deeper into darkness.

He reminded himself that Barsten remained his primary suspect; so many things pointed to her. But he could not rule out Bertha Grimes, the reader of romances, admittedly present at the scene of the crime through-out the entire period when it could have been committed. Witness or perpetrator? How could she be so unaware as to be no witness at all? There was an elusiveness to this lack of awareness, and he found it hard to be certain that her appearance as an unpretentious, almost stupid country woman was not just that: an appearance, a very sophisticated guise of unpretentiousness, a brilliant lie. Stimson didn't lie, she didn't even talk; and it remained difficult to countenance the possibility that an eighty-two-year-old, wheelchair-bound, diabetic double amputee could be a murderer. But there was that persistent viciousness in her history and he had proved to his own satisfaction that she was as mobile in that wheelchair as any ambulatory patient, even as mobile as Martin. Martin, however, was a more likely candidate. He didn't merely have the strength and medical knowledge; he was an obvious liar, sleazy as slime. Petri remembered the slime in his dream. Dreams, of course, had nothing to do with reality. But he knew in his gut that Martin was covering something up.

What to do now? Yes, he was deep in the dark. But as he pulled into the station, a couple of moves, at least, were clear. He could ask Mitchell to check all the three new suspects—Grimes, Stimson, and Martin—for priors. And he had already set the scene for follow-up with Hank Martin. It would be interesting indeed to see what the little man would have to say in the morning after a whole night to reflect upon the sins of his soul.

## THIRTEEN

## *Tuesday, March 29th*

Petri arrived at Willow Glen to see Hank Martin with some new information. None of it was really startling. Bertha Grimes had no record whatsoever of a prior arrest or any association with an investigation. Martin, as expected, had a very lengthy record of public intoxication and disturbing the peace. He'd spent many a night in jail. But there was nothing major: no burglaries, no weapons charges, no serious assaults. Mildly intriguing, however, was the matter of Mrs. Stimson. One night, eight years before, she had phoned the station charging her husband with assault. When the policemen arrived at the house there was no evidence she was harmed. Strangely, it was her husband whose face was covered with scratch marks. No action had been taken. But it was odd, Petri thought, that the woman should have called for help when she, herself, was the apparent assailant.

This time he found Hank Martin in his room. Hank was there deliberately. It would not be long before he had another roommate, but since Tim O'Hara's death a day and a half before he had had the bedroom to himself. That was fortunate. Hank did not want anyone to hear what he would have to say.

"Well, Mr. Martin," Petri began, "you've had a whole night to think about what you're going to tell me."

"Could you please close the door?" Hank asked.

Petri looked at him. He must have had an uncomfortable night. The man had begun to appear his age, bleary-eyed and even more tremulous than the day before. Petri shut the door. "Yes?"

"I've got nothing much to say," Hank muttered.

"Yes?"

"I mean, I really didn't cover up anything important."

"Yes?"

"It's not like it's any big deal."

Petri waited for the squirming man to open up.

"The only way I covered up, really," Hank continued, peering at the floor, "was when I told you I liked him. I didn't like him."

"Go on."

"That's all."

"And why didn't you like the victim, Mr. Martin?"

"Because he got all the attention," Hank blurted. "Especially from Heather. She wouldn't give me the time of day, but she was always hanging around him."

Petri was struck once again by the strange power the crippled young man apparently had had to affect others. But the information clearly fit into the picture he was developing of life in Willow Glen. "So you were jealous of him?"

"I suppose you could call it that," Hank admitted, still staring at the floor.

"Jealousy is a very common motive for murder, Mr. Martin."

"I didn't do it," Hank whined. "I told you I didn't do it. I never even really touched him."

He was still holding back, Petri thought. "What do you mean, never *really* touched him?"

"Nothing. I didn't mean anything."

"I'm fed up with your continuing cover-up," Petri snapped. "I'm afraid I have no choice, Mr. Martin, except to take you down to . . ."

"I only hit his gurney," Hank broke in. "I never touched him."

Petri had been prepared for an admission of murder, not this kind of hostile action. "You hit his gurney?" he repeated dumbly.

"Yeah." Hank looked miserable.

"With what?"

"With my cane."

"You mean you actually went up to a crippled man, lying there totally helpless, and you hit his bed, his only support, with your cane?"

The question was rhetorical. Needing time to think, Petri did not press for an answer. For Hank the two minutes of silence were unbearable. Finally the detective asked, "And what else did you do to him?"

"Nothing. I told you. I never even spoke with him. And I never touched his body."

"I don't believe you, Mr. Martin."

"But it's true!"

"How can I believe you, Mr. Martin? You're a liar, remember? You've already lied to me twice."

Hank raised his hand and laid it over his heart. "I swear to God it's true." The hand was less tremulous now.

Fortunately for Hank, less fortunately in terms of finding a solution to the murder, Petri did tend to believe him. He found this little man totally offensive, but the action he described did seem more in tune with his character than murder. "Is there any other piece of information you're withholding, either about yourself, or the victim, or anyone else," he asked, "that might even possibly have a bearing on the crime?"

"Nothing. I swear it."

"Mr. Martin, you remain my number one suspect in this case. *Anything* you do to clear yourself of suspicion will be to your benefit. If anything comes to your mind, you just . . ."

"If I find out who he is," Hank interrupted, "I'll grab him and bring him to you."

Petri had had all he could take. "Aren't you afraid, Mr. Martin?"

"No. Why should I be?"

"Because if you're not the murderer, someone else is, and maybe you're next on that someone's list. Aren't you afraid that some night— maybe tonight—when you're alone in this room—maybe when you're asleep—somebody's going to come in and drive a pair of scissors into your heart, Mr. Martin?"

"Nah, I'm not afraid."

"You're lying, Mr. Martin."

"No," Hank protested. "I'm not."

"Yes, you are. You're lying because you're a liar and you're lying because you're a coward. You're a bully, Mr. Martin, and all bullies are cowards."

Petri turned on his heel and walked straight from the room without looking back.

He stopped when he got to the nurses' station, went in and sat down. Damn! Now where? If Martin was telling the truth—and he suspected the little creep was—then it was another blind alley. There was Stimson, but that was a narrow alley indeed. Vicious, yes, but so old and crippled. Still, she could sure work that wheelchair. Vicious, but why would she have accused her husband of assaulting her when she was the assaulter? Paranoia, probably. Yet something about it gnawed at him. Petri extracted her chart from the rack.

He began with the admission note, again reading "This seventy-four-year-old retired nurse . . ." when his eye was caught by the date on the right upper corner of the page: August 13, 1980. It struck a chord. Petri looked to see if there was anyone in the vicinity of the nurses' station. The nurse and aide were elsewhere. Only Mrs. Kubrick was around, strapped in her geri-chair. He picked up the phone, dialed the station, and asked for Sergeant Mitchell. "Bill," he asked when they were connected, "you know the prior on the Stimson woman—not the prior but the report of that incident—you don't happen to remember the date of the report, the incident, do you?"

"Sure," Mitchell answered. "I've got it on my desk still. Wait a minute. Here it is. August 8, 1980."

"Interesting," Petri told him. "I'm over here at Willow Glen, looking at her chart. She was admitted here five days afterwards."

"Sir?" There was a tentative tone in Mitchell's voice.

"Yes, Bill. What is it?"

"Well, I don't know why you're interested in her, but since you are, there is one little thing you might want to know about that incident."

"Yes."

"I wasn't directly involved, so I don't really know anything more about it, except that it was unusual from a procedural point of view. The chief directed that it not be put in the log at the time. He had it added to the log a couple of weeks later, just before it was transcribed into the computer. He occasionally does that—probably no more than once a year—when he doesn't think an incident ought to get into the newspapers."

"Why didn't he want it to get into the papers?"

"No idea, except her husband's a bigwig in town."

"Thanks, Bill." Petri hung up appreciatively. His sergeant was turning out to be very competent indeed. It had been a good move coming to New Warsaw. But he wondered why the chief had wanted to keep it out of the papers. Small item, yet another little question left dangling about Mrs. Stimson. He was becoming quite curious about her. He could ask around: Simonton, the staff, old neighbors, her husband, other patients, Dr. Kolnietz. But what could they tell him that he didn't already know— that she was a mean old lady who could whip a mean wheelchair and once was a nurse? Probably not much. They couldn't tell him whether or not she had stabbed Stephen Solaris, and *why*. Only she could tell him that, and she wasn't talking. He wanted to get inside her mind—at least a little inside—the way he'd gotten into Hank Martin's. But how do you search out the inner self of someone who won't speak, who refuses to be searched out?

Search! That was it. He could do a search. He had no idea what he would be searching for, but what better way to get into the mind of someone who wouldn't talk than to search her belongings, the things closest to her, the things in her closets and drawers, the intimate things that might reveal the character of their owner? Yes, a search should be next. But there were problems. Petri ticked them off, one by one, his mind forging ahead like clockwork, racing against impatience. They were solvable problems, he calculated; the question, however, was the speed with which he could overcome them. He was on a roll again and wanted a shortcut. And, whether he liked it or not, Mrs. Simonton was the key to the shortcut. As he shot up to the front office, almost running, he was painfully aware of his failure to nurture a relationship with the director of Willow Glen.

"Well, Lieutenant," she said when he burst into her office, "you seem excited. What's up? And would you like some coffee?"

It was welcoming—more than he deserved or expected—leaving him feeling all the more chastened. "Yes. Please, if you don't mind." He decided to get it over with quickly. "You'll be glad to know Ms. Barsten isn't my only suspect anymore. Not that she's off my list."

"Indeed, I am. And most curious. Who else is on your list?"

"Mrs. Stimson, among some others."

She was relieved, and she was pleased to see this new flexibility in the young lieutenant. "You may not be barking up the right tree, but it doesn't feel like a wrong one."

"I've gathered she's not necessarily the nicest lady in the world."

"That's a fair statement. But how did you get on to her?"

"I wish I could tell you through my brilliance," Petri said wryly, "but it was Mrs. Bates. The reason she had summoned me was to tell me she felt badly that she had not given a more balanced view. Then she proceeded to do so. In several ways. It was quite an eye-opener. She is a very clever woman."

Well, the world is indeed full of surprises, Mrs. Simonton thought. If Georgia had been more successful than she herself in influencing Petri's one-track mind, she was clever, all right. Far more clever than she looked. There might be a lot of potential there. A sentence flitted through her head: "Come with me and I will make you fishers of men." Why did these absurd Bible verses keep coming to her? But she filed the information away for future use. She and Georgia Bates might just do a little fishing together. "In what way did she open your eyes?" she asked Petri.

"She was the one who told me that she'd observed Ms. Barsten having sex with the victim on the night of the murder. She wanted to let me know additionally that she'd walked around the nurses' station three times that night without Mrs. Grimes ever noticing her. She told me Mrs. Grimes reads romance novels at night with such ferocity a bomb could go off without her noticing it. I interrogated Mrs. Grimes later, and it checks out. It's at least conceivable that someone could have murdered the victim right next to her without her looking up. Not just Ms. Barsten. Anyone."

Mrs. Simonton wrote herself a note on the pad on her desk. She would have to deal with Bertha on this. "What's that got to do with Rachel Stimson?" she asked.

"Mrs. Bates also pointed out how I'd been underestimating the patients. She made it clear that others may be having sexual lives. She suggested some of them might have had medical or medically related training and that some of them might also have seen a psychiatrist. Frankly, I never thought about any of these things."

"And?"

"And so I started going through the patients' charts much more thoroughly. Mrs. Stimson's is quite revealing. She's clearly a violent person. She's able to get around. And she used to be a nurse."

Mrs. Simonton thought about Rachel Stimson: the Saturday night rages and those furious eyes. But an amputee in a wheelchair? "It's startling," she said to Petri, "but that's mostly because of the wheelchair. God knows I've seen her *look* murderous."

Petri told her of the reports of Rachel's strength and his own observation of her silent skill in maneuvering the chair. Simonton digested it and nodded. "What now?" she asked.

"Now is when I need your help. When I tried to talk with her yesterday afternoon, she wouldn't say a word. So I'm stuck with trying to probe someone who won't talk. One of the few ways I can think to do that is to search her room."

"For what?"

"I don't know. That's part of my problem."

"But how can I help?"

"By giving me permission. I haven't asked her yet, but since she won't talk to me in the first place, I doubt that she'd give it. I could get a warrant eventually, but that would take up valuable time. I was hoping you could help me. You told me sometimes you allow patients to have scissors and sometimes you don't. You must have authority to search their belongings."

Mrs. Simonton sat back, inhaling her cigarette deeply. She could see it might, indeed, take time to get a warrant on such vague suspicion to search for nothing in particular. The question of her own authority to search the patients' rooms, however, was ambiguous. A few patients were committed by the court to her care, but almost all of them, like Rachel Stimson, were there supposedly of their own free will, even though usually there was no place else for them to go. Still she was responsible for them, and more often than not that meant the aides packing and unpacking their drawers, going through their clothes to see which were clean and which needed laundering, as well as searching for sequestered medications, hidden food that had begun to smell, and knives or scissors that might be dangerous. But the authority to do so had never been subject to legal test. She would be liable if she didn't exercise it, but theoretically she might be liable if she did. And if there was trouble, it would be with just the wrong person. Hubert Stimson was not only a power in New Warsaw, he was one of the major benefactors of Willow Glen.

"I don't know," she said. "I just don't know. There are so many factors to be considered. One of them, Lieutenant, which you may not be aware of, is that Rachel's husband is something of a big shot in town, a member of my board, and one of my regular financial contributors."

"I've been learning he's apparently an important man," Petri said, "although I didn't know he was on your board. Maybe there's another piece of information you can give me. I had Mrs. Stimson checked for priors, and lo and behold, like Ms. Barsten, there was a record of domestic violence. Eight years ago she phoned the police one night charging her husband with assault. When they got to the house, they couldn't find any evidence she'd been assaulted. No sign of injury. In fact, he was the one who showed signs of injury. He had scratch marks all over his face. So we didn't do anything. But there's something intriguing. Do you know it was only five days after that incident that she was admitted here?"

"That *is* intriguing," Mrs. Simonton agreed, "and all the more so because I wasn't aware of it. But I'm not sure what to make of it; as far as I know, she wasn't forced here."

"What do you think would happen if we asked Mr. Stimson for permission to search her belongings?"

Mrs. Simonton was quick to respond. "He wouldn't give it. He's a suspicious old bastard."

"You don't like him?"

"No. I don't have to, thank God. It's pretty much a pro forma board. But he's pompous and . . . I don't know how to put it into words . . . there's something not—not *good*—about him." Petri was surprised by the intensity of her tone. "I don't know how else to express it," she said. "And it's just a gut feeling I have. But it feels real. I mean it."

The disconcerting possibility he might have yet another suspect flitted through Petri's mind. A visitor, an elderly man, an important man, slinking into Willow Glen at four o'clock in the morning? It was a bizarre notion, but this was a crazy place and a crazy case with an increasing number of weird angles. Still, for his own sanity, he'd best stick to the matter at hand. "Well, are you going to help me?" he asked.

Mrs. Simonton lit another cigarette. The idea of a double amputee being a murderer was still startling. But as she had said to Petri, he was barking up the right sort of tree. There was something ugly about both Stimsons. This was one of those times she wished she didn't have responsibility—or not so much of it. She could easily be hurt. At the very least Hubert Stimson might stop his donations. But she not only had a responsibility to protect Rachel's legal rights; she had a responsibility to protect all her patients.

"Yes," she decided. "I'll help you. First you must ask her for her permission in my presence. If she refuses it, I'll have to back her up and you'll just have to get a warrant if you're to continue. But if she keeps her usual angry silence and says nothing, you have my permission to search her room—again, only in my presence. Okay?"

"Okay. Now?"

Having made up her mind, Mrs. Simonton wanted to get it over with. "There's nothing more important to either of us than getting this resolved, is there? Yes, now."

As they walked to the wing, Petri commented, "She's never said a word to me when I've questioned her. She looks alert, but she must be pretty much out of it."

"Rachel's unpredictable, but no, she's not out of it. Usually she won't talk, but when she does, she's quite lucid. And often foul-mouthed."

They passed Crazy Carol in the corridor and found Mrs. Stimson alone in her room, sitting in her wheelchair facing the doorway. Except for a brief flicker in her eyes that might or might not have been a reaction to them, her facial expression was impenetrable.

She had no lap robe today and in spite of himself, Petri glanced down at the hem of her skirt and the empty space beneath it. He pulled himself together. "Good morning, Mrs. Stimson," he said. "I'm Lieutenant Petri of the police department. You'll remember that we spoke yesterday. That is, I spoke. You wouldn't answer my questions."

Silence.

He tried again. "I need to talk with you, Mrs. Stimson. I need to know more about you. I need to ask you some questions and it's hard to learn about someone who won't talk."

Silence.

Well, it was what he had expected, though not what he'd hoped for. Okay, on to the next step. "This is a police investigation," he said. "It's essential that I learn about you. If you won't talk, the only way I can do that is to search your room. Do I have your permission to do that?"

Rachel still did not answer. Petri realized that what was bothering him most was not her lack of response but her eyes. They seemed to be looking *through* him. One second they were totally blank, dead, just like Crazy Carol Kubrick's. The next moment he felt them penetrating him with an intensity that was—or was it his imagination?—naked malice.

He swallowed. "Do I have your permission, Mrs. Stimson?" he repeated.

Now he wondered whether he saw a flicker of fear, but if so it was gone in an instant. "Since you are either unable or unwilling to respond to me," he said, "I am going to take the liberty."

Despite his thoroughness, the search was brief. She had, he noticed, relative to other patients, few possessions. No photographs. No get-well cards. No family mementos. A bureau with three drawers. He emptied them out one at a time. Underclothes, nightclothes, cotton blouses, sweaters. He did not unfold them, but he laid each one on top of the bureau and felt it separately. There was nothing, not even jewelry. He felt her sheets. He lifted the mattress. He looked under her bed, under the nightstand. He rummaged through the nightstand drawer: hairpins, a handkerchief, an old bottle of perfume. Not even a pen or stationery. No handbag. She could have been a hermit. He went into the bathroom. Two toothbrushes. Two tubes of toothpaste. One hairbrush. He went to the closet. "How can I tell which are her dresses and which are her roommate's?" he asked.

"I can't tell you without checking the name tapes," Mrs. Simonton replied, "but you have my permission to look at Mrs. Kubrick's clothes as well."

He smoothed his hands over each dress and skirt. He checked the pockets of the two coats hanging there. He emptied every shoe. He surveyed the shelf. There was nothing.

He was strangely disappointed, given the fact there was nothing specific he was looking for. He came back to the center of the room and gazed around it. He realized he had only searched half of it. "Her roommate—what's her name? Kubrick?" he said to Mrs. Simonton, "you gave me permission to go through her clothes in the closet. May I go through the rest of the room as well?"

Mrs. Simonton reminded herself that Carol was clearly one of those patients who was not responsible for herself. And that there was no way she could be implicated in murder. But she saw no harm in letting Petri continue. "Yes, you can search it if you want to."

On the opposite side of the room, Petri again went through the night-stand, looked under it, looked under the bed, felt the sheets, the mattress. Nothing. He went to Mrs. Kubrick's bureau. He lifted each piece of clothing from the top drawer. Then the middle one. Then the bottom one. "Holy Christ!" he exclaimed.

Mrs. Simonton was startled. "What is it? What's wrong?"

"What's *wrong*? Look! Look!"

With both his hands Petri had lifted up the clothing on the left side of the drawer. On the bottom lay a rumpled square of brown linen, the adhesive still taped to it, and two white, powdered plastic gloves.


Hank had been sitting in his room for the past hour, nursing his rage. That stupid pig of a lieutenant. How dare that pig call him—him, Hank Martin—a coward? Maybe he hadn't been a fighter pilot, but so what? He was no coward.

Why did they all think he should be afraid of the murderer? First it had been Mrs. Simonton with her speech in the dining hall. Then it had been Peggy. Now it was the pig detective. He even tried to make himself afraid. He recollected Stephen's body lying there that morning with the scissors stuck into his chest and Peggy screaming. No, no fear. Then he tried to imagine the murderer stabbing his, Hank's, chest with the same pair of scissors. At first it was difficult because he had no picture of the murderer in his mind. But then he fantasized a huge, burly man with a black hood over his face, an executioner. Still no fear. The executioner simply stuck the scissors in and it was over. That was that.

Hank exerted himself. He imagined that the scissors were twice as large, that they were almost a large pair of shears, that the executioner had to use all his strength to shove them in between his ribs. No, still no fear. Hank Martin was a man without fear!

He was no coward and no bully. Imagine, calling him a bully! It was the pig detective who was the bully. Like all the other police. All the pigs were bullies. And all his life he'd been picked on by them. He'd always been their victim. He'd been the victim of them and all the other bullies. Just because he was small. He remembered the times he'd been forced down on the sidewalk, being pummeled, squeezing his legs together, trying to protect his vital parts.

And then a fantasy did come to him. One without exertion, a fantasy unbidden. Suddenly Hank saw himself stretched out on the gurney, na-ked, in a small room with the same burly, hooded executioner. Only now the executioner did not have the same huge pair of scissors. He merely had a small—almost tiny—razor blade, tucked daintily between his thumb and forefinger. The executioner delicately approached Hank's naked penis with the edge of the blade and slowly . . .

With a whelp of sheer animal terror Hank shot up from his chair and whirled around the center of the room searching for protection. There was no one. Where was Tim? Why wasn't Tim O'Hara there? But Tim was dead. Tim had died. Why did he have to die? Wasn't there anyone? "Oh, Jesus," Hank wailed. "Jesus. Jesus. Help me. Please. Help me. Help me."

Petri and Simonton had walked back from Rachel Stimson's room in stunned silence. Even when they were back in her office they sat together speechless. "Do you think Mrs. Kubrick did it?" Petri finally asked.

"Lieutenant, I think that there are only two patients on C-Wing who could *not* have done it. One is Mrs. Grochowski, who's paralyzed from the neck down and totally bedridden. The other is Carol Kubrick. She's always restrained, night and day, except when she's being walked." Mrs. Simonton smiled. "I know you're well aware that we can get careless, and Carol has gotten out of her restraints. But believe me, that's rare indeed."

Petri not only believed her, but added, "And that was the night of her screaming fit. She was given a sedative a couple of hours before the murder, which would have put her doubly out of the picture. So I suppose someone else put the wrapping and gloves there."

"I would suppose so."

"And that could have been anybody. It could have been Ms. Barsten. It could have been Mrs. Grimes. It could even have been you, Mrs. Simonton."

"Certainly. Theoretically."

"But I also suppose Mrs. Stimson would be the most likely candidate," Petri mused out loud. "And if Mrs. Stimson did put them there, it tells us something else."

"What's that?"

"One of the criteria of insanity, we're taught in our training, is when a criminal makes no attempt to hide his tracks. If he—or in this case, she—tries to cover up, it's a sign she knew what she was doing was wrong. If Mrs. Stimson really did put them in Mrs. Kubrick's drawer instead of her own, it would probably be because she didn't want them found in her possession. She may not be as out of it as she appears."

"I had suggested that," Mrs. Simonton said mildly.

"I want Mrs. Kubrick moved to another room. Can you do that?"

"Yes."

"I'd also like a guard posted by Mrs. Stimson's door. Could you assign your security guard there until I get down to the station? I'll see to it that we provide round-the-clock coverage. Will that be all right?"

"Certainly." Mrs. Simonton could see that he was itching to move into action and was on the verge of leaving. "Lieutenant, I'd like to call Heather to let her know you've got another suspect. She's off duty for the next three days, and I hate to think of her sitting at home worrying that you're still about to put her in jail."

"No!" Petri said firmly, almost harshly. "For all I know she could have put the wrapper and gloves there. Ms. Barsten is not off the hook by a long shot. I appreciate you giving me permission to search Stimson's room, but I would also appreciate it if you'd keep quiet about all this until we've got things more pinned down."

Mrs. Simonton swore under her breath. An hour earlier he'd been all smiles, telling her that Heather wasn't his only suspect, and now with some real evidence against Stimson he was still behaving as if the girl were on the top of his list. There were moments when she quite liked him—his drive, his conscientiousness, his analytic mind. Even, for a while there, what she thought was a new and welcome flexibility. But the next moment he'd turn callous and officious. Maybe he needed to be, maybe he was just doing his job, but he certainly had the capacity to make her wax hot and cold in response to him. And she kept having the feeling that for some reason, not at all clear to her, he actually had something personal against Heather. She recollected all too vividly, however, that when she'd tried to confront him on this before it had done more harm than good. "Whatever you say, Lieutenant" was all she answered as he turned to leave, not hiding the coldness in her response.

When he got back to the station, Petri was discomfited to learn that the chief had left to have lunch with a colleague in the next county and would not return until midafternoon. He would have liked to have shared his excitement with his boss. But it helped to bring Sergeant Mitchell up-to-date, to talk with another professional. And there was something else he could do to prepare himself before the chief got back. After asking Mitchell to arrange for policemen to be assigned around the clock to Mrs. Stimson's room, he phoned Dr. Kolnietz. He told the psychiatrist about his discovery of the morning and asked to speak with him about Stimson.

"We've been through this before, Lieutenant," Kolnietz reminded him. "I can't even tell you whether I have such a patient without her written permission."

"You did have her as a patient," Petri said. "You were called to Willow

Glen several years ago to consult because of her violence. I've seen your report in her chart."

"I still can't speak with you without her permission."

"Look, Doctor," Petri said testily, "we're talking about a very different case than that of Ms. Barsten. Mrs. Stimson won't even talk with me. She's not going to sign a permission. Your own report suggested she may be psychotic, and if that's true, she's not even competent to sign. Everything I know about her husband says that he wouldn't give permission either, even if he had the authority to do so. So I've got no other choice than to get a court order to talk to you. That takes time, and meanwhile someone else may get murdered because you're being so rigid. For Christ's sake, can't you bend just a little bit?"

Kolnietz found the line of argument persuasive. Still, he probably would not have bent had he not remembered Rachel Stimson quite clearly. "Hell, I don't even know whether she's competent to sign," he said, "but it begins to look as though we're falling into the habit of having lunch together, Lieutenant."

And, indeed, he was unwrapping his sandwich when their talk began. Petri wasted no time in getting to the point. "Why is she violent? What makes her tick?"

"Hate."

"*Hate?*"

"Yes. She is possibly the most hateful person I have ever seen. Usually I wouldn't even remember a patient I saw for a single, one-hour consultation three years ago. But I remember her. She was filled with hate. It seemed to govern everything she thinks or feels."

Petri was taken aback by the simplicity of this—this monosyllable. *Hate?* Surely it should be more complicated. "In your report you were unclear whether or not she was psychotic. Why? What do you mean by psychotic?" he asked.

"Ah, Lieutenant, that's not an easy one. When she talked to me, Mrs. Stimson was quite lucid. She knew where she was. She knew what day, month, and year it was. She was largely capable of taking care of herself. She could plan and make logical decisions. Many psychiatrists would not have called her psychotic."

"So, if she committed a crime, you think she is the kind of person who would have sufficient forethought to attempt to cover her tracks?"

"Very possibly."

"Then why did you say maybe she was psychotic?"

"Because hatred so drives her life."

They were back to hate. "What is psychotic about that?"

"Many psychiatrists would say, nothing. But it's a horrible way to live. Hatred is a normal emotion. It's a reasonable response to a serious insult. But when it consumes someone, as it seems to with Mrs. Stimson, it gets to be in control of the personality. It begins to take leave of reality. It develops a life of its own. Her hatred was not rational. At least not any longer. It was no longer a reasonable response to an insult. She no longer governed it. It governed her. I happen to believe it's possible to call a way of being like that psychotic."

Petri could understand. But he had a strange sense he was being sucked into a quagmire. "What makes such a person so hateful?" he inquired.

"I don't know."

"You don't know?"

"That's right. I'm a psychiatrist and should know about such things, but I don't. Psychiatry doesn't know. No one knows, except perhaps God."

His sense was right. It was a quagmire. "Lord, don't you know anything!"

"Oh, we know some things. We know the process. But not enough to explain it. There's a sort of economics to the soul. It's the equivalent of the way the rich get richer and the poor get poorer. People who are love-filled tend to become filled with even more love. People who are hate-filled tend to become even more hateful. But we really don't understand about the dividing line between them—why one person goes one way and another another way. To what extent it is people's childhood experiences, to what extent it is their later experiences, to what extent it is their heredity and genes, to what extent it is their free will, to what extent it is the intervention of strange cosmic forces or God, we simply don't know."

"I don't believe it."

"Well, you had better."

The lecture was hardly clarifying. "Isn't there *any* explanation?"

"Not really. Sometimes, close to the dividing line people who seem to be going one way change their direction. Sometimes someone seems to be headed for good, but then seems to go bad. Or vice versa. Sometimes somebody seems to be bad, but then suddenly moves toward goodness. It's unexplainable."

Petri thought about the malice-filled woman in the wheelchair. "Could Mrs. Stimson still turn around?"

"I don't believe so. As I said, turn-around experiences tend to occur when people are close to the dividing line. My impression of Mrs. Stimson was that she had long since crossed the dividing line. It seemed to me that hate had long become her way of life."

Petri leaned back in his chair to reflect. He had the feeling, thanks to the psychiatrist, that he had succeeded in getting slightly into the woman's mind. But only slightly. There was still not a hint of motive. He sat forward again. "Do you know of any reason why she might have wanted to kill Stephen Solaris?"

"No."

"Except hate?"

"That's right," Kolnietz answered. "She seemed to hate just about everyone, so it wouldn't surprise me if she hated Stephen. But I don't know why she might have hated him in particular."

Petri continued to probe. "The other day you told me that at the deepest level Ms. Barsten was, in your opinion, not capable of committing murder. Would you say that at the same level—at the level of the soul, you called it—Mrs. Stimson is capable of committing murder?"

"Yes."

"She has a murderous sort of soul?"

"Yes."

"But you don't have the foggiest idea why? None at all?"

"Not really. I do have one other possible piece of information. But it really doesn't explain anything. It won't answer your 'why.' "

"What is that?"

"Mrs. Stimson has been married for many years. It would be hard to be married to her husband for those many years and not be hateful."

"Tell me more."

"Well, as you know, I was asked to consult on Mrs. Stimson's case by Willow Glen. After the consultation, Willow Glen instructed me that all bills were paid by her husband. So I sent him the bill for my services. He phoned me and asked for a copy of my report. I told him that it was personal—a confidential medical matter between me and Willow Glen. He insisted upon seeing a copy of the report. He told me that since I was billing him for it, it was his property. I told him the gist of the report. I tried to be very accommodating. I told him that all the report said was that I was unable to suggest any intervention by medication or ordinary psychotherapeutic attention that would likely be productive—or cost-effective—in controlling, limiting, or decreasing his wife's violent behavior. He continued to insist that he wanted a copy of the written report, that he had paid for it."

Petri was intrigued. The rich and powerful Mr. Stimson, always backstage or in the wings, continued to be part of the act. "What happened then?"

"We got in a little—but real—kind of fight about it. Maybe it was my fault. But I told him that Willow Glen was the contracting party, and that if he wanted to fight with Willow Glen over getting a copy of the report, he should do so. But I made it clear I was not going to give him one. He said he would refuse to pay my bill. I told him he was free to try to do that, but I also explained I was free to send the bill to a collection agency. Within the week he paid it. But it left a very bad taste in my mouth. He came across to me as an extraordinarily controlling individual. To be perfectly frank, in our very brief interaction, I found myself disliking him deeply. I even felt a bit sorry for his wife. I found it difficult to understand how anyone could live in an ongoing relationship with him."

"But Mrs. Stimson has."

"Yes."

"Then how does she stand it?"

"That gets back into the same 'I don't know' area, Lieutenant. All I do know is that the old adage, 'Birds of a feather flock together,' tends to hold true in psychiatry. Healthy people tend to stay married to healthy people. Sick people tend to stay married to sick people. While being married to Mr. Stimson might make a normal person hateful, I simply cannot tell you why anyone would make the choice of staying married to him as opposed to the choice of leaving him. And I certainly can't tell you that Mr. Stimson made his wife that way. Some psychiatrists think they can tie up all the loose ends. Maybe you'd like to try to talk with them. But in my own experience with relationships, there are always loose ends, things untied, which I do not understand."

Petri reminded him of the weekly Saturday night fights, predictable as clockwork, and told him how Rachel Stimson had been admitted to Willow Glen only five days after the police had been summoned to the Stimson home. "Do you think her husband somehow railroaded her there?"

"Yes and no."

Another unclear response. But Petri was becoming more patient. "Could you explain the 'yes' part and explain the 'no' part?" he asked.

Kolnietz obliged. "I too would certainly imagine the timing to be more than accidental. I imagine the incident with the police did precipitate her admission. Probably it was even his idea. But I doubt that she objected to it. She's a very strong-willed woman. I doubt that she would stay in Willow Glen unless she wanted to."

"But why would she want to?"

"Birds of a feather not only flock together; it's often difficult to separate them. It would seem that eight years ago the Stimsons' relationship reached a point where it was no longer possible for them to live together.

But neither were they able to live apart. Willow Glen was probably an acceptable compromise for both of them. It gave them the space where they didn't actually have to live together but also the opportunity for them to continue their ongoing fight with each other on Saturday nights."

"You mean they actually like to fight?"

"Yes. Even depend on it. Sick, isn't it?"

On one level it was confusing, but on another it had a strange kind of logic. From the start Petri had found Dr. Kolnietz frustrating and today, as usual, he had been unable to pin him down to anything black and white. Yet slowly he was beginning to feel the psychiatrist's ifs, ands, and buts were more clarifying than confusing, paradoxically more to the point than vague.

He turned to Kolnietz. "Mrs. Stimson wouldn't say a word to me either yesterday or today," he said. "I need her to talk. I don't think I have the skill to make her talk. I suspect you do. I do think that she may be the murderer. But as far as I know, she had no relationship whatsoever with the victim. She had no motive. I need her to talk, and I think that I need your help to get her to talk. Would you help me? First I have to get my chief's permission to formally interrogate her, but I think he'll give it to me. I'd like to do it tomorrow. If you're willing, I would like you to be present. It would not be a psychiatric interview, it would be a legal interview. It wouldn't be your responsibility. It would be mine. But I believe that you may be able to get her to talk when I can't. Would you please help me?"

Kolnietz heard the younger man's acknowledgment that he needed help as a request of unexpected humility. He found he was impressed, even moved. "Oddly enough, my eight A.M. patient tomorrow canceled," he answered. "Maybe it's a sign—I don't know. Actually, I wouldn't oblige you unless I wasn't strangely interested myself. Yes, I'm willing to help in your interrogation."

"Can we meet that early at Willow Glen then?"

"Yes, I'll be there at eight," Kolnietz answered. "But there's one thing, Lieutenant."

"What is that?"

"It may not be very nice. Please be prepared to be hurt."

Mrs. Grochowski's eyes lit up when Mrs. Simonton came into her room. "Edith, it's so good to see you again!"

Mrs. Simonton almost blushed with pleasure. She would have been equally glad to be there were it not for the circumstances. "I'm terribly sorry about Tim, Marion," she said. "I should have come yesterday, but I had to go to the capital for one of those damned state commission meetings. It must be very hard for you."

Tears came involuntarily to Mrs. Grochowski's eyes. "Yes, I'm grieving, Edith. But do you know who's been consoling me? Young Peggy."

"*Peggy?* Peggy Valeno, the aide?"

"Yes, she's coming around, Edith."

It was no accident Mrs. Simonton was unable to hide her surprise. She remembered thinking that it would take a miracle to turn Peggy around. Had one actually occurred? Why? And how? For the first time she found herself wanting to think more deeply about this matter of miracles. But this was not the occasion. She had more urgent business. "I'm afraid that Tim's death is not the only reason I came to see you today, Marion," she said. "I'm afraid I have to give you a roommate again."

"Well, of course you do. I've expected that since poor Stephen was murdered. You haven't justification to keep the other bed in this room empty. And it doesn't matter to me now that Tim's gone. In fact, I'd feel safer with a roommate."

"I can understand that; I know it must still be scary for you. But between you, me, and the lamppost, there may be some progress made in solving it soon. I'm afraid the roommate I have for you won't seem like much protection, however. Unfortunately I have to stick Mrs. Kubrick in with you tonight. Maybe for the next few nights. But it's only temporary, and I'm sure in the next few days we can find someone better. Is there someone on the wing you'd particularly like?"

Mrs. Grochowski was intensely curious. What progress was being made in solving the murder? And why was Crazy Carol being moved? She was aware Carol was Rachel Stimson's roommate. Was Rachel under suspicion? Quite possibly, since Rachel had come to be one of the candidates in her own mind. But she knew Edith would have told her if she didn't have reason not to. "No," she said, "I can't think of anyone offhand."

"Perhaps Georgia Bates?" Mrs. Simonton suggested. "Her roommate's just about to be discharged, and she also seems to be coming around."

"Does she?" Mrs. Grochowski could no longer contain her curiosity. "Georgia's coming around doesn't have anything to do with the progress in solving the murder, does it?"

"Possibly." Mrs. Simonton looked at her friend keenly. "You don't happen to know something I don't know, do you?"

Mrs. Grochowski grinned. "I suspect that each of us knows a few things the other doesn't, Edith. But yes, if Georgia Bates's coming around has something to do with solving the murder, we might indeed make good roommates. Let me have a chat with her. Anyway, it's interesting timing that you should see me today because I've been thinking of asking to see you."

"Oh?"

"I've hesitated because I know how busy you must be with this terrible affair."

"There you go again, you and your neurosis! You know I always want to see you when you need me, Marion." Mrs. Simonton had been standing all the while, but now she pulled the rocker up to the bed. Marion Grochowski was not one for idle conversation. "What's up?"

"Oh, a couple of things. For one, I was just wondering how you were doing, besides the murder."

Why was she being so circumspect? "Except for that Willow Glen goes on pretty much the same as always," Mrs. Simonton answered, waiting.

"And cold-fish McAdams, how's she doing?"

"Also the same. She's very efficient. I couldn't run the place without her. But yes, she's the same cold fish as always."

"No, I haven't noticed her warming up either." There was a short pause. "Should something strange ever happen to me, Edith, just remember McAdams, would you?"

Mrs. Simonton was startled. The request seemed to have come out of nowhere, but she knew that it was quite deliberate. And important. "Something strange?" she asked uneasily. "What do you mean?"

"Oh, nothing in particular."

Mrs. Simonton could tell the other woman's casualness was feigned. "Are you suggesting Roberta McAdams had something to do with the murder?"

"No. No suggestions. No accusations. And anyway, that's not really why I wanted to talk to you. What I really wanted to ask you about was the wine."

"The wine?" The sudden switch of subject was dizzying.

"Yes, the wine you let Tim keep so we could have communion together. I'm sure it was cleaned out with his other possessions, and that's fine. The wine itself wasn't precious to me. But the communion was. I'll miss that terribly. I'm not sure I can do without it. Edith?"

"Yes? How can I help?"

"I feel it's a terrible imposition, Edith, but I was wondering if I could ask you to take communion with me from time to time?"

Mrs. Simonton was stunned. It was not merely a proposal she had never received before, but one which she would never have conceived. "Of course, I'll get you some wine," she replied, buying time, "but surely there are other people here you could share it with."

"You're right," Mrs. Grochowski acknowledged. "In time, there'll be Heather. There's young Peggy. And maybe even Georgia Bates as she comes along. Indeed, some day we might even be able to make it a real big party." She smiled at the thought. But then her face turned serious again. "But as we've said, they're all just coming along. None of them are really ready yet. But you are."

"Ready? Ready for communion? What on earth are you talking about? I'm just an ordinary person."

Mrs. Grochowski snorted. "Stop that foolishness, Edith. You know perfectly well that you're not just an ordinary person. You've grown deep with God."

Mrs. Simonton's mind raced. A part of her knew that, willy-nilly, whether she liked it or not, she had indeed been growing toward God with all these strange thoughts of prayer and miracles and Bible verses. But another part couldn't possibly believe she'd grown very far. She stalled. "Marion, I'm not even a Christian. I don't know what I am. My husband was Jewish. For all I know that makes me a Jew. I can't celebrate communion."

"Why not?"

"Well, I don't even know that I believe in it. I mean, I don't know that Jesus was the son of God. Of course I believe what he taught. To tell you the truth, sometimes I even read the Gospel of John and I cry over it. But that doesn't make me a Christian. They wouldn't let me take communion."

"They? I'm not talking about they. I'm talking about me, Edith. *I* want *you* to take communion with *me*."

"But I don't know how."

"I'll teach you how."

For the first time in years, Mrs. Simonton wanted to run. Not from Mrs. Grochowski. She loved Marion. Not even from the room. Just from some place that didn't even exist. "I'm not ready," she protested.

"But you *know* God! Don't you?"

Mrs. Simonton pretended the question was rhetorical. "Do I know God? How the hell do I know if I know God? Who knows God?"

"Shut up, Edith," Mrs. Grochowski commanded. "Quiet yourself. Just sit there. Don't say anything until the words come to you."

More than a minute passed in silence. Then, very quietly, Mrs. Simonton said, "I don't *know* God, but I do ache for Him."

"As I told you, you're ready."

"I'm not." Mrs. Simonton backpedaled. "I don't believe in it. Eating His body, drinking His blood. Ugh, symbolic or not, it's cannibalism. And I don't believe in—in what you Catholics call it—transubstantiation—anyway. It's not His body. It's not His blood. It's just wine and bread. It's meaningless."

"You're scared, aren't you? What are you scared of?"

For a moment her heart seemed to stop still. "Of God," she said. "I'm scared of God. How could I be ready for Him yet? He wouldn't want me, not for His bride, not for anything. I don't care about the cannibalism part. I don't understand it. But for me it would be like sex. I just don't think I'm ready for that intimacy yet. It would be like having sex with God."

Mrs. Grochowski glowed with joy. "That's exactly what it's like, Edith. Why do you think I need it? It's not literal sex. But it's not metaphorical either. It's a mating of the spirit. And you are ready."

The silence fell between them. Mrs. Simonton felt like a young girl. "You'll teach me how?"

"Of course."

Mrs. Simonton stood up, a young girl no longer. "I've got to get back to work now. You've given me a lot to think about. But yes, Marion, I'll get you a bottle of good red wine for your drawer. When you want communion, just call me and, yes, I'll come."

She returned to her office but it was a while before she could settle down to the papers on her desk. A lot had happened that day, beginning with the search of Rachel Stimson's room. Then there had been that strange, brief little interchange with Mrs. Grochowski about McAdams. What had Marion meant by it? It was disquieting. But neither of these things was nearly as disquieting as this business about communion and God. It was not only as if she were no longer really in charge of Willow Glen; worse, it was as if she were no longer in charge even of herself. She reached for her paperwork to maintain some semblance of control.

As soon as the chief returned, Petri briefed him thoroughly to explain his request for permission to conduct a formal interrogation of Mrs. Stimson in the morning. To his surprise the permission was not so quickly forthcoming.

"So, what you are proposing is that sometime before the murder—minutes, hours, days, or weeks—Rachel Stimson wheeled herself into the supply room and obtained, in secret, a pair of scissors and two gloves," the chief said, reviewing Petri's information. "She kept these in her possession until approximately four-thirty that morning, when she took them with her and wheeled out to where the victim was lying on his gurney. At that point, presumably when Ms. Barsten was out for her walk and Mrs. Grimes absorbed in her reading, she stabbed the victim in his chest, directly penetrating his heart, and then, without any awareness on the part of Mrs. Grimes, wheeled herself back into her room and hid the gloves and wrapper in her roommate's drawer. And that she did all this without any motive of which you are yet aware."

"Yes, sir," Petri said, feeling somewhat foolish, yet wondering why the chief was being so much more rigorous than when he'd agreed to the Barsten interrogation.

"Well, it's possible. But I certainly wouldn't say it's probable. Do you really think that a double amputee would have the strength to reach out of her wheelchair and stab to death a man lying on a gurney some distance away from her?"

"Probably not most of them. But this woman, yes. Everyone comments about her unusual strength. It requires extraordinary strength for her to get from her wheelchair to the bed and back, yet she does it routinely. I've deliberately watched her whip around in that wheelchair, and she's something. The doors to the bedrooms open inward, and they're quite heavy. As I observed her, it didn't take her more than a couple of seconds to lean forward far enough in her chair to grasp the knob, turn it, pull that heavy door out in front of her without it hitting the foot of her chair and whiz out of the room. And the knob was at just about the same level as the victim's gurney. She's one strong woman."

"Okay, okay, but wouldn't the victim have screamed out when she stabbed him, even enough to rouse Mrs. Grimes?"

"I honestly can't say. I would think so myself except for several things. The medical examiner's of no help in this regard. He's unable to offer an opinion as to how loud—if at all—the victim might have screamed were he stabbed in his sleep. And it is likely he was asleep at the time. Not only was it night, but as you remember, he'd just had sex. And as far as we can tell, it does take a lot of noise for Mrs. Grimes to look up from her reading."

"And Dr. Kolnietz can't give you a clear reading on whether she's mentally responsible?"

"No, sir. He says that most psychiatrists would say she's not psychotic, but he himself is unsure."

The chief sat back and rubbed his gray temples. It was damned complicated.

It was the woman's husband who made it so. Hubert Stimson was a powerful man—wealthy, connected, a man with sharp-witted lawyers at his beck and call. If she was interrogated without requesting a lawyer, they'd be able to argue she wasn't responsible enough to refuse counsel. If he tried to enlist Stimson's cooperation, he knew the man well enough to know he'd want a whole battery of lawyers present and it would be a week before they could even do the interrogation, while in the meantime three of his limited force were required to guard Rachel Stimson's door around the clock. And that was the irony of it. The chief had not told Petri this, but the mayor had called him that very morning to ask why the case hadn't been wrapped up. On cautious questioning, the mayor admitted that it was Stimson himself, who loved to wield whatever power he could, who was pressing him, hinting about forming a citizens' committee for action. Hubert Stimson was going to be the leader of the pack in criticizing the police for being too slow, but were he to learn that his wife was suspect, he would be the first to accuse the police of undue haste.

Still, Hubert Stimson was no longer quite as powerful as he liked to think he was. Age had a way of paring people down to their bones, and there were many who disliked his bones. Ten, twenty years ago, few would have openly voiced that dislike when the town was smaller and he played so big a part in running it. But at eighty-two, Hubert Stimson was no longer able to make all the crucial meetings, be on all the committees. Most of his cronies had died off; the agribusinessmen often didn't know his name; times had changed. There were many people in New Warsaw who would feel no sadness to see him taken down a peg.

And the chief was one of them. He was in no way a vindictive man, and had nothing specific against Hubert Stimson. Yet he could not forget the day eight years ago when he had been asked to keep that little domestic violence call his men had made to the Stimson home out of the papers. Indeed, he had done so, for he saw no need to make every one of New Warsaw's minor squabbles public. But there had been something in that request—a hint of a threat?—that had not felt entirely appropriate somehow. And the matter now at hand was so much more than a minor squabble.

"This is not quite as simple as interrogating the Barsten girl," he finally explained to Petri. "Her parents are neither wealthy nor well respected. Mrs. Stimson's husband, however, is both."

"So I understand, sir."

"Do you think I'm exercising a double standard, Tom?"

"I suppose you have to, sir."

"Do I? I don't always know," the chief confided. "Eight years ago I kept their little domestic squabble out of the papers. I wouldn't have done that for ordinary people. I think you do have to bend a little bit sometimes, Tom, but I'm never sure when."

Would Petri be in his position someday? the chief wondered. And if so would he do what was right—whatever in God's name that was? Should Mrs. Stimson reveal nothing in the morning but her husband get wind of the interrogation, there'd be hell to pay, and he, the chief, would bear the brunt of it. And should it prove her guilt, Hubert Stimson would probably also raise hell and see to it that the case be tied up in court for years. Meanwhile, however, his wife would be a ward of the court and the frightened residents of Willow Glen—and their families—might sleep just a bit more easily.

"I want you to be very careful," the chief said to Petri, "very formal and to the letter. Don't take any other action without informing me. But yes, Tom, you can do your interrogation."

## FOURTEEN

## *Wednesday, March 30th*

If Mrs. Stimson was surprised by the number of people crowding into her room, she didn't show it; her face was as expressionless as usual. Perhaps she had been prepared by the presence of the policemen who had been guarding her door ever since the preceding afternoon.

Petri introduced everyone. "I'm Detective Petri," he said to her. "I spoke with you yesterday. This is Sergeant Mitchell, also from the police. He has a tape recorder. Everything that is being said here is being recorded. And this is Dr. Kolnietz, whom you saw several years ago. He is a psychiatrist. I asked him to be here because I've had such difficulty communicating with you and I thought he might help us. Mrs. Simonton you know, of course. I wanted her with us not only as a witness but also so that there would be another woman in the room."

Mrs. Stimson looked at them blankly—or was it coldly?

"You are under suspicion for the murder of Stephen Solaris," Petri continued. "Anything you say may be used against you in court. Consequently, you have the right to remain silent. You also have the right to be represented by counsel, by a lawyer. Would you like me to call a lawyer?"

There was no answer.

"Do you understand what I have been saying to you?"

Rachel stared ahead, seemingly oblivious.

"Are you sure you don't want me to call a lawyer for you?"

Silence.

"Mrs. Stimson, can you tell me your whereabouts between four and six A.M. on Monday, March twenty-first, the time of the murder?"

No response.

"Did you know the victim, Stephen Solaris?"

Petri felt he might as well have been talking to a wall. He was glad he had brought Dr. Kolnietz, although the wall was so impenetrable he could not imagine what magic the psychiatrist could possibly exert.

"Did you have a relationship of any kind with him?"

There was no answer.

"Yesterday I found two gloves and a cloth wrapping in your room-mate's bottom drawer. Do you know how they happened to be there?"

Rachel's eyes blinked. But that was all; the blink seemed to signify nothing. Eyes have to blink, Petri thought. "Did you put them there, Mrs. Stimson?"

She continued to stare straight ahead.

"Have you had nurse's training?"

Silence.

"You used to practice as a nurse, didn't you?"

No response.

"What are your feelings toward your husband?"

The eyes blinked again.

"Mrs. Stimson, yesterday I had you checked for a possible arrest record. We have no such record. What we do have is a record that you called the police one night eight years ago, accusing your husband of beating you. Because you were not visibly injured, the police took no action. Within a week your husband had you admitted here to Willow Glen. Did you consent to that admission?"

There was no reply.

"You have a fight with your husband each week when he visits you here. Obviously something is quite wrong with your relationship. Could you tell us what it is?" Petri sounded sympathetic.

Rachel said nothing.

"Mrs. Stimson, did you murder Stephen Solaris?"

Rachel continued to look at him blankly.

"Why did you kill him, Mrs. Stimson?"

The expected lack of response continued. Petri changed his style in the vague hope it would elicit something more. "Let me tell you what I think," he said to her. "I think you wheeled yourself into the supply room and obtained the gloves and a pair of surgical scissors. Then sometime between four-thirty and five A.M. on Monday morning, March twenty-first, you wheeled yourself over to the victim while the aide, Mrs. Grimes, was reading. The victim was lying asleep on his side. With your gloved hands you plunged, very accurately, the sharp blade of the scissors into the victim's heart. Then you wheeled yourself back to this room and placed the gloves and the wrapping of the scissors in Mrs. Kubrick's bottom drawer. That is the correct sequence of events, isn't it?"

There was no response.

"Why did you hate Stephen Solaris, Mrs. Stimson?"

Still no response. Petri looked at Dr. Kolnietz helplessly.

Stasz Kolnietz closed his eyes, gathering strength for what needed to be done. Watching Rachel, he had realized she would have to be taunted into talking—the same way Stephen might inadvertently have taunted her into murder. He must have been some kind of wordless insult to her. That insult would have to be resurrected.

"Stephen's body was terribly crippled," Kolnietz began softly, his eyes still closed. There was a crooning quality to his voice. "To a stranger he would have looked ugly. But Stephen was not a stranger to the people in Willow Glen. They were able to see beyond his body. They were able to see his wonderful intelligence. They were able to see the will which overcame his limitations, that marvelous human will which allowed him to communicate. They were able to see his kindness. His love, despite his afflictions. His caring. His gentleness. His spirit. They saw the beauty underneath his crippled body. He was beautiful. He was a truly beautiful human being. No one has ever been more beautiful. He was so beautiful."

"SHUT UP!" Mrs. Stimson roared.

Petri was not only taken aback by her sudden eruption, he felt blasted against the wall by the pure rage in her voice.

But Kolnietz continued as if nothing had happened. "So beautiful," he intoned again. "With all his afflictions, he could have given up. He could have been retarded. He could have died some years ago. But the spirit of life was in him. He chose life. He chose love. What a magnificent spirit. It was so beautiful. He was so beautiful."

"WILL YOU SHUT UP!" Mrs. Stimson screamed. "HE WAS UGLY. HE WAS A CLAWED UP, DEFORMED WRETCH: UGLY, COVERED WITH SHIT. HE COULDN'T EVEN WIPE HIMSELF, THE SHIT WAS CAKED IN THE CRACK OF HIS ASS, ALL OVER HIS BUTTOCKS; A SHITTY LITTLE CREATURE, WHO CRAWLED OUT OF THE MUD, AN UGLY SHITTING BAG OF BONES."

"No, he was human," Kolnietz countered in the same gentle chant, almost a lullaby. "Fully human. More human than most of us ever become. A man. A true man."

"HOW DARED HE?" Rachel raged. "THE STUPID WORM WAS EVEN BE-COMING SEXUAL. HOW DARED HE REACH FOR THAT? THAT ENERGY? HE NEEDED TO CRAWL BACK DOWN INTO THE MUD WHERE HE BELONGED!"

"So beautiful," Dr. Kolnietz crooned on. "What a beautiful soul. A God-given soul. A soul created by God. Created especially for His glory. An example to men. An example for women. An example of how you could have been. An example of the glory of humanity. What a beautiful, beautiful soul."

"HE DESERVED TO DIE. THAT LIGHT. THAT DAMN LIGHT HE HAD. ALL AROUND HIM. IT WAS GROWING. IT HAD TO BE PUT OUT. I COULDN'T STAND THAT LIGHT ANYMORE. I COULDN'T STAND IT!"

"So you extinguished it, didn't you? It was an affront to you. You had to get rid of it. So you stabbed him, didn't you?"

Abruptly Mrs. Stimson's eyes, which had been blazing, shifted for a fraction of a second to craftiness, then to dullness. She looked at them blankly. There was no answer.

Kolnietz opened his eyes. "I'm sorry," he said. "I'm exhausted. That's all I can do."

"It's enough," Petri answered. He stood up, feeling strangely tired too. "Mrs. Stimson, there are formalities to go through, but you may consider yourself under arrest for the murder of Stephen Solaris. Your door will continue to be guarded. You will no longer leave this room. Any attempt to do so will be used as further evidence against you. Do you understand?"

There was no response.

The four of them—Petri, Mitchell, Kolnietz, and Simonton—shuffled back wordlessly to the Administration Center. They did not appear victorious; they looked more like a small band of drained soldiers in retreat, barely able to put one foot in front of the other. Their heavy silence continued even after they were all seated in Mrs. Simonton's office and she made them coffee.

Petri was the first to speak. "We police don't usually have a high opinion of shrinks," he said, "but I've changed my mind. At least about you, Stasz." The use of the first name seemed appropriate for two who'd been through a battle together. "Jesus, that was magnificent."

"I got her to open up for a grand total of ninety seconds," Kolnietz demurred.

"But it was enough. It's not exactly a confession, but it will do."

Petri sounded very subdued. Mrs. Simonton understood, and voiced her own feelings as she asked, "Did it shake you up, Lieutenant?"

Petri nodded. "I've never seen such hate. Naked hate. Never heard such hate. As Dr. Kolnietz said, it didn't last much more than a minute, but I'll never forget it. I didn't even imagine such hate existed."

"I did warn you," Kolnietz reminded him.

"Do you see it often?" Petri asked.

"No, not to that degree. That degree is very rare."

"But what causes it?"

"Didn't I tell you yesterday it was inexplicable?"

"Yes, but you've got to know *something*. I mean, that was raw *evil* I saw this morning. What on God's earth goes on in that woman's head?"

"That's the problem with evil, Tom." Kolnietz also slipped into a first-name basis. "It's inexplicable because it's always hidden."

"What do you mean?"

"We have an expression in psychotherapy: 'We're as sick as our secrets.' The evil are the sickest of all people because everything about them is secret."

Petri knew they were back in the quagmire, the labyrinth. Which came first: the chicken or the egg? But his logical mind wouldn't allow him to let the matter rest. "Why do they keep everything secret?" he asked.

Kolnietz smiled. "And for the last time, Tom, let me tell you that I don't know. People who come to psychotherapy expose their inner lives to us so we can learn what makes them tick. Evil people do not come to psychotherapy, so we don't get to see their inner lives, so we don't get to see what makes them tick—other than that little bit we might guess about them from their outside. Probably that's why they don't come to therapy: they don't want to be exposed. So you're left with only two choices. Either an evil person, for some reason, refuses to expose his inner life, or else, for the same reason, he may not even have one."

"There's one other possibility." The voice was Sergeant Mitchell's.

The others turned in surprise to the quiet man who had not spoken until now. "Yes, Bill?" Mrs. Simonton urged.

"The old woman might be possessed."

"Possessed?" Petri repeated dumbly.

"Yes. Demon-possessed."

Petri looked up at his sergeant with consternation. Was this some wild small-town superstition or had the man gone off his rocker? To his amazement, however, Kolnietz responded matter-of-factly. "Yes, I've had that possibility in the back of my mind. It was even there when I first saw her three years ago."

"There's something demonic about her, all right," Mrs. Simonton agreed.

Petri stared at them as if they'd all gone mad. "I told Tom yesterday," Kolnietz continued, unperturbed, "that hatred had taken control over her. It possessed her. But I'm not sure it's possible to tell whether someone's possessed by human hatred or demonic hatred. Not when they're that far gone. What do you think, Bill?"

Mitchell shook his head. "Doubt it's possible to tell."

Petri wanted to return to more rational ground. "It's obvious she hated

Solaris and wanted him dead," he said. "But why? And what was all this stuff about 'light'? Can you make sense out of this, Stasz?"

Kolnietz smiled. "Oddly enough, yes. Or at least some sense. Remember I talked about secrets? In a sense the evil—the hateful—choose to live in darkness. So they must dislike the light. And anyone who chooses differently must be an insult to them. I know Stephen. No one could have chosen light—truth—more fully. I think I can understand now why she hated him in particular."

"Yes, that follows," Mrs. Simonton commented, "but you're seeing it as symbolic, allegorical. Rachel spoke of the light as something physical, as if she could actually see it, as if it actually hurt her eyes."

"Maybe it did," Kolnietz replied. "And maybe she could. Some people can see auras, you know, and they usually don't seem to be terribly wacky. I've never seen one myself. But I doubt that the early religious painters invented haloes from nothing."

Petri found this talk slightly more reasonable than the possession business—but only slightly. "She also seemed to pick up that Solaris had a sex life. Do you suppose she'd seen him and Barsten in the act?" he asked, his curiosity overriding his squeamishness.

"Possibly," Kolnietz answered. "But I don't think necessarily. You can ask her, of course. I doubt that she'll answer you. But if she's the kind of person who could pick up on auras, then she could possibly have picked up on that too. Stephen was probably in love. That can give off a lot of energy, you know. But that's enough of questions." He stood up. "I've got to run. I mean, really run. I've got a nine-thirty patient, and I may be late as it is."

"Oh, Stasz, we're always in such a damn hurry, both of us, aren't we?" Mrs. Simonton said, getting up also. "So busy giving to the patients we never give to each other. Well, I want a hug, damn it. Give me one before you go."

Despite himself, Petri's eyes filled as he watched the embrace. It was brief, but there was nothing perfunctory about it. It occurred to him that they would have known each other for at least a dozen years, so this would hardly have been the first battle that they had gone through together. How many, he couldn't even guess. He was moved by their muted but visible affection, so different from the ugliness of the hatred he had just witnessed.

Kolnietz left and Mrs. Simonton sat back down. Petri's head was still reeling, and not just from what he had seen. There was this bizarre notion of demons, raised by his own sergeant and discussed so matter-of-factly by the others. He was full of questions—so many he didn't even begin to know how to ask them. How might the chief deal with them? he wondered, feeling very much in need of an older man's counsel. "Well, I suppose I ought to be going myself," he announced lamely. "I'll need to brief the chief as soon as possible. There's a lot we have to put to rest."

"Speaking of putting things to rest," Mrs. Simonton responded, "*now* may I call Heather to let her know she's off the hook, Lieutenant?"

Petri looked startled. He hadn't given Barsten a thought, and he was aware of the slight edge in the director's tone. "Oh, sure," he said casually. "I'd appreciate it. I'd do it myself if I didn't have to report to the chief right away."

He stood up and made a point of thanking her for all her help. There were indeed many things that needed to be done. But even as he and Mitchell were going out the door of Willow Glen, Petri could still feel the eyes of Edith Simonton behind him, faintly accusing him of some unspecified sin.

For the past twenty-four hours, Hank Martin had been wandering around the corridors of Willow Glen like a lost puppy. Frightened of being alone, he was using every excuse he could imagine to engage anyone in conversation. Now he found himself at Mrs. Grochowski's doorway trying to think of something reasonable to say. "I wanted to offer my condolences," he finally got out stiffly.

"Why, thank you, Hank. That's very kind of you."

"I don't know what else to say."

"There's nothing else you have to say."

Hank wanted to run. But he also wanted to stay, and it seemed to him there should be something more. Mrs. Grochowski broke the silence.

"You have my condolences, too, Hank."

"Why is that?"

"Well, Tim was your roommate."

"We weren't all that close," Hank stammered.

"Tim told me you didn't talk much. But then maybe that's because you're shy."

At that point, Hank did run.

He stopped when he got to the dayroom. He wished he could clear his head, but he could not. So many epithets had been hurled at him the past few days. "Cold," Peggy had called him. The detective had speared him with "liar," "bully," and "coward." And now the gentlest, yet somehow the strangest of all: "shy."

Hank would have denied each of them if he could. But the reality was too blatant. His only other choice would have been to take total leave of reality, and something—pride or perhaps some remaining shred of dignity—forbade him that exit. Eccentric, yes, but he would not be insane! Mrs. Grochowski had offered him condolences on the assumption that Tim's death was a grief to him. The reality, however, was that he hadn't cared a hoot about the other man. He hadn't even given a thought to his death until two days after the fact when, in panic, he'd turned to Tim yesterday for protection and Tim wasn't there.

"We weren't all that close," he'd told Mrs. Grochowski. What an understatement! They had lived in the same room for over a year, yet were not close. Why not? Certainly, there had been nothing objectionable about Tim. In fact, the man had been unfailingly kind. He couldn't remember anything Tim had done to make conversation difficult. He, Hank, had never moved out to Tim. He hadn't cared enough to do so. He simply hadn't cared about Tim.

Did he care about anyone? He always thought he cared about women. Yet he could not forget Peggy calling him cold and telling him that he reached out only for himself. He was cold and uncaring. That was the reality.

He also could not deny the reality that he was afraid. The fantasy of the executioner, razor blade in hand, approaching him—his genitals—returned less often today, so seemed more unreal. Yes, his terror had subsided to mere fear, but the fear stalked him ceaselessly everywhere he went. He could not rid himself of that feeling of unremitting anxiety, as if a pair of rats were inside his rib cage gnawing to get out.

"Maybe you're shy," Mrs. Grochowski had said. He had never thought of himself as shy. Pushy was what most people called him. You had to be pushy to get close to women—not that it had ever seemed to work for *him*. Yet she had made "shy" sound almost like a compliment, as if it were somehow all right to be timid. But shyness was a kind of fear, and fear was weak and feminine, wasn't it?

Suddenly Hank felt the fear tighten still further in his chest. Only there was no place left for him to run. He was trapped, and in that minute of motionlessness the three words—"care" and "close" and "fear"—came together. Maybe he was scared to care, to actually *be* close. What was he afraid of? That people wouldn't care back? He thought about himself caring deeply for someone—someone like Mrs. Grochowski, for instance—and he became aware that he was blushing.


Much later, whenever she would look back on this day, Mrs. Simonton would be struck by the irony of relativity. It would have been an important day in any case. The solution of Stephen's murder was a most significant event in the life of Willow Glen. But as she watched Petri and Mitchell leave she would never have guessed that an event far more important—relative to her own life—was about to occur.

So much had already happened in the past hour that before she called Heather, she needed to put things in perspective. She leaned back in her chair. Like the others, she had been shocked—even wounded, poisoned, on some deep level—by Rachel's murderous rage. There had been a venom in it that did have a demonic quality. But were there *really* demons? The question disturbed her despite her casual manner when the issue had been raised. What was most disturbing were the implications. If one were to allow for demons, one would probably also have to allow for angels. Could there really be some kind of cosmic struggle going on, with supernatural forces waiting in the wings, barely offstage? And if so, which side was she on?

At that point a very odd thing happened in Mrs. Simonton's head. It was like a voice that was not her own, but not truly a voice, because it was inaudible. It was as if the words were somehow written in her mind. The mechanism, the brain biochemistry involved, was unfathomable. But the message was irrevocably clear. Simple and definitive, it said, *"You are on the side of the angels."*

Period. That was all. No doubt. A statement of pure fact.

Almost as remarkable was the feeling that then flooded Edith Simonton's entire being. It was the feeling of being totally loved, of being utterly lovable and acceptable. Only it was more than a feeling; it was an *experience*. She was actually experiencing herself being totally loved. At the very same moment she was aware of having read somewhere about others who had had such an experience. But this awareness in no way detracted from her joy. "It's happening to me!" she thought with astonished delight, as wave after wave of joy filled her being.

On the heels of joy—no, it was a part of the joy—came her gratitude. She was unspeakably grateful. For what seemed like an eternity she lived in the ineffable paradox of being utterly undeserving and, simultaneously, unalterably *worthy*.

The eternity passed. Gently—as if she were a baby bird being replaced in her nest by a careful hand—she came back to earth. She was staring at the phone. Heather needed to be called. Mrs. Simonton glanced at her watch. It was no more than ten minutes since the two policemen had left. She grinned to herself at the incongruence of the momentary with the momentous, and picked up the receiver to dial, knowing that she would never be quite the same.

·     ·     ·

"Congratulations, you've solved your first murder," the chief said when he finished listening to the tape of the interrogation.

"I don't really feel I can take too much credit for it, sir," Petri said. He was feeling pleased—by the chief's approval, by the resolution of the case, by his own role—but the feeling was muted by his lingering horror at the rage he had witnessed and the ambiguities of the whole business. "It took a senile patient to point me in the right direction; it took Mrs. Simonton to allow me to do a search; and it took Dr. Kolnietz to get her to talk."

"Yes, but you were willing to listen to that senile patient, and it was your idea to do the search, and it was you who asked Kolnietz to help with the questioning. But you're right in one sense, Tom. I've never seen a major case solved by someone working alone. You succeeded precisely because you were smart enough to get the help you needed."

"Speaking of help, what do I do now?" Petri realized he'd not even given a thought to anything beyond the discovery, the naming, of the murderer.

"A whole bunch of things. The first is you take this tape and get five copies of the highest possible quality made. Sergeant Mitchell will tell you where, but go with him. That tape is your case. You lose it and you're out of a job. Give me one copy, keep one on your person, and put the original and two copies in the safe."

Petri smiled. "That adds up to five. I suspect you've got something in mind for the sixth."

"You're right." The chief smiled in turn. "That you take to Judge Michelwicz at his chambers in the county courthouse. Barge in on him if you need to. Have the arrest forms filled out first. Tell him we need a court order to transmit her to the State Hospital for the Criminally Insane."

"Doesn't she have to be tried first?"

"Jesus, no. We can't hold an eighty-two-year-old woman who's a double amputee in the jail. Nor can we keep patrolmen around the clock guarding her for months in a nursing home awaiting trial. He's smart enough to realize that, and he's got the authority to remand her to the state hospital for observation pending trial. But you may need to push him a little. He's cautious, like any good judge."

"Okay. And then?"

"Then go tell her husband that we've arrested her. Not before. He deserves to know before he reads it in the papers tomorrow. But Tom . . ."

"Yes."

"He's an s.o.b. Don't let him scare you."

Petri was suddenly acutely aware of what a novice he was. As a sergeant in New York City he'd worked with the scum of society: the prostitutes and pimps, the junkies and petty dealers, the purse snatchers. He'd come to New Warsaw to get clean from that scum, not thinking about the fact that there was another kind of deadliness lurking behind well-kept houses and large bank accounts that might even be more dangerous. "I can get scared. But not if you're backing me up."

"I'm backing you up."

"But how can you be so sure? I mean it's not even a full confession on the tape. It's a diatribe. She hated him, yes. But it's not really a confession, is it?"

"There are three types of murders, Tom. The most common is a crime of passion. Someone kills his wife's lover or two people are in a barroom brawl. The next most common is premeditated murder for gain. You kill your husband for his insurance policy or something. But then there's a third type."

"Yes?"

"It's something like rape. Many rapists rape because they hate women. It's not sexual. It's hate, almost for the sake of hate. It's crazy because in a sense it's motiveless. That's what makes it so horrible. There's a horrible kind of purity to it."

"But why are you so sure?"

"I heard the tape, Tom."

Petri was torn. He had been overwhelmed by Rachel Stimson's hatred himself. Yet if he'd learned anything from the past week and a half, it was to distrust certainty. He winced at the memory of Heather Barsten. "What if I can't handle her husband?" he asked.

"You can always refer him to me, Tom. You're not making the arrest on your sole authority. It's on mine. But not just on my authority either. That tape is there. It's not even in my hands. Hubert Stimson can do what he wants. Believe me, I've thought about it. He might want to stop us. He might want to hurt us. But I don't think he can. He's not the law. I think he's in a corner, Tom."

Heather was feeling calm when she arrived at Mrs. Simonton's office. Over the phone she'd been told she was being summoned for good news, not for bad. The best news she could think of was that the murder had been solved, so she was not surprised when the director told her of the search the day before and Rachel's explosive expression of hatred toward Stephen that morning. But then her eyes flooded with tears.

Mrs. Simonton was concerned. "Why are you crying?"

"I just remembered something," Heather explained. "On the night of the murder, after I gave Carol her shot, I asked Rachel if there was anything I could do for her. She didn't answer me. But when I turned out the light, just as I was going out the door, I thought I heard a faint voice saying 'Don't go.' It didn't sound like her—it didn't sound like anybody, it was so faint—but I asked Rachel if she'd said something. She didn't reply, so I decided it must have been my imagination and I left. I should have stayed."

Mrs. Simonton wondered about the mystery of it all. Had it been Rachel's voice? Or possibly even Carol's? Or might it even have been some spirit from outside or within her speaking to Heather, warning her of the impending danger? God knows, she thought. "You're very intuitive, Heather" was all she could say. "That's one of the reasons you're such a good nurse. But we'd probably get in a lot of trouble if we acted on all our intuitions when there wasn't any evidence to back them up."

"But if it was actually Rachel. . . ."

Mrs. Simonton encouraged her. "And if it was?"

"Then she must have been in torment," Heather continued. "A part of her must have wanted to be stopped."

How could they ever tell? Mrs. Simonton's eyes also filled. The hateful woman was so cut off, so isolated and alone. "Rachel Stimson is a soul in torment either way," she said. "The only difference, I suppose, is the kind of torment. For her sake, even though it might be more painful, I'd like to think there is a part of her which didn't want to kill. Somehow it seems more hopeful that way."

Heather did not look comforted. But there seemed nothing more to be said. Mrs. Simonton switched the subject. "How have you been?" she asked. "You must have had some torment of your own, knowing that Lieutenant Petri was suspecting you of murder. *I've* been in torment worrying about you, but I wasn't allowed to talk about the case until today."

"It was pretty scary at first," Heather acknowledged. "But then I talked to Mrs. G. and Dr. K. about it, and that really helped. I mean, they actually believed in me."

Mrs. Simonton picked up the hint of amazement in her words. "I've believed in you too, Heather. I wanted to tell you that, but I had to promise the lieutenant not to speak with anyone about the investigation. I'm sorry."

"That's all right. I haven't felt bad for the past few days. After Mrs. G. and Dr. K., I somehow just knew it would be okay for me. I've only been feeling badly for poor Stephen."

"Yes. That's concerned me too. I know how deeply you cared for him."

Heather's face clouded over. "Did you know why the lieutenant suspected me?"

Mrs. Simonton was grateful for the opportunity to get so quickly to the point of the other item on her agenda. "Yes, I know you had a sexual relationship with Stephen," she answered. But she was not prepared for what came next.

"I'm going to miss Willow Glen," Heather said. "And I'm going to miss you too."

"What? What are you talking about?"

"I know you've got no choice," Heather explained. "I realize you've got to fire me."

Mrs. Simonton was aghast. "Fire you? Fire you for what?"

"For having sex with Stephen."

The poor girl, not only having to worry about being falsely accused of murder but also assuming that she would be fired! Where did that assumption come from? "Heather, we've got two problems," Mrs. Simonton responded in measured tones. "Yes, your having had sex with Stephen is a problem, but hardly one I'd fire you for."

"You wouldn't?"

"No, I wouldn't and I won't. If you were a bad person, a bad nurse, having sex with a patient would probably be a reflection of that badness and would indeed be cause for dismissal. But you're the best nurse I have, Heather, and I think you're a very good person. I think you may have made a mistake with Stephen in this instance, but I don't fire a good person for a single, possible mistake."

"*May* have? A *possible* mistake?" Heather was astounded by Mrs. Simonton's tolerance.

"Yes, may have. Only you can tell what your motives were, and only you can tell to what degree they were mistaken. But, you see, not only do I know you loved Stephen, I loved Stephen; and I can understand what those motives might have been. Mind you, I am not condoning it. At the very least I think you made a mistake in not coming to talk with me about it first. I somehow doubt that there will ever again be another patient in Willow Glen with whom you might want to have a sexual relationship, but if there is, I expect—no, I require—that you come to me and discuss the issues with me first. Because there are a lot of issues involved, and it's too important a matter for someone to decide by herself."

There was a part of Heather that wanted to break down and sob with gratitude for the mothering acceptance she was receiving. But there was another part—familiar, but for the first time faintly unpleasant to herself—

that was distant, even irritated. It was as if it had an existence of its own and was sitting there staring at Mrs. Simonton with disbelief so haughty as to be indifferent. The sum of these two parts so disparate was confusion. Heather did not know how to respond.

Mrs. Simonton sensed her confusion and guessed its cause. "Which brings me to the other problem we have," she went on. "Why would you just assume that I would fire you? It's like the time you had your black eye last month and you never even thought of asking me for time off to see Dr. Kolnietz. Sometimes I think you see me as I am, Heather, but other times it seems you regard me as a mean old witch. What are we going to do about that?"

The mute confusion continued. But something Mrs. Simonton had just said was like an echo in Heather's mind of a sound she'd recently heard coming from a different direction. Something about transference. She surprised herself by the spontaneous request with which she broke the silence. "Would it be all right with you if I saw Dr. K. routinely, which would mean sometimes when I'm on duty?" Heather asked. "I mean, even if it's not an emergency? It's hard for us to set up regular appointments with my work schedule. I'd like to see him more often and more regularly."

Mrs. Simonton thought quickly. Was it a test? A testing of limits or a testing of her own genuineness? It could be a manipulation. But the problem of the girl's unrealistic perceptions belonged more in Stasz's bailiwick than her own. Administrators could be coaches, yes, but it was not their job to be long-term psychotherapists. And she wanted Heather's healing even more than her devotion to Willow Glen. The trust, the benefit of the doubt, could always be withdrawn if this were warranted. "Of course," she responded. "Just let me know in writing the schedule of appointments you arrange so I'll have it to refer to if need be. And be sure—as I know you will—to let your aides and the RN know when you leave and when you'll return."

Heather thanked her perfunctorily. Mrs. Simonton could tell how anxious she was to leave. Whatever its effect, her coaching was done. Wondering what might be going on in her nurse's mind but knowing it was a matter beyond her control, Mrs. Simonton let her go.

As soon as she had driven back to her apartment, Heather got undressed and into bed. The urge to be naked and nested was primitive, compelling. It was as if she needed to sort out her feelings, only there were none to sort out. She knew logically that she should be experiencing a sense of great relief—relief that the murder had been solved, relief that she was no longer under suspicion, relief that she was not going to be fired. But instead she was feeling absolutely nothing. Why? Why was she so empty of feeling? Was it because she had felt so much and now was simply depleted? Drained? No, it didn't seem like that. This was bizarre. The emptiness didn't seem so much a depletion of something as a something in its own right. How could an emptiness be a something?

Suddenly the image of a desert came to Heather's mind. As she lay on her bed, she imagined herself lying on the floor of a desert. Way off at the horizon there were dry mountains, but for miles around her it was dead flat. There was no vegetation, nothing, only emptiness.

Was she alive or dead? A vulture circled high overhead, slowly descending. No, it was a raven. The raven flapped down to the desert floor right beside her head. Then it began to peck at her left eye. She felt no pain. Yet she was conscious, fully so. She could have moved away if she wanted to, but she felt no need. She simply lay there, passively letting it peck away.

What a strange image! Why was she so passive? She was waiting. Waiting for what? For death? Tears began to flow gently down her cheeks. These were real tears. In her imagination she was lying on the floor of the desert but simultaneously she, Heather, was aware she was lying on her own bed shedding real tears. Why was she crying? She did not feel sorrowful. She felt only empty, waiting. Was she crying because something was dying? But then why didn't she feel sad? Unless it was something that needed to die?

Gradually, she drifted to sleep. And in her dreams she returned to the desert, waiting.


Although ostensibly retired, Hubert Stimson still maintained an office at the real estate company he had founded; and it was an elegant one. Lieutenant Petri thought it spoke of power. Was that why, when he asked to see him, he was invited here rather than to his house? "I must say I'm surprised to receive a visit from the police. That's never happened to me before in all my eighty-two years," Mr. Stimson said. "It's rather dramatic. What can I possibly do for you, Lieutenant?"

Petri noted how vigorous the man was for his age, noted the urbanity of his manner, and also noted that he had forgotten—or chosen to forget—the visit of the police to his home that night eight years previously, when Rachel Stimson had accused him of beating her.

"I'm afraid I'm the bearer of bad news," Petri told him. "Your wife has just been arrested for the murder of another patient at Willow Glen."

The skin of the elderly man's face, which did not look as though it had seen much sun, suddenly flushed. "Why, that's impossible. My wife is in a wheelchair. There must be some mistake."

"No, I don't think there is any mistake," Petri responded. "She had the strength; she had the expertise; she had the access; and she had the temperament. We found remains of the weapon in her room and this morning she admitted she hated the victim."

"What's wrong with that place?" The flush on Stimson's cheeks had descended all the way down his neck. "They should have restrained her. It's their fault. I ought to sue them. I'm going to contact my lawyers."

The urbanity had been quick to go, Petri noted. He said nothing.

Mr. Stimson changed his tack. "I'm sure you're mistaken, Lieutenant. It's irresponsible of you to make false accusations. I warn you, I'm not going to rest until justice is done."

"It is possible for the police to make mistakes," Petri acknowledged. "That's why we have the judicial process. Thus far your wife has only been arrested. But the evidence has already been independently assessed by Judge Michelwicz to be sufficient to take action. Still, guilt will not be established until the time of trial."

"Trial? There can't be any trial."

"Why not?"

Mr. Stimson avoided the question. He attempted to recapture his oily composure. "Were there possibly a trial, and were my wife found guilty, what in your opinion, Lieutenant, would happen to her?"

"By virtue of her age and psychiatric condition, I suspect she would probably be placed in a hospital for the criminally insane."

"Well, then, why can't she just be placed in such a hospital without having to go through a trial first?"

Petri noted how the man was talking of his wife as an object to be moved. There seemed to be no concern for *her*. "She can," he answered. "In fact, we're intending to do just that, since Willow Glen is no longer the appropriate place for her. But there would still have to be a trial."

"Why?"

"To be judged criminally insane, a person has to be judged a criminal, or at least incompetent to stand trial, and that judgment requires a judge and at least some kind of public legal proceeding."

"There can't be any trial. I won't allow it. I won't allow this sordid mess to be in the newspapers."

"I'm afraid, Mr. Stimson, it will get in the newspapers in any event."

"Why do you say that?"

"Every twenty-four hours the press reviews the arrest blotter down at the police station. They can report any arrest they want. It's inevitable that they're going to report an arrest for murder. And, as you know, they've shown particular interest in the murder at Willow Glen."

"You mean my wife's name is likely to be in the newspapers tomorrow?"

"Yes."

"But that's irresponsible. You mean that my wife's name can be in the newspapers just on your say-so?"

"No, that would not be a balanced way to look at things. As I told you, the evidence has already been assessed by the judge and, even before that, by my chief."

"I'm sorry, Lieutenant," Mr. Stimson said ingratiatingly. "I didn't mean to offend you. It's just that this has been so upsetting to me. You will, of course, do everything you can to keep it out of the papers, won't you? I'm sure that we can find some way that you would ultimately benefit in so doing."

Petri had seen it coming. "It's not a matter within my control, Mr. Stimson."

The elderly man's oiliness vanished as quickly as it had returned. "Well, it must be in someone's control. You know, don't you, that I'll have to call your chief in that case? It won't look good for you, Lieutenant. He's a friend of mine. All the influential people in this community are friends of mine."

"You can do whatever you feel you have to do, Mr. Stimson, as long as it's legal," Petri responded, standing up. There was something about the other man that made him want to get away as quickly as possible. And, fortunately, there was no plausible reason left to detain him. Stimson had to let him go.

On his way back to the station, Petri tried to put himself in Hubert Stimson's shoes. What would it be like to be informed that your wife of many decades had just been arrested for murder? Would it have helped if he'd tried to be more sympathetic? But it was not easy. He was startled to realize it was easier to feel sympathy for the openly vicious, hateful woman he had seen that morning. He also had a clear sense that no matter how he might have played the unpleasant scene he'd just gone through, the outcome would not have been any different. Whatever made Mr. Stimson tick, it was not something that seemed amenable to much in the way of influence—and least of all the influence of compassion.


Five minutes after the dinner buzzer sounded, Mrs. Simonton left her office for the dining hall. Two speeches in just over a week! she thought to herself. But this time the subject would be easier and, as she entered, another one of those unbidden fragments came to her mind: "It will be given unto you what to say."

As before, she rang Hank Martin's glass with his spoon to get their attention. "I have news for you which some of you may already have guessed. But I don't want any of you left in the dark. Mrs. Rachel Stimson has been arrested today for the murder of Stephen Solaris. The case has been solved. As long as she remains on the premises, a policeman will be guarding her door. I do not anticipate this will be for very long. You are no longer in any danger. I thought you would like to know that."

"Why? Why did she do it?" The question was Georgia Bates's. It was natural she would want to know, Mrs. Simonton realized, now that she was apparently almost an ex officio member of the New Warsaw Police Department.

"I'm afraid I'm not at liberty to tell you any more. Rachel would not have been arrested if there were not strong evidence, but she's only been arrested and I cannot discuss the evidence until the time of the trial. I'm sorry, Georgia."

It was Hank Martin's turn. "I feel I'm still in the dark," he said.

Mrs. Simonton was surprised. It was unlike Hank to be involved. Usually he seemed uninterested, almost oblivious. "That's true," she acknowledged, "but then we're less in the dark than we were. Besides," she added, "we're always somewhat in the dark, aren't we?"

"What do you mean?" Hank queried.

Mrs. Simonton was startled. Why had she said that? What did she mean? "I guess there's always some mystery in life," she stumbled in reply. "But that doesn't make it meaningless. Something is mysterious when we don't understand the meaning of it, but just because we don't understand the meaning doesn't mean that there isn't any."

"Now I'm really confused!" Hank exclaimed.

Georgia came to the rescue. "I think I know what Mrs. Simonton is saying. Sometimes I ask myself why I'm here, why I'm alive, and I don't have an answer. But just because I don't know the answer doesn't mean there isn't any answer. Maybe my life is meaningful even though it seems like a mystery to me from the inside of it."

Mrs. Simonton looked at her gratefully. "That's exactly what I meant," she said. Then she looked at the whole group. "And I would like you to remember it. You may be confused at times, but each and every one of your lives is meaningful." Suddenly she was not embarrassed by the power. "Don't you forget it," she added. "And God bless each of you."

She walked out of the dining hall and when she was out of earshot down the corridor she whistled to herself in amazement. The brief meeting had come to a totally unexpected conclusion. She felt as if she were a puppet dancing to invisible strings. But what extraordinary choreography! The whole day had been the same. Never had she felt she understood less or felt so content to let it be that way.

## FIFTEEN

## Thursday, March 31st

Hank Martin stopped at Georgia Bates's door. "Is it all right if I come in?" he asked. "I promise I won't touch you. I want some advice."

Georgia looked at him skeptically. A promise from Hank the Horny not to touch was questionable. But it was also out of character, and somehow he looked different, almost sheepish. She took a chance. "Come on in," she said.

Hank hurried to the point. "I would like to court Mrs. Grochowski," he explained when he was seated. "I don't think I've ever courted anybody before. Laid hands on them, but I guess you wouldn't call that courting, would you?"

"No, I wouldn't." Georgia was tempted to laugh. The notion of Hank courting anyone—much less Mrs. Grochowski—seemed ridiculous. Yet there was something about his seriousness that told her this was not a time for ridicule.

"So I don't know anything about it. I thought I would ask you for your advice. How does one go about courting?"

"Why on earth ask me?"

For a moment Hank reverted to his familiar self. "Because you're so sexy, my love." Then he realized he didn't want to go that route anymore. He regained his seriousness. "You have a kind of dignity like Mrs. Grochowski," he answered.

"I am hardly an expert on the subject." Georgia smiled, pleased by the comparison. "I've not been into sex or romance much in my life. My husband courted me, but that was a very long time ago. And there were many times since I wished he hadn't. It was my only experience."

"Still, I want a woman's point of view."

"Well, why don't we start with the word 'court,' " Georgia began. "I suppose that we got the word from what went on in the courts of kings and queens. There were lots of rules of etiquette. Courtship was a kind of dance of communication according to those rules."

"What are the rules?"

"Good heavens, I don't know. But I do know that good manners were also developed in the courts. I suppose the rules are the rules of good manners. So I would advise you, if you want to court Mrs. Grochowski, to do so with good manners."

"What are good manners?"

"You haven't seemed to know much about that subject, have you, Hank?" Georgia couldn't resist the barb. "Good manners are mostly a question of respect. When you are dealing with someone in court, you are dealing with someone of very high rank, like a princess. Perhaps when you want to court someone, you have already placed that person in a position of high respect."

"Mrs. Grochowski is certainly in that position in my mind."

"Then you treat her with respect. I think that's all manners are. Treating people with respect."

"Like don't just reach out and grab them?"

"Yes, like that. Respect the integrity of their body. Respect their privacy. Respect their right to say no. But it's more than just that. You respect their personality. You respect their humor and their wisdom. You respect their history, their experience."

"How does someone get to know all that?"

"That's the point, Hank. Respect is getting to know all that. If a woman wants to be respected—and who wouldn't?—she won't want you to lay your hands on her until you have learned all that."

"It sounds like an awful lot of work to me," Hank commented.

"But what woman wants a lazy man? Besides, there are some people who happen to think that that sort of work is kind of fun."

"I don't know. I haven't done it before."

"Certainly not with me."

"Is there anything else you can tell me?"

"I don't think so."

Hank got up and limped with his cane to the door. "Thank you, Georgia," he said.

Georgia looked at him framed in the doorway and for the first time realized he was actually not an unattractive man. He was slender. He was small, but he kept himself well groomed. Why had she never noticed these things before? She could imagine him as someone's lover. "Good luck, Hank," she said. His seriousness had touched her.

After he was gone, Georgia sat in her rocker, bemused. She looked down at her hands. Yes, they were an old woman's hands. But that didn't mean they were ugly. It didn't mean that her life was at an end. Maybe she, herself, might even get interested in a little courtship some-day. The thought of there being romance again—even sex—in her life was most new and strange. But also entertaining. She smiled softly to herself.

Feeling that he deserved it—having completed the case—Lieutenant Petri had decided to sleep in that morning. He had just gotten up and was holding his coffee cup when the phone rang a few minutes before ten. It was Mitchell. "I thought you would want to know that they just brought Hubert Stimson into the hospital DOA," he announced.

*"What?"*

"Hubert Stimson's DOA at the hospital—you know, the husband of the woman you arrested yesterday."

"And the man I interviewed yesterday afternoon. Jesus Christ."

There was a long silence over the phone. Finally Mitchell asked, "Sir, are you there?"

"Yeah, I'm here. I'm trying to collect myself. I mean I just talked to the guy yesterday afternoon. How did he die? Was it suicide?"

"I don't think so. I don't know. All I know at this point is that the maid came in to clean and found him lying at the foot of the stairs. Apparently a big bruise on his head. Looks like an accident, I guess."

"Is he still at the hospital?"

"Yes."

"Well, call them and tell them to keep him there. I'm coming down. And, Bill, alert the chief. And phone the medical examiner, will you? I want him in on this one too. There's a question of suicide. Tell him I want blood levels on everything."

Was there anything else he needed to tell Mitchell? He noticed that his hand was shaking on the receiver. "Would it be possible for you to meet me down at the hospital, Bill?" he asked. "I'd kinda like to have someone to talk with."

"Sure, sir."

Petri hung up the phone. "Holy Jesus!" he whispered.

He shaved and showered quickly, and by ten-thirty he was viewing Hubert Stimson's body. The face that had been flushed with anger the afternoon before was now white with a tinge of green, except for the huge, swollen blue bruise over the left temple. For the second time in viewing a corpse, Petri felt squeamish—although it was a different discomfort from that when he'd first seen Stephen's crippled body. "It's probably an epidural hematoma," the medical examiner explained, pointing to the center of the bruise. "The skull fractured here, severing the temporal artery right where it courses through the bone. You can see where the artery's bled out on this side, but there's probably an even bigger bruise on the inside, which pressed against the brain and caused death by brain compression. Can't be absolutely certain until I do the autopsy, and I won't be able to get around to that until tomorrow. But I'll get an X ray now before they take him to the morgue, and I'm pretty sure it'll show the fracture. Doubt it'll show anything else. The skin's not broken, which makes it less likely that he was hit by someone. If the fracture's depressed, though, I'd have to rethink that. I've drawn the blood and just now sent it to the lab for toxicology. It'll take them a little while. Why don't you call me after one, and I'll have a pretty complete report for you."

"Let's go see the judge while we're waiting," Petri said to Mitchell. "He's going to need to know about this. It'll likely change the picture in his remanding the old lady to the state hospital today."

When they got to the anteroom of Judge Michelwicz's chambers, his secretary told them the judge would be in court until noon. They sat down to wait. Dozens of thoughts were swirling around in Petri's mind, but the one that kept floating to the top was the comparison between Mr. and Mrs. Stimson. In his own way the man now dead, when alive yesterday afternoon, had felt to Petri to be just as evil as his vituperative, murderous wife. But they were evil in such different ways. What might account for differing flavors of evil? The question raised a very dangling loose end. "Bill, you were the one yesterday who started that talk about demonic possession," he said. "You don't *really* believe in that sort of stuff, do you?"

"Well, yes and no," Mitchell answered, unperturbed.

Now his own sergeant was beginning to sound like Dr. Kolnietz, Petri thought. But he was becoming more patient with ambiguity. "Okay," he sighed. "Go on. Tell me more."

"It's not easy," Mitchell said. "Excuse me, sir, but are you a Christian?"

The question caught Petri totally off guard. "Hell, I don't know," he stumbled. "I mean, like all the Italian kids in my neighborhood, I was raised Catholic. Baptized when I was a baby. Confirmed and all that. My mother used to drag me to mass. But when I was in high school I put it all behind me. Haven't thought about it. I guess since it's not important to me, I'd have to say I'm not. But why? Why do you ask?"

"Well, it is important to most of the people around here. It's sort of the 'buckle of the Bible Belt,' you know."

"I've been picking up on that," Petri acknowledged. "So?"

"But we Christians aren't all the same," Mitchell went on. "We belong to different camps, so to speak. One camp they call the charismatics. For about five years my wife and I used to be in that camp."

Why was he being so roundabout? Petri wondered. Couldn't he say "yes" or "no"? That he either believed in this stuff or he didn't? But he bit his tongue and simply urged, "Go on."

"Well, the charismatics take the devil very seriously. They tend to think we're all involved in what they call spiritual warfare. They believe that many people with psychiatric problems are really afflicted by demons, so they go around doing a lot of exorcisms with each other. 'Deliverances' they usually call them. My wife and I participated in a number of them."

"You said you used to belong to that camp?" Petri prodded.

"Yup. We got out. Number of reasons. But a big one was that from our point of view they took this devil business too seriously. Or, in some ways, maybe not seriously enough."

Too seriously or not seriously enough! Was Mitchell deliberately speaking in riddles? "What do you mean?" Petri asked in frustration.

"They did deliverances all over the place. A lot of the time it didn't seem to us to do much good. It was too simplistic. After a while my wife and I decided they were often barking up the wrong tree, and we just didn't want to be involved with the possession business that way. We go to a more traditional church now."

"So you don't believe in demons anymore?"

"I didn't say that," Mitchell replied with equanimity. "I believe in them sometimes."

"But how can you?"

"I've seen them, sir."

"*Seen* them?"

"Yes, sir. You see, occasionally they were barking up the right tree. I've seen them. Sometimes. Sometimes they're real. Very real."

Petri had come to appreciate his sergeant's competence. Now he suddenly glimpsed the possibility that this quiet man might have faced depths of reality he himself hadn't even dreamed of in his brief twenty-nine years.

"Okay," he said, "let's go back to Mrs. Stimson. Do you think she's possessed?"

"Maybe. She's got some of the signs."

"Like what?"

"Like her pure hate. Like her filthy language. But there's no one or two particular signs. Sometimes—on the surface at least—they'll talk real pretty and loving—and you begin suspecting it for other reasons, like they do something out of character or they hear voices telling them to kill themselves. But none of these things prove anything. They just start you thinking in that direction."

"How about Mr. Stimson? Oh, I know you can't tell. You didn't see him alive the way I did yesterday afternoon. But he struck me as being as evil as her, although in a very different way. He didn't shout or swear or any of that stuff. He was oily. He would have bribed me if I'd given him the chance. In fact, I think he would have killed me if he could have gotten away with it."

"I know the type," Mitchell responded with recognition. "The power-broker type. Yes, sometimes when I've been with that type I've had the feeling that Satan's hanging around."

"But was he possessed?" Petri insisted.

"Maybe."

Petri's new found patience faltered. "Maybe, maybe, maybe," he mimicked. "It's like it's every third word in your vocabulary."

Mitchell smiled, unoffended. "There's something I haven't explained to you yet, sir," he said gently. "The only time I've ever actually seen demons for sure has been during those exorcisms when we *were* barking up the right tree. That's the purpose of an exorcism: to flush them out. But until you do an exorcism you can only guess that they're in there."

"But how about Mrs. Stimson? Could you do one on her?"

"That's the other piece I haven't explained to you," the sergeant answered. "The only real exorcisms I've ever witnessed were done with people who wanted to be healed—who wanted to badly enough that they'd let us do it to them. Maybe our Lord could do exorcisms on people who didn't want it, but I don't think ordinary folk can. I didn't see much sign that the old lady wants to be healed. I think what Dr. Kolnietz did with her yesterday was probably the closest we'll ever come to an exorcism with that one."

Petri finally understood. "So what you're saying is that even though she's still alive we'll also never know whether Mrs. Stimson is possessed."

Mitchell nodded. "Yes, sir. I think we'll probably never know."

An unobtrusive buzzer sounded at the desk that guarded the inner door. "Judge Michelwicz has returned to his chambers," the secretary said. "He'll see you now."

Ordinarily Georgia would have gone directly to her room after returning from lunch in the dining hall but Peggy blocked her way. "Hi," she announced cheerfully. "Mrs. Grochowski would like you to come visit her when you've got a moment."

Summoned again, Georgia thought. She hoped the summons would be more pleasant than the last one. But then a lot had happened since that time.

And, indeed, it was different. Mrs. Grochowski was all smiles. "You didn't need to come *that* quickly," she said, "but I'm glad to see you. Sit down, Georgia. I'm sure you've heard they've solved the murder."

"Of course. You know how rapidly word gets around here. Actually, I began to suspect it as soon as they moved Mrs. Kubrick into your room and they placed a guard outside Rachel Stimson's door."

"Were you surprised?"

"I hadn't thought of her before the fact. But no, I wasn't after the fact. I only spoke to her once, but she was very rude. Not a nice person, I'd say."

"So one would gather." Mrs. Grochowski looked at her visitor closely. "I've some reason to believe, Georgia, you may have had something to do with solving the murder. What did you do?"

"Only what you instructed me. I simply asked to see the lieutenant and explained that I hadn't given him the whole picture. I gave him a few suggestions to round it out, and he followed it up from there."

"That must have taken a bit of thought."

"Not much."

"It's fun to think, once you get started, isn't it?"

Georgia hesitated. "Well, yes and no. I've always thought, but generally only of those things I wanted to think about. But then I suppose you can't call that real thinking, can you? So I'm not sure it's all fun. Because it means you have to look at things you'd rather not see."

Mrs. Grochowski chuckled. "That it does. But after a while you get in the habit of it, and then it begins to become a challenge. A zestful kind of challenge. What kinds of things have you not wanted to think about?"

"Things like my age. I haven't wanted to face my age."

"But now, obviously, you can. Tell me, Georgia," and here Mrs. Grochowski was looking at her very intently, "are you able to think about *everything* now?"

"How can I answer that? I mean, there may be things I'm not even aware I'm not thinking about precisely because I don't want to think about them."

"Clever, Georgia, clever. Then answer me this: If there was something you didn't seem aware of, and I asked you to think about it, would you do so?"

Why was she being questioned like this? Georgia wondered. But it didn't take her more than a few seconds to answer, "Yes, I would. You're a sort of teacher for me."

Mrs. Grochowski beamed. "Then please call me Marion. You know, you've never used my first name. It's as if you've been a bit afraid of me. But now that you can think, and are ready to think of everything, there's no need to be afraid of me, is there?"

Georgia smiled back. "I guess not."

"And now that you're not afraid of me—and not, I hope, in awe of me either—I'm free to make a proposal to you, Georgia, because you're free to turn me down. As you mentioned, they've temporarily moved Carol Kubrick in with me. She is not the most entertaining of roommates. I've been wondering whether you would care to be my roommate. But before you answer, I want you to think. I am aware, for instance, that you have your bed by the window. Anyone in her right mind would want the bed by the window, and that includes me. In fact, since I can't move from this bed, as far as I'm concerned, I have to be by the window. It's necessary for my soul. So if you were to move in with me, you'd have to give up the window."

Georgia thought hard. She did *not* want to give up the window. It would be a real sacrifice. But then, why sacrifice anything if not for something better? Come to think about it, weren't all decent sacrifices selfish? And then there were different kinds of windows, she was coming to learn—windows through which you could look inside yourself as well as outside yourself. "I can't say that I'm not still in awe of you, Marion," she finally replied, "but, yes, I would be happy and honored to be your roommate."

"Fine. It's settled then!" Mrs. Grochowski exclaimed. "Why don't you tell Peggy about it and ask her to start the arrangements?"

Georgia practically bounced out of the room to do so, enormously pleased by the accolade she had just received.

Mrs. Grochowski was also pleased. Georgia was clearly indeed "coming along." Moreover, the presence of another woman in the room, particularly one so alert and vigorous, would provide her with a certain small measure of protection. If she calculated correctly, Roberta McAdams would very soon be visiting. Mrs. Grochowski was unclear as to how that uncomfortable visit would proceed. She anticipated, however, that after it there would be some likelihood she might need whatever protection she could get.


For the first time in his life, Petri recognized the meaning of the expression "like being on a merry-go-round." Last evening he had been up: the pieces seemed to be all neatly wrapped together and he was feeling buoyed by the chief's congratulations and his self-congratulations. A night's sleep later, and he was down: it felt as if the package had come unraveled or, more accurately, that there was a whole new set of pieces and the package needed to be rewrapped. Nor was it just a matter of up and down; it was also one of whirling all over town. First to the hospital, then to the judge, then to interview the maid at Stimson's house, then to the morgue and the medical examiner. Mitchell was hungry and he'd let him go. He himself was without appetite. It was four-thirty in the afternoon when he finally got to Willow Glen to inform Mrs. Simonton.

"It looks as though it was an accident," he said when he was seated in her office. "Apparently he fell down his staircase at home and hit his head. The doors were locked and the maid let herself in with her key and found him at the foot of the stairs. There was an undepressed skull fracture. No suggestion that he was hit by any object other than the floor. The broken edge of the skull bone tore through an artery and caused what they call an epidural hematoma. He would probably have been knocked unconscious by the blow; death by brain compression from the hematoma occurred about an hour later. The medical examiner estimates that he probably fell around one in the morning and was dead by two or two-thirty."

Mrs. Simonton looked at him piercingly. "You seem somewhat down, Lieutenant."

"I am," Petri acknowledged. "It was a shock. You see, I informed him yesterday afternoon that I had placed his wife under arrest. It's hard to see someone alive in the afternoon and see his dead body the next morning."

"Yes, I can see that. But I should think that after your years in the police force, you might be inured to that sort of thing."

Petri looked at her wanly. "You're always on the ball, aren't you? Yes, there is more. He was very upset when I told him. Not that he seemed to be concerned about his wife at all. What concerned him was that it would get in the papers. He seemed absolutely terrified of it. He even vaguely tried to bribe me to keep it out of the papers. I didn't like him."

"I never liked him either, you remember."

"He was so upset, my first reaction when I heard of his death was that it was probably suicide. They say it was an accident. But was it really? His blood alcohol was two point two. Tests can't find any other drugs, at least not yet. But two point two is high. He was drunk at the time. He didn't look to me like a heavy-drinking man. And while two point two isn't outrageously high, it's really very high for an eighty-two-year-old man."

"Go on, Lieutenant," Mrs. Simonton urged.

He finally admitted what was really troubling him. "Well, I have a feeling that I caused his death. It's not real guilt. I think he was a son of a bitch. And I certainly had to do what I did. They call it an accident. But I don't think he would be dead today if I hadn't talked to him yesterday."

"I suspect that's correct. But I'm not sure what you mean when you say 'it's not real guilt.' Do you mean you're experiencing 'unreal guilt'?"

Petri managed another weak smile. "It's whatever the hell kind of guilt a person feels when he thinks he's caused someone to die and yet can't be blamed in any real ethical sense."

"I understand," Mrs. Simonton said consolingly. "You don't deserve to feel guilty, but you still do because you're a responsible sort of person."

"Anyway, it doesn't seem much like an accident to me," Petri continued. "Probably he fell down the stairs because he drank so much. But why did he drink so much? To numb his terror that it would be in the papers? Or was he so terrified that he wanted to die? He reminded me of a cornered rat."

"Many people die when life backs them into a corner from which they can't get out otherwise."

"But was it an accident, or was it suicide?" He was back to the same theme.

"Ah, Lieutenant, you'd still like everything to be either black or white, wouldn't you? Maybe it's not possible sometimes to distinguish accidental death from suicide. In fact, it's equally hard sometimes to distinguish many natural deaths from suicide."

"How do you mean?"

"You were struggling with this in regard to Heather. The notion that people would wait to die on her shift was a foreign one to you. Can you accept the fact now that the time of natural death may be a matter of choice?"

"I guess so," Petri acknowledged grudgingly.

Mrs. Simonton chuckled. "Still not enthusiastic about it, eh? Well, if you assume it to be the case that people can often choose *when* to die their natural deaths, then it follows that on some level they also actually choose to die."

"I still don't understand."

"Life wears us down, Lieutenant. We get tired, and eventually we get ready to quit. There comes a time when the biggest part of us would rather die than live, and that point is a moment of choice of sorts."

"But old man Stimson sure didn't look ready to quit when I saw him yesterday afternoon."

"Let me try once again," Mrs. Simonton plowed on. "Life wears some of us down very early. Others of us it wears down very slowly and gradually. Sometimes it wears us down very suddenly. It would seem, perhaps, that life had suddenly trapped Mr. Stimson—or maybe he had trapped himself with his own need for respectability. It all depends on how you want to look at it. It's seldom clear. But it does seem that life had suddenly gotten a death grip on Mr. Stimson last night."

At that moment understanding suddenly got a grip on Petri. It was nothing he could put into words. A door had been opened. His mind had instantly jumped into a new territory—one for which he didn't yet have a map, or even a name—but it was a place filled with a kind of light that felt very good to him. "Wow," he said. "I think I've got it. Thank you."

There was a long pleasant pause. Then Petri began to laugh heartily. Mrs. Simonton was amazed by his unaccustomed lightheartedness. "What's so funny?"

"I used to have a mentor, an old detective when I was back on the force in New York City, a wise old bird. Most of the things he said made perfect sense. But there was a quote he used to throw at me from time to time—I think it was from Judge Oliver Wendell Holmes—that never meant a thing to me. I think I just finally understood it."

"And what was it?"

"If I remember it correctly, the old judge said, 'I don't give a fig for the simplicity this side of complexity, but I would die for the simplicity on the other side of complexity.' "

It was Mrs. Simonton's turn to laugh. "You're right. I think you've got it."

But the lighthearted moment passed. "I need to tell Mrs. Stimson," Petri said grimly. "I'd prefer it if you'd be willing to do it with me."

"Of course."

"Do you suppose she might be relieved? I imagine it's hard to be relieved when you're under arrest for murder. Still, I'd be relieved if I was unhooked from that man. But God knows how she thinks. She's insane."

Then he remembered Dr. Kolnietz's telling him that most psychiatrists would probably consider her sane. "Actually I don't know whether she's sane or not," he added. "It depends upon your point of view. I guess that's another area where it just isn't all black and white, is it?"

"You're learning. Yes, you seem to be learning, Lieutenant."

"Trying to. Or rather, being kicked into it. But what do you think? Do you think she'll be relieved?"

"I'm too smart to even hazard a guess," she replied as they got up to go to C-Wing. "You're right that some people are relieved when the death of a spouse frees them from a dreadful marriage. The death can give them an opportunity to live again. But other people can thrive on terrible marriages."

"How could she possibly thrive on a marriage to that man?"

"She's eighty-two, isn't she?" Mrs. Simonton continued on their way down the corridor. "She's lived into a ripe old age off it. I think your friend Dr. Kolnietz would tell you that some of the very worst marriages are the most stable ones. There are husbands and wives whose psychopathology fits together like a hand in a glove. They may murder each other daily, but you can't pry them apart with a crowbar. I have no idea whether his death will be liberating for Rachel, or whether it will be like stabbing a crowbar into her life. Or perhaps something else altogether. God knows."

They nodded at the uniformed policeman by the door and went in to see Mrs. Stimson. She sat in her wheelchair, as usual doing nothing, just waiting.

"I have some bad news for you, Rachel," Mrs. Simonton said. Her voice was matter-of-fact, but Petri could detect an undercurrent of sympathy in it. "Your husband died last night. He fell down the stairs at home. It was a head injury. As far as they can tell, he was knocked unconscious right away, so there was no suffering."

Petri had expected that Rachel would simply not respond. But he was surprised. "You're lying," she said venomously. "I don't know why you're lying to me, but you're lying. He's not dead."

"I'm afraid he is, Rachel," Mrs. Simonton said.

"No he's not. He's not dead. The turd will be here to see me Saturday night. He always comes to see me Saturday night."

"He died, Rachel. He won't be seeing you Saturday night."

"Yes he will. He'll be here Saturday night. He damn well better come. He wouldn't dare not come. I know him. He'll be here."

Mrs. Simonton had borne the brunt of the visit and Petri felt it was his responsibility to do what he could to help. "Mrs. Stimson, as you may remember, I'm from the police," he said. "It's my job to look into deaths, to even make certain that they've occurred. I talked to your husband yesterday afternoon and he was alive. This morning I saw him in the hospital and he was dead. Later I saw his body again at the morgue. I know this is difficult news to hear, but I assure you, Mrs. Stimson, your husband has died. He is dead."

"GET OUT OF HERE, YOU LYING MOTHERFUCKERS!" Rachel screamed. "GET OUT. GET OUT. GET OUT NOW OR I'LL RIP YOUR FUCKING BRAINS OUT!"

There was nothing to do but for them to leave.

When they returned to Mrs. Simonton's office they both felt as assaulted, almost raped, as they had the morning before. Finally breaking their numbed silence, she commented, "At first blush, it would seem more likely to be the crowbar, wouldn't it?"

He didn't care to admit it, but Petri was too upset to continue a philosophic discussion of death and marriage and evil and relationships, no matter how much he now realized this woman had to teach him. He retreated into details. "I'm afraid I've got bad news for both of us," he said. "Yesterday I asked the judge to remand Mrs. Stimson to the State Hospital for the Criminally Insane for observation pending trial. He told me he'd take it under advisement and let me know today. But today I had to tell him about her husband's death, and he said it's changed the picture. No one even knows if they've got any other family at all, or even who the executors of their estates are. He's got his staff questioning the lawyers around town. We'll probably know something tomorrow, but until we do it looks like we're stuck with her. You with her here at Willow Glen and we with our limited force having to guard her around the clock. He says he isn't going to remand her anywhere until he knows more about where things stand. I'll let you know, as soon as I do, what's happening."

"Of course."

Petri suddenly became aware of how quiet it was. There were no typewriters clacking outside the door. "This place really shuts down at five, doesn't it?" he remarked.

"If you mean by this place the Administration Center, yes," Mrs. Simonton responded. "But if you mean Willow Glen, no. Life always goes on at Willow Glen. And death," she added.

The hell with philosophy. "It's time for me to shut down," Petri said, standing up. "It's been a difficult day."

Mrs. Simonton was sympathetic. She had unfinished business, however, and she held him. "I've come to like you, Lieutenant," she said. "You're conscientious. You're flexible. You learn. But there's something that bothers me about you. You were strangely heartless yesterday. You'd practically accused Heather of being the murderer. You were really on her case. Yet when you learned she wasn't the murderer, you never even gave a thought to letting her know she was no longer under suspicion. How come?"

Petri needed to be left alone. Why wouldn't she lay off? "I probably would have told her when I got around to it," he protested lamely.

"I'm not sure. What have you got against her?"

"I don't have anything against her."

"Yes, you do. Think about it, Lieutenant."

Damn her, Petri thought as he drove home. She said, "Think about it," and much as he didn't want to, he did. He thought about it all evening until he fell asleep. He had to admit there was some truth to her charge. He'd gotten stuck on Heather Barsten like glue. He'd been overfocused. Even when this had been brought to his attention, he'd had trouble letting go of her. And now, as Mrs. Simonton pointed out, when he knew she was innocent, he'd failed to treat her with concern. He'd failed even to be reasonably polite. It was true. It was as if from the very beginning he'd been out to get her. Why? Damn Mrs. Simonton! Why had he been out to get Barsten? Not consciously. But it did seem as though he'd had something against her. What? Why wouldn't the dragon lady leave him alone? It had been a bad enough day and now the evening, if anything, was worse.

## SIXTEEN

## Friday, April 1st

The dream came back. And even as he was dreaming it, Petri was dimly, simultaneously, aware that it was the same old exasperation that would soon explode into rage, horror, and shame.

He'd just finished painting the living room of his apartment. It was thoroughly white, clean. He turned around and saw the spot on the wall. He painted over it. He put the lid on the can and stood up. The spot was back. The same dark-green slime began oozing down the wall. He tore into the wall, ripping off slabs of Sheetrock. He dug through the boards into the insulation, trying desperately to get to the source of the oozing slime.

Only this time he suddenly broke through the wall to the other side. He enlarged the opening so he could step across into the next room. It was a small room. The floor was covered with ancient grimy linoleum. There was nothing in the room but a small, old-fashioned bathtub raised from the filthy linoleum on four short, dirty little porcelain feet.

He woke up.

As the ending of the dream was different, so was his feeling upon awakening. There was no rage, no terror. There was, however, the same shame, only mixed with an extraordinary sense of deep sadness. What in God's name was going on? Petri wondered. He knew that the dream was significant, even that it represented some kind of breakthrough. Of course, he'd broken through the wall. But why that funny little room on the other side? What was the meaning of the bathtub?

And then he remembered.

Drenched in sweat, he looked at the alarm clock. It was only four A.M.

He couldn't call Kolnietz at that hour, could he? Was it an emergency? It felt like one. But it wasn't fair to the psychiatrist. He'd just have to wait three or four hours to phone him. Christ, how could he possibly wait that long?

After visiting Mrs. Grochowski, Heather went in to see Georgia. "I'm back from my three days off," she announced.

Georgia felt almost as excited as a young girl. "And a lot's happened in those three days," she exclaimed.

"So I've heard."

"Heather, I'm sorry I got you into trouble. I had no business telling that lieutenant about your personal life."

"I never even held it against you at the time," Heather responded, "and Mrs. G. told me you more than rectified it. She also told me the two of you are going to room together."

"Yes. Whoever thought someone as smart as her would ever want to room with a foolish old woman like me?"

"After lunch, I'll ask Peggy to come in and get you started with the move. Maybe even I'll be able to help." Heather glanced around to assess the extent of the job. She noticed that the picture of the young girl in the swing was gone from the dresser and had been replaced by one of Kenneth and Marlene. But she did not comment upon it. She was thinking about Peggy. Mrs. Grochowski had also told her of the relationship growing between her and the young aide. For a flash Heather had felt resentful, in fact, jealous. Was she, herself, becoming expendable? But the feeling had passed quickly, to be replaced by that strange passivity, that emptiness that had been pervading her for the past two days. So what? Good for Peggy. So what if she was expendable? So what about anything? She no longer had any idea what she was supposed to do, who she was supposed to be. She was waiting to find out.

Georgia noticed her abstraction. "You don't seem yourself, somehow. What's going on?"

"I don't know," Heather answered. "I just don't know."

On the dot of ten Ms. McAdams strode into Mrs. Grochowski's room, clipboard in readiness for her biweekly rounds. "And how are you feeling today?" she asked.

It was the moment Mrs. Grochowski had been dreading for days. "I'm feeling quite fine, Roberta," she answered.

Ms. McAdams was startled. It was the first time a patient had ever used her first name. But she hid her surprise by making her customary mark on her checklist. "Do you have any complaints about the staff?" she proceeded down the list.

"Yes, I do."

It was also the first time she had ever known Mrs. Grochowski to complain about anything or anybody. What was going on? Again she acted as if nothing was out of the ordinary. "Oh? Which member of the staff is that?"

"You."

*"Me?"*

"Yes, you, Roberta."

Ms. McAdams knew instinctively that whatever was coming would be worse than difficult. But she was a master of composure. She became cold, as cold as she would possibly need to be. "And what complaint or complaints do you have about me?"

"You're unfriendly, Roberta. You're emotionally distant."

"I don't believe the staff should be personal with the patients."

"Oh? Why not?"

"Things work more efficiently when distinctions are not blurred."

"Roberta, our paths have crossed ever since you've been here, for four years now. Don't you think it's time you started treating me as a human being?"

"I respect you as a human being."

"It doesn't feel like it." Mrs. Grochowski looked at her closely, amazed at how opaque the young woman was. "Who are you, Roberta? I know this isn't easy for you. But I'll let you go if you just tell me one thing about yourself which lets me know you're human. Please. It's very uncomfortable for me not knowing whether you're a robot or not."

"I told you I don't believe in familiarity between patients and staff." Ms. McAdams turned to leave the room.

Mrs. Grochowski fixed her in her tracks. "You haven't even finished your checklist, Roberta. You're being derelict in the performance of your staff functions. What are you so afraid of?"

Ms. McAdams could not bear the taunt. Afraid? She turned back to look at the older woman lying in the hospital bed. "What specifically would you like to know?"

"Anything, just anything, that tells me you've got a soul."

Ms. McAdams said nothing. For an entire minute they stared each other down, the one standing and vigorous, the other paralyzed and helpless.

"Where do you go, Roberta?" Mrs. Grochowski asked, finally breaking the silence. "Do you go south to St. Louis or north to Minneapolis?"

"I don't know what you're talking about."

"Where do you go for sex? If you're human, you have to have sex. Where do you go for it? You're such a hidden person I suspect you wouldn't want to do it here in New Warsaw. Where do you go?"

Mrs. Grochowski thought she detected fear, but she couldn't be sure. She wasn't even sure her guess had been correct. "Why are you doing this to me?" Ms. McAdams asked.

"It's terrible sometimes for a person like me to be so helpless," Mrs. Grochowski answered her. "For instance, when I'm lying here in an empty room knowing there's a murderer about. All I could do was wonder who it was and whether I'd be next. As I wondered, I thought it was probably you, Roberta."

"But now you know it wasn't. Now you know it was Mrs. Stimson."

"Yes, probably it was Mrs. Stimson. I should have thought more about her. And I tried to feel badly that I misjudged you, Roberta. But you know, I couldn't. Because there's still a lingering doubt in my mind. Yes, it was probably Mrs. Stimson. But you hated Stephen too, didn't you? And even when I assume it was Rachel Stimson for certain, I'm still worried about you, Roberta. I'm worried about what you might do someday. And I felt I needed to do whatever I can to protect myself and others."

What was the expression on McAdams's face? Mrs. Grochowski wondered. If there had been fear, it seemed to have faded. What she saw now was a faint supercilious smile, almost a smirk. The woman's voice was incongruously flat, calm, as she said, "I don't have to listen to your ridiculous, brain-damaged meanderings."

"No, you don't, Roberta," Mrs. Grochowski answered. The viciousness had not surprised her. "You can walk out on me any second, any time. But you won't be able to wipe me out of your mind. You'll have to come back here every two weeks with your checklist, won't you? And even if you choose to skip over me and fake your list, you'll be aware of doing it, aware of me. There's no way you can avoid me. You'll always be aware that there's someone in Willow Glen who knows who you are."

The arrogant smile became more pronounced. It was almost as if it were a game McAdams had begun to enjoy. "And just what do you suppose I might do with this awareness?" she asked.

"It seems to me you have three choices, Roberta. The one I hope you'll take is to seek healing. Dr. Kolnietz is a very good psychiatrist. But you can go some other place to see somebody else if you desire. Please. Please get help. Anybody can be healed if they want to badly enough."

The expression was unchanged. "And what exactly are the other choices?"

"You can move out of town to get away from me. Or you can kill me to get rid of me. But Roberta . . ."

"Yes?"

"I'm not so stupid as to put myself in any greater jeopardy than I need to. I've let people know that if anything untoward should happen to me, they're to think of you."

Ms. McAdams looked at the last item on her checklist. "Do you have any requests?"

"Yes. Please get help, Roberta."

McAdams wheeled around and strode from the room.

The chances were slim, Mrs. Grochowski mused when she'd left. And if Roberta McAdams moved to another town, another state, what would be accomplished? Except to put the problem elsewhere? Although maybe, at least, it might be delayed a little bit. "Dear God," she thought, "I hope I did the right thing."

Kolnietz could not resist the joke. "We've got to stop meeting like this, Lieutenant," he said, feet up on his office desk, in between bites of his sandwich.

But Petri was in no mood for humor. "I'm sorry to take up another one of your lunch hours. And I probably should have told you over the phone that it isn't police business. It's personal business. I'll pay you whatever your fee is. But I was desperate. I needed to see you. I've got to talk with you."

Kolnietz took his feet off his desk, hiding his surprise. For whatever reason, Petri had switched himself to the role of patient, which was a more honorable estate than police officer. It required greater courage and deserved the utmost respect. "Tell me what's up."

Petri recounted his repetitive dream and this morning's unexpected new ending. "I wondered why the bathtub, and then I remembered."

"Go on."

"I was an only child. My father left my mother soon after she had me. I don't even remember him. She never remarried. She never even dated. I think I was a substitute. She doted on me. Too much."

Petri's voice seemed normal, but Kolnietz could feel his tension. Whatever he was about to say wouldn't be easy. "Keep going," he urged gently.

"The bathtub in my dream was the same as in the grubby little apartment where I grew up in Newark, New Jersey. My mother liked to bathe me when I was young. I don't know how young I was when it started. It seems to go back as far as I can remember. Anyway, when the bath was finished, she'd dry me off. Then she'd sit me on the edge of the tub. She'd kneel down on the floor and take my penis in her mouth and she'd suck on it until I became erect."

He was blushing now. "Keep it up," Kolnietz said. "You're doing just fine."

"I enjoyed it. I can remember that. I enjoyed it a lot. It felt good. Yet I also always seemed to sense that there was something wrong about it. I looked forward to it, but I felt bad about it at the same time. Then one evening when I was about twelve—maybe I was eleven—I came in her mouth. It was the first time I'd ever had an orgasm. In one way it was wonderful. But I didn't know what was happening, and even more it was frightening and disgusting. And that was the last time we ever did it. I don't know whether she was the one who stopped it or whether I was. I honestly can't seem to remember."

"I understand," Kolnietz said softly.

"It was right after that, I think, that I started to hate her. I'm not sure, but I can remember from about thirteen on I not only couldn't stand her to touch me, I didn't even want to be near her. We lived in the same little apartment until I was twenty-one, but I wouldn't even talk to her unless I had to. For the next three or four years after I moved out I'd occasionally drop by the apartment—not to see her, but just to use it as a place to crash or get a free meal. I haven't been back since. I haven't seen, spoken, or written to my mother for the past four years. She doesn't even know where I live, and I don't even know whether she's alive."

There was a long pause. The story was out—at least the bare bones of it. But what was its meaning? Kolnietz wondered. And how best to explore that meaning? He decided for the moment to let his new patient take the lead as far as possible in exploring it for himself. "So this dream led you to remember a sexual relationship with your mother which you had forgotten," Kolnietz said neutrally.

"Well, that's sort of funny. I can't truly say it was something I'd forgotten," Petri responded. "It's kind of like I knew it all along, but I just never thought about it. It's like it's been sitting in the back of my mind for the past fifteen or twenty years, and for some reason I wanted to keep it back there. It isn't so much I couldn't remember it as I just didn't want to think about it."

"Excellent," Kolnietz said appreciatively. "That's a very good description of the way these things usually work."

Emboldened, Petri continued, "But even though I didn't think about it, I have a sense now that it did a lot to govern my life. I'm pretty sure it has a lot to do with why I've put so much distance between me and my mother. Maybe it even has something to do with why I came out here to the Midwest—to get away from her."

There was another long pause. There was obviously a great deal more here to examine, but Petri seemed to need a push. "I wonder why you might have had this particular breakthrough dream at this particular time?" Kolnietz questioned.

"I wondered that myself. I think it may have to do with the murder and Mrs. Stimson. I think maybe because of what she did to me, I've thought about my mother as if she were evil. Certainly I've treated her that way—as an untouchable who deserved to be punished. But then the other day when you got Mrs. Stimson to open up, I saw real evil. I mean, it was pure hate. I don't think my mother should have done what she did—I think it hurt me—but I don't think she was evil. In fact, as I've been examining it all morning, I've realized for the past fifteen years I've treated her pretty shoddily. Yet she just took it. She never seemed to hate me back."

"So?"

"So maybe it's time for me to forgive her. I mean, I really don't know who the hell she is. I might not like her if I talked to her, but I haven't talked to her all these years. I think I owe it to her to at least be willing to do that."

"So?"

"I've been thinking maybe I'll write her. And, depending on how she responds, maybe I'll go back to see her sometime this summer and try to find out something about who she is."

Kolnietz was moved. Petri must indeed have been examining this all morning. He'd already done a lot of work. There was obviously some real healing going on. But he seemed remarkably comfortable under the circumstances and the psychiatrist had the uneasy feeling that there was still more, that something was missing. "I can understand why Mrs. Stimson's real evil called your image of your mother as evil into question," he said. "And that your dream was helping you to deal with the discrepancy. But you saw Mrs. Stimson's evil Wednesday. I wonder why you didn't have the dream Wednesday night? Why last night instead?"

"Hell, I don't know."

Well, maybe and maybe not. The response was too quick. There was something Petri didn't want to look at. "What happened to you yesterday?" Kolnietz asked.

"I spent the whole day dealing with Hubert Stimson's death. Did you hear about it?"

"Yes," Kolnietz answered. "Mrs. Simonton called to tell me about it. But go on."

"Well, there's really not that much to say. I went to the hospital to see the body. Then I talked to the person who found him. Then to the judge. Then to the medical examiner. Then Mrs. Simonton and I informed Mrs. Stimson."

"That's all?"

"Well, Mrs. Simonton and I talked a little bit afterwards."

"What did you talk about?"

Suddenly Petri blushed. "She criticized me for having something against Heather Barsten. I realized she was right. I'd been so quick to get on her case and so reluctant to let go of it. I was wondering why all evening, but I couldn't come to any answer."

"Does the dream give you the answer?"

Petri was still blushing. "It does, doesn't it? I guess this oral sex thing has been a real hot button for me. I guess automatically I saw Ms. Barsten as being evil for having oral sex with the victim because I saw my mother as being evil for doing oral sex to me."

"It does make sense, doesn't it?" Kolnietz commented with a kind, teasing grin.

"Jesus, your unconscious can really screw you up, can't it?" Petri said with consternation. "I mean, how can I ever be a good detective when this sort of thing can happen to me and I'm not even aware it's happening?"

"But you are becoming more conscious," Kolnietz consoled him. "All serious prejudices are unconscious. You've not only just overcome a serious prejudice; you've become aware of how you can be prejudiced. You're well on your way to becoming a better detective, not that you were bad before. You were just human. And young. But the point is, you're growing."

Petri was still not ready to let himself off the hook. "I not only reacted to her like a righteous prude; I was ready to crucify her for it. Where do we go from here, Doctor?"

Kolnietz picked up on the use of his professional title. "What do you mean?"

"Are you going to be willing to take me on as a patient?"

"Why should I?"

"Well, I know you must be awfully busy, but I respect you and I really need therapy."

"Why do you need therapy?"

Petri looked exasperated. "Why do I need therapy? My God, I've just realized that I was an incest victim, that it's screwed up my relationship with my mother, and that it almost caused me to make a serious mistake in my work—and you ask me why I need therapy!"

Kolnietz put his feet back up on his desk and gave him a wide grin. "It's highly likely that you'll need therapy some day, Tom," he said, "and if I'm still around when that day comes, whether it's next week, next year or the next century, I'd be honored to work with you. But you've told me nothing to indicate you need to keep seeing me now."

"I haven't?" Petri was amazed.

"All of us are screwed up and neurotic, but a few have the good fortune—and perhaps you are one of those few—to be able to grow out of it quite naturally on their own. The time to get into therapy is when you're *not* growing; when you're stuck. That's why Heather's been working with me: because she's stuck. You've been stuck, but you seem to be becoming unstuck by yourself. Your healing not only seems to have begun; at this point it seems to be proceeding with unusual rapidity."

Petri felt oddly disappointed. All morning he had been gearing himself up for being a long-term patient, and this surprising verdict of health came as a letdown. But he had to acknowledge that the psychiatrist's judgment made sense. Things did seem to be moving very fast for him. "Why might I be one of those few who become unstuck by themselves?"

"Hell, Tom," Kolnietz exclaimed, "once again we don't really know the answer to questions like that. Only little glimmerings. For instance, you may remember me telling you that Heather's mother didn't love her, didn't regard her as valuable. So she's stuck feeling not valuable in relation to men. Possibly you're becoming so easily unstuck because—despite how she truly did hurt you—your mother really *did* love you. I don't know. What I do know, young man, is that my lunch hour is up and I've got another patient waiting. I'll send you a bill. And don't feel rejected. If you're having trouble dealing with all this—if you still think you ought to get therapy—give me a call anytime. Tomorrow even. Next week. Anytime that you get stuck."

Kolnietz had lied. His next patient was not due for another four minutes. He wanted the time to savor what he had just witnessed. It was one of the things that kept him in the business. More often than not, people refused to grow at all, and even those like Heather who did have the courage to seek therapy usually moved at a snail's pace. What a privilege it was to see the unconscious *really* at work, producing a dream such as Petri's, and to witness such a rapid, graceful leap forward. Ballet had always bored him, but for the first time in his life Kolnietz could imagine the pleasure someone might take in watching it.

•     •     •

Mrs. Simonton was happy to put down her paperwork when Petri showed up at Willow Glen at the end of the afternoon. She eyed him quickly. "Well, Lieutenant, you look considerably better than you did this time yesterday."

"I'm feeling much better," Petri acknowledged, "and part of it's your fault."

"Oh?"

"You kept bugging me yesterday about why I'd been so much on Ms. Barsten's case. I kept thinking about it and this morning I figured it out."

"Oh?"

"I realized I'm not without my own sexual problems."

"Oh?" Mrs. Simonton raised her eyebrows for the third time.

"And beyond that it's none of your business," Petri said with a smile. "I took it up with Dr. Kolnietz and he performed instant psychotherapy on me. But I do want to thank you for pushing me on it. You were right. I was not being fair to Ms. Barsten. I was hung up on her, but I'm not any longer."

Mrs. Simonton thought again of how much she was beginning to like this young man. So he'd asked Kolnietz for some personal help. Smart. "But I'm sure you didn't come here just to thank me for straightening out your sexual life," she teased.

"As usual, you're correct. I talked to the judge this afternoon. He's found out the Stimsons, as might have been expected, are represented by Stefanovski and Underhill. Underhill, in fact, has been their estate lawyer and is named as the executor in both their wills. They have no close relatives. He's setting up a funeral service Sunday afternoon at the Lutheran church for Mr. Stimson and expects a lot of the townspeople to turn out. Everyone knows, of course, that Mrs. Stimson is under arrest for the murder. A number of curiosity seekers will probably be at the funeral hoping to see her there. If she attends. If she does, of course, I argued it would have to be under guard, to which both Underhill and the judge agreed. They also agreed to leave it ultimately up to your judgment whether she should or shouldn't attend. And finally, the judge has issued an order remanding her to the State Hospital for the Criminally Insane on Monday for observation pending trial. Underhill has listened to the tape of the interrogation and he's agreed not to fight this, but he will be appointing one of the younger lawyers in the firm to start representing her as soon as she's transferred to the hospital."

"All of which sounds eminently reasonable, of course," Mrs. Simonton commented, "except the part of my having the responsibility of determining whether she should or should not go to the funeral. Not that that's unreasonable; I'd just rather not have it. I suppose we ought to tell her the gist of these things. Shall we do it together again?"

"I guess so," Petri agreed.

The guard at Rachel's door had nothing significant to report. "She just sits in her wheelchair, staring into space," he told them, "except when she's in bed, eating, or in the bathroom."

"It's a dull job," Petri commiserated, "only it has to be done. She could kill somebody else if she wheeled herself out of there." The policeman seemed pleased by this affirmation of his importance.

Mrs. Simonton took the lead in talking to her. "Rachel, your lawyer, Mr. Underhill, has been appointed to look after your affairs. This is Friday afternoon. Monday you will be transferred to the state hospital for observation." Realist though she was, somehow she could not bear to spell out that the hospital was specifically for the criminally insane. "Mr. Underhill will see to it that you will be well represented by counsel from his firm. Do you understand?"

Rachel sat in her chair, apparently oblivious to what had been said.

"Your husband's funeral will be at the Lutheran church on Sunday afternoon. Do you think you will want to attend? Particularly since you will be under guard?"

Rachel exploded. "GET OUT OF HERE, YOU FUCKING LIARS!" she shrieked. "HE'S NOT DEAD. DON'T YOU REALIZE I'M IN CHARGE? HE'LL BE HERE TOMORROW NIGHT LIKE HE'S SUPPOSED TO, THE LITTLE PRICK."

They left. There was no point to doing anything more. They didn't even go back into Mrs. Simonton's office. "It's early," she said surprisingly when they reached the foyer. "But I think I'll go home anyway. Willow Glen can do without me occasionally."

"I should hope so," Petri said to her.

She told the receptionist that she was leaving and asked her to inform Ms. McAdams. At that moment she didn't even feel like telling her own deputy. "God knows what she'll do when her husband doesn't show up for his usual visit tomorrow evening," she said to Petri. "I'll ask the staff to be on the alert. At the moment, it looks as if I'll probably decide she shouldn't attend the funeral. But I'll come in Sunday morning to talk with her and make a final assessment."

"Thanks," Petri said.

They parted in the parking lot. Mrs. Simonton was not feeling uplifted. Who could after talking with Rachel and witnessing the power of the human will to reject reality in favor of itself? Yes, there was reason for her sadness. But the world was larger than just the Stimsons. After Petri had driven off and she was getting into her own ancient Buick, Edith Simonton became simultaneously aware of several things. One, of course, was how uncharacteristic it was that she was leaving early. But why shouldn't she? After all, she was on the side of the angels, wasn't she? Another was that it was still light out. The snow was gone. Everything was still brown and the stubble left in the cornfield across the road was stark and sterile. But even though the sky was cloudy, there was a hint of balminess in the late-afternoon air. The ache inside of her felt very different from her customary one. Maybe I'm even getting a touch of early spring fever, she thought as she started up the old engine.

## SEVENTEEN

### Sunday, April 3rd

Mrs. Simonton had a restless night and awoke early, worrying about Rachel Stimson. Hubert Stimson's funeral was at one o'clock and she had a decision to make. How in the hell does one make that kind of decision? She guessed Rachel would still be denying the reality of her husband's death. Should she be sent to the funeral in order to break down that denial, to help her adjust to the reality? Or should she be allowed to have that denial and not be put through the ordeal of leaving Willow Glen for the first time in eight years to attend a public event under guard? Obviously the answer was to do whichever was the more humane. But what in God's name was that?

In any case, the decision couldn't be made until she talked with Rachel again. She was down at C-Wing by seven-thirty. "What on earth brings you here so early on a Sunday morning?" Heather asked with surprise.

Mrs. Simonton was pleased to see her looking well rested. "I've got to talk with Rachel to find out if she should go to her husband's funeral this afternoon," she explained. "How's she been doing?"

"I don't know. I haven't been in to see her yet, but I don't think so well," Heather replied. "The night nurse reported that about seven yesterday evening—which is when her husband should have come for his weekly visit—she began to wail 'Why isn't he here?' Apparently she wailed that same question—nothing more—every fifteen minutes or so until about ten. Then she stopped. Either the nurse or the aide checked her every two hours after that. She never got into bed. She refused to. She wouldn't talk. Just sat in her wheelchair. She never seemed to sleep. Susan thought of calling the doctor to order a sedative, but decided not to. A half an hour ago, when Betsy took her breakfast, she refused it. Turned the tray over on her, in fact. All over her uniform. I was just about to check on her myself."

"No, it doesn't sound so good," Mrs. Simonton acknowledged. "I'll check her because I've got to try to talk with her anyway."

She ambled down the hall and nodded to the patrolman standing outside her door. Entering, she saw that Rachel was sitting in her wheelchair next to the far bed, with her back turned to the door. Mrs. Simonton walked across the room to stand at her side. She realized with a start what a small woman Rachel was physically. Her body looked quite petite now the life had gone out of it. Because it had. With her head leaning forward against the edge of the bed, it was quite clear that Rachel Stimson had died.

Kenneth and Marlene Bates were feeling guilty that they had not been to see Georgia for three weeks. Their visits were always so difficult. Still, it bothered them that they'd been reluctant to come to her side after the murder. The feeling had remained even after Kenneth's call and his mother's mean put-down. This Sunday they went to the early service at church and drove straight to Willow Glen afterwards, hoping to get the ordeal over with as quickly as possible. They were surprised to find her room occupied by two other patients. Puzzled, they went to find Heather at the nurses' station and learned Georgia had been moved to Mrs. Grochowski's room.

Georgia got up from her rocker when they came in. She introduced them to Mrs. Grochowski, but allowed no room for small talk. "We can visit in the dayroom," she announced, and led them out. They did not even have time to notice that their picture was sitting on her dresser.

She didn't bother to introduce them to Hank Martin when they got to the dayroom. "I'd like to talk to my children here alone," she said to him. "You'll be a dear and leave us, won't you? Why don't you go down to my room and talk with Mrs. G.? It'll be a good opportunity for you, Hank. A-courting you will go."

Hank went out docilely. Georgia took an overstuffed chair and motioned them to the sofa. "How come you've been moved, Mother?" Marlene asked.

They missed the gleam in her eye as Georgia replied, "They just move you around like cattle in this place."

"How are you feeling, Mother?" Kenneth tried again with forced cheerfulness.

Georgia was unable to resist the temptation. "How do you think I'm feeling, being put in this concentration camp?"

"I see nothing's changed," Kenneth said.

"But things do change. I know I've said that sort of thing to you many times over the past year. But this is the first time I've been teasing."

*"Teasing?"*

"Yes, I'm teasing you."

"What do you mean?" Kenneth literally did not understand.

"The fact of the matter is that I am feeling quite fine, thank you. Indeed, I am enjoying myself quite immensely in this concentration camp."

"Enjoying yourself? Are you serious?" Marlene spluttered.

Georgia was delighted by their confusion. "Yes, I'm quite serious. And I'm quite happy to be here in Willow Glen."

"But what's happened? What's different?"

"A great deal's happened. There was a murder, for one thing. It's not every day that one's involved in a murder, you know."

Kenneth and Marlene glanced at each other uneasily. This did not seem to be the person they had become accustomed to over the past two years, and they were at sea. If she was, in fact, different, they knew neither the nature of the change nor how long it might last. It would be best to be quite careful. "We've been very aware of the murder," Kenneth said in measured tones. "You know that from my phone call. We were even considering taking you out of here, but when I asked if you were in danger, I was informed it didn't seem so. That was when the police came to see me because you'd been involved in some way."

"Did the police come to you?" Georgia smiled with pleasure. "Yes, I *was* involved. In fact, I helped to solve it. I didn't know who did it. But I helped put them on the right track. They had suspected the wrong person, but I set them right."

"We read Thursday that it had been solved," Marlene said cautiously. "We were so relieved."

"Yes, it was another patient. She was not a very nice person. For a while some of us didn't feel quite safe. But then they put a guard by her door. They don't need him anymore, however. She died a few hours ago."

"*She* died? You mean her husband died, don't you?" Kenneth contradicted her. "It was in Friday's paper."

Georgia continued to be delighted. "No, I mean exactly what I said. She died as well. This morning. Sometimes we patients at Willow Glen can know things even before they get into the newspapers. But you said that the police came to see you, Kenneth. Was it that nice young lieutenant? When was it?"

"It was about ten days ago. And yes, it was a young lieutenant. Petri, he said his name was."

"And I suppose he wanted to know if I was senile?"

"Well, sort of," Kenneth answered, blushing.

"Well, I'm not senile. I never was senile." Georgia paused. Then she continued, "No, that's not exactly true. I was going senile, but I changed my mind."

"You changed your mind?"

"Yes, I changed my mind. Senility does have to do with the mind, doesn't it? So if one changes one's mind, one can become unsenile, can't one?"

Kenneth and Marlene gaped at her. Georgia continued to take secret pleasure in their confusion, but by now she had a touch of remorse. "I know I seemed senile," she said. "And I know I hurt you. I blamed you for all kinds of things that were my fault, not yours. I'm sorry, and I hope you will forgive me. I don't expect you to forgive me very quickly, because I've been quite mean to you. But I hope you will in time."

Marlene looked at Kenneth, then piercingly at Georgia. Something was indeed very different about her mother-in-law. But some of her pent-up frustration surfaced as she probed. "Just why were you mean to us, Mother?"

"Because I was old and tired and I wanted to be here. But I hid this even from myself, and I certainly wasn't able to tell you that. I felt you wouldn't understand. What it amounted to was that I pretended to be senile, and then I accused you of forcing me here. It was terribly dishonest and unfair of me. I am sorry."

"You pretended to be senile?" Kenneth asked.

"Yes. Or, at least, I sort of pretended it. Perhaps a better way of putting it would be to say that I let myself become senile. But I've stopped letting myself any longer. I am not senile now. Maybe someday I will become senile. But I don't intend for that to happen for some time."

"If you're really not senile, then you can come home with us," Marlene said.

It was exactly what she had been anticipating. "No," Georgia replied firmly.

"Why not?"

"Because I don't want to."

"You don't want to? Don't you want to live a normal life? Don't you want to be with your grandchildren?"

"No. Those are just the kind of expectations which made me feel I couldn't tell you what I really wanted. But I am a grown-up woman now. I can tell you what I want."

"You don't want to be with your grandchildren?" Kenneth was aghast.

"No, not particularly. Maybe someday I will. But not now. I know it may sound harsh, but I'm tired. I spent many years taking care of you, Kenneth, and your brother and sister. Were I to leave here, you would want me to take care of your children from time to time. Adolescents still require lots of care in their own way. You would want me to house-sit for them. They are very nice children, what I've seen of them, but they're not my responsibility. They're yours."

"We wouldn't expect you to care for them," Marlene protested.

"Oh, yes, you would. Maybe not at first. But after a while you would expect me to be the doting grandmother. Maybe someday I will be a doting grandmother. Things change. For the moment, however, I just don't feel up to being a doting grandmother."

"But don't you want to lead a normal life again?" Kenneth asked.

"God forbid. I lived a normal life for many, many years. Now I am much more interested in leading an abnormal life."

"You mean you want to stay here?"

"Haven't you heard what I've said? That's exactly what I've been trying to tell you."

"But don't you want your freedom? Don't you want to be free to leave here?"

"No, I don't want to leave. Not at the moment, anyway. But I am quite free to leave here." Georgia was frustrated with their obtuseness. In the most decisive of tones she continued. "I can leave any time that I want. As you pointed out to me, Kenneth, all I have to do is to sign a form. They might hold me long enough for me to see a psychiatrist. I would tell the psychiatrist that I was born in 1912, and that I am seventy-six years old. And that it's early April, 1988. It's all very simple, you see. He would have to let me walk right out. But I don't want to walk out. I know it may be hard for you to believe, but Willow Glen is really quite an interesting place. We even make the newspapers. Besides which, I've made friends here."

"But it's so expensive," Kenneth protested. "You could live much more reasonably at home with us or in an apartment again."

"Kenneth, I know that I have done you and Marlene great wrong," Georgia answered firmly. "But I want you to get something straight. When your father died, he left me a good deal of money. I earned that money. It is mine to do what I want with. I know you have my power of attorney. I am glad you do. I trust you, and I would just as soon not worry about my investments. Frankly, I have more important things to think about. But having my power of attorney doesn't mean that you are in control of my life. Maybe if I really do become senile, you will be. But for now if you do not use your power of attorney in the way that I want you to, I will get it away from you within a week."

Kenneth and Marlene quickly stole another glance at each other. What were they to make of this? It was such brand-new behavior. She was speaking this morning with a strength and authority they had never seen before.

"I am in Willow Glen," Georgia went on, "because I have decided it is where I want to be. I know that that is difficult for you to understand. It would be for many people. But it is my choice. And it is my choice to spend my money to exercise my choice. As I said, things change. It is quite possible—even probable—that as time goes by I may well want to develop a relationship with my grandchildren—your children—but it will be done on my terms and not yours."

It was indelibly clear by now that their mother, once apparently senile, confused and unpleasant, had undergone some kind of metamorphosis. But two years of accumulated resentment compelled Marlene to ask, "How can we trust you, Mother? You've been pretty miserable to us. How do we know you really know what you're doing? How do we know it isn't some new kind of game?"

"I apologize, again, for the hurt I have caused you by falsely blaming you for putting me here," Georgia responded. "I mean that. It was a great sin. So great, as I said, that I do not expect any immediate forgiveness. But I am no longer dishonest. I am being quite up-front about my wishes. Frankly, I don't care any longer whether you think it is normal or abnormal for me to want to be here. This is where I want to be. It is my choice. And you will simply have to learn how to respect that choice. I am too old to fool around any longer. It is my life to do what I want with."

Then Georgia paused for a moment. "That's not precisely true," she added. "My life is not entirely mine to do what I want with. It's more properly a matter between me and God. God can appoint one every so often, you know."

"God?"

"Oh, I don't want you to go off thinking that I am senile again. Forget it. Just remember that at this point in time—this relatively brief moment—I am in control of my life. Do you hear me?"

"We hear you, Mother," Kenneth answered, "but I'm not sure we understand it all yet."

"I wouldn't expect you to. But I do hope you will continue to be willing to visit me. And maybe someday you can even bring the children. Now what would be a good time? By the way, I think it might be good for me to get an appointment book. Would it be possible, Marlene dear, for you to buy me one between now and our next visit? I'd very much appreciate it. It would help me to keep track of things just in case I do start getting senile someday."

Marlene agreed and they set a date for their next visit two Sundays hence.

Once they had pulled out of the entranceway and were driving back along Route 83, Kenneth said, "I don't understand it. Why on earth would she *want* to stay there?"

"You've got me," Marlene replied.

"I mean, it's such a waste of money."

"Would you rather she was nasty like before?"

"No, of course not. But it's as though she's just exchanged one form of craziness for another."

"I'm not sure of that," Marlene said. "Is she crazy or is she just not meeting our expectations?"

"But damn it," Kenneth burst out, "they're *normal* expectations, aren't they?"

"Yes, they are," Marlene said. "I don't understand it either. She's certainly changed—for the moment at least. But she certainly isn't normal."

They lapsed into silence, both trying to sort things out in their own way. And there was so much to sort. Obviously the murder had something to do with it all. But what? How had it come about? It was not right for her to be uninterested in her grandchildren. They wouldn't really expect her to house-sit, would they? What *should* they expect from her? As Georgia had suggested, it was going to take them time to adjust—a good deal of time.

Hank Martin's heart was beating so fast he wasn't sure he could move. For a moment he seriously thought that this might not be good for his health. But somehow he now knew life was about more than safety. And somehow he managed to propel himself into the doorway. "Would it be all right if I came in?" he asked, forcing his voice to stay calm.

"Of course, Hank," Mrs. Grochowski replied. "Come and sit down."

Hank did so. "I know it's awfully soon since Tim's death," he began, speaking the words he had rehearsed in his mind over and over. "If it's not appropriate, you just tell me so and kick me out. But I was wondering if I could pay court to you."

Mrs. Grochowski was startled. While Hank had never behaved inappropriately with her, she'd heard all the tales of his sexual misconduct. He had sounded like a rather stupid man. And, still grieving, she felt no desire whatsoever for sex or romance. On the other hand, she had a profound distaste for prejudice. For years she had trained herself to be open to life's unexpected and often oddly packaged gifts. No, she was not going to close any door unnecessarily. "Pay court? What a wonderful phrase," she responded with a careful welcome. "But that's not the sort of thing I can just answer yes or no."

"You can't?"

"No, we don't even know enough about each other to have a courtship. If you got to know me—even a little—you might decide you didn't want a courtship."

"Oh, I don't think I would ever feel that way," Hank proclaimed.

"Oh, but you might," Mrs. Grochowski cautioned him, thinking that his innocence was rather endearing. "And I might decide that I didn't like you well enough to want further attentions. That would be hard on you, wouldn't it, Hank?"

"I don't know. I can't tell what I'll feel in the future."

"Exactly," Mrs. Grochowski exclaimed. "We can't tell what the future will bring, can we? That's why I can't tell you simply that yes, you can pay me court. But if you're willing to take the risk, why, yes, I would be willing for you to *begin* to pay me court."

"Really?"

"Really. But remember, we must each be free to stop at any time."

"The trouble is that I have never paid court—even begun to pay court—to anyone before," Hank confessed. "I've just tried to put the make on them. I never had good manners. I've always been self-centered. I wasn't raised to have good manners."

"You weren't?"

"No, I was raised in the slums—the west side of Cleveland. Down by the mills. And then, as you suggested, I'm shy. You know you were the first person who ever told me I might be shy. I got to thinking about it, and realized you were right. So I don't even know how to begin to pay court."

"Yes, you do."

"I do?"

"Yes, you've already begun. You've begun to tell me about yourself. You've begun to tell me about your childhood. Tell me some more about that," Mrs. Grochowski suggested, thinking that Hank seemed perfectly intelligent, and authentic to boot.

"Well, I never really thought that there was much to tell. We Irish kids were always getting in fights with the Polish ones. I was small for my age. I remember one time when . . ."


Petri came to Willow Glen shortly after Mrs. Simonton called to tell him of finding Rachel dead. "So I didn't have to decide whether or not she should attend the funeral," she said. "Rachel made the decision for me. I've contacted Mr. Underhill and he's making the arrangements with the mortuary."

"We'll have to get an autopsy again, you know," said Petri. "I daresay they won't find anything, but we can't let a murderer just die without an autopsy, can we? What do you think it was, a heart attack?"

"Probably. Or possibly a stroke. Being a diabetic she would be particularly susceptible to either. You don't seem to be so surprised this time, Lieutenant."

"I've been trained," Petri smiled. "You've whipped me into shape. I doubt if ever again I will assume the timing of a death to be accidental. Eight years in here, strong as an ox, and the first time her husband doesn't show up for their weekly Saturday night fight, she dies the next day. It's dramatic, but no, I don't think it was accidental. I'd even give you three-to-one it was a heart attack."

"Oh, why?"

"Because it would stand to reason that she would die of a broken heart."

Mrs. Simonton beamed at him. "You are starting to talk like a psychiatrist, aren't you?"

"But what a strange heart! It still boggles my mind that such a hateful relationship could be so important to her."

"It does mine too, Lieutenant. For those of us more fortunate, sustained meanness seems hard to fathom. Why would anyone want to choose a life of hate? But think of the times you have hated someone. It's not easy to let go of that hate. It tends to feed on itself. It's like a bone that you want to keep gnawing on even though there is hardly a shred of meat or even tendon left. There's a lot of energy in it."

Petri remembered his all-too-recent feelings about his mother.

"Some people—though very few—seem to be able to live long lives on pure love," Mrs. Simonton continued. "But others—and we've had some here before—seem to be able to live into a very ripe old age on pure hate."

What was it Kolnietz had told him about good and evil? That it was like the rich get richer and the poor get poorer? "I don't think I told you," Petri said after a pause, "but this is the first murder case whose investigation I've been in charge of. I am sure I wouldn't have told you. I wouldn't have wanted to seem like a tenderfoot."

Mrs. Simonton appreciated the confession of what she herself had long since surmised. She was liking him more and more. It was time to use his first name. "You really didn't seem that way, very often, Tom."

"I had pictured it as being classical," Petri continued, "with all the evidence I had brilliantly accumulated being presented dramatically in court, my name in the papers, citations. But then as it turns out, my first real murderer is an eighty-two-year-old woman in a wheelchair who doesn't have any legs. I know she's guilty, but I don't have even a clear confession. There isn't even a motive that would make sense to the press. And then she dies a natural death four days after her arrest and before she can be brought to justice."

"A bit unsettling, eh?"

"Well, right now it seems more ironic. But you're right, unsettling and humbling." He realized how eager he was to share all his feelings and thoughts with this wise and tough woman. She too had been a mentor to him. "Still, while the case hardly conformed to my fantasies, I've learned more these past two weeks than I would ever have dreamed."

"Such as?"

"Such as things you've taught me—that death is seldom wholly accidental. What looks like natural death or accident may often be suicide of a sort. That people can choose when to die. But don't get a swelled head. You've hardly been my only teacher."

"Oh, I've got colleagues?" Mrs. Simonton asked with mock surprise.

"Yes, but you're not entirely in good company. Rachel Stimson taught me a lot about hate. And how people who may be judged sane are really insane. But someone else taught me the corollary to that."

"Oh."

"Mrs. Bates made it quite clear that someone who looks senile may actually be more competent than I am."

"That *is* humbling."

"But maybe the hardest yet the most important lesson was taught to me by Stephen." Petri realized he no longer thought of him as "the victim." It felt strange to be developing a relationship with a corpse. "Because he was so disfigured on the outside, I wrote him off as a reject. It took me a long time—and other people's eyes, yours, Heather's, Kolnietz's and, in a different way, Rachel's—to see him as he really was. He actually was a leader, wasn't he?"

Mrs. Simonton did not answer the question directly. "You're going to make a very good detective, Tom. You *are* a very good detective."

"And people who look like sourpuss bureaucratic administrators may be very wise philosophers and teachers."

"Well, we have quite a mutual admiration society going on here, don't we?" There was an odd touch of gruffness in her tone.

"It *is* a bit hard to say good-bye," Petri smiled, standing up. "But I may drop by Willow Glen every so often to see what real life is about."

"I'd like that, Tom. There's always coffee. See you around the campus."

Petri did not leave Willow Glen immediately. He went down to Rachel

Stimson's room on C-Wing. The body had been taken from her wheel-chair and laid upon the bed. He too noted how small it seemed now that the hate had gone out of it. Then he questioned the patrolman who was still guarding the door. His report matched Mrs. Simonton's. "You can go back to the station," Petri said. "There's no need to stand guard over a dead body. She can't hurt anyone now."

At the nurses' station Heather, as he had hoped, was sitting writing notes in a patient's chart. He cleared his throat. She looked up. "Well, Lieutenant," she said, "are you still keeping tabs on me?" There was a slight bite in her voice.

He tried to make a joke of it. "Yes. I interrogated Mrs. Simonton and the patrolman in depth. You apparently didn't go near Mrs. Stimson. It would seem you do have an alibi this time, Ms. Barsten." He smiled at her.

She did not smile back. "Is something I can do for you then, Lieutenant?"

"Yes, there is." He fished two letters from inside his jacket pocket, put back the one with a stamp, and handed her the other. "I wanted you to have this letter," he said. "I wrote it to you yesterday."

"What's it about?"

"I felt more comfortable writing you than saying it in person."

"I'll read it," Heather said coldly, and dismissed him by returning to her charts.

Walking out, Petri was only mildly disappointed by her response. He'd hoped for something better but had not expected it. He felt for the other letter inside his jacket. He would stop by the post office on his way home and put it in the box outside for the morning's mail. It was a letter to his mother.

## EIGHTEEN

## Monday, April 4th

Heather threw the letter onto Dr. Kolnietz's lap. "Just look at this," she said with outrage. "Just look at it!"

Kolnietz read:

Dear Ms. Barsten:

I would rather call you Heather, but I do not have your permission yet.

I very much owe you an apology in suspecting you of murdering Stephen Solaris. I did you an injustice. I not only seriously misjudged you, but I am sure I also caused you a good deal of unnecessary pain. I am sorry.

I have been laboring under a large number of stereotypes. Some of those stereotypes have started to go. I am sure that I have many more of which I am not even aware. But I hope that perhaps you might be willing to help me get rid of them too.

I was wondering if I could make my apology to you in person as well. Ideally over dinner. I must warn you beforehand that the lives of detectives are such that we must break about ten percent of our social engagements because of emergencies that we are called to work on. But with that forewarning, may I take you out to dinner some evening? Please call me at home or at the station to let me know.

I hope that I will be hearing from you soon.

Sincerely and apologetically yours,

TOM PETRI

Kolnietz handed the letter back to Heather. She stuffed it into her purse. He said nothing. Getting no reaction, Heather said, "The nerve of him, the absolute nerve."

"I am not sure I understand."

"You don't understand? You don't understand the gall of that man, practically arresting me, thinking that I could have murdered Stephen, and then having the nerve to ask me out for a date?"

"In the letter he is apologizing very clearly," Kolnietz said mildly.

"Oh sure. Apologies are cheap. And then to ask me out for a date after what he did to me!"

"He doesn't seem to be an arrogant sort of man."

"Well, you can have him if you want him."

"So you're not planning to go out to dinner with him?"

"I certainly am not."

"How are you going to answer the letter?"

"I'm not even going to bother. That will serve him right."

Kolnietz was actually aware of his muscles tensing before the leap. He pounced. "It seems that we have come to a moment of truth. Finally! For many months now we have been talking about the tapes in your head, the tapes that dictate that you should take up only with weak, passive men; men who are potentially violent men, men who are antisocial, men who are on the fringes of society and the law."

"So?"

"But you have not wanted to acknowledge the reality of these tapes, have you? You explain them away. You keep telling me that it is not a matter of these tapes, but a matter of opportunity. You say that you would like to go out with a better type of man, but such men just don't seem to be around. They just don't seem to be available. So you don't have a choice. But if you did happen to run into a good man, you would certainly choose to go out with him."

"That's right," Heather said. "I would."

"That's *bullshit*. I'm not saying you didn't believe it. Only now it's been exposed for what it is. Because now a very different kind of man is very politely asking you for a date, and you're just going to flatly reject him. Yes, he misjudged you. But considering the facts, probably any detective unfamiliar with the workings of a nursing home would have done likewise. Moreover, he had the intelligence to correct his mistake and has the grace to acknowledge it. Here you have the very opportunity that you've been telling me you've been waiting for, and you throw it away. You're full of it, Heather."

"But I don't like him," Heather protested.

"Why don't you like him?"

"Because he was mean to me." She sounded like a four-year-old.

"We've been over that. He wasn't mean to you. He was just doing his job. He was wrong, and now he's very humbly apologizing to you. That's hardly meanness."

"But I still don't like him."

"Why?"

"Well, the chemistry just isn't right. It's a matter of chemistry. Our chemistries don't fit."

"Oh. Does he smell bad?"

"No." Heather did not smile.

"Then why don't your chemistries fit?"

"I don't know. You can't explain a thing like chemistry."

"Do you have some kind of intuition that he's a bad man?"

Heather grabbed at the lifeline. "Yes."

"But intuitions are always based on at least some little observation or complex observations. What have you observed that would indicate he is a bad man?"

"I can't think of anything at the moment. Not now, the way you're hassling me."

Kolnietz was unrelenting. "As a psychiatrist, I'm supposed to be a specialist in intuition and a trained observer of people. What I have observed of Lieutenant Petri is that he is a hard worker, that he is intelligent, that he is able to revise his thinking with new information, that he is able to ask for help when appropriate, that he is grateful when he receives it, that he is friendly when the circumstances allow, and that he is capable of changing and growing. He also happens to have a good job which is this side of the law and a career in which he has clearly moved ahead. Why do you think he is a bad man?"

"I don't know," Heather wailed. "I told you, it's chemistry."

"What creates chemistry?"

"How should I know?"

"Do you think it's possible that tapes create chemistry?"

"Fuck you. I don't have to take this crap!" Heather shouted, jumping from her chair. She strode to the office door and turned the knob.

"So you don't even have the courage to stay in the same room with the truth," he shouted back at her.

"It's not the goddamn truth." But she had stopped by the door.

It was long enough for Kolnietz to continue more softly. "You can walk out of here, Heather. Therapy's going to work only if it's according to your own free will. But I want you to realize something. If you walk out of this room, you're also walking out on me. I'm not the greatest, but I think I am a pretty good man. I love you. I think I've tried my very best to be of help to you, and I don't think I've ever really hurt you. I think I've been a faithful therapist for you. But now you're about to walk out on me. You're not only sacrificing one good man, Petri, for your neurosis. Now in the same breath, I think you're about to sacrifice another. It seems to me it's a pretty high price to pay to keep a neurosis that you don't even want."

"Go to hell," Heather answered.

She slammed the door behind her, grabbed her coat off the waiting room rack, and ran out into the parking lot. She got in her car. "Go to hell," she repeated to herself. "Go to hell. Go to hell." Then she began to bang her head against the steering wheel.

At first Kolnietz had the fantasy she would come back. He sat in his chair, waiting numbly. After several minutes, he looked at his watch. Of course it would take her a few minutes to calm down, wouldn't it? No need to get alarmed for another five anyway. Now he waited anxiously. He checked his watch three times before the five minutes were up. Then he watched the hand circle another sixty seconds. He felt so helpless. He got up, crossed the room, sat down behind his desk, laying his forehead down on her chart, not even aware it was her chart. "Please, God," he moaned, "don't let her run away. Please, God, don't let her run away. Please, God, don't let her run away." He moaned it over and over and over again. It was like a chant.

He had no idea how long he repeated the chant. All he knew was that the moment finally came when it was clear he had lost. He began to cry. At first he wept silently, the tears pooling on his cheeks and beginning to drip on the chart. "Damn," he wailed. "Damn, damn, damn." Then he sobbed. He raised his arms above his head, laying them flat on the desk, with his nose ground into her chart, mucus blending with the tears, his diaphragm spasming uncontrollably.

When he first felt the hand soft on the back of his neck, it registered only as a neutral weight. Then as a kind of interruption. Why couldn't he be left alone with his grief? It was a full minute before he consciously wondered what a hand was doing on his neck. He looked up. Through his tears, all blurry, he saw Heather standing at his side, erect in her starched white uniform. "What's the matter?" he asked, stupid in his disbelief.

"I came back," she said.

"But I didn't hear anyone come in." It was as if he were testing the presence of an apparition.

"I came back," she said again.

He sat up and looked at her in focus. "I couldn't give you up," she said. "I got in my car. I wanted to, but I couldn't. You were right. It wasn't worth it to give you up."

He was still putting her in focus when she left his side and went over to take her usual chair. And she began to giggle. It was surrealistic. "Why are you laughing?" he asked in total confusion.

"Because you've trapped me. You've backed me into a corner. I've only got two choices. One was to scream at you and run out of this room and never come back. The only other is to laugh."

"You mean I've won?"

"Yes, you've got me. I'm defeated. It doesn't feel great. Part of me is saying 'oh shit.' But part of me is laughing. Laughing at myself. I've held out for so long."

"You actually mean I've won?"

"Yes, you're right. I don't know about chemistry. But I acknowledge that maybe my tapes are what create it. I guess I even admit it—admit that I'm the one who creates the bad chemistry."

"And that maybe if you alter the tapes, you can alter the chemistry?"

"Yes, for the first time I see that. For the first time I really see that my choice of men has been my choice. You've won."

"Then we've both won. Thank God." Kolnietz began to cry again, only this time they were tears of joy. The struggle was over. Tears of joy mixed with tears of fatigue and relief.

It was still hard to believe, but witnessing him crying, the sense that she was actually loved deepened in Heather. She would have wept herself had she not felt so light, almost playful.

Finally, he dabbed his eyes. "So what are you going to do?"

"Maybe I'll take him up on his dinner invitation."

"If you did, that would be to change the tape."

"Yes, it would."

"It's scary to use a new tape. It's like doing things totally differently than you've ever done them before."

"Still, I have that choice too, don't I?"

"Yes."

Heather smiled. "Well, maybe then I'll just take it out of pure perversity."

The hour was up. Kolnietz stood and, as usual, Heather followed suit. But then something unusual happened. Quite spontaneously, mutually and naturally, they moved toward each other and, for the first time, hugged. "I'll see you next Monday," Heather said.

When she had left, Kolnietz sat down behind his desk and put his feet up on her tear-soaked chart. It was his lunch hour. No Petri this time. No emergencies. But he didn't reach into the drawer for his sandwich. Nor did he move to write a note in the chart. That could wait. He wanted to savor the moment.

The battle was over. Thank God. There would be other battles with other patients, but this one was over. Oh, it would not all be smooth sailing with Heather after this, but the outcome of the race was no longer in doubt. She had won.

Then, as his tears dried, he thought of his wife. Ex-wife essentially. The outcome of his marriage was also not in doubt. That struggle had been lost. And his future was uncertain. But in this regard, at this moment, he experienced an unusual absence of fear. As he did with every single feeling he had, he examined this one. Why was he feeling such calm? A major part of it, of course, was the triumph he had just shared with Heather. And the release that comes with tears. But there was something more. Something small, but significant. What? It was another hug. He remembered the pleasure he had felt last week at the time of his brief reunion with Edie Simonton after the interrogation of Rachel Stimson. It shouldn't take a murder to bring about a reunion; reunions could be planned. As soon as his wife got out of the house in a couple of weeks, he'd have the old bat over for some of his homemade linguini with clams and wine. Hopefully the boys would warm up to her. They needed somebody like her around. And he did too, whether the boys kept their distance or not. The future was uncertain, but he was going into it with friends.

Mrs. Simonton had two tasks to do: one pleasant and one unpleasant. She'd scheduled the unpleasant one first. She went out to the waiting room where Mrs. Grimes had been summoned from home. "Please come in, Bertha."

She began gently. "Bertha, you've worked here for me a long time. It seems like almost endless nights. You've always done your work well. Not inspired, maybe, but well. You're a good and honest and hardy person. You've come through snowdrifts when no one else would."

There was a pause. Bertha waited, stolid as always. She knew she had not been summoned from home for a compliment.

"But now we have a problem," Mrs. Simonton continued. "I understand that not only are you a reader, but you read with great concentration. So much concentration that Stephen was murdered ten feet from you while you were reading. It could not have happened were you more alert. I am afraid that such a lack of alertness simply cannot be tolerated."

Bertha seemed neither surprised nor offended. In her usual phlegmatic way she simply said, "Well, I've been thinking about resigning. Sam's got a bid on the farm. We're going to retire down to Florida."

"When are you planning to do that?"

"Should be about two months from now. Expect the closing will be in six weeks."

"When do you want to resign?"

"About a month."

"So you'd like to work for another month?"

"Yup. Then I'll have a month's vacation time. We'll be well set, Sam and me."

"If I let you work for another month, can you promise me that you won't read on duty?"

Bertha looked dismayed.

"I wouldn't want to tell everyone that they can't read on the night shift," Mrs. Simonton said. "It's just that your concentration is so good, Bertha, I have to ask it of you. Willow Glen could have been sued because of your lack of attentiveness. Not only that, but we would have lost the suit." She saw no point in rubbing in the fact that Stephen might possibly still be alive, beginning to learn how to use his computer and open new worlds, were it not for her carelessness.

"How 'bout if I don't read except when the nurse is with me in the station?"

"Can you truly promise me to do that without fail?"

"Yup."

"Then that's a good compromise. We'll be missing you, Bertha. I hope things go well for you in Florida."

"Should have lots of time to read. And it will be warm," Bertha answered, getting up, instinctively knowing there was nothing more to be said.

It had gone more easily than she had expected, Mrs. Simonton thought. She flipped the squawk-box after Bertha's departure and called for Peggy. The life of farming people could be hard, she realized: Bertha might need the fantasy and the romance her novels gave her.

"You wanted to see me?" Peggy asked, standing at the open office door and interrupting her musing.

It was her usual greeting, but Mrs. Simonton saw a visible difference in her. "Yes, sit down, Peggy," she said. "I know your six months aren't up. But there's been a change in you, Peggy; just in the past week. The reports come in to me from all over. You seem to care now."

"I'm trying," Peggy acknowledged. "It's sort of like a game. Whenever I go into a patient's room I say to myself, now try to care. It's kind of fun."

"Yes, it's a good game. And because you're playing it, I think that we can put you on permanent hire, if you would like to continue working for Willow Glen."

"I'd like that."

"How did you make the change, Peggy? Why did you start playing the game?"

"Because of the murder. Well, it wasn't just the murder. If it had been another patient, I don't think it would have mattered to me. But it was Stephen. It's such a shame that he had to die."

"Yes, it was a shame."

"I hope his arms and legs are all straight now."

"Yes, I hope that also."

"Well, I suppose I'd better get back to work now."

"I suppose so.'"

Mrs. Simonton was acutely aware of how much Peggy had left unsaid, but she knew how difficult it was to talk of things of the heart. And it was a matter of the heart that was at issue. One thing more, however, did need to be said. "Peggy, the game won't always be fun. Sometimes when you care you can get your heart broken. When that happens I hope you'll feel free to come to talk with me about it. Because I don't want you to stop playing the game. It's the only way there really is to learn. In fact, it's the only game in town worth playing."

"Thank you, Mrs. Simonton," Peggy said. "You're okay."

"And thank you, Peggy."

It was only six weeks ago that she had thought it would take a miracle to turn Peggy around. Was that why she'd been feeling so well these past few days? No, it was a lot more than that. She'd seen miracles before. She also thought of how much she'd enjoyed seeing Stasz Kolnietz again. But that was just another little piece, and what was going on was something very big. For years there had been a heaviness upon her, and now it felt lifted. Not just temporarily. Of course the biggest single cause was that extraordinary "experience" she had had last week, the "voice" telling her so unequivocally that she was indeed in a deep relationship with God. But it also had to do with so many other things and so many people over so much time. She had gone through a long, long tunnel and finally come out the other end. What was it she had come through? Marion Grochowski would probably call it the Dark Night of the something or other.

At this thought Edith Simonton recollected that some time in the not-too-distant future Marion would be summoning her to her first communion. Perhaps it was childlike, but at the age of sixty, she found the prospect strangely exciting.

Roberta McAdams was also contemplating the future. Only she was doing it by using her computer, which was always the way she thought best. She would, of course, erase what she had written, but she still instinctively inputted it in code. A simple code. The screen in front of her as she sat at her desk, larger than any other in the Administration Center, now contained five such inputs, widely separated from each other:

S

M

S & K

S & T

S & KG

The *S* stood for stay. The *M* stood for move. *S & K* meant stay and see Kolnietz. *S & T* meant stay and obtain therapy out of town. *S & KG* signified stay and kill Mrs. Grochowski.

Those were the alternatives. Basically, they were the ones Mrs. Grochowski had given her. Except the simple one of staying. Surely there must be others. But she had been racking her brain for twenty minutes and had failed to come up with another—with one that was wholly positive. Each had negative consequences. So it was not a question of evaluating positives; it was one of choosing the least of five evils. She had no choice but to think in terms of negativity.

She looked at the top one: *S*. That was what she basically wanted: to stay. But as Mrs. Grochowski had pointed out, the woman's very presence would be an insult to her, knowing what she knew. Ms. McAdams moved the cursor under and slightly to the right of the *S* and punched in an *X*.

The next alternative was *M:* move. She didn't want to move. It would mean sending her resumé out, interviews, finding a new home, checking the rates of different moving companies, packing and unpacking: an extraordinary amount of hassle. She moved the cursor under and to the right of the *M* and punched in *X*.

Next was *S & K:* stay and see Dr. Kolnietz. She didn't even have to think; it was a matter of instant recoil. She had listed it only out of her lifetime habit of being methodical. She punched in another *X* with her cursor.

Next was *S & T:* stay and go out of town for psychotherapy. Again the recoil was instant. Again she punched in an *X*. But it did have to be considered purely because it was a theoretical alternative. She had long ago learned that if you didn't look at all the alternatives, you could make a mistake. And even the tiniest mistake might be fatal in this world where everyone was a potential killer.

Last was *S & KG:* stay and kill Mrs. Grochowski. It did not require much thought to realize that murder was inherently risky. She punched in her fifth *X,* and sat back to survey the results. The screen now read:

$$S$$
$$X$$
$$M$$
$$X$$
$$S \& K$$
$$X$$
$$S \& T$$
$$X$$
$$S \& KG$$
$$X$$

Yes, all the alternatives were negative. Now it was simply a matter of rating the negativity. "Weighting," they called it in statistics.

She went back to the beginning. Simply staying was negative because Mrs. Grochowski's presence would be an insult. How much of an insult? She would have to skip those twice-monthly visits, yet fake the reports. Two lies a month. Not a large problem in itself unless Mrs. Grochowski called her on it, and somehow she suspected she wouldn't. But there was more to it than that. Mrs. Grochowski had a roommate now. She'd have to go into her room at least sometimes to see Georgia Bates, who was such an old busybody to boot. Mrs. Grochowski had been right; there would be constant reminders. Ms. McAdams inputted another *X* under the option of simply staying, of doing nothing.

What about moving? It was an unpleasant thought because of the hassle, but there was, in fact, nothing else against it. She had no particular attachment to Willow Glen or the town. She would have no trouble whatsoever getting a similar job elsewhere; indeed, she would be able to have her pick of places and their computer systems. The negativity could all be categorized under the hassle factor and, while it was large, it was also manageable. She decided, for the moment, not to input an additional *X.*

Stay and do psychotherapy with Dr. Kolnietz? The alternative was only theoretical. There was nothing wrong with her. She had no reason to need therapy, and what went on inside her was nobody's business. Then there was the expense and the time. Besides, she couldn't abide the man. He was so ordinary. She should let someone so ordinary lord it over her, fiddle with her, make her submit to his mercy? She immediately typed in four additional *X*'s under the alternative.

Stay, but go out of town for therapy? Same objections. Even more time required. The only reasons would be the guarantee of privacy and that she could, undoubtedly, find someone more controllable. But the fact remained, she didn't need therapy in the first place and it would be putting herself in enormous jeopardy. She typed in three additional *X*'s.

Stay and kill Mrs. Grochowski? She'd made her initial *X* because murder was inherently risky. But in this case it was more than that. Mrs. Grochowski had threatened her. If anything happened to her, people had been told they should think of her, Roberta McAdams. Of course, she could have been bluffing. No, Mrs. Grochowski was not the kind to bluff. She inputted another *X*.

She sat back and surveyed the picture on the screen as it had developed:

S
XX
M
X
S & K
XXXXX
S & T
XXXX
S & KG
XX

She had done her duty; she'd been thorough and listed *all* the alternatives. But some alternatives were simply illogical—basically unthinkable. Her computer demonstrated the fact. Quickly she erased *S & K* and *S &T*. The screen now read:

S
XX
M
X
S & KG
XX

Those were her only real options: stay, move, or stay and kill Grochowski. At this point it looked like moving on was the best—or the least negative— of her alternatives. Yes, that was probably what she should do. But there was no need to make an immediate decision. She manipulated her cursor and erased the remaining input. She would sleep on it and go through the now-abbreviated process again. Things had a way of changing overnight. In fact, she could sleep on it for many nights. Probably she would move. But at this point, she just wasn't sure.

The wing was quiet when Heather got back from seeing Dr. Kolnietz, and she sat down at the nurses' station to think. So much had been happening. Not just external things like the loss of Stephen, his murder. Internal things as well. Why had she suddenly asked Mrs. Simonton if she could see Dr. Kolnietz on a more regular basis? Was it because Mrs. Simonton had been so understanding at the time? Or was it that Dr. K. had told her something about his own troubles, in his own vulnerability making himself less threatening? Or had her work at Willow Glen become less important? Or had therapy become more important? Or had *she* become more important? All the threads were so interwoven.

Then had come that odd feeling of passive waiting, the strange fantasy of herself lying on the desert floor, the emptiness. What had she been waiting for? Could it have been for the session she had just had with Dr. K.? It was almost as if she had had some sense of what was coming. But how could she have sensed something that hadn't happened yet?

She realized that passive feeling of waiting was gone now. In its place she had a sense of calm but powerful energy. The nurses' station seemed smaller and she herself larger. Might she ever work someplace else? she wondered suddenly. Could she be anything other than a licensed practical nurse? Would it be feasible for her to go back to school? To study what? She had no idea. That itself was a new notion. Not that she would act on it. It was just a possibility, and there were so many possibilities. Almost too many.

Yes, she could change her tapes. She reached for the telephone, then pulled back. She took Petri's crumpled letter from her purse and reread it. She reached for the phone again. Again she pulled back. The silliness of her behavior struck her and she remembered how she had laughed at the end of her session with Kolnietz. She started to giggle all over again. This time she dialed the police department and asked for Lieutenant Petri.

He came on the line. "This is Heather," she said cheerfully. "I thought I would take you up on your invitation to dinner. I thought it would give me an opportunity to make you grovel."

Petri chuckled. They set a date and he took down her address.

As she hung up the receiver, she heard a noise down the corridor. An aide was pushing a frail elderly man in a wheelchair toward her and a middle-aged woman walked beside them. This would be the new admission to fill Tim O'Hara's empty bed. She glanced down at the papers on the counter. The woman must be the patient's daughter. When the family's names were imprinted in her mind she looked back up. But before she was able to welcome them, she saw Carol Kubrick reach out from her geri-chair and grab the sleeve of the old man's daughter. "Have you seen my purse?" she whined. "Do you know what they've done with my purse? Someone's stolen my purse. Where's my doctor? I want to see my doctor. Why won't they let me see my doctor?"